GW00672002

# THE KING OF SCANLON'S ROCK

First Published in Great Britain 2022 by Mirador Publishing

Copyright © 2022 by David Luddington

*All rights reserved. No part of this publication may be reproduced or transmitted, in any form or by any means, without permission of the publishers or author. Excepting brief quotes used in reviews.*

Any reference to real names and places are purely fictional and are constructs of the author. Any offence the references produce is unintentional and in no way reflects the reality of any locations or people involved.

*A copy of this work is available through the British Library.*

ISBN: 978-1-914965-84-5

Mirador Publishing
10 Greenbrook Terrace
Taunton
Somerset
UK
TA1 1UT

# THE KING OF SCANLON'S ROCK

## BY

## DAVID LUDDINGTON

~ OTHER BOOKS BY THE AUTHOR ~

Return of the Hippy
The Money That Never Was
Schrodinger's Cottage
Forever England
Whose Reality is this Anyway?
Camp Scoundrel
The Bank Of Goodliness
The Rose Well Files

## ~ PROLOGUE ~

Dear Your Majesty, King of England

I hereby give my official formal notice that the island known as Scanlon's Rock will be leaving your majesterial domain and will now be the Independent Kingdom of Scanlon's Rock. Forthwith.

I formally tell you that we will make a border and have our own passports as soon as I can get the printer to work. This is nothing against you personally, it's just that I don't want anything to do with your tax and laws anymore. You're welcome to drop by for a cup of tea next time you're visiting your Dukedom of Cornwall and you can meet our new President. I am going to be King.

Yours sincerely

Jim Sullivan – King of Scanlon's Rock

PS you might remember me from the Royal Variety Performance in 1994, I'm the leader of the Spartans rock band. You shook my hand afterwards and asked me what I did.

## ~ CHAPTER ONE ~

SIR OLIVER FROGMORTON'S MAHOGANY DESK dominated his office. I'd always been fascinated by desk choices within the Civil Service. Mine was a half metal, half chipboard affair just large enough for a computer terminal, a telephone and three piles of paper. But then, I was just a Research Analyst, not a Permanent Under Secretary. And while Froggy's monster desk lay completely devoid of paper, in my little windowless office, four floors below, my desk suffered under the weight of pink folders, grey box-files and random missives from above. The Prime Rule of the Civil Service, the size of the desk is in direct proportion to the height of the job and inverse proportion to the amount of work carried out on it.

Froggy waved me to a seat opposite his desk. A chrome and canvas affair, a good three inches lower than the leather sofa-on-wheels in which he sat. At least mine was just the right height for me to rest my chin on his desk should I so wish.

"Well, John," he started. "How did you get on at the Chipping Sodbury Geographical Society?"

"One fell asleep, two walked out, and one stood up and declared his name was Bob and that he was an alcoholic."

"Ah, I see. So how many were actually there?"

"What, including Bob?"

"Yes."

"Two."

"I see. Never mind, *ad astra per aspera.*" He waggled a mouse and squinted at an oversized, curved screen.

"Huh?"

"Sorry, I keep forgetting they didn't do Classical Languages in Comprehensive Schools. Through adversity to the stars."

"*Hbe chughbI Qapla Hbe,*" I said.

"Sorry?" He studied me across the top of his glasses. "Is that Welsh?"

"Klingon, if you cannot fail, you cannot succeed."

"I see." A frown fluttered across his forehead, and he returned his gaze to his computer screen. "I have you booked for a talk with the Oswestry Greengrocers' Guild next week. You'll be delivering a session on how to identify trends in banana crops in India using historical data. I'm told they're really looking forward to your talk."

"Yes, I've been meaning to ask, when am I going to get something... erm, more appropriate to my position?"

As I said the words, I knew I'd given him the opening to attack, but I was so fed up with the cavalier way the Civil Service has of sidelining those who don't quite fit, that I almost welcomed the inevitable acerbic response.

He didn't waste the opportunity. "Oh, you mean your position as a Research Analyst for the Foreign, Commonwealth Development Office?"

"Yes."

"Maybe when you stick to researching the data we need you to research, instead of going off-piste and digging up long forgotten, and inherently troublesome, information with no regard as to the consequences such revelations can create for the Foreign Office, and indeed government as a whole."

"I see," I said. "You're still grumbly about the Hossain family."

"I'm the Permanent Under Secretary to the Diplomatic Service. I am not grumbly, as you call it. I don't need to be grumbly when I can do vindictive career realignments instead."

"But wouldn't it sometimes be more diplomatic to—"

Froggy slapped his hand on the desk to cut me short. "I'm the Head of the Diplomatic Service, I don't have to be diplomatic. I have people for that. That's your job. And telling a family from Bangladesh they can settle in the UK, when they clearly can't, is neither diplomatic nor your job. Have you *any* idea how much trouble that's caused?"

"But they had a copy of a letter, signed by Churchill's Private Secretary, confirming that because of their grandfather's bravery in the Royal Navy, that he was to be made a British citizen in order that he could be awarded the George Cross. That meant they themselves are British citizens."

"And just how did they happen to have that letter?" Froggy demanded.

"Well, I found a copy when researching their claim."

"Exactly. *You* found it. It wasn't your job to find that. In fact, it was precisely your job to *not* find it. You're supposed to be looking for grounds to reject claims. Heavens above, where would we be if we looked for reasons why foreigners could just turn up here demanding citizenship? I mean, what next? Somebody turns up with a note from their local witch doctor and we say, oh, how wonderful, come on in?"

"But this was from the Prime Minister of the day. Able Seaman Hossain rescued twenty—"

"I heard your argument at the hearing." He leaned forward and steepled his fingers. "The hearing where, as you will recall, the panel ruled that just because a copy of a letter exists in our systems, doesn't prove it was ever delivered to the gentleman concerned. Maybe Churchill had a change of mind? Maybe he was drunk when he dictated it?"

"But the George Cross was actually presented, therefore, he must have been granted citizenship." I'd been down this road before and knew it led nowhere.

"And here we are again." He raised his hands as if expecting applause. "This is the attitude which keeps you touring the church halls of the shires. And I have to say that, were it not for the fact that your father's service to the Foreign Office will be forever honoured within these walls, that you are not touring the Job Centres instead. Are you sure your future lies in the Diplomatic Service? You still have some good years in front of you, I'm quite sure you could find something more aligned with your peculiar talents. Have you considered asking for a transfer to our new offices in East Kilbride? I hear Glasgow can actually be quite pleasant at times."

I slumped deeper into the chair. "I'll try to stick to accepted policy."

"Good." Froggy shook his head slightly and turned to squint at his computer screen. "Well, as it happens, we *do* have a little annoyance which might be within your narrow skill-set." He pushed a sheet of paper to me. "This was addressed to the King, but the Palace forwarded it to us to deal with."

I scanned the letter. "How can he have a king *and* a president in a kingdom?"

"That's your problem with this? Some pop singer wants to declare independence on a lump of rock off the coast of Cornwall, and your first concern is a constitutional anomaly?"

"Well—"

Froggy snatched the letter from my hands and stared at it. "The man's clearly an idiot. His bit of rock is well within UK territorial waters, so there's no discussion, no question. Apparently, he has a house down that way somewhere, so do you think you can manage to track him down and tell him no?"

"Just no?"

"Just no. Nothing else, no commas, no PowerPoint presentations, royal decrees or state visits. Just say no and get on the next train to Oswestry."

I shrugged. "Easy."

"Now," Froggy said, "I have a luncheon engagement with Sir Guy Serrick, so unless you have any more business, or even if you do, I think our business is concluded for the day."

I returned to my particular dark corner of the basement and logged in to the FCDO intranet. My schedule blinked a little bell icon, indicating that somebody had made an entry. I pulled it up and noticed that I'd already been issued with a travel warrant to Penzance, and a room had been booked in something called a Moto-Lodge near the village of Trekenwryth.

Another file in my in-box gave the details of the island and the full background from the FCDO legal department. I skipped the body of the file, I'd read that later, and went straight to the summary notes. The island was known as Scanlon's Rock and lay 11.97 nautical miles off the low water mark of the coast at Little Didney, a small fishing village on the south coast of Cornwall. That seemed cut and dried. Not quite the definition of '*Well within*' that Froggy had asserted, but at 11.97 miles, that was still regarded as within UK Territorial Waters limit of twelve nautical miles. The new owner was listed as one James Sullivan and he took possession only two months ago. He hadn't wasted any time.

James Sullivan? Froggy had said he was a pop singer. Jim Sullivan, of course. Rock God, a legend. Jim Sullivan and the Spartans. I was going to get to meet Jim Sullivan. Okay, this wasn't looking like too bad a job now. I wondered how he'd take to being referred to as a pop singer. He wouldn't like that. Then I realised I was going to have to tell him he wasn't going to be able to declare independence for his bit of rock in the English Channel. Maybe not such a good job. Sullivan wasn't exactly known for calm reason. Or calm anything.

Open Maps told me the Trekenwryth Moto-Lodge lay some five miles inland from the coastal village of Little Didney, and nine miles from Penzance station. That was hardly convenient. While I could take taxis, of course, the aggravation and the paperwork involved in recording and justifying each separate trip just wasn't worth it. I decided to take my own car, then find a place closer to the village. I should be able to claim the mileage, but if not, hey, I was going to get to meet Jim Sullivan.

I went back to the file I'd been sent. Sullivan owned a house on the coast, just west of Little Didney. Spartan's Nest, a retreat come recording studio he'd bought twenty years ago.

I did a search for places to stay, closer than Trekenwryth, and apart from a couple of twee B&Bs, the only place which looked reasonable was somewhere called the Smuggler's Arms. Open Maps placed it near the harbour in Little Didney, so that seemed perfect.

I treated myself to a coffee and a KitKat from the vending machine on the floor above, then settled down to investigate the technical detail of the file. Although now far behind me, my philosophy degree had at least taught me to assimilate information efficiently, even if I had never needed it beyond filling a tick in the box on my FCO application form. And I still lived in hope that one day it would come in useful other than being able to quote Socrates at inopportune moments.

This text was particularly dense, but after dredging through it, I discovered very little of any substance. Everything seemed oddly vague and lacking detail.

Sullivan had acquired the rock for an undisclosed sum from one Marek Werner, a tech billionaire, one of the New Kings. Founder of the MySexRated social media app. It also seemed that he was currently the subject of several financial investigations, by the look of the footnotes. I tried following up on the references, but they ended in a foggy cloud of shell companies and hedge funds.

I switched my gaze to the large plastic clock on the wall. The one that deleted, one by one, the remaining minutes of my life. I stared at the clock for a moment, as it appeared to be trying to tell me something. *Jane*, oh hell. I was going to be late for my sister's birthday lunch. I grabbed my coat as I scurried for the door and shrugged it onto my shoulders just as I hit the staircase. One year, I promised myself, one year I'd make this on time.

~ * ~ * ~ * ~

THE TAXI DROPPED ME BY the door to the Melchester Hotel. I swiped my card in the driver's machine, and without checking the little screen, ran for the hotel door.

"My name's Cabot," I told the head waiter. "I have a reservation with Mrs Straithwick."

He led me to the table. "Mrs Straithwick is already here," he said, his voice laced with a disdain they must train in head waiter school.

"Thank you," I said, and slipped from his control as I spotted Jane. "Sorry." I settled into the chair, circumventing the waiter's offer of help. "Affairs of state." I gave my best big brother smile.

"You're a Research Analyst in the Foreign Office," she scolded. "Don't give me that. You forgot again, didn't you?" Her words scolded, but her eyes smiled.

The waiter poured wine into my waiting glass, then faded away in the way only waiters and Cheshire Cats can manage.

"How could I forget my little sister's birthday lunch? It's the highlight of my year."

"Oh, dear, are things that bad, then?"

"Froggy has me running around the countryside giving talks to Women's Institutes and school geography clubs." I picked up the oversized menu and studied it.

"Yes, I did hear about your little contretemps over that family from Bangladesh. Perhaps if you weren't quite so difficult, he might be a little more accommodating?" She broke a bread roll onto her side plate and nibbled at a corner. "You never know, you might even get an overseas posting."

"That would involve going abroad," I said. "You know how foreign travel disagrees with me. Especially if it involves aeroplanes or boats."

"I know, but maybe if you tried it…"

"I think that's one of life's little opportunities which has left me behind. Although, he did give me an almost-overseas assignment." I tilted my wine glass in her direction. "Happy birthday, sis." We chinked glasses.

"An almost-overseas assignment? How does that work?"

The waiter re-materialised. "May I take your orders?"

I ordered beef rump with filled Yorkshire pudding, and Jane, Scallops Vieiras with chorizo. He unnecessarily topped up our glasses then slid out of sight again.

"I have to go down to some forgotten part of Cornwall. There's a bit of a hoo-ha over a little island off the coast. So it's almost overseas."

"Pirate smugglers?" Jane asked with a smile.

"No, I have to tell Jim Sullivan he can't declare UDI on his island."

*"The* Jim Sullivan? Oh, yes, I think I read somewhere he'd bought an island. I didn't realise he wanted to declare independence. What a wheeze!"

"Yes, well, he's out of luck." I sipped at the wine. It was a bit sweet for my taste, but it was a favourite of Jane's. "The place is just within the twelve-mile limits, so that's going to spoil his day."

Our meals arrived and a pair of waiters rearranged plates, cutlery and dropped crisp white serviettes onto our laps. They left with a well-rehearsed, "Bon appétit."

We ate in comfortable, sibling silence, for a while until Jane could no longer resist broaching the annual subject of my love life. Or lack thereof.

"So, have you been seeing anybody in the last year?" she asked. I was always fascinated by how long she managed to put off that question each year.

"Nobody will have me," I said. "Who's going to want a fifty-year-old A-grade civil servant? Maybe when I get my B grade."

"If you'd played the game a bit more, you could have been a C or even a D by now."

"Not with Froggy on the top desk. Anyway, enough about me, how's Gerald?"

She allowed the change of subject. "He's in Beijing at the moment. Negotiating a deal for some new tanks for the Department of Defence, or something."

"We're buying tanks from China? I hope he keeps the receipt."

"I probably wasn't supposed to say anything. Don't tell."

"Don't worry, nobody listens to me anyway. Besides, haven't we got enough tanks already?"

"Apparently not. Somebody complained the army has more brigadiers than tanks. Or maybe it was helicopters. I can't remember. Anyway, he'll be back in London next week some time, for a day or two. Then up to St Andrews for a golf exhibition match, then he's off to Saudi."

We finished our lunch and parted ways in separate taxis with the usual farewell of, "Until next year." And, "Don't be late next time," added Jane from the cab window as it slid into the afternoon traffic.

I headed back to my flat to prepare for the trip to Cornwall. A change of suit and a spare shirt should see me through. How long could it take for me to say, "No," and for Jim Sullivan to throw one of his famous tempers and dump me in the sea?

# ~ CHAPTER TWO ~

MY AGEING VOLVO PLODDED THE miles to Cornwall in its usual business-like manner. I should really upgrade, but as it rarely moved from its allocated garage space underneath my apartment building, there seemed little point. London traffic didn't really invite driving for pleasure.

The warmer spring weather had generated a flow of holiday traffic, which made the journey slower than I'd anticipated. At one point it even came to a complete stop for twenty minutes while police cleared an overturned caravan from the road. I marvelled at the collection of stuff the caravan had contained before it had emptied itself all over the carriageway. The passengers scurried like ants collecting for a nest, trooping to-and-fro with various kitchen goods, table lamps, what looked like a knitting machine, an office chair, a stepladder and all manner of cardboard boxes brimming with more stuff. As they finally dragged the remains of their weekend away to the side of the road, the police waved us past, and I settled back into the drive.

I eventually left the A30 on the Trekenwryth road and stopped to consult my map. A mild breeze tugged at the edges of the map as I laid it across the bonnet of the car, and I had to secure it with a couple of handy rocks. I took advantage of the break to pour myself a coffee from my flask and a cheese sandwich from my Tupperware box. I nibbled at the sandwich as I studied the map. Little Didney lay about fifteen miles due south of where I'd stopped, but the tangle of lanes between here and the village would probably add another five. I traced a couple of options with the tip of a KitKat finger and settled on what looked like the easiest to remember. I finished my coffee and folded myself back into the driver's seat.

The roads turned out to be even more tortured than they'd appeared on the map, but I trusted the route I'd memorised, and half an hour later, a sign appeared in front of me announcing, 'Welcome to Little Didney' underneath which, somebody had added, 'The Birthplace of the Original Cornish Pasty'. The word 'original' had been underlined in a splash of red paint.

Another sign, a hundred metres later, warned me that the roads were unsuitable for automobiles and tractors from this point and an arrow pointed to a gravelled parking area.

I followed the advice and parked up next to the only other vehicle, a ride-on rotavator with an armchair tied to where the seat should be. I remembered that Open Maps had positioned the Smuggler's Arms about half a kilometre downhill near the harbour. I took my overnight case from the boot, double checked I'd locked the doors, then set off down the hill into the village.

The main road sloped downhill on a semi-cobbled surface, which I guessed could prove tricky on a rainy day. Fortunately, the sky held the promise of a nice sunny day. As the buildings started to crowd inwards, I realised the wisdom of the sign advising against trying to bring cars down here, let alone a tractor.

The road continued to narrow as it descended, and by the time the small harbour came into sight, it was little more than a walkway. Just before the waterfront, the road forked, and I turned to the right as Open Maps had directed. The Smuggler's Arms appeared a short walk along the harbour front. A handful of wooden bench-type tables sat outside, and a chalk board by the door spoke of local ales and homely food. A sign on the closed door gave the opening times of 'Mid-morning to Late'. I checked my watch. If one counted mid-morning as being the median point between sunrise and noon, then eleven thirty should be well into opening time.

I knocked on the door and waited.

After a minute, I knocked again, this time more forcefully. A faint voice called from somewhere inside. I pushed the door and put my head inside, straining to hear. Nothing.

"Hello," I called.

A voice drifted back. "We're not open. It's Tuesday."

I looked back at the sign. No mention of Tuesdays. I tried again. "Hello, anybody there?"

"Who's that?" The voice seemed to come from the back of the bar.

I stepped inside and waited for my eyes to adjust to the gloom. The smell of stale beer and wood smoke hung heavy in the air.

"I'm looking for a room," I called.

A head popped up from behind the bar. A tangle of white hair surrounded the head and under the chin yet left the face itself cleanly shaven. The only dark hair belonged to a pair of eyebrows perched unnaturally high on the head. He looked vaguely like a startled daisy.

"You'll do," said the man. "Just the job. Come on down here." The head disappeared below the bar again.

I stood for a moment until the voice called again, "You comin' or what?"

"Oh, yes." I picked up my bag and followed the sound of his voice.

Once behind the bar, I saw an open hatch in the floor and a dimly lit room below.

"And mind the third step," the voice called up.

"Is it loose?"

"No, there isn't one."

I counted the wooden steps carefully, clutching my bag in one hand and a wobbly banister in the other. When I counted three, my foot searched the void, then found contact with another step.

"I thought you said the third step was missing?"

"It is, it's the third step up from the bottom. We always count steps upwards, these parts, don't know which way you count 'em up London."

I negotiated the missing third step and found the floor. The concrete felt safe and stable when I reached it.

"What you bring that down here for?" The man pointed at my bag.

"It's my overnight bag. I want to stay a couple of nights."

"In my cellar?"

"That wasn't the plan." I cast my eyes around the cellar. "Do you have anything... more, erm, bedroom-like?"

"Of course I do. It's a hotel. Wouldn't be much of a hotel without a bedroom now, would it?" He wiped his hands on an apron which looked like it had been used for gardening. "I'm the landlord, Sam Goodenough." He thrust his hand towards me.

"My name's Cabot, John." I reluctantly took the hand, forming a cup-shape to minimise the contact points.

"Give me a hand gettin' this barrel up, will you? Only I've buggered me knee." He pointed to a metal beer barrel near the bottom of the steps.

I tugged at the barrel, and it didn't move.

"Thems is heavy beasts, you go careful now," he added.

I dragged the barrel to the bottom step and looked at him, expecting at least some help. It didn't come, so I bumped it up onto the first step.

"You might want to take yer jacket off," he said. "Don't want to go spoiling a nice jacket like that."

"It's okay," I said, and humped it another step.

The missing third step proved tricky, but once past that, I found a system and soon nudged it the last step up onto the floor.

Goodenough followed me out of the hatch. "I normally use the hoist to drag them up, but you seemed set on doing it like that. Don't forget your case." He nodded down the hatch.

I headed back down again and collected my case.

"What's wrong with your knee?" I asked, as I brushed dust from my suit.

He lifted his leg and flexed it. "Twisted it when the step broke. You look like you could use a beer?"

"Thanks, yes."

He poured a pint from a pump marked Doom Bar and slid it across the bar at me. "That'll be four-fifty then. We take Chipcoin, if you'd prefer."

He pointed to a sign behind the bar which said, *'Chipcoin Accepted Here.'*

"Oh, I thought… never mind." I found a five-pound note and handed it to him.

The note disappeared in Goodenough's pocket, but no change was forthcoming.

"What's Chipcoin?" I asked. "Is that a crypto currency?"

"Local currency. I can exchange some for you, I give the best rate in town."

"Um, no thanks. You said you had a room?"

"You're in luck. Just had a cancellation on the Bridal Suite. How many nights?"

"Just the one. I'm not sure I need the Bridal Suite, though. It's just me."

"Take it or leave it." He pulled a key from under the bar and dropped it in front of me. "Tis the only room I've got left. First floor. I'd help you up with yer bag, only—"

"I know, you've got a knee."

I found the room at the top of the stairs. A large pink porcelain sign with a floral border informed me this was the Bridal Suite, in case I'd been in any doubt. I let myself in and unpacked my spare suit and shirt, then settled with my laptop to check my emails. Nothing of any consequence. A quick change of tie, and I headed downstairs.

Goodenough was standing on a chair and fiddling with a big-screen television, high on the wall.

"Everything alright with the room?" he enquired, as he fiddled with a cable behind the screen. The screen blanked, then presented a myriad of coloured lines before turning black again.

"Yes, it's all fine, it's quite…" I struggled for the right adjective, then settled for, "charming."

A fizzing noise from behind the television caused Goodenough to start. He wobbled on the chair and shook his hand as if it he'd just burnt it.

"Problems?" I asked.

"Just needs a…" He tapped the side of the unit and it flickered into life.

"There we go. Got a load in tonight to watch football, there'll be a riot if this don't work." He aimed the remote, and the screen filled with menu options in what looked like Chinese.

"A Chinese match?" I asked.

"What? No, Truro v Exeter. It's just hooked up through a Chinese satellite. Poor country publican can't afford Sky Sports' prices. It's criminal."

"It probably is," I said. "I'm looking for a place called Spartan's Nest. Jim Sullivan's place?"

"It's down yonder." He pointed vaguely at the door. "Down past old Ben's workshop, then keep goin' till you get to the Hundred-Year Tree, and you'll see a path, well you would, but it's all overgrown now. Anyways, up along that path to where Tom Pengelly's top field used to be—"

"Used to be?"

"Well, the field's still there, 'course it is, but it ain't no longer Tom's. Don't rightly remember who's got it now." He froze, mid-contemplation.

"Can I drive there?"

"What? Oh yeah, just go up round the top o' the village, road drops down to the coast, you'll see it there in front of you."

"I'll do that then," I said.

"Wouldn't bother if I was you."

"Why?"

"'Cause he ain't there. He went over to the island yesterday. There's a couple of trays of pasties over there." He waved the TV remote control towards a table by the door. "You wouldn't just pop them on the counter, would you? Only I've got a frozen shoulder."

"A frozen shoulder?" I lifted the trays, they were still warm, and headed to the bar. "How did that happen?"

"Pullin' pints for the cricket club, Ben reckons."

"Is Ben your doctor?"

"Ben? No, he's the butcher. He knows more 'bout joints than any doctor. While you're stood there, you might as well put those in the cabinet there. Don't want 'em to get cold."

I transferred the pasties to the glass warming-cabinet on the bar. "Can I get a ferry?"

"No ferries here. Nearest one goes from Penzance."

"And that goes to Scanlon's Rock?"

"No, that one goes to the Scilly Isles. Help yerself to one o' those if you want. Original Cornish they are, from Pengelly's Bakery. Beef's so fresh, the animal don't know it's dead yet."

The pasties did smell tempting, so I took one and tried it. Delicious. "So how do I get to Scanlon's Rock?" I asked, chasing pastry from my lips.

Goodenough paused for a moment, then said, "You want to be asking for Tegan Tretheway, down the dock. She goes over at times." He waved a hand at the cabinet. "You need to turn them around. Gotta have the handle facing front. So as when I take one out with the tongs, it's the right way round for the customer to grab a'hold."

I set about turning all the pasties round. "Tegan? She has a boat?"

"Could call it that. Not much good for nothing apart from carting folks to-an-fro."

I closed the door on the glass cabinet a second time and started for the door. "Thanks."

"Don't mention it. You can leave the money for the pasty by the till on yer way."

## ~ CHAPTER THREE ~

I HEADED EAST ALONG THE waterfront to where the tiny harbour nestled its fleet of little boats. The harbour itself was mostly natural rock, supplemented in places by generous helpings of concrete to make it more boat friendly. It had clearly grown up over many years, as needs had demanded.

Docking space was sparse, and afforded mostly by a wind-torn concrete jetty extending some fifty metres into the water, a pair of fishing boats lay one each side of the jetty. Neither of them seemed much bigger than the average cabin cruiser on the Thames. I felt seasick just looking at them and found myself unconsciously shuffling backwards. Slightly away from the dock, several smaller boats bobbed against their moorings, and just beyond those, a larger boat lay at anchor. This was altogether a grander affair, gleaming white with flashes of glass and clearly designed for recreation rather than work.

I noticed somebody on the nearest fishing boat unloading plastic crates onto the jetty. He was a big man, well clear of six feet and with a build that strained the thick, blue cotton shirt. Wiry black hair pushed its way from under a blue woollen hat and curled across the top of a weather-beaten face.

"Good afternoon," I called as I approached.

The man paused, straightened, and studied me. "Afternoon," he responded.

"I'm looking for somebody called Tegan. Do you know where I can find her?"

"Ain't no Tegan hereabouts." He returned to shifting crates.

"Mr Goodenough, from the pub," I pointed back the way I'd come. "He said she could give me a ride over to Scanlon's Rock."

The man paused again, removed his hat and scratched at his head. "You a tax man?"

"No, I'm from the Foreign and Commonwealth Office."

"I'm guessing you're in the wrong place then, we got no foreigners here. Unless you count the Dibnals up Shore Street. They're from Sidcup."

"I just need a lift over to Scanlon's Rock. I have some business with Mr Sullivan. I can pay."

"Pay is it? Well. You're in luck. Here she comes now." He nodded seaward to where a tiny boat pushed its way towards the dock, its outboard motor puttering through the little waves.

My stomach immediately harmonised with the motion of the boat as it approached and threatened the return of the Cornish Pasty. I hadn't the faintest idea about how long it would take a little boat like that to cover the twelve miles to Scanlon's Rock, but any time longer than about five minutes was far too long. I started mentally rehearsing my excuses to Froggy as to why I'd skipped on the assignment.

The boat bumped against an old tyre tied to the concrete some six feet below where I stood. Tegan stood and tossed a rope up onto the jetty where the man caught it with effortless nonchalance, and tied it to a bollard. She clambered out of the boat and scurried up some rough-hewn steps, landing on the jetty with the ease of a ninja panther trained in parkour.

"Fella' here to see you, Tiggy. Says he's a government man and wanting a lift out to Scanlon's Rock. He ain't a tax man, I asked him that, he said no. I didn't drop 'im in the harbour like you said."

"Well done, Jake," she said.

Tiggy stood a few inches shorter than me and a good foot less than the man. She wore jeans, and a faded blue T-shirt which showed stark against her tanned arms and face. Her once dark hair, now streaked by sun and time, fell loose, stopping just short of her shoulders in a rough cut.

She studied me with suspicion in her green eyes for a moment, then said, "You must be Mister Cabot?"

"Yes, how did you know?"

"This is Little Didney, not much happens here that everybody don't know about. I can take you in the morning, but I'm done for today. Just had a stag party out and I need a break. And a shower. You won't believe... no, you probably don't want to know."

I looked down at the tiny boat, bobbing furiously on the perfectly calm water below, then out to sea where a smudge lay just below the horizon.

"Is that it, there?" I asked.

"That's it. They say on a blue moon you can hear the bell of the Vagabunda calling."

"The Vagabunda?"

"A supposed wreck out there somewhere."

I studied the boat once more. "Maybe I'll wait for him to come here."

"Suit yourself, but as I only took him and a crate of Jack Daniel's over yesterday, I doubt we'll be seeing him back here till Thursday."

"Is there anybody else who might take me? Perhaps somebody with a slightly bigger boat?"

She followed my gaze, then a smile spread over her face. "That?" She pointed at the boat bobbing vigorously on non-existent waves. "You thought I go over to Scanlon's Rock in that?"

"Well..."

"That's just my dinghy." She pointed to the large white boat anchored out in the harbour mouth. "*That's* my boat over there. The '300', I just use the dinghy to get to that."

"I see." I studied the boat, it seemed to sit more solidly in the water than the dinghy. "I can pay you. It's government business."

"Government business? Five hundred then."

"Five hundred? That's a bit steep," I said, although, as I'd never hired a boat before, except for a rowing boat on the Serpentine in Hyde Park, I had little basis for that assessment.

"Do you see any other boats available?"

My eyes skated across the harbour. "Hmm, I'll give you a requisition chit. Oh, and I'll need a receipt."

"If you want a receipt, it'll be six hundred."

"Oh, well, if that's the rate…"

She sighed. "Come on, I'll take you. Jim's expecting you anyway."

"How…?"

"As I said, this is Little Didney." She turned to the man. "Tell Dad I've gone over again, Jake. I'll drop by the Smuggler's when I get back." She slipped back down the steps and stood in the centre of the boat expectantly. "You coming or what?"

My descent of the steps was markedly slower and when the boat wobbled violently under my feet, I had to fight hard to resist scrambling straight back up again.

As soon as I'd settled on the forward bench seat, Jake unhitched the rope and tossed it back in the boat. Tiggy opened up the engine, and the bow lifted slightly as it pushed its way out to sea. I gripped both sides of the boat tightly, doing my bit to keep it steady and afloat.

"Relax," Tiggy said. "Enjoy the ride. And anyway, they do say that drowning is the best way to go."

I concentrated on the white boat ahead of us as it grew in size. Not quite quickly enough, but at least it didn't appear to be bouncing up and down.

We eventually drew up at the rear of the boat and Tiggy tied a rope to a deck cleat, then held the ladder rail to keep the boat from twisting out.

"Up you hop," she said.

Moving from one wobbly platform to another wobbly platform was one life skill I'd missed out on so far. I tried hard not to think about what would happen if the two boats drifted apart while I was halfway through the manoeuvre. I was sure I'd seen that in a Laurel and Hardy movie. I set my foot on the little platform and climbed the short ladder with at least some grace and without getting wet.

"Do you want a hand?" I asked.

Tiggy laughed and shook her head. "I think I can manage," and suddenly she was on the deck alongside me.

The boat seemed to be about two-cars' length, maybe a bit more, and about twice the width. The deck on which we stood was small with a curved seat in the back, doors to an inside area in front, and another ladder to the roof.

"Come on up," Tiggy said, and slid up the second ladder.

I followed and found myself in an area resembling an open-top sports car. A pair of seats and a dashboard and a steering wheel all made it comfortingly familiar. With just a little imagination, I could kid myself we were on the M25 rather than the middle of the ocean.

I settled into the seat without the steering wheel and Tiggy dropped into the driver's seat and turned a key. The engine started thrubbing somewhere below us.

"How long will it take?" I asked.

"Half an hour, if I take it easy. Twenty minutes if you don't mind it being a bit bouncier."

"Half an hour's fine. Even an hour, if that's easier."

A smile broke across her face. "You're not a boat person, are you?" she said.

"You spotted that then. Truth be told, I'm not very keen on aeroplanes either."

"For somebody from the Foreign Office, isn't that a bit of a problem? I mean, isn't that what you do? All over the world, boats and planes and stuff?"

"How did you know I was from the Foreign Office?"

She stared at me for a moment as if disbelieving I could ask such a stupid question, then smiled and said, "Oh, bless."

I turned to study the approaching island. Slightly less smudgy now, but still too far away. And it was moving. I switched my gaze to the inside of the boat. This upper deck was small, the two forward seats and an L-shaped sofa arrangement would seat another three people, maybe four, but beyond that, it wasn't really much different to a modern car. Just a couple more instruments and a ubiquitous lifebelt hanging to the rear to remind me of the fragility of our existence on this vast ocean.

"You alright?" Tiggy asked. "You're looking a bit green. Try looking at the island."

"No, I'm fine," I lied. "Just curious about the boat. The last ferry I was on was the Isle of Wight ferry. But that was basically a British Rail waiting room sat on top of a barge. Nowhere near as sporty as this."

"That's because this isn't really a ferry. I just do the odd run to-and-fro Scanlon's Rock when needed. Plus the occasional stag party, of course. It's supposed to be a fishing boat."

I looked down at the lower deck. "Isn't that what it is? It looks like a fishing boat. But then, I'm hardly an expert, I'm only going on the one I saw in Jaws."

"This is a sport fishing boat; it's actually meant to be a trawler."

"How did you end up with a wrong boat?"

"His fault." She pointed a finger towards the island. "Jim Sullivan. About six months ago, he came to Little Didney to make a video for his new release. A concept album about Vikings. Anyway, he wanted to hire a boat to shoot a Viking Funeral. Dad rented him mine for the day and the silly idiot set it on fire."

"Isn't that pretty much how a Viking funeral works?" I asked.

"Apparently so, but it was supposed to be all special effects. Anyway, to avoid any legal aggro, he offered to buy Dad a replacement. So off he went and bought a fishing boat off some Hollywood type, without a clue what he was doing." She waved an arm around, indicating the boat. "And here we are, one boat. How am I supposed to trawl for sardines on a pimped-up penis extension like this?"

"Couldn't you just refuse it? Or swap it? I don't know how these things work."

"I expect I will. Just haven't got round to it yet."

I looked back towards the island. The smudge had materialised into sharper focus now, showing sandy coloured cliffs rising from the sea, topped with a cap of green. With nothing to fix a sense of scale, I didn't know how close we were or how high the cliffs. A small, or enormous, promontory extended from the western end of the island. It hosted what looked like a beach and much kinder slopes than the sharp cliffs of the main body of the island.

"How far now?" I asked.

"About five minutes. Soon be on dry land." She grinned.

I tightened my grip as the boat turned a bit and leaned as it went. The engine strained, then settled as she pointed the nose of the boat towards the little sandy beach. The boat bounced a bit more now that we were crossing the waves at an angle.

"Is that where we're going?" I pointed at the beach.

"Pirate's Cove. The only place *to* land. Unless you fancy clambering up the cliffs."

"Not particularly."

The engine noise dropped away to a faint vibration through my feet and the boat drifted around 180 degrees. Tiggy turned a switch on the dashboard, and I heard a short rumbling noise, then the boat jerked slightly. I guessed the anchor was down.

"Is this as close as we get?" I asked.

"This is a boat, not an amphibious landing craft. Time to get back in the dinghy."

"Oh, good."

The little dinghy skimmed across the waves and shivered to a halt within three feet of dry sand. I sat for a moment, not sure what to do, then Tiggy jumped out with the end of a rope in her hands.

"Out you get then. I'm not pulling this up onto the beach with you sat in it."

I took my shoes and socks off, then pulled my trousers up over my knees and slid off the side of the boat into the sea. The cold water stopped short of my knees and the sand felt solid as I waded to the beach. Once there, I found a rock on which to sit while I replaced my shoes and socks.

"I probably should have thought this through and brought more suitable footwear," I said.

All Tiggy said was, "Hmph," and set off for a cut leading upwards between the rocks.

At one time, maybe a century or two before, somebody had cut rough steps in the track leading upwards and a trace of them remained. I was grateful for each and every one as they appeared. Although the climb was only about twenty metres, I made a vow to take the stairs in the office in future.

On arrival at the top, a brisk wind from the west reminded me there was nothing between me and North America. I scanned the view. I'd had the idea, for no particular reason, that I would arrive in some sort of harbour with people and houses and vehicles. So the view laid out in front of me was all the more disconcerting.

To the west, the cove where we had arrived continued out to sea, culminating in a pointy bit, which I guessed to be the westernmost reach of the island. Above the cove, trees covered the headland, obscuring anything laying beyond, although a tall, slender building reached clear of the trees, and could well have been a lighthouse.

Straight ahead, facing south, stretched nothing but pastureland, although, it was not possible to determine if that continued to the southern edge of the island as the ground rose slightly, then fell away beyond my eye-line.

Looking to the east showed more promise, where what looked like a clutch of buildings, far in the distance, stood grey against the blue of the sky.

"Stunning, isn't it?" Tiggy said.

"It's certainly dramatic." My eyes searched for a road. "What now?"

"We wait for a number forty-two bus, it goes straight there."

"Huh?"

"We walk, you daft wocki. No roads here." She turned and set off east towards the buildings.

I fell in behind her and tried to keep up while we followed a barely visible trail in the grass.

"Is it very far?" I managed to ask.

"The island is only a couple of kilometres long. Nowhere is very far."

I processed the information. Two kilometres, that's about a mile and a quarter. Roughly the distance from my apartment block to St James's Park. Not that I'd ever walk that, not when I could get an Uber for the price of a macchiato in Colston Coffee.

I realised she was increasing the distance between us and hurried my pace. Not easy in shoes designed for London pavements.

"That big guy on the quay — who was that?" I tried to keep the concern out of my voice.

"Who, Jake? You don't want to worry about him. Great lunk, he's my big brother. He gets a bit over-protective at times, that's all, but he's harmless. Mostly. Unless you're a taxman."

"Do I look like a taxman?"

"Not really, but then you don't look like somebody from the Foreign Office, either."

"How is somebody from the Foreign Office supposed to look?"

She stopped and studied me. "Well, if you don't mind me saying, you don't look much like somebody who travels a lot."

"That's because I don't," I said. "In fact, I've never been further than the Isle of Wight."

"John Cabot?" she mused. My name sounded slightly odd with the Cornish burr. "Wasn't he the great fifteenth century explorer?"

"Yes, we're supposedly distantly related. Great-great something of a twentieth cousin second removed, I think."

"You didn't inherit the explorer genes then?"

"Actually, he wasn't much of an explorer anyway. He tripped over Canada while he was looking for Asia. Totally the wrong direction. So mostly, he was just famous for getting lost."

She shrugged. "I'd have thought foreign travel was pretty much the point of working in the Foreign Office? But hey, what do I know? Just a fisherman's daughter." She turned and continued her march. "*London's foreign to me.*"

I skipped a step to keep up with her. "It wasn't really what I wanted. But both my father and grandfather were in the Diplomatic Service, so it was sort of expected."

She stopped so suddenly I nearly collided with her. "That's the way it goes. I always wanted to be an explorer, growing up. Nowadays, I'm lucky if I can make it as far as Newquay for a night out with the girls." She nodded towards my shoes. "They're holding up well."

"Church's. Not really made for this, although they do make..." But she'd gone, and I was talking to a gorse bush.

I spotted something moving up ahead. Hiding in the grass and moving in quick spurts to avoid being seen.

"There's somebody out there," I called, pointing to where I'd seen the movement.

Tiggy stopped and turned to look at me. "Where?"

"Just there." I pointed to the grass tufts which concealed the figure. Or figures. "I think there's more than one."

Tiggy turned and held her hand to her eyes, shielding against the low sun. "Nah, nothing there."

I'd seen this movie; it didn't end well for Jon Voight. I squinted into the light. Something moved. "There! Did you see that? There's two, maybe three people out there. Hiding."

She looked again. "You mean the people with the big ears and fluffy white tails?"

"What?"

"Rabbits. There's a whole heap of rabbits bouncing around over there, if that's what you meant."

"Rabbits?" I queried.

"Yeah, if you're not used to the open landscape, scale can be tricky. Not like you've got any cars or phone boxes as a reference point."

I admired her tact. She'd do well in the Diplomatic Corp. "Ah, of course." I had to almost run to keep up with her as she turned and resumed her march.

As we drew closer to what I'd thought were buildings, they showed themselves to be just large rock formations. I guessed it to be around fifteen metres at its tallest point, but, as I'd recently discovered, estimating scale wasn't one of my strong points. Maybe about the size of my apartment block.

"Mount Scanlon," Tiggy said. "And if you look way in the distance over there," she pointed to the east, "you might just see the old mine buildings. It used to be an old tin mine, many years back. The wheel house is still standing."

As we cleared the rocks and crested a slight rise, a modern structure came into view. An anomalous wooden structure, looking for all the world like a lodge from a caravan park.

"Government House," Tiggy announced.

"Government?" I queried.

"Jim had it built. It's what they call a Wikihouse. Comes in bits, like a giant Lego set."

We followed the track as it led around to the front of the house. Another Wikihouse appeared to be under construction just to the west of Government House.

"More people moving in?" I asked.

"That's going to be a Chinese restaurant. Jim's obsessed with Chinese food, it's pretty much all he eats. He's hired a chef to run it."

It seemed a very random choice for the second build on an uninhabited island, and I wondered what I would have chosen had the choice been mine. Failing to immediately come up with an alternative, I decided maybe it wasn't such a stupid idea after all.

We rounded the front of the main house to where a semi-cobbled area fought a losing battle with nature. In the centre of the cobbled splay stood an ancient Land Rover Defender. We climbed the three wooden steps up to a large veranda, then round a corner to the front door, a large double-glazed affair. The door slid open as we approached it.

"Oh, it's you, Tiggy," said a very large man in corduroy trousers and a threadbare green pullover. "Is this him?" He nodded in my direction.

"He says so."

"Doesn't look much like an ambassador."

"That's because I'm not," I said. "I'm John Cabot, and I'm just a Research Analyst."

"Best come in then," he said. "I'm Jeeves." He turned and walked up the hall in the unspoken expectation that we'd follow. His steps carried a weariness that belied his limber appearance. He continued talking even though he couldn't have been sure we were there. "Name's Jim actually, but when I came to work for Mr Sullivan, he said we can't have two Jims, as that would be confusing, so he calls me Jeeves. Don't mind really, as Jeevesing is what I do mostly and he can call me Polly if he likes, as long as I get paid. He's through 'ere in the sun lounge waitin' on you."

He pushed a door open and stood to one side.

Jim Sullivan sprawled on a wicker sofa, facing a full height window taking the complete southern wall. Although he had his back to the door, some sixth sense must have told him we were there as he unhooked a set of headphones from his head and turned towards us.

"Hey, Tiggy," he said, aiming a remote control at a Hi-Fi unit in the corner. He eased himself clear of the sofa and turned to face us. "You seen that boat out there?" He pointed to the window. "Big red thing, been plodding up and down all morning. One of your mates?" The London East End accent, immediately familiar from dozens of TV and radio appearances.

Tiggy moved to the window. "Where?"

"Just..." Jim peered out to sea. "Ain't that the thing now, would you believe it? It's gone. Looked like it was towing something."

"Doesn't sound like anyone from round here. Could be a French trawler."

Jim seemed to notice me for the first time. "You must be the much-talked-about Mr Cabot."

"John," I said. I was in the same room as Jim Sullivan. The only time I'd ever seen him in the flesh before had been from half a mile away from the back of Wembley Stadium. He'd been a bouncing dot on a distant stage.

Jim moved with the grace of an athlete and the fact he had nearly twenty years on me did nothing for my self-confidence.

He waved towards another sofa and slid back into the one he'd just left. I sat, my knees clicked.

"There's a beer in the cooler." He pointed to a glass-fronted fridge. "Help yourself. Or something stronger if you prefer."

"Bit early for that," I said, then realised how that might sound. "For me, that is. I mean, technically, I'm still at work."

"So am I." He waved a whisky glass in the air. "It's when I do my best work, when the edges of reality are slightly faded. There's some weed in the box there, if you'd rather." He pointed at a carved wooden box.

"No thanks."

"You sure? You look like you could do with unwinding a bit. Nice shoes."

"Really, I'm fine, thanks." I sat my briefcase on my lap. It felt comforting.

"Well, at least take off your tie. I'm going to ban them on the island, first thing I'm going to do when I declare this a sovereign state." He waved his whisky arm around.

"Yes, about that…" I clicked open the briefcase and dived inside. Papers gave me purpose and control. The piece I wanted was on top, but I fluffed for a moment anyway. "The Foreign, Commonwealth Development Office have reviewed your request, and… unfortunately… as the coastline of Scanlon's Rock, the land mass in question, falls within the twelve nautical mile limit, as defined under the Territorial Sea Act of 1987, then—"

"Yeah, yeah. Blah-de-blah." Jim swung his feet to the floor and turned to face me. "You guys really need to start talking to each other."

"Who?" I queried.

"Had HMRC down here a couple of weeks ago. Wanting to seize the island under an Unexplained Wealth Order."

"Really? Nobody told me that."

"They didn't get very far. Idiots didn't realise it had changed hands, they thought it was still owned by that tech magnate."

"What happened?"

"What happened? Tiggy's brother, Jake, dumped the pair of them in the harbour and they went back to London with their tails between their legs. And now they send a..." He studied me. "What are you?"

"I'm a Research Analyst with the Foreign, Commonwealth Development Office."

"That sounds very important." He refilled his glass from a bottle of Jack Daniel's on the table, then pulled the little box to him and started rolling a joint.

"Not really. I just analyse details and documents and prepare reports for the important people."

"Probably the perfect job for somebody who always wanted to be a librarian but thought the excitement might be too much."

"My parents were both in the Diplomatic Service and it was sort of expected."

"You ever jumped out of an aeroplane?"

The random question caught me for a moment. "I've never actually been in an aeroplane, so I'm certainly not inclined to jump out of one which has left the ground."

"I'm having a zip-wire built down there." He waved towards some cliff tops just visible through the window. "Quick way down to the beach. I can sit here, and when I feel like a quick dip... down we go. You should come along and have a go. When I've built some more of these as guest houses." He waved his whisky glass around to indicate the building in which we sat.

"Tiggy told me they come as a construction kit," I said. "Easier than bricks out here, I guess."

"And cheaper. And... they're green. As in eco-good, that is. I didn't mean green in colour, obviously. You can paint them any colour you like."

"Is it just you here?"

"And Jeeves," he said. "And Cindy, of course, my current wife. Although, she's in L.A. at the moment, buying socks."

"Socks? In Los Angeles?"

"There's a little place off Newport Beach which sells socks, handmade from locally grown hemp. Zero carbon footprint apparently. Cindy's very into saving the planet."

I took a sheet of paper from my briefcase. "I'm supposed to give you this." I handed it to him.

He took it from me and, without looking at it, screwed it into a ball and threw it perfectly into a bin at the far end of the room.

"Get your coat," Jim said. "I want to show you something."

I straightened my suit jacket. "I only have this."

"Really? Oh well." He turned to the door. "Jeeves!"

Jeeves appeared instantly in the doorway. "What?"

"Where's the Landy keys?"

"I hid them."

"I wish you'd stop doing that. I'm only driving to the other end of the island, not Basingstoke."

"Yes, sir. But Basingstoke doesn't have fifty-foot cliffs into the sea."

"And stop calling me, sir." Jim turned to me. "He only calls me *sir* when he's got the 'ump with me."

"Yes, sir," said Jeeves.

"Where are the keys?"

"In the muesli box."

"We have muesli?"

But Jeeves had gone.

Jim emptied the last of the whisky from his glass, lit the joint, and headed for the door. "Bloody, muesli. He knows I can't stand the stuff."

I followed Jim through to the kitchen, where he opened random cupboard doors until he found a box marked 'muesli'.

"Gotcha." He pulled a set of keys from the box, then called, "Jeeves, you're fired."

"Yes, sir."

## ~ Chapter Four ~

THE ANCIENT LAND ROVER DEFENDER bounced across scrubland and rocks with the surefootedness of a mountain goat, only without the padding. I was beginning to feel more seasick than I had on Tiggy's boat.

I sat in the back, which gave me plenty of room in which to bounce around like a marble in a tumble dryer. Tiggy sat in the front alongside Jim, and they chattered to each other, but the noise of the vehicle filtered out any audible dialogue.

"Where are we going?" I called.

Jim turned and said something I couldn't make out, then he pointed vaguely in front, smiled and talked some more. All without watching where we were going.

I just smiled and nodded until he turned back to face front. I decided not to ask any more questions.

As Tiggy had said earlier, nowhere is very far away on an island which is only two kilometres long. I managed to glean we were heading further east, the opposite end from the pointy western bit where we'd landed.

I grabbed the little handle in the roof as we skimmed the edge of a cliff, scattering rocks and scree over the side as we went. I sucked in a hard breath. The drop looked precipitous, and I doubted my vice-like grip on the handle would have done much to save me, but it made me feel I had at least some control.

We stopped a few feet away from the edge and Jim said, "Out you hop, we're here."

I climbed out of the vehicle and flexed my fingers. They ached from the grip I'd maintained on the handle. The wind tore at my jacket, and I buttoned it down as far as it went.

"Where are we?" I asked.

"This is the point of the island which is the closest to the mainland." Jim walked to the cliff edge and set his gaze northwards towards England.

I kept back a couple of steps. I always had this feeling that, when close to precipitous drops, somebody was going to run up behind me and push me off.

"Look out there," he said, pointing towards the mainland. "How far away would you say that is?"

It seemed a strange question, but I gave the answer I knew to be correct. "It's exactly 11.97 nautical miles. Putting us just inside the twelve-mile Territorial Waters limit."

"Yeah, you'd think, wouldn't you?" He stared out across the sea. "I mean, that's what it looks like, doesn't it? 11.97 nautical miles. Give or take." He turned to me. "But that's not actually the case. When did you say they measured it?"

"It was defined in the Territorial Waters Act of 1987, when the limit was changed from three miles to twelve."

"So, in 1987, when your act was laid down, this point here was 11.97 miles from that point there?" He pointed at the grey smudge along the horizon.

I nodded, unclear how I was supposed to respond to that.

"And do you remember what else happened in 1987?" he asked.

"Um…" I trawled my mental filing cabinet. "Margaret Thatcher was re-elected, Reagan challenged Gorbachev to tear down the Wall, Coventry City won the FA Cup—"

"Okay," Jim waved a hand to interrupt my flow. "Let's say more specifically, in October—"

"Ah October, yes, Black Monday, the Wall Street Crash which sent—"

"No, before you give me a newsreel for the whole year, here's a clue, how about when weatherman Michael Fish promised everyone there would be no hurricane?"

"Yes, and then along came the biggest storms in 200 years," I said.

"Exactly, taking with it a sizeable lump of the shoreline." He waved his hand to the distance. "Just over there. You see it?"

I stared into the distance. "No, I don't."

"My point exactly."

I was beginning to see where this was going. "And you think that was enough to increase the distance?"

"There we go." He patted his pockets and came out with a joint. After several failed attempts to get the lighter to hold against the wind, he gave up and returned the joint to his pocket.

"How do you know?" I asked.

"Because I measured it. I had a little… erm incident with Tiggy's fishing boat."

"Yes, she mentioned it," I said. "Something to do with a Viking Funeral?"

"Yeah, not one of my better ideas. But hey, did you see the YouTube numbers? Anyway, long story short, I had to buy her a new boat, and I got a good deal with a pal of mine who had one for sale. All the bells and whistle, including… the very latest satellite navigation system. Accurate enough to find you within your own shoes."

Tiggy turned away from the view to face me. "And when I was playing with it, to find out how far I needed to go before I could serve drinks on a stag party, I discovered that Scanlon's Rock was *actually* 12.11 nautical miles offshore. I even got the Commodore to check it on *his* boat."

"The Commodore?"

"Commodore Saltby. Ex Royal Navy. Been here since the Armada. What he doesn't know about the local waters wouldn't make a splash in his brandy glass. Anyway, he's got a Russian Satnav, far more accurate than the American-based systems, they purposely degrade their signals, did you know?"

"No, I didn't."

"Hmm, well, his came out the same. There used to be a sandbank about eighty metres wide before the storms. You can still see it on some of the old postcards."

I stood in silence, trying to process this. "I see," I said finally.

"Cool," said Jim. "Just need you to pop back to your bosses and let them know, then I can get on with designing my flag. I was thinking of a guitar against a dolphin? Or a weed plant? What do you think? Or should it be a seal? There's lots of seals here."

"I'll certainly look into all this," I said. "But if what you say is right, there are still other conditions which need to be fulfilled first."

"Really? Always more paperwork with you lot." He turned away from the wind and tried once more with the joint. This time, the lighter caught, and he breathed deeply. A smile settled over his face, and he offered it to Tiggy. She shook her head, so he continued to smoke.

I stared across the sea towards the far coast. "It's certainly spectacular. Do you plan on living here full-time?"

He thought for a moment and pulled deeply on the remains of the joint. He crumbled the last of the ash to the wind and pocketed the paper. "Probably," was all he said. He headed back to the Land Rover. "Hop in, I'll take you back to the cove. Save your shoes."

After several whiskies and a joint, the drive was surprisingly smooth and sedate. In fact, at points, we came to a standstill as he seemed to forget what he was supposed to be doing. I watched him go as we stood on the beach.

"Is he going to get back okay?" I asked. "He seems a bit... um..."

"I think high is the word you're struggling for," Tiggy said. "And yes, he'll get back just fine. His driving's more of a worry when he's straight. Fortunately, those times are rarer than getting through to your doctor on the first call."

"He's like this most of the time?"

"To be honest, Jim has a tendency to being a bit manic at times. Then at others, especially when he's been on the wacky baccy, which, to be fair, is most of the time, he gets very laid back. He tends to walk a tightrope between cannabis, Jack Daniel's, and coffee."

"You can't have a tightrope between three points. Only two points. Or two tightropes between three points."

"I bet you're fun at parties. Come on, we need to get going."

We wasted little time getting the dinghy in the water and out to the '300'. Tiggy seemed quite concerned about a growing black mess on the eastern skyline.

Once aboard the boat, Tiggy fired up the engine, and we swung out to sea in quite a violent curve and a fair bit of bumping over waves.

"Might be a little uncomfortable, I need to beat the weather," she said, as she took aim for the shore. "Hold on to your lunch."

The boat bumped across the tops of the waves. At this speed, it felt more like a car racing over a ploughed field rather than a boat. Uncomfortable, but not as unsettling to my system as rolling waves.

"You alright?" Tiggy asked.

"Actually, yes," I replied. "Does Jim stay on the island much?"

"More and more. Now he's building those Wikihouses, aren't they great?"

"They certainly seem easy."

She swung the boat in a wide arc to aim at the harbour. "Might get a bit choppy for a moment, we're crossing the run of the tide."

The bumping now added a rocking movement and at once my stomach swirled as if trying to match the movement. I gripped the edge rail next to my seat, trying to slow the movement.

As we approached the little harbour, Tiggy pointed out where the spit of sandbank had been.

"It stretched from the western end of the village out in a curve to about there." Her hand pointed to a point in the sea, roughly in line with the harbour and about a hundred metres out. "Folks just went out of their houses after the storms, and there it was, gone."

The little jetty was now free of fishing boats, so thankfully, we were able to moor directly to something solid and physically attached to England.

"What do I owe you?" I asked.

Tiggy looked at me and considered the question. "If you go back to London and get them to reassess the position of Scanlon's Rock, then you owe me a pint, job done. If you don't, I'm going to hit you with a bill so big, it will make the invoice for the Dunkirk evacuation look like sofa change." She smiled and watched my eyes.

"Deal." I offered my hand, and we shook. Her handshake was firm, and I felt callouses against my skin. It made me feel oddly uncomfortable.

I headed back to the Smuggler's Arms for a shower and food.

The shower proved trickier than expected. The setting between ice-bath and napalm was a point so fine, I would have needed an electron scanning microscope to find it. In the interests of preserving my skin, I settled for a cold shower. A change of shirt and fresh tie made me feel human again, and I went downstairs for dinner.

The restaurant area of the bar was essentially just more bar except with placemats instead of beermats. I ordered fish and chips with a pint of Doom Bar, and settled at a table with my laptop to assemble my notes while I waited for my food. I emptied my short-term memory onto a Word document, making sure I included the details of the distances Jim and Tiggy had claimed. Once satisfied that I'd forgotten nothing of importance, I closed the laptop and slipped it into its bag.

The bar hummed with activity. A group of four played the noisiest game of dominoes I'd ever heard, and regular cheering erupted from some darts players at the far end.

I appeared to be the only person in the place wearing a suit and tie, with pullovers or denim being the dominant attire.

The meal arrived and looked delicious, with homemade chips, and fish, probably not long off the boat. I was about to tuck in, when my table turned dark.

I looked up to discover the cause, and saw a huge man settling into the seat opposite me. He had a face which looked like it had been carved from driftwood and which cracked into a smile when he caught my gaze. Not the sort of smile that says how lovely to see you, but the sort one might expect from a lion which has just cornered a rabbit and wants to savour the moment.

"Hello," I said, and held out my hand. "I'm John, have we met?"

"Name's Branok." He engulfed my hand in his and I braced myself for the permanent destruction of my fingers, but his grip was remarkably gentle. "Branok Tretheway."

"Ah, you must be…" I studied the man for a moment, trying to take a quick guess at his age. I settled at around sixty and said, "Tegan's father?"

My guess seemed to take him by surprise.

"She said you was as sharp as a rook."

"What can I do for you, Mr Tretheway?"

I took aim at a chip with my fork, but Tretheway's hand covered mine, preventing it moving.

"You can call me Branok. Most folks do. Or Bran, up to you, I'll answer to both."

"Okay, Branok." I nodded my head towards my plate. "Mind if I eat while we talk? I hate cold chips."

He gave a small grunt and moved his hand. "I hear you been out on the rock."

"Yes, I had some business with Mr Sullivan. Tegan very kindly took me out there."

"Point is, we're not so keen on people comin' down from London tellin' us what we can and can't do 'ere."

"I see, well, I'm afraid I can't really discuss the reason for my visit. It's confidential. But just to reassure you, it in no way involves any sort of directives concerning Little Didney. It's just a private issue between Mr Sullivan and the Foreign Office."

"Not much private round here."

"I'm beginning to realise that."

"Jim's a good man, and while he ain't got no dead in the graveyard, he's part of this place as much as the tide."

"I understand, but really, there's nothing to worry about. It's just an administrative matter."

"Administrative matters is what they called it when they took the fishing and gave it to the French."

"Leave him alone, Dad." Tiggy closed on my table. She grabbed a chair from a nearby table and sat down with us. "Let the poor man eat his fish and chips."

"Just explaining how it is," Branok said. He seemed sulky.

"I'm sure John understands," she said. "He has the details, and he's going back to London to get them to change their mind." She turned to look at me. "Isn't that right, John?"

"Well, I'm certainly going to re-evaluate the data on which the original rejection was posited and should a review be necessary, it will be given full consideration."

Tiggy turned to her father and smiled. "See, it's all going to be alright."

"That wasn't exactly what—" I started.

Tiggy put her hand on my arm and pressed gently.

"That's alright then," said Branok. "Revenue men, and oil people, and now Foreigner Office people, don't know what it's got to do with them anyway. Not like we get many foreigners here nowadays, not since Brexit."

"Go get me a drink, will you, Dad? I expect John would like another one." She turned to me. "Wouldn't you?"

"I wasn't really going—" The hand squeezed again. "Yes, please, that would be lovely," I finished.

Branok lifted his bulk clear of the table and headed to the bar.

"Don't worry about him," Tiggy said. "He doesn't do well with change. Just do what you can."

"I promise." I pushed my half-eaten meal to one side. "What did he mean about the tax people and oil people?"

She looked at me like I'd just asked where babies come from. "You really didn't do your homework, did you? As Jim said, we had a couple of bailiffs from HMRC trying to put a seizure notice on the island until they realised it had changed hands. And there's been oil company people in and out of here for months."

"How do you know they were oil people?"

"Oh, they pretend to be tourists, of course. But it's not difficult to find out who people really are."

"I suppose," I said. "Everybody leaves digital trails across the internet these days. Social media makes it easier to track people down if one knows how to do it."

"Digital trails?" Tiggy questioned. "Don't be daft. Old Sam Goodenough just went through their suitcases while they were out."

"Here ya go." Branok reappeared and dumped two pints on the table. "I'll be off now. Early start if we're to get out there before the Frenchies tomorrow." He headed for the door, nodding goodnights to people as he went.

"Frenchies?" I asked.

"Endless squabbles between our boats and the French over fishing waters, and at this time of year, the pilchards are on the rise and things can get heated."

"Are pilchards still popular?" I supped at my beer tentatively, I hadn't planned on a second.

"More popular than ever, it's just that you won't find them called pilchards in posh restaurants."

"I don't understand."

"The pilchard was always associated with simple foods for ordinary folks."

"Tinned pilchards in tomato sauce," I said. "Yes, I remember them well. Served on toast, mostly."

"Part of our heritage, but then people started to take exotic package holidays to far-away places like the Costa Brava or the Algarve, where they had wonderful local delicacies like sardines on open barbecues. And when they came home, this is what they demanded. Suddenly, everybody wanted expensive, imported sardines and nobody wanted the poor humble pilchard anymore."

"So, what happened to change that?"

"Nothing." She smiled and sipped at her beer. Her brown eyes sparkled over the top of the glass, flashing with the same tones as the ale. "What most folks don't know, is that pilchards and sardines are the same fish. So the Cornish fishermen eventually started calling them sardines, and all of a sudden, they're back on the menu in all the best restaurants."

"It's all about the spin, I suppose."

"Exactly, you say 11.97 miles, we say 12.11." She smiled again and watched my eyes with an intensity I could feel in the back of my skull.

I took another large drink of my beer.

# ~ CHAPTER FIVE ~

I SET OUT FOR LONDON early in the morning. My head buzzed with questions which only a deep search of the department records would solve. The journey back went smoothly, and I hit the city before the evening exodus started. I grabbed a latte and humus salad wrap from Colston Coffee on the way into the office and managed to slip in just before the front reception closed for the evening.

My initial search turned up no more than I'd gleaned a couple of days ago. Data taken from satellite imagery put the distance at 11.97, consistent with the original information. However, oddly, no dates for the images were present.

The ownership of the island just showed as James Sullivan with the previous owner as Marek Werner, and no details of any sums paid or how. Again, unusual. Searching for Werner directly ended up in multiple entries, most of which were completely unintelligible due to redactions. That was *not* unusual. At my grade level, even the code to the local Wi-fi was redacted.

I did, however, manage to find entries in the HMRC records which showed an action being instigated against a redacted person to take possession of a redacted estate in a redacted area of Cornwall as part of a larger action against said redacted individual. I decided it was safe to make assumptions about the redacted bits.

One of the useful perks of being a Research Analyst in the FCDO was the fact that, even if I couldn't access high-level data, I did have low-level access to lots of different departments. A search through the Department of Energy and Climate Change's records turned up a geotechnical study hinting at the possibility of shale gas deposits at the western reaches of the English Channel. I looked for any information about exploration licences being put out to tender and found that several had been issued. I checked the company involved. Redacted.

By the time I'd finished, most of the building was closed and I had to leave via the security desk.

"Working late, Mr Cabot?" commented the guard as he checked my card.

"The lower the pay grade, the longer the hours," I said.

"Ain't that the truth?" He returned my card to me and pressed the button unlocking the door. "You have a good evening, Mr Cabot."

"Thank you, Ted. I plan to."

I stepped into the late evening lights of King Charles Street and called up an Uber.

~ * ~ * ~ * ~

THE CRISP MORNING SUN DID nothing to assuage my feelings of looming trouble, and I entered Sir Oliver Frogmorton's office with even more trepidation than usual.

"Ah, John," he greeted. "I trust your pirate pop singer has now been disabused of his ambitions of empire?"

I settled into the little chair facing him across the desk. "Things turned out to be a just a touch more complicated than anticipated," I said.

He gave a large sigh and leaned forward on his elbows. "Why does this not surprise me?"

I pulled out a copy of the satellite images of the coastline at Little Didney and turned them towards him. "These are supposed to be the latest images, but there are no dates on them."

He scanned them briefly, then pushed them back across the desk at me.

"And just how does that impact on the little job with which you were entrusted?"

"Mr Sullivan disputes the measurements. He claims the island is 12.11 nautical miles from the low water mark, and not 11.97, as our data indicates."

"Well, as he seems to have done such a good job convincing you of his cartographic skills, perhaps he'd like to remeasure the whole of our coastline for us. Of course, we may then discover that we're too close to France and we're all going to have to learn French."

I ignored his jibe. "It's to do with coastal erosion." I turned the printouts back to him. "These images show a sandbar from which the baseline was taken when establishing the low water mark. However, this no longer exists."

"So he says."

"I saw it myself. It isn't there."

"Am I to take this to mean that you failed to convey to him that his piece of rock falls within UK territorial waters and that he remains subject to UK legislation?"

"I just think we need to do another measurement. I've also been trying to trace the previous ownership so I could see if any previous applications had been made, but everything is very vague and most of it is not available under my access authority."

"Didn't we have a discussion, only a few days ago, where we talked about your tendency to conduct your own research into areas counterproductive to the smooth functioning of this department?"

"Yes, but—"

"And how you promised me faithfully that you would stay rigidly within the parameters of your brief?"

"I know, but—"

"Enough," he said. "You will go back to your office, and you will prepare a statement explaining that after further investigation, his application for independence is, without option of appeal, rejected. Immediately. You will then take that to him and deliver it personally. Do I make myself clear?"

I nodded.

He continued, "And when you return, you have two choices, either present to me his signed acceptance of this, or your written request that you be transferred to the East Kilbride office. I believe they need somebody to oversee the digitisation of old written records. That should be well within even your somewhat limited skill set, heaven help them."

"But that's actually only *one* choice. A choice is a singular noun implying two possible..." I looked at his face and decided now might not be the time to continue this.

I gathered the printouts and left the office.

I spent the rest of the day feeding the ducks in St James's Park and wandering idly through the West End. I had an odd feeling of seeing the area as if for the first time. The crowded streets with everybody in a hurry, the shops with their endless sales and discounts, the traffic dancing a beautifully choreographed ballet through traffic lights and roundabouts. So familiar but at the same time, slightly alien. I wondered if Froggy was serious in his threats to send me to East Kilbride if I failed to get Sullivan's acceptance. I didn't ponder that long, though, as I knew he wouldn't hesitate. I'd seen him do the same thing to others on more than one occasion. While my lowly rank in the Civil Service offered a certain security, in as much as I was unlikely to be dismissed unless I actually killed somebody, and only then on camera, I had no defence against being moved from place to place on the whims of the more senior officials.

I'd been to Glasgow before. Just the once, to the Immigration Office at the airport, helping to set up data management systems to allow better processing of passenger information of foreign nationals. And although a perfectly lovely city, it wasn't London.

I went back to the office briefly to contact the Hydrographic Office to request up-to-date images on the coast around Little Didney. They told me they would provide hard copies and courier them up to the FCDO within five working days. I settled on that and was about to leave for home when I had a change of mind. I rang them back and said I needed the data urgently and that I would drive down to Taunton to collect it personally in the morning.

Taunton was on my route back to Cornwall, so it would only be a ten-minute diversion. I then telephoned Tiggy to book a boat trip back over to Scanlon's Rock and asked her if she could arrange another meet with Jim Sullivan.

~ * ~ * ~ * ~

BY MID-AFTERNOON THE FOLLOWING DAY, I arrived back in Little Didney with the maps and a statement for Sullivan to sign, relinquishing his claims on independence.

Goodenough checked me back in to the Bridal Suite and I unpacked my overnight bag, after which, I headed down to the bar for a snack.

The bar was closed, but Goodenough let me settle at a table with a sandwich, a beer and my papers. I spread out the sheets from the Hydrographic Office and studied them. Although they were very large scale, and clearly showed the changes in coastline from the previous sets I'd seen, I couldn't find a way of measuring accurately enough to get within the hundred metres or fewer necessary to pin this down.

My phone rang, and it was Tiggy letting me know she'd fixed up a meeting with Jim and I needed to be at the harbour in two hours. I thanked her and went back to my sandwich as I tried to think through the problem of the maps. I could ask the Hydrographic Office to do an accurate distancing for me, but that would take time and if Froggy got to hear of it, I'd be on the next bus to Glasgow.

Goodenough wandered over and planted another beer on the table, unbidden.

For the briefest of moments I thought it might be a generous gesture for a weary traveller, then he said, "I'll put that on yer tab."

I looked up at him. "Who around here would know the shorelines better than anybody else?"

"That'll be the Commodore. Born on the sea, he knows the coastlines here better than the crabs."

"Where would I find him?"

"Got a workshop up behind the Duty-Free shop. While you're there, can you pick up Elisse?"

"Who's Elisse?"

"He'll know, just ask for Elisse."

I gathered up the maps, drank as much of the beer as I could, and headed out. I found the Duty-Free shop just along the harbour front from the Smuggler's Arms. The shop looked new and not open yet. I pressed up against the window to cut the reflected light. Sparsely stocked shelves held a varied assortment of goods, ranging from alcohol to cheap electrical gadgets such as chargers or plug adaptors. A little wicker basket held an assortment of round disks of varying sizes but all a similar grey colour with some sort of patterning I couldn't make out. It seemed a very random shop, considering this was a Cornish fishing village and not part of some international airport.

A glance at the sign above the shop told of its sudden appearance. A badly fitted, and clearly free-hand painted sign announced, 'Little Didney International Seaport - Duty Free Shop'.

I continued around the side of the shop to find a small alley. I followed this and came to a large oak door, which had one time, clearly belonged to something grander than this workshop. It was open, and offered a view of a room, with walls covered in pictures of ships. They mostly depicted scenes of naval battles covering all eras and navies. A mix of watercolours, oils, prints, and some photographs. A huge table occupied the centre of the room. The central part was painted mostly blue, with greens and browns covering some raised areas around the edges. It resembled a model train setting, except this was mostly sea. Miniature castles bristled along the coastlines and tiny ships sat on the blue of the sea.

A man sat at a large workbench, hunched over a brightly lit magnifying glass and studying something locked in a small vice.

He must have heard me, as he called, "Come on in, young man, I won't be a moment."

I moved a little closer and saw he had a miniature cannon. He pressed a button on a small device which resembled a TV remote control. The cannon gave a little crack and the glass in a small window in the opposite wall shattered.

"Ah," he said. "I might have to adjust that." He looked up and peered across the top of his glasses at me. "You must be John Cabot, the minister man. What can I do for you?"

"Commodore Saltby?" I asked.

"That's me."

"Mr Goodenough said you'd be able to help me understand some hydrographic charts."

He placed his tweezers on a small leather pad and removed his glasses. "I would have thought that you'd have people for that back in London?"

"We do, but I'm not convinced they're being as forthcoming with their help as might be appropriate. Given the situation."

He smiled and turned to a little gas burner under an old kettle. He clicked the flame into life. "Seems like a very careful way of saying you think they're trying to hide something. Tea?"

"Um, yes, thank you."

The Commodore took two mugs from a shelf, held them up to the light, then wiped them on a yellow duster. He stood with them in his hands as he studied me. "You're not a normal government man, are you?"

"I'm not sure…"

He planted the mugs on the bench and dropped a teabag in each. "Last lot of government men came down here, thought they were dealing with a bunch of half-witted, country folk. Cornwall's been dealing with government men for centuries, and they always think they can call the odds. Milk and sugar?"

"Milk, just a touch, no sugar. Thank you."

"Came along here, with all their clipboards and iPhones, telling us how they were going to take possession of the rock. Didn't work out too well for them this time either."

"I heard."

He looked at me, then flicked his head back with a little, "Huh." The kettle whistled, and he poured water into the mugs, squished the tea bags and removed them, then handed one of the mugs to me. "Milk's over there." He nodded to a carton on the bench.

I studied the mug. It bore a gold braided crest, a spear with crown, laid on a red background, and the legend, HMS Gladius. "I'm just a research analyst in the Foreign Office," I said. "I can't take possession of anything. I'm so low down the ladder, I have trouble keeping possession of my own parking space." I tipped a little milk into the mug, sipped, and set the mug on the big table.

"Don't put that there," the Commodore snapped. "That's Cadiz." He waved at the workbench. "Put it there." He motioned to a vacant corner of his workbench.

"Cadiz?" I scanned the diorama. I now recognised it as the Atlantic coast of south west Spain, reaching down beyond the Straits of Gibraltar, with Morocco in the south. Around forty or fifty, miniature battleships grouped facing each other. Each ship was beautifully detailed, down to tiny people on board. "This must be Trafalgar," I said.

The Commodore smiled over his mug and nodded. "Man knows his history. Changed the face of naval warfare, this one." He pointed at the ships. "You see how the British ships are in two columns heading straight at the French line?"

I looked more closely. The French ships lined up so their sides faced the oncoming flotilla. "Yes, so their cannons pointed at the English."

"Correct. Up until then, opposing navies had always lined up side-on, so their cannons would aim at the enemy. They'd chuck cannonballs at each other that way, until one side sank more of the other's ships, forcing a retreat. Nelson changed all that. He drove head on and split the French line in two. The French lost most of their fleet, with not a single loss on the British side." He sank the last of his tea and rinsed the cup. "You said you had some charts? Show me." He cleared a space on the bench.

I unrolled the charts and looked for something to weigh down the corners. I picked up a round lump of pitted metal, about three or four centimetres in diameter. "Alright to use one of these?" I asked.

"About all they're good for. That's swivel gun shot, there's a box of them somewhere. Came off a Spanish wreck out near St Michael's Bay."

I stood back and pointed at the charts. "I got these from the Hydrographic Office today, so they're about as up to date as they can be."

He studied them for a moment, then aimed a wooden ruler at various points, explaining each as he went. "Here's the headland, and that's Trellyan Cove. And here," he planted the ruler along a shaded part, then drew a line with pencil. "That's the sandbank, now submerged since eighty-seven." He looked me straight in the eye. "Now, exactly what is it you want to know?"

I studied the pencil line and had to force myself not to go in search of an eraser. "I want to know how far away Scanlon's Rock is." The line on the map captivated my attention.

He squinted his eyes at me as if trying to see a different answer in mine. "Hmm, the sandbank marked the point the baseline cut across the harbour, but now that's gone, officially, the baseline reverts to the low water mark on the shore, here." He aimed the ruler at the headland. "This chart is a scale of one to ten thousand. That's ten centimetres to the kilometre. So..." He placed his ruler against the chart where the sandbank was marked. "Now, that's 260 metres back from the previous baseline."

"Meaning?"

"Meaning..." He tapped at keys on an oversized calculator. "Scanlon's Rock is exactly 12.11 nautical miles from the new baseline. Though I'm not sure that's the answer you wanted. Your tea's getting cold."

I drank the tea as I studied the charts. "And you're sure?"

"Son, I have sailed these waters sixty-years, man and boy. So, yes, I know. I also happen to have the finest Russian satellite navigation system ever produced. Far more accurate than the British systems. The Yanks purposely degrade the signals from their satellites, you know?"

"So I understand. Why a Russian system though?"

"Came off a Russian trawler, as they called it. Three years back, wrecked on the Dragon Point one night."

"I never heard about that," I said.

"Nor would you have. The Royal Navy position was that no Russian vessel could ever get that close, the Russkies denied all knowledge. Ipso facto, it didn't exist. The locals had the thing dismantled and scattered halfway across the county before anybody could decide that it might be there at all."

"It was dismantled?"

He looked surprised I should question this. "The Cornish have been doing this for centuries. They're very good at it." He shrugged and supped the last of his tea. "Anyway, I got the satellite navigation unit, but I don't know where the rest went. Although, there are rumours that old man Goodenough has a surface-to-air missile in his attic."

That reminded me. "I nearly forgot, Mr Goodenough asked me to pick up Elisse?"

"Elisse? Yes, quite right, she's over there." He pointed to a ship's figurehead sat on the floor. It stood about a metre high and represented a sorrowful looking woman with gold, flowing hair.

"That's beautiful," I said.

"Rumour has it, it came off the Vagabunda. Branok fished it up in his nets a few years back, thought I might like it for the Argo."

"The Argo?"

"My motor yacht. I spent many hours restoring her," he nodded towards Elisse. "But, in the end, she didn't seem right for the Argo. And as Sam's been after her for years, I finally gave in to him. She deserves a good home, where she'll be admired by all. You tell him to look after her."

I lifted Elisse carefully. She wasn't quite as heavy as I'd expected. "I will, and thanks for the help." I turned to leave.

"That'll be fifty quid," the Commodore said.

"Fifty quid? For your help?"

"No, for Elisse, fifty quid. Help's free. She's not leaving here on tick. I know what he's like."

"Ah." I put the figurehead down as I rummaged in my pocket. "I'll need a receipt to show Mr Goodenough."

"A receipt, is it? Well, in that case, it's eighty."

I looked at the notes in my hand. I figured not getting a fifty pounds back was preferable to not getting eighty back. "Okay." I handed him a fifty note.

I turned to go, then paused by the door. "You're sure the island is 12.11 nautical miles from the low water mark?"

The Commodore sighed, then picked up a white peaked cap from a peg on the wall. "You'd better come with me, son."

I followed the Commodore down to the harbour. We walked the harbour wall around, and out into the water. A long, low motor launch bobbed at a buoy, some twenty metres from the harbour wall on which we stood. I scanned the boat. It looked more like it should be chugging the Thames while Bertie Wooster sipped cocktails and entertained young flappers. Everything on board seemed to be made of polished pine, shiny brass, or pristine white paint. A few coils of white rope lay in strategic locations.

"She's beautiful," I said.

"The Argo, named after Jason's boat. Once belonged to Agatha Christie. I found it in a boatyard in Wallingford. Terrible state it was. Taken me twenty years to restore her."

He guided me down some slippery steps carved in the wall to a small, white, clinker-built dinghy. The little craft wobbled side to side with every breath I took. I gripped the sides and wondered if I could hold my breath for the trip over.

The Commodore unhitched the rope and settled in the seat. The boat wobbled again as he picked up the oars and set them in the rowlocks. He pulled at the oars with a strength which belied the fact that he must be at least in his late sixties.

We arrived at the rear of the Argo, where a set of white wooden steps led up to the deck. I climbed the steps, hearing the words of my school gym master, when he was teaching me to scale the climbing frame, 'Three points of contact at all times'.

Once on board, the Commodore pointed to a deckchair. "Take a seat, make yourself comfortable. This is nowhere near as fast as Tegan's boat."

"That's fine by me."

He patted the top of the polished wood instrument panel in the wheelhouse. "Can't rush an old lady like this one. It's improper."

He turned a key, pressed a button, and a rumbling rose up through my feet. Slow, comforting, and unexciting. As we gently made our way out of the harbour, it reminded me of one of those Dinner Cruises I'd been bulldozed into taking on the Thames. All part of the welcome for the Ambassador of Guatemala on a 'Friendship Visit', designed to show the joys of London. Not much of a joy, trying to eat Lobster Bisque on a moving boat. That had cost me a new dinner shirt.

A fishing boat overtook us, and the Commodore waved to the skipper as they went. "That's the Pelican, Branok Tretheway's boat. He'll be out for the day now. Back on the early tide. You see here, the tip of the harbour wall?" The Commodore pointed with a small wooden rod. He had a polished wooden pointing stick, of course he did. "This is still six-point-two metres back from the base line. You can see the beach over there," pointing again. "That's where the low water mark is furthest south in this area. Representing the base line."

He turned the wheel, and what seemed like ten minutes later, the boat responded by turning towards the beach.

"You see that number there?" He pointed to an instrument in the control panel. "The one which starts 49? That's our position north. The higher the number, the further north we are. If you watch that, you'll be able to work out which is the southernmost point of the shore."

I was sure he was right, but I didn't really understand.

As we neared the beach, the pointing stick came out again. "You see the remains of that jetty?" He aimed the stick at some upright bits of wood, just breaking the surface of the water. "That's where the sandbank used to start. Now we'll follow the line of where it went." He turned the wheel once more, and we both waited patiently while the boat eventually responded. If Agatha Christie had owned this thing, I could quite see how she had so much time to write all those books. What else does one do while waiting for a boat like this to get anywhere?

We skimmed the beach, surprisingly close, then turned south-east, the bow pointing to open sea.

"If you look into the water here on the port side, you might be able to make out a different colour to the sea. That's the remains of the sandbank."

I craned my neck over the side and stared. Just water.

"The other port side," the Commodore said.

I moved to the other side of the boat and studied the water. Now I could see a difference. A slightly lighter hue to the water, nothing dramatic, but I supposed to somebody who knew what they were looking for, significant.

We chugged along a bit further out to sea, then the Commodore silenced the engine. "Here is where the sandbank ended." He picked up his glasses from the string around his neck and planted them on his nose. He squinted at the numbers on the satnav unit. "Now, if I deduct..." he tapped at numbers on an oversized calculator, "...there, we are exactly 11.97 nautical miles from the northernmost point of Scanlon's Rock." He pointed to the grey smudge of the island sitting just below the horizon. "Now, should the land of Great Britain finish here, then indeed, Scanlon's Rock would be within its limits."

I nodded.

"But, of course, it doesn't," he said. "It actually finishes back there." He aimed his pointing stick at the coast behind us. "QED, Mr Sullivan's island is indeed outside of the United Kingdom's territorial waters limits."

# ~ CHAPTER SIX ~

GOODENOUGH WASN'T AROUND WHEN I returned to the Smuggler's Arms, so I left Elisse on the bar and headed down to the harbour to meet Tiggy. I checked my watch as I arrived on the waterfront. Exactly two hours since Tiggy had said to meet her in two. There was no sign of her. I tried to suppress my irritation, reminding myself this was Cornwall, and not London. That didn't stop my right foot from tapping in impatience. There was, however, a man who looked like a refugee from Woodstock. His long hair, flashed with white, tangled in natural semi-dreadlocks across his shoulders. His slim build, and a face which looked more carved from rough tree bark than flesh, gave a general appearance of a life well lived. He also had a cow on a lead.

He saw me watching him and returned a smile of unnaturally white teeth and eyes so clear and blue as to rival a new-born kitten's. He looked vaguely familiar, but I couldn't think why. I nodded a smile in return, then scanned the harbour mouth for any signs of Tiggy's boat.

A thin trail of white streaked inwards from behind the headland. As I watched, it grew until I could make out a boat skimming the waves heading in our direction. The man pointed at the boat and said something I couldn't hear. He smiled again.

As the boat drew closer, I recognised the lines of the '300', Tiggy's boat. It headed straight in to a vacant spot against the dock and settled gently against the fenders. I noticed the deck of the boat was almost level with the dock now. I guessed the tide must be higher today.

Tiggy jumped off the bow of the boat as it touched. She carried a rope, which she looped around a bollard with practised ease. She waved a brief acknowledgement in my direction, then went to talk to the man with the cow. Much pointing at the boat and the cow, but I couldn't hear what they were saying. I moved up to them.

"But you have to take her," the man said. "It's a surprise for Jim's birthday."

"A surprise?" Tiggy replied. "You bought Jim a cow for his birthday? How much have you had to smoke today, Stringy?"

Stringy, that was it. I knew I recognised him from somewhere. Stringy Cordell, Jim's guitarist in the Spartans.

"Just a..." He held his thumb and forefinger close together as if holding an invisible pea. "Little teeny bit, you know, keeps the goblins quiet."

"What on earth induced you to buy a cow?" Tiggy asked.

"I know how much Jimbo likes fresh milk on his Sugarpuffs. I thought... well... Milk, cows, sort of go together. Cut out the middleman."

"There's a middleman between cow and Sugarpuffs for a reason, Stringy. How did you two ever even *form* a band?"

"Ah, come on, Tiggy. You gotta take her. I can't take her home, they got rules in my apartment."

"Against cows?"

"Well, cats actually, but I'm sure cows are in the small print. I know I'm not allowed to open a fish shop. She'll be cool, really. I mean, look." He pointed at the cow, who was looking decidedly cool and nonplussed.

"It'll panic," Tiggy said. "The moment we start to move, it will panic. Do you really want to be on a small boat in the English Channel with a panicking cow?"

"No, she won't panic. Promise. I gave her a bit of my magic bush to keep her calm."

"You got your cow stoned?"

"I think we should call her by her name," Stringy said. "Ermintrude. Not right to keep calling her the cow, like she's not a real person."

Tiggy threw her arms up in the air and walked around in a tight circle. "I don't need this." She turned to face him. "Right, you get her on the boat, and you keep her calm. I'm having nothing to do with it. And if it kicks off, you're both getting out and walking."

"You're a hero. Just hang on to this a mo." He handed her the cow's lead rope. "I'll go get Dylan and Zebedee." He set off to the far end of the harbour.

"Dylan and Zebedee?" she called after him.

"Chickens, they make eggs. The other half of the breakfast."

Tiggy held the rope and watched him go, then turned to me. "And what have you brought for the show-and-tell table?"

I held up the roll of charts. "Just some hydrographic charts that show the underwater topography."

She looked at me, then shook her head. "I suppose I should be grateful. How are you with cows?"

"I know they are a major contributor to greenhouse gases. Oh, and they kill more people each year than sharks."

"I was thinking more in terms of whether you're any good at looking after them, but I think you probably answered that."

The squawking of chickens drew my attention, and I turned to see Stringy marching back with a wheelbarrow, in which sat a cage containing a pair of chickens. "All set," he called as he drew up alongside the '300'. "We can go now."

"Just one small problem," said Tiggy. "How do you propose getting this," she indicated the cow, "onto that?" pointing at the boat.

"Easy, I got this." He picked up the end of a wide plank and dragged it to the boat. "The farmer let me have it. It's for getting them into trucks, but truck, boat, Ermintrude won't know the difference." He dropped one end on the deck of the boat. "There you go."

"That's too much of a drop down into the boat," Tiggy said. "It can't get down there. I'll have to turn the boat so the dock is more level to the rear deck."

After boat juggling and plank juggling, the cow actually crossed the plank quite happily. Bribed by a small bunch of greenery which Stringy held out for her, and only let her have once she was safely on the deck.

The cow took up most of the small lower deck and stood nose towards the inner door to the cabin and her rear end just fitting inside the aft railing. Ermintrude seemed quite content, unnaturally so. Probably something to do with the nature of the bush with which Stringy had been bribing her. We left Stringy to look after his charge, and I went up to the upper deck with Tiggy.

Tiggy took the boat out of the harbour very slowly and edged it into the thankfully now calm, open sea. I settled into the passenger seat, fixed my eyes on the horizon and tried to pretend I was sitting on a bench on Bournemouth sea front. It didn't work. My stomach rotated gently in time with the movement of the island.

"Try not to think about it," Tiggy said.

"About what?"

"About feeling seasick and that horrible squirly feeling you get like your head's in a tumble dryer and you're about to throw up your breakfast of fried bread, runny eggs—"

"Not helping," I said.

I heard her chuckle over the wind and concentrated on making the island grow bigger.

After a while, I'd just managed to convince myself we were in reality, just in a sports car on a slightly bumpy road, when a loud thump came from below and the boat wobbled from side to side. It felt, for all the world, like we'd just lost a wheel from my imaginary car.

I grabbed the little handrail in front of me. "What happened?" I asked.

"Felt like we hit something." Tiggy throttled the engine back to a gentle purr, and the boat bobbed gently as it drifted. She peered over the bow as far as she could from her position, then scanned the water each side of the boat. "Nothing there. Have a quick look from the lower deck, will you?"

I negotiated the little ladder with possibly an excess of caution, but it was moving, as was the inside of my head and stomach. I landed on the lower deck and immediately saw the problem. The cow was lying down on the floor with Stringy sat on the semi-circular rear seat, resting his outstretched legs on the cow's rump.

"What happened?" I asked.

"She fancied a lie down," he said. "Must be coming on to rain. They do that, you know, lie down when it's going to rain."

"Oh, is she alright?"

He gave a little shove with his foot and the beast grunted. "Yeah, she's cool. Are we nearly there yet?"

"Don't think so." I headed back up the ladder.

"Well?" Tiggy asked as I appeared up top.

"Ermintrude fell over. Stringy thinks she's getting ready for rain."

"Nothing to do with the dope plant he's been feeding her all morning, then?"

"Ah, yes, hadn't thought of that."

"How are the chickens?"

"I don't know, they're quiet. Can we go a bit faster now? As she's asleep." My desire to get off this insane version of Noah's Ark and onto something more solid was becoming urgent.

"Don't see why not. Hold tight." She pushed the throttle lever forward, and the back end of the boat bit into the water, pushing us forwards.

I slumped back in my seat, gripping the side of it with one hand, and the little deck rail with the other. The rocking movement of before had now been swapped for a more violent thumping and bouncing, as we broke through the tops of the little waves, rather than riding over them. I wasn't sure which sensation was worse, as although I was no longer feeling queasy, the buffeting made it feel like the boat could disintegrate at the very next bump.

Fortunately, the increased speed meant my torment was short-lived, and we soon slid into the shore of Pirate's Cove. Tiggy played with the controls and the boat drifted through a one-eighty turn, and very gently idled sideways to a gentle bump as the bow grounded out.

"You'll have to walk from here," she said. "It's only a couple of feet deep." She slid down the ladder. "Come on, Stringy, time to wake your cow up."

"Yeah, cool," I heard him say. "Wakey wakey, Ermintrude."

I climbed down the ladder to the now very overcrowded bottom deck.

Stringy shoved at Ermintrude, who blinked an eye at him, then snuffled and laid her head down again.

Tiggy dragged the plank to the boarding point at the rear and swung open the little gate. The plank splashed into the water.

Tiggy looked at me. "You can test it out."

"Thank you," I said. I sat down to remove my shoes and socks and pulled my trousers up over my knees.

Tiggy nodded towards my shoes. "I thought you were going to bring walking shoes this time?"

I held the shoes up. "These are they."

Her brow crinkled fleetingly. "They are these, are they?" She shook her head. "They look just the same as the ones you had on the other day?"

"I know. They're great, aren't they? Church's make a range of—"

"I'm sure they're quite wonderful." Tiggy cut in and flapped her hand towards the plank, indicating I should hurry up.

I stepped down the plank and into the water, which lapped around the bottom of my rolled-up trousers. I waddled the five metres to the shore, trying to keep bag, shoes, and trouser bottoms as dry as possible. Once on the dry sand, I sat down to replace shoes and socks and watched as Stringy finally prodded Ermintrude into a standing position, then led her down the plank with the temptation of more of her now favourite vegetation.

Once Stringy and Ermintrude were ashore, Tiggy took the boat out, secured the anchor, and then came in on the little dinghy. By the time she came back, Stringy and his menagerie had negotiated the cut to the top of the cliff and had disappeared from sight.

When we'd climbed to the top, they were just visible in the distance. Stringy carried what looked like a long stick, and the chicken cage had been tied to the cow's back. They plodded along in a strange Quixotic pastiche.

"How was London?" Tiggy asked.

"Oh, the usual. Shops, pavement cafes in the rain. No cows or boats."

She smiled. "Are you sure you're in the right job? Only, tell me to shut up if you want, but you really don't seem cut out for this whole diplomat business?"

"Funny you should say that, it has been mentioned to me before. But parental expectations and all that." I stopped for a moment to catch my breath while pretending to take in the view. "My father was a hero in the Diplomatic Service."

"A hero?"

"Yes, he helped smuggle a British agent out of North Korea when he was ambassador there. They hid him in the embassy car during a diplomatic visit to the Sino-Korean Friendship Bridge."

"I can see how that would be a lot to live up to. My dad was a hero too. Not like *your* dad though, but he was able to down seven pints of Goodenough's special scrumpy and still beat Porth Cullen in the inter-pub skittles league. He's got his own tankard with his name on it behind the bar to commemorate it. Although, it's engraved Brandon, instead of Branok. Have you ever tried to text the name Branok to an engraver? Auto correct's going to start a war one day."

I pondered the idea of having my own engraved beer tankard behind a bar somewhere. The idea seemed strangely beguiling, yet somehow scary at the same time.

"I suppose I should have rebelled and done something different. But it's difficult when everything is laid out for you like a train track and you've got the Flying Scotsman pushing at your back. I had a vague notion of being a private detective, but that was never going to happen."

"Private dick, huh?" She studied me as if weighing me up for my stated vocation. "Yeah, I can see that. You're certainly tenacious enough." She nodded towards my feet. "You'd need some better shoes though; you won't catch many philandering husbands in shoes like those."

I followed her gaze and realised I had my foot in one of Ermintrude's recent deposits. I removed my foot and pushed my shoe around on the grass. "Not that sort of private detective. More the resourceful one who spends his time trawling through dusty old records in secret libraries to find the secret last will and testament left by great uncle Peabody."

She shook her head and started walking again. "So, you really want to be Peter Parker, Spiderman's secret identity?"

"You can scoff, but when you want to prove that the local shepherd does *not* have droving rights through your front room, you'll thank me."

We fell to silence as we plodded. Walking over land like this necessitated much concentration to avoid more of Ermintrude's pancakes, or ankle-ready rabbit holes.

I felt we should have been able to close the distance on a septuagenarian guitarist and a cow, but somehow, we couldn't, and by the time we arrived at Government House, they were nowhere to be seen.

Jeeves spotted us as we rounded the front of the house. "Oh, it's you two," he said. "You took your time."

"John's got some new walking shoes." Tiggy pointed at my feet, as if they explained everything.

"Don't look much like no walking shoes I've ever seen," he said. "Best follow me. See if you can keep up." He turned and headed for the main door.

I noticed the half-constructed Wikihouse/Chinese-restaurant-to-be had moved on a fair bit since my last visit. "That's coming on," I said.

"Like mushrooms. He's got another one started over yonder." He nodded in the direction of the cliff. "Guest house, he calls that one. Hope he's not expecting me to butler to guests."

We had to negotiate our way round Ermintrude, who was parked by the door, before we could enter. I couldn't work out if she was being curious, or just bloody-minded, as she kept moving in my way each time I aimed for the door. A surreal version of the Pavement Dance pedestrians play on Oxford Street on busy days.

We found Jim and Stringy in the lounge. They each had a glass of something toxic-looking and the room lay heavy with the scent of cannabis.

"Ah, the man from the ministry," Jim greeted. "Have you met Stringy? He plays guitar with the band, allegedly." He waved his glass in the direction of a couple of armchairs. "Take the weight off, you look knackered."

I took the cue and sat, briefcase securely on lap. "Yes, we met in the village," I said.

"Stringy's brought me a birthday present. You'll never guess what it is."

"A cow?" I suggested.

"Aw." Stringy looked at me with sad puppy eyes, "You've ruined the surprise now."

"You bought me a cow?" Jim looked suddenly alive. "I thought you'd just got me the chickens?"

"Yeah, but you can't have chickens without a cow."

"I know." Jim stood and pointed at Stringy. "See, the only guy who really gets it. That's why we're so cool. Where's my cow?"

I looked towards Tiggy. She shrugged and shook her head slightly as we watched the pair head for the front door.

"You may have a bit of a wait," she said.

"Gives me chance to organise my papers." I opened the briefcase and spread some of the files on the small glass coffee table. I found my label maker and printed off some sticky labels to identify the contents of several of them.

I glanced up to see Tiggy watching me carefully, she looked confused. "It'll make things easier for Jim to file them later," I explained. "For future reference."

"You know we have pens in Cornwall now? If you'd asked, I could've found you one."

I picked up one of the files. "But labels make it easier to change, if necessary. Labels peel off again. Have you ever tried to identify the contents of a file which has been written on, then crossed out a dozen times?"

She seemed lost in thought for a moment, then simply said, "No."

"Well, if you had, you'd appreciate the value of one of these." I held up the label maker briefly before dropping it back in my briefcase.

"I'm just saying there should be an instruction manual," Jim said, as he came back into the room.

"You can't have an instruction manual for a cow," Stringy said. "They're just cows. That's all they do."

"But how do you feed it? And the milking, how does that work? I remember having an instruction manual when my folks bought me a gerbil for my eighth birthday. You know, how to feed it and where to keep it where it could stay warm but couldn't get into the electric toaster."

"Toaster?" asked Tiggy.

"Yeah, it was complicated, bit of a misunderstanding about the 'Keep Warm' setting," Jim said. "Hey, you must know how to milk a cow?"

"Why do you say that?" Tiggy bristled. "Is it because I catch fish for a living or because I'm female?"

Jim stared at Tiggy, and his mouth moved slightly as if rehearsing what to say. Finally, he settled on, "Because you know Tom Pengelly, the farmer."

"I also know you, that doesn't make me an expert on making pop songs."

"Pop songs?" Jim looked ready to explode. Or about as ready as somebody who lives in a perpetual haze of cannabis and Jack Daniel's will ever look. "I don't do pop songs, I'm a rock god, a national treasure. It says so in Classic Rock Magazine. Pops songs, pfah." He collapsed into an armchair and reignited his joint. "You must be mixing me up with Justin Bieber." He blew a cloud of smoke across the room and sank deeper into the chair.

Tiggy smiled. "There we go, my point exactly."

Jim's face flicked into confusion briefly, then he gave a little shake of his head and looked at me. "So, what did you bring me?"

I opened the briefcase on my lap. "I have an official response to your request for the secession of this island from the greater United Kingdom—"

"I meant for my birthday," Jim interrupted. "But hey-ho, let's get this done, then I'll have two things to celebrate."

"Hmm," I wasn't quite sure how he was going to take this, so I took one of the files I'd prepared and handed it to him. At least his hands would be occupied.

Jim looked at both sides of the folder, as if looking for the Cliff Notes, then said, "What's that then? My island divorce decree absolute? When do I get my letter from the King?"

"Are you familiar with the Montevideo Convention of 1933?"

"No, but I'm sure you're going to tell me all about it." He tossed the folder onto the coffee table.

"The good news is that it looks like you might be right about the position of Scanlon's Rock," I said.

"I really don't like good news, bad news conversations. They're always just ways of people dumping shit on you. Nobody ever says, the good news is you've just copped a million, but the bad news is I broke your favourite mug. It's always, you've got to pay out twenty grand in damages to a hotel for the swimming pool you trashed, but hey, at least I didn't break your mug."

"Yes." My carefully rehearsed piece about appeal processes, or maybe trying to open a dialogue with the UN crumbled. I shuffled the piles of papers in front of me, vaguely hoping for a way to spin this in a more positive way. I failed.

After a long, awkward silence, Jim said, "Well? What's your shit?"

I breathed deep and focused. "Even allowing for some area of dispute over the territorial waters issue, there are still other factors which prevent your application from being successful. The Montevideo Convention provides that a sovereign state must fulfil certain other criteria. For example, it must possess a permanent population, and you've only just moved in. It needs a government, and the capacity to conduct international relations. You have to have a currency and a legislature. Trade with other countries. Maybe give it a year or two and try again?"

"Okay." Jim eased himself out of his chair and collected a bottle of Jack Daniel's and two glasses from a Chinese cabinet. He poured a generous measure in each and placed one in front of me. "Is that all?"

"Well, maybe some other details, but in essence, that's the thrust of the convention."

He took a large sip of his drink and stared out of the huge window for a while. He seemed to be searching the horizon for answers, and then after what seemed like minutes, he turned.

"What's the bit about conducting international relations?"

Despite hours of preparation and obsessive research, Jim continued to throw me with his responses. I'd expected a temper tantrum or threats of lawyers. Even one of his famous rantings about governmental oppression, instead, I got a simple, clear question about a relatively minor issue.

"Um, that means..." I sought the words. As a civil servant in the FCDO, we spoke all the time of conducting international affairs without ever really needing to define the term. It was just that. International affairs. But how does one explain it? "I suppose the best way of explaining that is that you need to be able to, and have the infrastructure, resources, personnel, etcetera, to negotiate on a government-to-government basis via some diplomatic structure. One government's diplomats negotiate with—"

"Yeah, yeah. I got that. You don't need to go on. It's like when I get my tour manager to negotiate with Virgin Atlantic over shipping our gear to Canada for a gig. I don't get on the phone to Richard Branson myself."

"Yes, I suppose that's a fair analogy. You need a diplomatic structure that is recognised by at least one other sovereign state."

"Cool." He flapped his hand towards my glass. "Drink up. There's someone I want you to meet."

"Who's that?"

"It's time you met the President of Scanlon's Rock."

# ~ CHAPTER SEVEN ~

I FOLLOWED HIM OUTSIDE AND clambered, somewhat reluctantly, into the back of the Land Rover alongside Tiggy. Jim jumped in the passenger door and sat for a moment.

"You alright?" Tiggy asked him.

"Yeah. Oh, I'm driving." He tried to stifle a giggle and failed. "I forgot. Hang on." He shuffled across to the driver's side, doing battle with handbrake and gear stick on the way.

"Would you like me to drive?" Tiggy offered.

"No, I've got this." He searched his pockets and came up empty. "Did I give you the keys?"

"I think you left them in the door."

"Oh, yeah." Jim climbed out of the Land Rover and walked round to the passenger side to retrieve the keys from the door lock. "I don't know why I lock it really. It's not like anybody's going to nick it out here." He clambered back in and turned the key. The engine reluctantly spluttered into life.

"Is he alright to drive?" I asked Tiggy, under cover of the noise of an engine complaining about being in the wrong gear.

"He'll be fine. Anyway, what's he going to hit?"

As we set off, I soon realised that my fear of colliding with something was the least of my worries. We bounced along a rough track, keeping close to the cliff edge as we went. Far too close for my liking. I grabbed the seat with one hand and the door handle with the other. Not that either would save me if we went over the edge, but somehow, I felt I was doing my bit to keep us alive.

Tiggy must have noticed my stress, as she said, "Don't worry, he likes to follow the edge when he's stoned. He can't get lost that way."

"That's a comfort."

We followed the cliff edge for about five minutes, then veered onto an almost-track and eventually into a small copse of trees. When they broke, the lighthouse loomed in front of us. The once white tower climbed out beyond the treetops, faded red rings snaked around it every couple of metres or so. We slid, slightly sideways, to a stop on a gravel patch in front of the door, a large wooden affair, and the only part of this building which looked to be upwards of the nineteenth century.

The lighthouse door swung open as we decanted the Land Rover, and a heavily bearded face peered out. When he saw who it was, the rest of the man stepped out. Grey hair straggled from his head and melded seamlessly with an equally straggly beard. A pair of hooded eyes stared out from the bundle of hair. Despite his apparent age, the man moved easily. As he left the doorway, a dog followed by his side. A large mutt whose distant ancestors had probably once met a German shepherd.

Jim held an arm out towards me. "John, meet Walter Tyler, the President of Scanlon's Rock. Everybody calls him Watt."

"Watt?" I checked.

"Yeah, nobody's quite sure if he got the name as a shorthand of Walter or if it's 'cause he's deaf as a post and says, what to everything."

"I ain't moving," Watt's voice growled, adding to the Wookie-like image.

"Don't worry, Watt," said Jim. "John's not a revenue man. He just came here to tell us we can't declare independence."

Watt chuckled. A rough, gravelly laugh that sounded like it began in a deep cave.

"Better come inside." Watt turned and headed back to the door. "Wind's coming about, be rain with it."

We followed him into the lighthouse, and I scanned the room in which we'd arrived. It was circular, as expected, but beyond that, it bore no resemblance to anything I'd envisioned a lighthouse to be. For a start, there was no spiral metal staircase going up the centre. In fact, it took me a moment to locate the stairs. A simple archway to my right with the stairs just visible as they commenced their climb. The walls were mostly clad in timber of varying colours and ages. Clearly having been added to over many years until little sign of the original brickwork remained. On top of the wooden cladding, shelves crawled around the room at random points and sometimes, crazy angles. I guessed fitting shelves to walls, which were not only concave, but narrowed as they rose, presented certain challenges. Each shelf strained under the weight of hundreds of books. In the few spaces between the shelves, assorted shells or bits of driftwood decorated the last available flat surfaces.

The furniture competed with the walls for chaos, with several stuffed armchairs and a couple of ancient sofas spilling their insides from worn chintz or threadbare velvet. A table, wooden and clearly home-built from driftwood, graced the centre position of the room.

Watt flapped a hand towards the seats. "You can sit, or you can stand. All the same to me."

I chose to sit, and the floral armchair threatened to swallow me as I sank into it.

"Is it still working?" I asked Tiggy.

"The lighthouse? No, shut down years ago. The light's still up there, but it doesn't work. The light-room is now a greenhouse for..." she paused and glanced at Jim. They exchanged silent cues, and she continued, "... for seedlings and... special plants which need... lots of light... and warmth... and... Do you garden?" she asked me.

"No. I live in an apartment with no outdoor space," I said.

Watt picked a bottle of Jack Daniel's and a glass from one of the shelves and handed them, without a word, to Jim. Jim smiled, nodded, then retreated to a wooden rocking chair. He poured a generous measure into the glass, reignited his joint and disappeared in a cloud of smoke.

"Do you live here?" I asked Watt. "I was told the island was uninhabited?"

"Twenty years, coming on," Watt said.

"Watt lost his fishing boat back in a storm in 2003," said Tiggy. "The whole town thought he was dead. No trace of him. Parts of his boat washed up way down on the Lizard, so the coastguard reckoned he'd been swept out that way. They gave up after three days. Two years later, a bird watching group came out to the island, and there he was."

I turned to Watt. "You'd survived two years?"

Watt went on to explain how he'd rescued enough of his fishing nets to rework and catch a few fish. The island, although not bountiful, supported a small variety of edible plants, and the old mine works held a plentiful supply of water. By the time he'd been discovered, he'd grown to love the isolation and decided to stay. The locals from Little Didney helped restore enough of the old lighthouse and ferried necessary supplies over as and when. And all the time, Watt tended to the island, gathering plastic and other flotsam washed up on the beaches and rocks while keeping an eye on the wildlife that lived there.

"And you've really never felt the need to go back to the mainland?" I asked.

"Nuthin' there for me 'ceptin' taxes and bits of paper."

I turned to Jim. "You said you were the only ones here?"

"Nah, you asked who lived at Government House. You didn't ask who lived in the lighthouse."

"Is there anybody else on the island I don't know about?"

"No, I think you're pretty much caught up."

"But how does this help your case?" I asked.

"Permanent population, you said, there he is."

I turned to look at Watt. He sat at an old table and seemed to be polishing a small flattish stone with a file.

"A one-person permanent population?" I thought for a moment. "Okay, you could have an argument. There's a precedent, a village in the U.S.

somewhere, Nebraska, I think, has a listed population of one. So, yes, a population can be one person. That still leaves the other issues—"

"Yeah, government?" Jim cut in. "You can put Watt down as the President." He wagged a finger at me as though directing a secretary to notarise the minutes.

"I thought *you* were the head of state?" I asked.

"Yeah, I'm King." He looked at Tiggy. "Tiggy can be Minister of Fisheries and Boating. Oh, and Women's stuff."

"Women's stuff?" Tiggy frowned. "Do I get a palace? I'm not doing it if I don't get a palace."

"Sure, although you might have to share it with Ermintrude."

"I share a house with my brother Jake and Dad, so that probably won't be much different." She smiled.

"There you go then," Jim said to me. "Sorted, we have a government and a population. What else you got on your list?"

This was rapidly turning into a career ender. "You have to demonstrate the ability to conduct economic activity, separate to the country from which you are intending to secede, both internal and external."

"In English?"

"Money," I said. "You need a currency, and an exchange mechanism."

Jim took a long pull on his joint and stared at the ceiling. After an elongated silence, he said, "I've got a printer, I can probably knock some up. I could have my face on it."

"It doesn't quite work like that."

"Hmm, you might have to leave that one with me. But apart from that, we all good?"

"No," I said.

"Typical paper clip counter," Watt said. He picked up a wooden bowl of what looked like small, flattish pebbles and settled at an old wooden table. "Always something else." He took a file from the bowl and set about polishing one of the pebbles.

Tiggy noticed me watching. "Ammonites," she said. "Little fossils of ancient creatures. The area is rich in them. Watt collects them and carves them all down into the disk shape." She picked up another wooden bowl from a shelf and handed it to me.

I took the bowl from her. It was half filled with a collection of small, grey disks. Similar to the ones I'd seen in the window of the Duty-Free shop. I picked one out and examined it. It was about the size of a pound coin but with tapered edges, like miniature discus. It had a pattern in the surface I couldn't make out.

I squinted closer and held it towards the light. It looked like a picture of a worm.

I turned the ammonite in my hand. "It's beautiful."

"He's been doing that ever since he got stranded here," Tiggy said.

"Had to do somethin' to save me from the crazy," Watt said.

A banging sound on the front door snagged Watt's attention. He headed into the kitchen, returning with a fish, which he took to the front door. He opened the door, tossed the fish out, then closed the door and returned to his seat. "Like I said," he continued, "livin' on yer own can do funny things to yer head. Look at Nietzsche, he sat on his own for so long he thought he'd killed God."

I stared at Watt and then turned to the door. "Um," I started, unsure quite how to reconcile the strange exit of the fish with Nietzsche. I found no words and pointed at the door with another, "Um."

"That'll be Clarence," Tiggy said.

"Clarence?"

"He's a seal. Comes to the door for fish. He's learned how to ask for them by banging on the door."

"Clarence the seal? Oh, good. I was slightly worried something weird was going on for a minute."

A smiled flickered across her face and she said, "What do you think?"

"About Clarence?"

"No, about the ammonite disks." She pointed at the bowl of disks I'd forgotten I was holding.

I picked a handful from the bowl and watched them as I let them tumble back. "They're all different?"

"Yeah, handmade." Jim seemed to come back from his cloud of smoke. "Each one's unique, no two the same."

I resisted my natural urge to correct the tautology and stayed silent.

"You can 'ave one if you want," Watt said, without looking up from his work. "Choose one."

"Really?"

"Course."

I sifted through the bowl of disks and found one which looked like a tiny, and very skinny, octopus. "Can I have this one?" I held it towards him.

He looked up and squinted in my direction. "Echinoderms. What you got?"

"You have to give him something in exchange," Tiggy whispered. "It's how he survives here. People bring him stuff he needs, and he swaps these."

"Oh, sorry," I said. "I haven't really got anything." I dropped the little disk back in the bowl.

Watt squinted at me again and his eyes travelled downwards. "Them's is good shoes. They'll do."

I looked at my feet. "They're Church's. I can't give you—"

Tiggy put her hand on my arm. "Just do it. You've got another pair just the same."

"They're not the same, these are—" I started, then felt her hand squeeze my arm, fingers biting into my forearm.

She gave me a forced smile, but the eyes threatened. "You'll offend him," she said, quietly, but very firmly.

Time stopped while the whole world waited to see if I was going to disappoint this old man who had nothing and who seemed to have become fixated on my shoes.

The pressure became too much, and I relented. As I bent down to remove my shoes, I felt the world breathe again.

I handed the shoes to Watt. He grunted and took them from me, then kicked off his boots and slipped them on his feet. He held a foot up and studied it. "Proper toff."

I picked the disk back from the bowl and slipped it in my pocket. I had a spare pair back at home, so the loss wasn't too critical. I just wasn't looking forwards to squelching my way back to the Land Rover in my socks. I comforted myself with the thought of putting in my expenses claim for this, and seeing the look on Froggy's face. That alone would be worth the discomfort.

"Well done," Tiggy whispered.

"He stung me for a chest freezer," said Jim. "You got off light."

Watt gave one of his deep laughs, which descended into a coughing fit. "Swapped some for a load of ice from a French trawler a few summers back," he said, as soon as his coughing allowed. "Helped keep my fish longer. That was till I got the freezer."

Jim wagged a hand in my direction. "What else you got on your little list?"

I pulled out my file and scanned the notes I'd made.

"You'll still need to gain external recognition from at least one other state."

Jim pondered, then, "You might have to leave that one with me. Is that it?"

I checked down my list again. "Just about. You'll need an ambassador, so you can negotiate with other countries, but that's just a formality."

"I can do that," Jim said.

"No, not if you're the King, you'll need somebody else."

"Tiggy?"

Tiggy shook her head. "Uh-uh. You can leave me out of this."

"What about you?" he asked me. "You know all this stuff. You can do that."

"I could, if I didn't already have a job in the FCO, and a nice flat in Pimlico, and if I wanted to live on a windswept rock in the middle of the English Channel."

"I'll build you a Wiki-embassy all of your own. I've got a contract for ten of them, so they need using up."

"Did I also mention I get seasick in the bath, and I'm allergic to mud? And nature in general?"

My mind wandered to the inevitable conversation I'd soon be having with Sir Oliver Frogmorton on my return. How on earth was I going to explain all this? I needed to find some way to kill this off, or I was going to spend the rest of my career checking immigration applications in a windowless office in East Kilbride.

"I think we should be getting back soon." Tiggy pulled back a floral print curtain from a small, circular window. "Watt's right about the wind. Don't want to get stuck here overnight, I've got a hen party booked for the morning."

The thought of being stuck on this rock in the middle of a tornado, or whatever was coming, removed the last of my resolve to continue this negotiation.

"Okay," I said and thrust a wad of paper in Jim's direction. "If I can just get your signature on this to confirm I've explained everything, and that you withdraw your request, I can get back to solid land."

Jim waved a dismissive hand towards the papers. "I'm not allowed to do paper. Not since the gig in Jerusalem. You have to send it to my legal representatives."

I sank into the armchair. I could stay and argue, but then I'd probably end up stuck here overnight. Not a pleasant thought, and still no certainty he'd sign anyway. On the other hand, if I went back to London without a signature, I'd have Froggy's anger to deal with, and goodness knows where that would lead.

Tiggy stood and looked at me. "I don't know what you're planning, but I'm leaving now before this weather front hits."

I eased myself out of the chair, hoping Jim would say something to stop me. He didn't. He just took another hard pull on his joint and appeared to melt in a haze of smoke.

I turned to Tiggy. "Is Jim driving us?"

"Don't be daft. It's only a short walk from here."

I looked at my feet. "But I haven't got any shoes."

"You'll manage. Pretend you're on holiday."

"I never go barefoot on holiday." I looked again at Jim, but he'd drifted off somewhere quite different to the rest of us. Watt sat at a table, chipping away at a small piece of wood with a knife and seemed to have no further interest in anything else.

"Well?" prompted Tiggy.

"Yes, of course. Okay, right, let's go." I gave a passing glance back towards Jim as we left, but he was going nowhere for some time.

Dusk settled across the trees as we left the lighthouse, making the ground dance with long shadows. I picked my way very carefully across the lumpy terrain until we came to the cut down to the cove. Fortunately here, the sun cast its dying light full to the slope, and we threaded our way to the little sandy beach without mishap. Not that I was able to relax yet, as we still had a sea to cross, and little daylight left with which to find our way.

~ * ~ * ~ * ~

WE ARRIVED BACK IN LITTLE Didney harbour at about eight-thirty, by which time the moon had taken control of the sky, dodging the evening clouds.

I held bits of rope for Tiggy as she secured the '300' to a bollard.

"You back up to London tomorrow?" she asked.

"Yes, I think so. No point in hanging on. Gives me a chance to prepare my report for Monday." I looked at my feet. "And I have to buy shoes."

She stood and studied me for a moment. The moon cast enough light to stand her in a dark silhouette where I could only just make out her expression. She looked angry.

After just long enough a silence to make me feel oddly uncomfortable, she said, "John, has a woman ever invited you to go for a drink with them before?"

Odd question, especially as her expression didn't convey any sense of an invitation. More like a challenge.

"Can I count my sister in the list?" I asked.

"Yes," she replied, with no hesitation.

"In that case, one."

"Hmm, figures. I'll meet you in the Smuggler's in half an hour." She swung a rucksack across her shoulder and disappeared into the shadows of the evening.

I hurried up to my room and showered away the island mud from between my toes, and rinsed off the general sticky feeling the salty sea air had left me. Fortunately, I had too few clothes with me to get in a stress about how to present myself for this meeting. Clean shirt, change of tie and clean trousers, and job done. Just enough time left to stoke the panic flames about whether this was an actual date, or was I to be the next offering in a wicker-man party.

I made my way downstairs to the bar exactly twenty-three minutes after the time Tiggy had said, half an hour. I didn't order a beer, assuming I would wait and order for both of us when she arrived.

By nine, Tiggy had still not showed, so I weighed up ordering on my own or just going up to my room with a snack. I opted for the snack and bedroom and just as I was about to stand, Tiggy arrived. She had a bottle in each hand, which she set on the table as she sat down.

"Sorry, got caught up." She pushed a bottle towards me. No glass, just a bottle of something calling itself, 'Proper Job'.

"Cheers." She held her bottle out for me to chink against.

I obliged and took a taste. Slightly tangy, citrusy even. "Cheers," I returned.

"So, John Cabot," she said. "Tell me about yourself."

"What's to tell? Middling civil servant, sliding into middle age, and wondering what happened to the last twenty years."

"Married?"

"No."

"Never?"

"Never."

"Gay?"

"Not that I'm aware. What's with all the questions?"

She fixed my gaze, as if looking inside my head. "You're a puzzle. I like puzzles."

"Thank you, I think. What about you?" I asked, keen to deflect any more of this interrogation.

"Married or gay? No and not decided." She sipped again from the bottle. "Indian or Chinese?"

"For what?" I asked.

"Food, which do you prefer, Indian or Chinese?"

"Um, Chinese... No... Indian. Probably Italian."

"Football or cricket?"

"Chess."

She smiled. "My old granddad tried to teach me chess."

"Tried?" I queried.

"He gave up. Said I was too impulsive. What's your life goal?"

"To not end up in East Kilbride."

"That's oddly specific."

Sam Goodenough appeared and dropped a plate containing a pair of Cornish Pasties on the table. I tried to catch his eye to query the arrival, but he disappeared.

"Sorry," Tiggy said. "I should've asked, but Sam said you liked the pasties, and I was hungry, so..." She waved a hand at the plate.

"No, that was very kind of you. Thank you."

"That's okay. What are you going to say when you get back to London?"

"Ah." I stopped, pasty poised just before taking a bite. "Did Jim set you up to find out?"

"Why? Because an attractive woman asked you out for a drink?" She smiled and flicked a challenging eyebrow upwards.

"Pretty much. My life doesn't run like that."

"Actually, no. My idea. So? What are you going to say?"

I thought for a moment, then, "Just the facts. That I conveyed the information to Jim, he wants to refer it to his lawyers."

"What happens then?"

"I don't know. That's out of my pay grade. I assume they'll issue a formal rejection, then carry on as usual. I guess he'll still get a tax bill each year and have to pay rates on his island." I bit into the pasty. "And his cannabis hobby will still be illegal."

"You have to stop them." For the first time, Tiggy looked really concerned.

"Why are you so worried? Surely the great Jim Sullivan's not worried about a tax bill? Is that what all this is about?"

"No, that's nothing to do with anything. Look, can you come back to the island with me tomorrow? Let me show you something."

I drank a bit more of the beer. I could grow to like this one. "What's to see? I thought I'd seen pretty much everything."

"I'm not sure you really saw what you think you saw. Give me tomorrow. You can't do anything until Monday anyway. Deal? I did buy you a beer and dinner, you owe me."

"I thought you had a hen party to do?"

"I do, but they'll want to be in the bar by lunchtime. You can have a lie-in, meet you at one?" She finished her beer, took her pasty from the plate, and left.

# ~ CHAPTER EIGHT ~

THE BRIGHT MORNING SUNLIGHT PIERCED the gap where the chintz curtains wouldn't quite meet, forcing me to wakefulness. I lay for a moment reorganising my day from the way I'd planned it to be.

Another trip to the island had not been on my original list. In fact, the only item *on* my original list had been to leave this place at the earliest opportunity and head back to sanity. Now, I had a morning to kill and another two sea crossings to contend with. And I didn't even want to think about what delights lay in store once back on the island. More mad hermits and sentient seals?

I showered, dressed, and headed downstairs to ask Sam Goodenough to arrange an extra night. I found him in the bar with a huge stack of crisp packets in front of him.

"Ah, just the man," he greeted. "Bring that other box over here, will you?" He pointed to another box of crisps near the door. "Only my hip's giving me trouble this morning. It's the new moon, you see."

I collected the box of crisps and planted it on the counter. At least it was a lot lighter that the beer kegs.

"If you're just going to stand there gawping, you can give me a hand with these," Goodenough said. "Grab some o' them labels."

"I was just going to ask—" I started.

"You can ask and label, can't you?"

"Erm, yes."

"Here, take a label off this sheet and stick 'em on each packet." He pushed a sheet of little 'Special Offer' labels at me.

"I need to stay an extra night. Slight business complications." I peeled a label from the sheet and stuck it on a crisp packet.

"Not there," he said. "Stick it here." He demonstrated by repositioning my label over the sell-by date.

"They've expired," I said.

"That's why they're on offer."

"But you can't stick a label over the expiry date."

"Where'm I s'posed to stick it? Can't put it over the ingredients in case somebody's allergic to potatoes, they gotta know that stuff. And if I stick it over the maker's name, I get infringement of trademark lawyers comin' after me. This is the only legal place to stick a label. If I want to stay legal. You want an extra night, you say?" He tossed the packet of crisps on the pile and picked another from the box.

"Yes, just one more night. Bit of a change of plans."

"There'll 'ave to be a surcharge. Short notice. You've stopped labelling."

"Sorry." I took another packet and a label, ensuring it fitted neatly over the sell-by date. "Why a short notice surcharge? I'm already here?"

"There you go then, can't get much shorter notice than that. You're never going to do all those if you take so long over each one."

"How much?"

"Twenty quid," he said, tossing another pack onto the pile.

"Fifteen," I said. "And I want a pasty and a beer for lunch included."

He looked at me and grinned. "You just mind you put those labels straight. I'll go enter you in the diary 'afore somebody double-books the room."

It took me another twenty minutes to label all the crisps, and Goodenough showed no sign of returning. I stacked them on the counter and went off into the village to buy shoes.

The village of Little Didney contained an eclectic selection of shops, but no shoe shops. I could find seventy-five varieties of fudge, Cornish Pasties with various fillings and pastry types, including one pasty claiming to be the 'Original Cornish Pasty' dating back to 1536. Something else well past its sell-by date. I could buy fresh fish, local scrumpy, models of boats made out of seashells or spare parts for my outboard motor. But no shoe shops.

The closest option I could find was a charity shop, Save Our Seals, selling mostly Barbara Cartland books and VHS movies, but with some second-hand clothing. They had a small collection of footwear, which predominantly consisted of women's stilettos or children's trainers. Although, after an exploration behind a shelving unit, I found a box of men's shoes. Including a pair of green lace-up boots, which were in my size. I looked at them but didn't try them on. They seemed in good condition, no sign of wear, just a deep scuff across the toe of the right boot. Apart from that, no other damage. I should try them on, but I fell short while wondering who had last worn them. I pondered my alternatives. I could drive to Penzance, but by the time I'd got there, and found somewhere to park, then found a shoe shop, I'd be late for Tiggy. So that was out. I could struggle on with my town shoes, but they hadn't fared well with my first island visit, another foray would destroy them.

That left me with this pair of green, pre-worn boots. Maybe nobody *had* worn them? They could have been bought in error and never used. Somebody had bought the wrong size. I settled on that as the narrative to tell myself, and paid for them without trying them on. A little supermarket, a few doors up, stocked a spray disinfectant. I think it was meant for toilets, but would probably also kill 99.9 percent of all possible footwear germs. I had to stop myself worrying what the missing point one percent was.

I took my purchases back to my room and sprayed them until they were quite damp inside, then held them under the hand-dryer in the gents' toilets of the bar. Eventually, I managed to slide them on to my feet and lace them up. They were still slightly damp, but it was a good damp.

I had just enough time for a coffee and a sandwich in the bar, then headed down to the dock to meet Tiggy. Predictably, she was twelve minutes late.

"Fit?" she asked.

"As I will ever be, before risking my life on the oceans again."

She smiled and scanned me. "Here." She moved to stand right in front of. me "Your tie's not straight." Her face, inches from mine, her breath touching my skin as she spoke.

I felt her fiddling with the knot. I couldn't understand what was wrong with it, I'd been tying ties since I was five and could do a Windsor Knot blindfolded.

A sudden snatch and she held up the tie. "That's better," she said. "It's Saturday, for heaven's sake. Nobody wears a tie on Saturday."

I reached out to take the tie from her, but she pulled back and stuffed it into the top of her rucksack. "You can have it back on Monday."

"I won't be here on Monday," I protested.

"Shame. Get in the boat." She glanced down at my feet. "Nice boots, well done."

"I found them in the charity shop." I clambered over the edge of the dock and stepped onto the rear deck of the '300'.

"Thought I recognised them," she said, dropping into the boat with the ease of a gymnastic cat.

"Huh?"

"Eric Merchant. Trampled to death when a herd of cows got spooked in a storm one night. His wife emptied his wardrobe down at the Save Our Seals. I got his Barbour back home. I bought it for Jake, but it was too small. You should put a lifejacket on today. It might be a bit squally."

I looked at my boots again and fought a desire to pull them off. Instead, I pulled a lifejacket unnecessarily tightly round me and settled in the seat.

Tiggy fired up the engine and puttered out of the harbour into the open sea. I looked towards the island. Little white horses skittered across the tops of the gentle waves. This was going to be a bit bumpier than last time. I heard the engine wind up and the stern dug into the water as the propellers found purchase. I grabbed the sides of the seat and we lurched forwards, skimming the tops off the waves in an envelope of noise and vibration.

Fortunately, the trip was rapid and within twenty minutes of leaving the harbour, we slid to a halt against an orange buoy moored offshore from Pirate's Cove. We clambered into the little dinghy and rode the waves in to the beach. Once the dinghy was secured, we set off up the gravelly path.

"Jim coming to collect us?" I asked, hopefully.

"No, I haven't even told him we were coming."

"Where are we going?"

"Seal Bay. Right at the east end of the island."

I looked to the east, beyond Mount Scanlon, which still lay in the distance. "Oh, goody."

"How are the boots holding up?"

I looked at my feet. I'd actually forgotten I had them on. "Surprisingly comfortable."

"That's good. I expect the rumours about them being haunted are nonsense anyway."

I studied her face as she turned and set off at a brisk, stomping pace. I thought I saw a grin.

We skirted Mount Scanlon, with its fierce granite shapes pushing up out of the grassy surrounds. I had a completely irrational urge to climb to the top. I reminded myself it would be an idiotic thing to attempt, as not only was I not good with heights, but I struggled with three flights of stairs in the office on the frequent days the lift malfunctioned.

Once past the mount, the old mine works came into view. Several tumbledown buildings gathered around deep gouges in the earth and rusting machinery lay scattered. A tall chimney reached up beyond the remaining structure of one building, and metal framework clung tenaciously to the end wall. Probably where the machinery had been to lift the buckets or whatever they used.

"Don't get too close," Tiggy said. "There's some very deep pits there, and not always easy to see."

I veered away from the mine area and noticed the grass giving way to sea a short distance in front of us.

"Is this the end of the island?" I asked.

"Pretty much. There's a cove down here. It's a steep drop, so watch your step."

"Is everything round here a trap to kill me?"

"Just keep an eye out for the killer rabbits and you'll be fine," she said, with a mischief in her eyes.

I smarted at the reference. "Are we going down there?"

"Yes, you'll be fine, as long as you watch where I step."

I watched very closely. Mostly out of self-preservation, but also, a guilty part of me didn't actually object to watching somebody as fit and agile as her displaying such physical grace.

As she slid from rock to rock, and path to a grassy mound, I fell so far behind her that I was beginning to have difficulty remembering where she'd stepped, so my descent slowed. She landed on the tiny, gravelly inlet, and turned to watch me, hands planted on hips in Gym Mistress fashion.

"Don't get much chance to practise my rock-climbing in Pimlico," I said, slithering to a stop in front of her whilst trying to remain upright and look cool all at the same time.

"That's alright, I used to race my brother up and down the Bosigran over Penrith."

I looked around. The sea sparkled in the sun, a greeny blue becoming clear, as it lapped around the boulders making up the tiny cove. The beach, if it could be called that, was no bigger than a couple of parking spaces and consisted of rounded pebbles of varying sizes and colours.

"Is this what you wanted to show me?" I asked.

"One of the things." She sat on a large rock and tucked her feet up under her. She seemed to have morphed from ninja to pixie.

"It's very nice, but a bit far for a picnic."

"Funny you should say that." She shrugged her rucksack from her shoulders and dived inside. "Peckish?" She held out a white paper bag.

I took the bag and retrieved a Cornish Pasty. "Ah, perfect." I held up the pasty. "I think I'm developing an unhealthy addiction for these things."

"Pengelly's finest. Did you know his pasties were mentioned in the court of Henry the Eighth? Apparently, there was an accident with a delivery, they had to send out replacements. There's a letter to Jane Seymour, apologising for the first damaged batch, it still exists."

"From Pengelly's bakery?" I bit into the crust.

"So he claims." She broke open her own pasty. "You can always tell a Pengelly's Pasty, it has only eighteen crimps instead of twenty."

"And that's important?"

She looked at me as if she couldn't believe that somebody so stupid could actually carry on breathing. "Of course it is. Wars have been fought for less. Pengelly claims the original ones were made by his ancestor who lost a finger while chopping beef, hence eighteen crimps, not the twenty that fully-fingered bakers made later."

"So, what's so special about this place?" I scanned my surrounds again.

"What do you see?"

I felt I was being tricked, but couldn't see the catch. "Nothing, just rocks and sea."

"What about litter?"

I studied the area, and my confusion grew. "What litter? There is none."

"Exactly. What about contamination in the water?"

I looked at the crystal-clear water which strained to reach my feet. So clear that the pebbles under the water seemed emphasised. "None?"

"Don't you think that's unusual for a UK shoreline?"

"I don't really do beaches."

"I guessed." She took a couple of cans of Tribute from her bag and handed one to me. "But you'd probably notice if one day there weren't any more cigarette stubs or chewing gum patties on the pavements outside your local McDonald's?"

"Probably. Disgusting habit." I cracked the tab on the can and sipped at the fizz before it covered me. "I guess it depends on what we're used to seeing."

"This island has so far escaped the worst of human pollution, but some still gets here. Huge amounts of plastic are washed up every day."

I looked around again. "What happens to it?"

"Watt comes out collects it. He's been doing it since the day he arrived. You see those mussels?" She pointed at some shell things stuck on some of the rocks.

"Yes."

"They're a prime diet of shags, those things." She pointed to a small group of birds clustered on a large rock about fifty metres offshore. They looked a bit like geese, standing with their wings outstretched. "The problem is poachers take these mussels and other molluscs to sell to restaurants who don't ask questions. And now, the shag is endangered here, and other places. The lack of their natural diet also drives them to try eating stuff they never should. Plastic and waste. They're dying."

"I didn't know." I stared again at the shags.

"Why would you? Watt keeps an eye on all this. He chases off the poachers when he can, but they're persistent. You see that rock?" She aimed the last corner of her pasty at a dark lump just visible beyond the small headland which formed the tiny bay.

I squinted into the sunlight bouncing from the sea. "Yes."

"You can just make out some shapes on it? Slightly darker?"

"I think so." I narrowed my eyes even more and thought I could detect some darker blobs.

"Grey seals. We're very lucky to have those here. The UK has nearly half of what's left in the world, yet there are still less of those here than red squirrels in Britain."

We sat for a few minutes in silence. I watched the sea splashing rhythmically on the rocks at my feet. It was almost hypnotic.

"You finished?" Tiggy asked.

I looked at my now empty beer can and paper bag. I nodded.

Tiggy reached out to me. "Give those here." She took the can and bag, scrunching them up, and stuffing them in the rucksack. "Come on." She stood and set off up the rocks, gliding from one to the other like a liquid cat.

I followed as best I could, but she still had to sit and wait for me at the top.

"They really should put escalators on these things," I puffed as I straightened at the top.

She smiled and turned away. "Come on. Mind the rabbits."

We headed back inland and into the mine area.

I panted for breath, trying to keep up with her, but she just bounced along, keeping up a running commentary as she went.

"This mine went out under the sea. Best part of a mile, so they say. The water that seeps in to parts of this is filtered through the rock. Makes it drinkable."

"You said it was tin?" I checked.

"And arsenic. There's talk of them opening up a lot of these old places again."

"For tin?"

"Yes, it's in demand again because of all the electronic shit being made these days."

I stared at the ruined buildings and the remains of the wheelhouse as we passed by. It seemed crazy that anybody would think of re-opening a place like this, but I knew enough about the way dwindling natural resources drove mining across the world to understand the potential.

As we came to the southern cliff top, a sharp breeze cut across the sea and made me nervous about going too close to the edge. The drop to the rocks below was sharp and fatal. It looked to be about the same height as the view from Courteny's Rooftop restaurant in Belgrave Road, and that was eight floors up.

"That's The Eye." Tiggy pointed to a rock that looked like half-a-mile south, but I had no way of validating that.

The reason for the name became clear as I made out the shape, a large grey mound with a huge hole in the centre.

"It's said that sirens used to lure boats there. They'd offer to lead lost ships to safety and at the last moment, they'd sit in that hole and call for the ship to come to them, which would then wreck against the rock."

"We have a local pub, the Morpeth Arms on Millbank, that's haunted. Used to be a prison, the cells are still under it somewhere. No sirens though. Unless you count the police cars which go up and down most nights."

"Idiot," she scolded and turned back to look out at The Eye. "They were probably seals. They can get quite big."

I studied the sea around The Eye, scanning for anything siren-like to break the surface. But nothing.

"Come on, then," Tiggy said. "We'll drop in on Jim before we head back. You never know, he might have signed your bit of paper."

# ~ CHAPTER NINE ~

JIM'S HOUSE WAS ONLY A short walk from the viewpoint for The Eye, and as we approached, I found my way blocked by Ermintrude. This seemed to be a favourite trick of hers, standing in front of me and predicting which way I would go. Only this time, it was a narrow part of the path to Jim's front door, running between some brambly bushes and a wooden storage shed. The gap was just big enough for a human, or a cow, but not both. Ermintrude seemed to know this and gave a lopsided sneer as I approached.

"Just give her a push," said Tiggy. "She'll move."

"That's easy for you to say. You're not the one wearing haunted boots."

"Oh, yes, I forgot. Don't look her in the eye."

"Not helping," I said.

The cow studied me, and her gaze drifted to my feet. Perhaps there was something about the boots that provoked cows? They didn't have to be haunted, that was ridiculous, but maybe the colour or smell or something set off their attack impulses.

"Oh, for goodness' sake." Tiggy brushed past me and slapped the cow on the rump, followed by a short shove. The cow grumbled, but took the hint and ambled off into a nearby patch of little yellow flowers.

"I was just going to do that," I protested.

"I know."

I followed Tiggy to the front door, where she called a, "Yoo-hoo, anyone home?" and just breezed in the door.

We passed Jeeves in the small hallway.

"You're not supposed to let yourselves in, you know," he said. "That's my job. Letting people in."

"Sorry, Jeeves." Tiggy flashed a smile at him.

"It don't do, takin' a man's work. It's only the passion for constant improvement in my life that stops me jumping off the edge of the cliff."

"I'll bring you some fudge over, next visit."

"You mind you do."

We found Jim in the lounge. He and Stringy sat in big leather gamer chairs facing what looked like an episode of Seal Team on the huge television. Stringy jabbed at a button on the control pad he held, and something exploded on the screen.

"That wasn't fair," said Jim. "I was distracted."

"Tell that to the widows of the hostages."

Jim stabbed a button, and the words, 'Game Aborted' replaced the mayhem.

"Oi, you can't do that," Stringy protested. "I was ahead."

"That's how war goes." He swivelled in the chair to face us. "Ah, I see you've brought our favourite civil servant back. Didn't recognise you there for a moment, without your tie."

"I was giving him the tour."

Jim stiffened, and his eyes narrowed. "Which tour?"

"Not that one."

"Oh, that's okay."

I looked at Tiggy and clearly, my consternation showed.

"He doesn't want you to know about his secret Dr Evil missile base," Tiggy said.

"You any good with an M16 assault rifle?" Jim asked me.

"Not really," I said.

"Shame." He pressed another button on his control and the big screen went blank. "Stringy keeps getting me killed every time we break the door down." He extracted himself out of his seat and moved to the leather sofa. A glass of JD, and a ready rolled joint, awaited him on the coffee table. "Sit, sit, I'm too wasted to be looking up at ya all the time." He waved a hand at the chairs, then lit the joint and flopped back in the chair.

I sat, as instructed.

Tiggy disappeared for a moment, then returned with two beer cans, she handed one to me. I took it before I realised I had.

"I threw your bits of paper away," Jim said.

"Oh." The randomness of the statement caught me short.

"Well, no point beatin' around the bushes and you gettin' your hopes up for a deal." He flapped a hand at the smoke which encircled him, probably so he could see me in order to gauge my reaction.

"Would you like another set?" I asked.

"You would, wouldn't you? You'd go and get another set, and I'd throw those away as well, and we'd keep this going till somebody died. Good on you. Determination and persistence. I admire that. Wish my accountant showed a bit more of that in trying to get my taxes down. How'd you fancy being my accountant?"

"I don't know anything about being an accountant," I said, then immediately regretted my hasty answer. What if he was genuine, and I'd just turned down the chance to be Jim Sullivan's accountant? I pushed the thought away.

"Nor does Jerzy."

"Cindy not back yet?" Tiggy asked Jim.

"Nah, she's flown on to Rio, there's a big protest there about climate change. It's her latest thing, global warming and saving the ice caps."

Tiggy wandered over to the big window overlooking the sea. "Have you seen that boat again lately?"

"Yeah, it was up 'n down there again earlier. Treasure hunters, I'll bet. What d'ya reckon? Looking for the Vagabunda?"

Tiggy scanned the sea-line. "I still reckon it's a new French trawler. I need to see it. But from what you said, it's too big to be legal in these waters."

"Sunken treasure, that's what it is. What say we get some diving kit and have a go? We could beat them to it?"

Tiggy turned and looked at Jim. "Have you ever been deep sea diving?"

"I did some snorkel fishing off Saint Martin once. Can't be much different."

"It's not really something you just want to *'have a go'* at," she said. "I'm not going scuba diving with you. People die doing stuff like that."

"Stringy, you'll come with me," Jim said. "I'll sort the kit, Tiggy'll drive us."

Stringy looked up from loading a small pipe. "I'm gonna pass on that one, mate. Me fags'll get wet."

"Can you get some pictures of it next time?" Tiggy asked.

"No problem. Hey, you two coming to my birthday party?"

"I thought your birthday was yesterday?"

"It was, but I wanted to wait for Cindy to get back before I have a party."

"When is it?" asked Tiggy.

"Um, the twenty-fourth. You gotta come, there'll be cake."

"I know your cake."

"To be fair, I did ask you if you wanted your cake with or without," said Jim.

"I thought you meant cream. Okay, I'll see if I can make space in my social calendar," said Tiggy.

Jim looked to me. "You can come." He studied me, then flapped a hand and said, "Just wear something... more...not that."

"I'm afraid I'll have to pass anyway," I said. "Sorry, but I'll never get the time off. We have to schedule our holidays on the rota twelve months in advance."

Jim looked at me as if I'd been speaking Martian. "How do you know where you want to go a year in advance?"

"I always go to Bournemouth."

"Did a gig there in... ninety-five, August it was. I remember it because the temperature got up to thirty-three. We were playing outside, and the wasps were everywhere."

"I'd have missed that; I was there in June."

Jim looked puzzled, then shrugged and went back to his glass.

Tiggy drank the last of her beer and looked at me. "You finished? We should make a move, might get to see some dolphins if we go now."

I put my half-finished can down on the table. "Really? I never knew there were dolphins in the Channel."

"There's a Bottlenose pod gets around here. Not as many as once were, too much shipping in the area for them. I sometimes take people out on trips to spot them, but we keep our distance."

We said our goodbyes to Jim and Stringy, although they were already back in Afghanistan, scrapping with the Taliban.

We took the dinghy back to the '300' and Tiggy took us round the western headland with the lighthouse and out into the Channel south of the island.

We cruised to-and-fro a while, seeming to creep further away from the island with each turn. As we meandered ever southward, the waves seemed to get bigger.

My unease grew as the ocean around us expanded on all sides, leaving the relative security of Scanlon's Rock far behind. The waves pushed more and more persistently at the boat, which actually seemed to be shrinking in size the further away from land we drifted.

Tiggy constantly scanned the sea around us and was clearly oblivious to the mounting danger.

"I'm really not bothered about missing the dolphins," I said, as nonchalantly as I could manage.

"Not a problem," she said, keeping her eyes to the horizon.

"I don't want to put you to any more trouble. I've had a very interesting day and—"

"Gotcha," Tiggy said, and turned the boat across the waves in a tight one-eighty.

I held tight to my seat, but risked a glance to see what had caught her interest. No dolphins, just a red boat in the distance.

"We weren't looking for dolphins, were we?" I asked.

"What? Oh, well... we *might* have seen some. But no, not entirely."

"Is that the trawler Jim saw?"

"Looks like it. You got a camera on your phone?"

"Yes, but I'm not much good with it. Pictures of trees, mostly."

"Trees?" Tiggy's gaze remained locked on the red boat. "In London?"

"Yes, they cover twenty percent of the area of London," I said. "In fact, the UN has designated London as a forest."

Now she turned to look at me. "London? A forest? You been on Jim's magic leaves?"

The boat kicked, and I pointed to the sea. "Shouldn't you be watching out for tsunamis?"

"Forest." She shook her head and turned back to the sea. "Just point and click while I get us close."

She pushed a lever forward and the front of the boat lifted, obscuring the red boat in the distance. I gripped both sides of my seat and squinted my eyes against the sea spray which now attacked my face. I wondered how I was supposed to take photographs when I didn't dare let go of the seat.

We bounced along in a flurry of noise, spray and general discomfort for what seemed an age, but my watch said three minutes, then the engine slowed, the boat sank back into the water, and we turned a lazy quarter circle.

"There she is," said Tiggy.

I wiped spray from my eyes and looked up to see a large red boat about a kilometre away. It looked like a huge leisure boat except it had a flat, low deck at the rear with some sort of structure overhanging the back end.

"French trawler or treasure hunters?" I asked.

"Neither." Tiggy powered down to tick-over, and we appeared to drift. "It's a survey ship."

"Surveying what?"

"The seabed. You see those booms out behind the ship?" She pointed to what looked like some logs being towed behind the vessel. "They're firing sonic pulses at the seabed to read what's down there. Listen."

I tried to tune out the gentle puttering of our engine and the wind. I heard a dull thud, like the muffled kick of a bass drum. I continued listening, and the sound repeated about every ten seconds.

"What are they looking for? Wrecks?"

"No, it's geological. Are you getting pictures?"

I'd totally forgotten that. I fumbled my phone from its case and called up the camera app. I couldn't really see the screen, so I just aimed and kept clicking.

"They're not supposed to use those in protected fishing waters," Tiggy said. "It confuses the hell out of the fish. No wonder Dad's catches are down lately. How are you doing?"

"A bit queasy, and wet, but otherwise okay."

"I meant, how are you doing with the photos?"

"Oh, that, pointing and clicking."

"Good, I'll do a closer pass, then we'll get back."

She pressed the lever forwards, and the engine responded, pushing us in wide ellipse towards the boat. I kept aiming my phone at the survey ship as it grew in my field of view, then we veered away, and I saw a grey smudge of England in the distance. I tucked my phone away and gripped the seat as the engine shifted in pitch and the bouncing began all over again.

Once back, we managed to get a mooring on the dock, so I was spared the trauma of shifting into the dinghy in the wobbly water.

Tiggy tied off the rope and threw her rucksack over her shoulder. "Back to London tomorrow?" she asked.

"Yes, I'll take an early start to avoid the traffic."

"Send me those photos, I want to report it to the Environment Agency."

"Of course."

Tiggy stood in front of me and appeared to be struggling with a decision.

Then, without warning, she stepped forwards with arms outstretched. I froze as she wrapped her arms around me in a hug.

I raised my arms slightly, thinking I should reciprocate, but I wasn't sure that was the right thing to do.

"You take care now," she said, as we disengaged.

"What do you mean?" I felt unable to move, not sure as to how to respond.

"You're a good man in a bad world. Don't let it chew you up." She touched her fingertips to her lips, then waved as she strutted off towards the village.

I stood for a moment, watching her go, then I turned to gaze at the sea. The evening clouds were gathering, and the early moon bounced from the harbour water. I looked to the horizon and the grey shadow that was Scanlon's Rock. It looked remote and vulnerable. The stretch of water between here and there threatened with a nonchalant malevolence. I didn't trust water, and probably never would. Although, the last couple of days had perhaps assuaged my fears a little.

I turned back to see where Tiggy was headed, but she'd gone. I felt oddly alone. I gave a little huff to myself to shrug off the feeling and made my way back to the Smuggler's.

After a long shower to clean the salt and mud from my pores, I folded my shirts and set them in my case. As I was doing so, I realised Tiggy hadn't returned my tie. I tried to tell myself it was just a tie, and I had dozens, but the annoyance still niggled. I looked at the haunted boots and wondered what to do with those. I was never going to need those in London, that was for sure, but it seemed wasteful, and somehow callous, to just throw them out. I wondered how I could put them in the case. They would disrupt the order and I would also need to cover them in something. I couldn't put dirty walking boots in a case with clean shirts. And then there was the tie. The place where the tie should be taunted me.

I closed the lid on the case. I'd go downstairs and have a snack. I was probably just hungry, and it was making me twitchy.

The bar seemed busier than usual, and a small stage had been set up at the far end. I ordered a beer, and fish and chips, then sat as far away from the stage as I could.

A poster on a wooden pillar near my table explained the stage. We were readying for one of the Smuggler's Arms Famous Karaoke Extravaganzas.

I pondered cancelling my order and running, but hunger pangs said no. I could do this. I could just sit here and eat my meal and listen to the singing. I didn't have to engage in any way.

My meal arrived at the same time as the karaoke started. An unfortunately large young woman singing '*I Will Survive*'. I concentrated on my meal and savoured the beer. The next act was altogether more disturbing. It took me a moment to recognise the Commodore. He wore a tight black mini skirt over stockings and topped off with an ultra-tight skinny top, which struggled to contain an enormous pair of falsies. Weirder still, he was carrying the hose and brush from a vacuum cleaner.

It was only when the music started, Queen's '*I Want To Break Free*', that I understood. I ate and tried to ignore. I cringed and supped at my beer. I smiled and noticed my foot was tapping, and when it finished, I clapped politely. I paid and slipped away before the next one started, a middle-aged couple who looked like they were either badly ageing rockers or about to attempt Grease. Either way, I'd tried, and I could now at least tick, '*watch a karaoke,*' off my bucket list.

I made my way upstairs and faced the suitcase dilemma with a bit more aplomb. I found a plastic bag in which to wrap the boots and stuffed them in the bottom of the case. I then layered my unused folders over that and finally, my shirts. I tried not to think about the missing tie.

The sound of the karaoke rumbled through the wooden floor, so settling down with a book was out. I found my phone and tried to work out how to send the pictures of the boat to Tiggy. I scrolled through the images. A few good shots, but also quite a few of the sea, the inside of Tiggy's boat, and several of my feet. There were, however, enough decent pictures to identify the vessel. I even had a lopsided image of the name, the Xerxes.

If I'd thought to bring my laptop, I could probably have accessed the Maritime & Coastguard Agency intranet and traced the owners. I'd give that a go as soon as I got back. I clicked 'send' and the images headed out through the internet to Tiggy and my own email account at home.

I managed to tune out the karaoke just enough to fall asleep in front of a movie on the television.

# ~ Chapter Ten ~

My early start on Sunday morning paid off, and by midday, I was back in my apartment. I unpacked my case and sorted out a corner of the hall cupboard for the haunted boots. I poked a frozen lasagne in the microwave and settled down with my laptop to collect the photos I'd emailed myself.

I looked again at the ship, the larger screen brought it into clarity, and after comparing it with images of hydrographic survey vessels on Wikipedia, there was no doubt about its purpose.

I logged into the Maritime & Coastguard Agency intranet. My access level allowed me to see that survey ships were likely to be operating in the Plymouth and Portland Shipping areas, but any further detail was beyond my level. The constant pinging of the microwave reminded me that lunch was ready, so I shut the computer and laid the table with plate and cutlery. A quick dive into the fridge yielded half a bottle of Chardonnay, which I couldn't remember opening. Not the perfect pairing with a beef pasta dish, but then, there was probably very little meat in a supermarket lasagne anyway, so it would do. The lasagne was severely burned on the edges but still frozen in the middle. I contemplated giving it another blast, but then a sip of the wine reminded me when I'd opened it, so I abandoned the whole idea and went out to find somewhere to eat.

I'd remembered a new seafood restaurant had opened just off Claverton Street, so I thought I'd give that a try. I ordered Mediterranean Sardines with roasted peppers. Three large sardines came with a Jenga-like construction of half a dozen perfect-cut chips and some pepper trimmings floating in olive oil. As I ate, I vaguely wondered where the sardines had actually originated. I left the restaurant as hungry as I'd entered it and picked up a sandwich in a Tesco Metro on the way back.

Once back in my apartment, I tried accessing the DEFRA records to see what complaints had been filed about illegal maritime activities in the seas around Cornwall. There were dozens of filings concerning French and Dutch trawlers using proscribed nets or boats, but nothing about survey ships. I gave up and spent the afternoon with an old Basil Rathbone Sherlock Holmes movie.

~ * ~ * ~ * ~

I ARRIVED IN THE OFFICE early on the Monday. I knew any extra-curricular research of my own would likely lead to an early termination as soon as Froggy realised I was back.

I logged in again to the Maritime & Coastguard Agency intranet, but as before, my access stopped as soon as I tried to find details of the Xerxes. I picked up the phone and called Derek Ball, an old contact in the MCA.

Derek answered the call at first ring.

"Hi, Derek, it's John from the FCO, I need a bit of help."

"Oh, hi, John, haven't heard from you in a while. I thought you'd been posted to Beijing or something."

"No, still stuck in the research section. I need your help with an investigation we're doing. We've had a tip-off about a ship we think might be involved in people smuggling. Trouble is, I can't access the details. Cross departmental communication is a nightmare."

"Tell me about it. It's easier for me to get to talk to an admiral in the Russian navy than the harbour master in Littlehampton. What's the name of your ship?"

"The IRV Xerxes. It's going under a Panamanian flag."

"Give me a moment."

The line deadened for a minute, then, "That's odd, it was locked. I had to over-ride the security protocol. What do you need to know?"

"As much as you can tell me, really."

"Well, as you say, it's Panama registered, and currently leased to Valdez Oil. It's been cleared to operate in the western Channel from Plymouth Sound out to Longships. I'll tell you what, I'm going to piggyback your access alongside mine for twenty-four hours so you can gather what you need. After all, we're all supposed to be working for the same government, aren't we?"

"Don't tell that to the politicians. That sort of talk is high treason."

"I know what you mean. Catch you soon."

After I disconnected the call, I went back to the MCA portal and found I could now access all the details I needed. I owed Derek a drink. If either of us still had a job after this.

It didn't take me long to discover that Valdez Oil had been granted licences to explore for oil and shale gas deposits over an unusually extended range. The licences themselves also appeared to be quite loose, although this was out of my area of knowledge. I checked through the opposition concerns to the exploration, and quite a few marine conservation groups had petitioned against the operation, but had been largely ignored or overridden.

I came out of the MCA portal and logged into the Department for Business, Energy & Industrial Strategy system. My access level cleared me here for most things, so I had little trouble tracking down what I needed. Valdez Oil was owned by a convoluted mess of shell companies and offshore entities. Not unusual in the oil sector. What was more interesting was the one name which stood out when I cross-referenced the directors with the Members of Parliament's Register of Interests. Sir Guy Serrick. I may not remember when I opened a bottle of chardonnay, but I knew that name. Froggy's lunch appointment of the previous week.

I opened up the FCO Social Media, Authenticate, Recognise & Trace system, or SMARTs, as we referred to it. Strictly speaking, this was one of these 'Grey Tools' which sat somewhere between the Foreign Office, the Home Office, and the security services. Designed to use social media platforms to identify undesirables, or Persons of Interest, then to track their movements and contacts. One fed in basic data, or photographs, then SMARTs trawled over twenty different social media platforms, making connections and joining dots.

I fed in the profiles of Sir Oliver Frogmorton and Sir Guy Serrick, and SMARTs ran through her algorithms. A few minutes later, with her usual efficiency, I had a list which ran to several pages. As usual, the significant connections appeared first.

They had both been present at Rotherby's Gentlemen's Club last week. Several posts appeared with one or other of them in the background of other people's posts. A couple of other posts were flagged as 'Possible Identification' where the facial recognition was not confirmed. They seemed to be enjoying a leisurely lunch and serious conversation. Their phones were also tagged as being in the same vicinity at the same time on multiple occasions and places, including the House of Commons bar. Locations visited by each, but at different times, also proved interesting. Geo-location revealed they had both visited Little Didney at various times over the last few months. Widening the parameters put Froggy at three Procurement meetings where the name Valdez Oil appeared in the minutes and also at a gala dinner in Riyadh, given by the Saudi prince with executives of Valdez in attendance.

Froggy had also spent time at a private island in the British Virgin Islands, which had also been visited by Guy Serrick, as well as the previous chancellor and the current Minister for Energy. There was no way to trace the owner of the island, but many years' worth of social media posts from hundreds of individuals holidaying on the island listed Valdez Oil as their employer. The majority of the posts praised their company's generosity in providing the facilities.

I logged out of SMARTs just as my desk phone bleeped. I guessed it was either Froggy, wondering why my report wasn't on his desk, or the King with my O.B.E. I figured it wasn't worth the risk and they could both wait.

I rang Jane.

"Who's dead?" she greeted.

"Nobody. I *can* ring just to say hello to my little sister."

"Of course you can, but you never do. What's wrong?"

"Nothing, I just fancied a chat. How about catching lunch?" I asked.

"We only did my birthday lunch a few days ago, and your birthday's not till July. So, I ask again, what's wrong?"

"I think I'm about to get dragged off to the Tower for treason. Or at least, sent to East Kilbride. Much of a muchness, really."

The line went silent for a while. "I see," Jane said, eventually. "We'll never get a table at the Melchester at this short notice."

"There's the 'Men of Essex' on Tachbrook Street. I've never been in, but it looks okay. We could try that."

"I've never heard of the place. Is that some sort of pub?"

"Just tell the Uber driver, they'll know. Twelve?"

THE 'MEN OF ESSEX' TURNED out to be a fairly ordinary pub in a fairly ordinary street. This very ordinariness calmed my growing paranoia. Even if we *could* have secured a table in the Melchester, I would have been constantly looking over my shoulder. The 'Men of Essex' was exactly the sort of place that anybody from the FCO would *not* go.

For the first time in I couldn't remember when, I was early for one of our lunches. I chose a table towards the back of the room where passers-by in the street wouldn't be able to see.

Most of the customers appeared to be locals and regulars, going by the way they were greeted by the bar staff. Probably estate agents or insurance brokers, as those types of businesses seemed to be more in evidence in this area than ironmongers or butchers. Jane arrived exactly at twelve, probably as a statement to show me how it was done.

"Well, I must say, this is very... er... local," she said, as she wriggled her way into the bench seat opposite me.

"Yes, I wanted discreet. Are you alright there?" I noticed she seemed to be having difficulties with the concept of a combined bench and table seating arrangement.

"Yes, dear. Now, do tell me what's going on. You sounded terribly distressed on the telephone." She pulled a napkin from her Louis Vuitton handbag and wiped the table in front of her.

"A crisis of conscience."

"I'm not sure I'm the best person to help with that, after all, I *am* married to an arms broker. But you can try me."

"You remember I was supposed to be getting Jim Sullivan to drop his claim to independence?"

"Something to do with territorial waters, you said? They're very slow in here." She looked around for a waiter and spotted a young girl delivering a tray of food to a nearby table. She waved her hand and cooeed.

The girl dumped her tray on the table and came over. "Can I help, loves?"

"Do you have a menu?" I asked.

The girl pointed to what looked like a small Rorschach test stuck to the table. "You stick that into your phone," she said and headed towards the bar.

I smiled at Jane. "It's all very hi-tech these days." I pulled out my phone, scanned in the QR code and up came the menu. "That's clever. Would you like me to bring it up on yours?"

"No, you can tell me what they have. Do they have lobster?"

I scrolled through the dozens of screens of pictures of meals. "Doesn't look like it. They have scampi in a basket."

"I'm not eating anything in a basket. Or a bucket. What about mussels? They do a lovely Moules Marinière in the Melchester."

"You shouldn't eat mussels. You don't know where they come from."

"You watch too much David Attenborough. Well, you choose."

"Cornish pasty and chips. I developed a bit of a taste for them when I was in Cornwall."

"Whatever you think best, just as long as it arrives on a plate. Now, tell me what's going on."

I clicked on the image of a Cornish pasty and chips twice, a picture of a glass of anonymous red wine and a bottle of Budweiser.

"Well, it seems that the island *is* outside the limits, but Froggy's still insisting I force Sullivan to sign away his claim anyway."

"Hmm, the British Empire has never given up territory easily. I remember mother telling us about when they were in Qatar, just before we were born, and—"

"I think Froggy, and some of his chums, are taking freebies to allow Valdez Oil to explore off the coast of Cornwall," I blurted. It felt good to finally get the words out to somebody.

"Ah, I see."

"If I don't get Jim Sullivan's signature, I'm going to be sent to East Kilbride to count paper clips for the rest of my career. If I *do* get him to sign, I'm complicit in corruption."

"Are you sure it's not all quite harmless? Father used to accept tokens of appreciation from local officials when he was the ambassador. He had a monkey given to him once, one of those with a long nose, that was when he was serving in Malaya. He let it go, of course. Probably should have let it go in the jungle though, it attacked a traffic policeman at the Bukit Bintang junction in the centre of Kuala Lumpur. Took them five hours to untangle the traffic."

"This is a bit more serious than a big-nosed monkey. I think this is why they're trying to block the island from going independent. Valdez wants to drill in the waters around Scanlon's Rock, the government want the oil revenues, and Froggy and his mates want the consultancy fees. None of which can happen, of course, if the island's no longer part of the UK."

The meals arrived with a curt, "There ya' go," from the bored waitress.

Jane pushed at her pasty with a knife. She looked like she was checking it was dead. "I had one of these in Sidmouth once."

"These aren't the original ones." I cut my pasty in two. "Those only come from Pengelly's bakery and have just eighteen crimps. The usual ones have twenty."

"And *this* is why you're still single at fifty-two."

"Hmm," I grunted. "Getting back to the subject of my impending vocational crisis…"

Jane nibbled the tiniest portion of pasty from her fork. "You know the old Klingon saying, bISovbejbe'DI' tImer."

"When in doubt, surprise them?"

"Exactly."

I pondered the relevance of the quote for a moment. Then the germ of a plan broke through. "And *that's* why I come to my little sister with my problems."

"You're welcome." Jane smiled and waggled the fork at me. "This is not bad at all."

~ * ~ * ~ * ~

AS I RETURNED TO THE office, I heard my desk phone ringing from the corridor. I wondered if Froggy had a remote volume button for it, as it always sounded louder when he called.

I picked up the phone at the same time as dumping my bag and landing in my desk chair. "Department of Lost Hope, how may I help?"

"Cabot?" Froggy challenged.

"Yes."

"I've been trying to reach you all morning. Bob told me you were in earlier."

"Bob?" I queried.

"The security guard on the front desk. Bob."

"Oh, you mean Sid?"

"Sid, Bob, just come up here now and bring the papers." The line went dead, and I replaced the handset with the same care I'd give a primed hand grenade.

Here we go.

~ * ~ * ~ * ~

FROGGY STOOD FACING THE HUGE window as I entered his office.

"I seem to be missing your report," he said, as he turned to face me.

"I haven't had time to prepare it yet," I said. "I still need to collect some more background data."

Froggy approached his desk and indicated I should take the seat opposite. "That can wait. All I'm interested in at this stage is seeing that clown's signature on the letter rescinding his claim to independence." He studied me over the top of his half-moon reading glasses. "You do have it, I assume?"

"Well..." I started, knowing full well Froggy's hatred of answers which begin with 'Well'. "Not exactly. It seems the FCO's position on this is... how would one say? Less than sound?"

He placed his hands flat on the desk and leaned forwards. "Your opinion on the FCO's position is of absolutely no relevance to this matter. I take it you didn't get him to sign?"

"I assessed the situation, and in line with the current legal framework, his claim is perfectly valid. The island is outside of the UK's territorial waters. Encouraging a signature under those circumstances would not be appropriate."

Froggy chewed his teeth while staring at me. "You do realise that even if his damned island is outside the territorial limit, there are other factors he would need to fulfil? And that the chances of him doing that are negligible?"

"Of course, but that is his prerogative to pursue, not ours."

Froggy gave a stifled exhale of a breath too long held. "In that case, moving on, we have a problem of a completely unrelated matter. This office, alongside many others, is facing financial cuts. And it behoves us to shoulder our share of the responsibility and find departmental savings. That means a rationalisation of resources, and unfortunately, yours is one of the resources being rationalised. Vis-à-vis, your position is being combined with our office in East Kilbride."

"I see," I said. "And if I don't want to go to East Kilbride?"

"Then you will be offered the standard redundancy package commensurate with your position and years of service."

"Then I accept."

He looked puzzled. "What do you accept?"

"Redundancy."

~ Chapter Eleven ~

The conventions of the Foreign, Commonwealth Development Office dictate that anybody leaving office under any sort of cloud should vacate their office immediately and move to Gardening Leave to serve out their notice period. As I was leaving under a storm cloud that would make Hurricane Katrina look like a little fluffy ball of cumulus, my departure was decidedly rapid. Within twenty minutes of my conversation with Froggy, I was being escorted from the front door by Sid.

He held the door as I stepped out onto the pavement with my standard cardboard 'Leaving Box'. "Have a nice day, Mr Cabot."

"I will," I said.

Sid shuffled for a moment, holding the door from closing on me. "Sorry to see you go, sir." He looked away and let the door slip closed.

I stood on the bustling pavement and scanned for a taxi. The FCO occupied a busy main thoroughfare, so I didn't have to wait long before I was heading home from the office for the last time. A very odd feeling.

For the next twenty-four hours, I mooched about the apartment, doing some of the odd jobs I'd promised myself I'd do when I had time. They took nowhere near as long as I'd thought they would. Gardening Leave is a bit of a waste when one's garden consists of three potted plants in the hallway and a tray of beansprouts in the kitchen window.

By Wednesday morning, I was bored. Not just the ordinary bored, easily resolved by opening a few random Wikipedia pages, this was wall-climbing bored. The sort of bored that drives some to invade neighbouring countries or others to rearrange the books in the History Section of their university library by colour.

I'd planned to relax for a while. The Civil Service thirty-year redundancy package is generous, forestalling the need for hasty career decisions, so taking time out wasn't a problem. I'd planned to relax for a few days, then go down to Cornwall and talk with Jim and give him a few tips to help his bid for independence. Maybe combine it with a holiday. That had been the plan.

The reality was that by Wednesday afternoon, I was in my Volvo and well on the way to Little Didney with revenge on my mind. A dish best served cold, as Worf would say.

~ * ~ * ~ * ~

SAM GOODENOUGH LOOKED UP FROM dragging a carton of bottles across the floor. "Just in time," he said. "Give us a hand with this, I've gone and twisted my back."

I grabbed the opposite end of the box and was about to help when Goodenough straightened up and pointed at the bar.

"Just set it on top there, I'll get the empties." He slipped out through the back door.

I hefted the carton onto the bar and looked inside. It was full of bottles. I took one out to have a better look. It was a litre bottle full of a clear liquid. It bore a simple typed label which declared, 'Gin 45%'.

Goodenough returned with another, which he placed on the bar. This one contained empty gin bottles of various sorts. Mostly expensive labels, Plymouth, Bombay or Hendricks figured predominantly.

"You can't do this," I said, guessing where this was going. "It's fraud."

"Course it's not." He took a funnel from under the bar and transferred the unnamed gin to the one of the other bottles. "My regulars know what it is."

He pushed the funnel towards me. "You hang on to that, I spill more'n I pour."

"I don't understand."

"This comes in from the Frenchies, dreckly like. Boat to boat, out in the ditch. We're not really supposed to sell it, 'cause it's foreign, see? But I say that's racist, banning summat on its ethnic origin. So I say, sod 'em. I sell it anyway. But I have to put it in other bottles, in case the Revenue men come a knockin'."

"So you're not passing it off as expensive gin?" I poured carefully as I spoke.

"Course not, that'd be dishonest. I keep these on a different shelf." He pointed to a row of gin bottles behind the bar. "When my regulars ask for a Special Label gin, they get this. Saves them a few bob and it's a few more volts. We're just a poor fishing village, gotta scratch a penny where we can. You need to fill 'em a bit more'n that. Up to the top."

"But what if a tourist asks for one?" I slowly dribbled gin to the very top of the bottle.

"They get the real stuff." He pointed to a different shelf with prime label gins. "And they pay for it an' all, mind. You can get on with that? I'll go get the whisky."

I continued pouring, and he returned with another case and dumped it on the counter. "You'll be looking for a room, I presume?"

"Yes, but I'm paying for this one myself, so no surcharges."

Goodenough smiled. "You're like family now."

"Does that mean I get a discount?"

"No, better than that, family get a teasmaid in the room."

THE SMUGGLER'S ARMS BRIDAL SUITE was beginning to feel like a second home. Not knowing how long I'd be here this time, I'd packed two suitcases with a wide assortment of clothes. Even a dinner suit. I'd bought several changes of casual clothing and some new walking boots, of a similar type to the haunted boots, which I couldn't bring myself to wear again and which I'd dropped into a local charity shop in Lupus Street. Butlers Needing Homes. Apparently, redundancy and homelessness among Gentleman's Gentlemen, was becoming a problem in the City. I slid the empty cases under the bed and changed into a pair of green trousers and a checked shirt. I studied myself in the mirror, then changed again into a pair of dark blue trousers, a white shirt, and plain blue tie. Baby steps.

I tried to contact Jim to arrange a visit, but as usual, his phone was off, so I tried ringing Tiggy. She told me she was out for the day with a stag party of bankers. She did, however, suggest that her father was heading out to the island with the parts for another Wikihouse.

I found Branok Tretheway on the dock. His boat, the Pelican, took up most of the tiny dock wall. A fork-lift truck ferried large sections of a Wikihouse from a nearby lorry to the boat, where several men then manhandled them onboard.

Branok turned as I approached. "The government man," he greeted. "Here to tell us we can't put timber on a fishing boat, is it?"

"Not at all," I said. "I was hoping for a lift over to the island. Tiggy said you were going."

"She did, did she? More official directives?"

"No, I've resigned. I don't work for the Foreign Office anymore. I thought I might be able to help."

Branok scanned me up and down. "Okay, grab an end of that." He pointed at the section of Wikihouse, dangling from a harness attached to the forks of the fork-lift truck. "Jake'll show you where it's to go."

"Oh, that wasn't quite the sort of help I meant. More like administrative counsel."

"Jake!" Branok called.

"Yes, Dad?"

"Do we need administrative counsel?"

"No, Dad."

He turned to me. "Sorry, seems like we're up to date on administrative counsels. But if you want a ride over, you can give us a hand moving this lot."

I looked at the pieces of the Wikihouse propped against the wheelhouse of the boat. I scanned the boat, covered in makeshift fixes and random paint touch-ups. The smell of old fish and diesel oil already filled my nose, and even without any waves, the thing rolled from side to side like an inebriated Weeble.

"Okay," I said. My new life, seize it with both hands.

I seized the top rail of the Pelican with both hands and wobbled my way over it to land on the deck. I tried to look cool, but clearly failed as Branok called out, "Tis easier if you use the little steps." He nodded towards a set of steps against the rail I'd completely missed.

I shrugged, to indicate my nonchalance to unnecessary difficulties. "What are we doing with these?"

Jake slapped his enormous hand against the top panel. "We need to lay these flat across those hatches. And get rid of that tie. You get that caught in the winch gear and it'll 'ave yer head clean off."

I removed my tie and rolled it neatly before tucking it in my pocket. I studied the deck, where three raised hatches lined up between the wheelhouse and the back end. I looked again at the panels.

Jake anticipated my question. "Yeah, they're gonna hang over the edge of the boat, but it ain't no matter. We lash 'em down, they'll be fine. This is the fifth lot we've done. Easy as fallin' off a boat." He smiled.

The panel was much heavier than Jake made it look. Even though we never actually needed to lift it, just shuffle, slide and wriggle, it still took all my strength to keep it under some sort of controlled descent to lay it across the deck hatches. I hoped for a bit of a break between panels, but Jake offered no respite, and we went from one to the other to the next until they were all positioned. As soon as they were set, Jake threw a tangle of rope at me and told me to loop it through the guardrail, then back to him. I started untangling the rope. I lay it in a line across the panels, curled it round, and back the other way as I untangled. I became aware I was being watched and looked up. Jake and Branok were silently staring at my method.

"What you doing?" Jake asked.

"I need to untangle it to thread it through the rails," I said.

"Just wind it through and untangle as you go. We ain't got all day for you to tidy up two-hundred yards of rope." He shook his head and went back to shoving the panels into alignment against the rear deck rail.

As I threaded, Jake tied. I wasn't allowed to tie.

Once everything was lashed down and secure, Branok slipped the mooring rope and we chugged out of the little harbour. The journey over to Scanlon's Rock took far longer than in the '300'. The boat also rolled a lot more, so I spent most of the trip sat right up front, holding tight onto the forward rail, and fixing my stare on the interminably slow approach of the island. The wind tore at my face, pelting me with sea-spray and forcing me to squint. But I kept my position. Watching the island was the only hope of hanging on to my lunch.

"I got the perfect cure for seasickness," Branok announced at one point.

"What's that?" I asked, expecting to be recommended an old, folksy cure involving oysters, magic herbs, and probably whisky.

Instead, Branok said, "Sit under a tree," and they both erupted into giggles.

As we drew closer to the island, I noticed we were heading straight into Pirate's Cove. A timber and scaffold tube construction had been built on the shoreline. It vaguely resembled something between a jetty and a building site. We nudged up alongside the flimsy looking construction. I expected them to tie off as they did in Little Didney, but Jake jumped into the water and waded ashore with a rope and metal spike. He beat the stake into the ground with a rock and tied the mooring line. I guessed they didn't trust the makeshift jetty to hold the boat.

We nudged up against the flimsy looking jetty and manhandled the sections of Wikihouse with the help of the fishing rig arms and winch, onto a waiting trolley. Everything looked very precarious and likely to collapse at any moment. Although, I seemed to be the only one concerned, as proved by the ribbing I'd received when I'd suggested we pull the trolley with a long rope, rather than pushing, so as to not be on the jetty should it collapse under the weight.

I noticed Jim's old Land Rover Defender had found its way down to the beach and waited near the shoreline. Once a panel had been balanced on the trolley, it was pushed along a row of planks to the Land Rover, where, with more manhandling, it was set on the roof and tied down. The size of the panels reached well beyond the Land Rover, and, from a distance, it resembled a sort of surreal, giant coffee table.

Jim spotted me as I leaned into the trolley, helping to push the next set along the wooden trackway. "It's the man from the ministry," he greeted. "What brings you back here? More pieces of paper for me?"

"No," I puffed out the word. "I've come to help."

Jim paused and studied me. "You any good with a nail gun?"

I shook my head. "I was thinking more on the administrative side."

He patted his pockets until he found a half-smoked joint, glanced at it, then fired it up. "I'm not sure we have an administrative side for you to help with." He drew the smoke deep and held it as his eyes started to water.

"You said you wanted me to be your ambassador."

"I did?"

I nodded. "Yes."

"Was I stoned?"

"I think so. Probably."

"Oh, I say shit like that when I'm stoned. You might not want to pay too much attention to me." He paused and stared out to sea. "Although..."

I waited, but nothing more was forthcoming and as Jake was still pushing at the trolley, I figured it best to get back to the current task. I pushed.

Once the next panel had been secured to the roof of the Land Rover, Jim signalled me to get inside, and Jake headed back to the boat.

"You can hold stuff though, can't you?" Jim asked me as he nudged the vehicle towards the cut which ran up the cliff. "You know, if I've got the nail gun, you can hold stuff still, right?"

"I'm sure I can do that." Although, holding something while Jim had a nail gun on the go, wasn't really on the top of my 'Must Do' list.

I gripped the side of the seat as Jim pushed the Land Rover onto the cut. It looked like somebody had tried to widen the track a bit since the last time I'd been here. However, it was still not much more than a footpath and far too vertical for anything other than a mountain goat with a Sherpa team in support.

"So, why are you here then?" Jim shuffled the gears as we started to slip backwards. "Some secret MI6 mission to infiltrate my headquarters?"

"Not at all." I peered out my side window, hoping to see ground underneath my side of the vehicle. There was none. My heartrate increased. "And anyway, it would be MI5, not six. MI6 only deals with external threats and as your island—"

"You might want to hold tight," Jim interrupted. "There's a fair chance this could all go horribly wrong."

I held tight. The Land Rover bucked violently to one side, and I looked up to avoid looking at the ground, or lack of it. Looking up also turned out to be a mistake, as I watched the section of Wikihouse shift against its ropes. Ropes which I had been allowed to tie. I shifted my gaze to the sea and fixed on the horizon in the distance.

"That's the way to do it," Jim said as we bounced once more, then oddly, all felt calm. "Easy run now. What were you saying about your MI6 mission?"

"I was just… never mind. I've been made redundant and on enforced leave. Leaves me at a loose end for a while, so I thought I'd see if you needed help fighting the decision." I risked a look out at the ground. We'd crested the top of the cliff and were heading along reasonably flat ground.

"Hmm, I wasn't really planning on fighting anybody. I was just going to tell them all to sod off and leave me alone."

The Land Rover shuddered and appeared to drift towards the cliff edge and Jim wrestled it back.

"It doesn't really work like that," I said. "They'll still come after you for taxes and such. In fact, they might even want you to ignore them for a while, it will give them the excuse they need to seize the island against the debt. It's what they tried with Marek Werner, before they realised he'd sold it to you."

Another shudder and once more we drifted towards the cliff.

"That's tricky," said Jim.

"The Foreign Office has a special section devoted to tricky."

"What? Oh, no, I didn't mean that. I meant keeping this damn thing going in a straight line is tricky. The wind keeps catching the panel on the roof. It's a bit like a wing."

"A wing?"

"Yeah." He rummaged in the centre console box, one hand on the wheel, one in the box.

As Jim's total attention was now dedicated to the box, I felt it my duty that at least one of us looked out front to see where we were going. Not that it mattered much, as the Land Rover seemed to have a mind of its own anyway. And despite where Jim aimed the wheel, we continued to drift sideways towards the cliff.

He finally found what he was looking for and held up a half-smoked joint. "Knew I'd put it somewhere." He planted it in his mouth, then looked out the windscreen. "Whoops," he said, yanking the wheel away from the cliff. "Now, what did I do with my lighter?" Both hands left the wheel again as he searched his pockets.

The vehicle kicked and for a moment, everything felt very smooth and calm. Then a couple thumps, and back to bouncing.

"What happened?" I asked.

"I think we went airborne for a moment there. Cool, huh? You're gonna have to take the wheel for a moment, I've got a bit of a problem."

I looked down and saw that his hand had become trapped in his trouser pocket. It looked like it had slipped under the hand brake during the bump, and he'd slipped sideways against it.

I grabbed the wheel, it felt far too light. Jim wriggled and pulled and freed his hand, complete with lighter clutched in his fingers. He took the flame to his joint, pulled, and took the wheel back. "That's better," he whispered through a cloud of smoke. "You ever been hang-gliding?"

"No."

"Might get a chance in a minute." He flapped his hand to clear enough smoke to see where we were going. "Oh, that's where we are. I might get Jake to fix up something like this permanently." He pointed to the roof to indicate the panel up above. "It's a bit of a giggle."

We bounced across the meadowland of the island's midsection, occasionally jolting as the wind caught us. Eventually, we rumbled to a stop beside a stack of other panels to the west of Government House. In addition to Jim's residence, another Wikihouse had been completed and bore a sign announcing it to be The Dragon Palace – Chinese Restaurant. Just beyond that, another building looked close to completion.

"Your second building on the island is a Chinese Restaurant?" I asked.

"Yeah, cool, huh? I mean, you ain't going to get a Deliveroo out here, and you gotta keep up your standards. Far too easy to just sink into microwaved lasagne."

"You built these yourself?" I asked, looking at the buildings.

"Yeah, start to finish. Well, I had a bit of help with that actual construction bit. Not really my forte, that. Jake and some of his mates, they did that bit. But I told them where to build." He started towards Government House. "You coming? Jeeves'll make us a nice cup of tea. I've got a special blend, a secret recipe given to me by the Great Maharajah of Chalakudy. At least, that's who he said he was."

"I'd rather have Typhoo, or Yorkshire, if you have any," I said.

He stopped to look at me. "No, it's not my magic tea, if that's what you thought. Just tea, but hand-picked by naked Sadhu monks. They have to do menial work to repair their karma or something, so we're really just helping them on their way. My spiritual contribution."

"I'd still prefer Typhoo, if that's okay?"

He shrugged and headed to the house.

Jeeves greeted me with, "Oh, it's you again. You know your way now." He wandered off, leaving me in the hall.

I followed Jim into the lounge, where he poured two Jack Daniel's and pushed one towards me. I refused as politely as I could, and he took both glasses out through the patio doors onto the decking which overlooked the sea.

"You think they're going to screw me over then?" he opened.

"I'm certain of it." I settled into a swinging sofa contraption. I recognised my mistake immediately as I started to feel seasick again.

"Time for action then." He emptied the first glass and turned towards me. His eyes lit with an enthusiasm which slightly scared me. "I've been working on a plan which will make them stop all their silly games dead."

"I have a plan too," I said.

"Okay." Jim started on the second glass. "You go first."

I pulled a file from my bag and opened it on my lap. The papers threatened to blow away and each time I reached to catch a sheet, the sofa swing wobbled and tried to dump me on the decking. "Hang on a second, I've got this." I gathered everything up, but they were now in the wrong order.

"Don't need the detail, just give me the headlines," Jim said.

"Okay, given that the distance is now clarified, we just have to satisfy the other conditions of the Montevideo Convention. With Watt Tyler, you can now prove the island has a permanent population and I think we can cite Watt's little disk things as a currency. That would also then mean that when he swapped some of those for ice from that French trawler, that could, in the very truest sense, constitute an example of International Trade."

He looked out at the sea in silence. I waited while working out how to get out of this swinging chair in an emergency.

Jim turned to me. "I like that. It's a good plan. It's better than my plan."

"What was your plan?"

"I was going to buy a tank," he said. "I saw one on eBay, although shipping from Iowa is a bit expensive."

"Okay... Shall we circle back to that idea if my method doesn't work out?"

"Do you think I should buy the tank anyway? Like a backup, keep it in reserve?"

"Not unless you think your biggest threat is going to come from a platoon of World War Two infantrymen armed with revolvers. And what about ammunition? I doubt you'll find that on the eBay, 'customers-who-bought-one-of-these-also-bought,' offer."

"Hadn't worked that bit through yet." He flopped himself down next to me on the swinging sofa. The thing managed a stomach-twisting figure of eight movement that resulted in Jim covering his lap in Jack Daniel's. "I can see we're going to make a good team." He rubbed at the spillage with his sleeve. "You can be my minister."

"Minister of what?"

"I don't know, you choose. Oh, and I can't pay you anything yet, not until I open my bank. But you can have a house, I've got another three on the way." He held out a sticky hand for me to shake.

~ C H A P T E R   T W E L V E ~

I SPENT MY FIRST NIGHT on Scanlon's Rock on a camp bed in the Guest Wikihouse. The scent of newly cut pine boarding blended with the smell of the sea. An oddly relaxing mix. Even though my apartment in London had good sound insulation and heavy curtains, I had never before experienced a night quite so silent and black. At one point, I actually woke and finding I could neither see, nor hear a single thing, I panicked, thinking I'd been struck deaf and blind.

The downside though, I woke at half six, as the sun shot through the big window, piercing my eyelids and stabbing my brain with a billion candlepowers. As I buried my face in the pillow to wait for the flashing lights in my retina to stop, the squawking started. A high-pitched scraw-scraw sound that resembled Edward Scissorhands carving his name on a blackboard. I understood now how the CIA got people to talk. I'd've owned up to shooting Franz Ferdinand and starting WW1 if it would make all this stop.

I staggered out of the bed and blinked into the dawn exploding across the sea. A group of gulls swooped along the cliff top just between the window and the fierce blue of the sea. The high-tech, thermos-efficient windows, proved no defence against their squeals. I needed some heavy curtains if I was going to stay here for any length of time. And some earplugs. I turned to look at the room. And some furniture. A folding garden chair and picnic table weren't going to cut it if Jane came to visit.

Fortunately, the bathroom worked efficiently, and the solar-powered hot water system, surprisingly effective. Starting the day without a decent shower would have been a deal-breaker. After my shower, I headed across the little bit of field, avoiding Ermintrude, who seemed intent on finding out what I had in my pockets, and knocked on the door of Government House.

Jeeves opened the door, grunted, then turned and walked back inside. I followed him in. Jim was in the kitchen, he wore a red Chinese silk dressing gown with a huge, embroidered dragon across the back.

"Hey," he greeted. "Just in time for breakfast. We have Sugar Puffs." He handed me the box of Sugar Puffs and pointed to a cupboard. "There's a bowl in there. Milk's in the fridge, it's only UHT, I haven't figured out how the cow works yet."

"Thank you." I took the Sugar Puffs and poured a small portion. "I haven't had these since I was... twelve."

"My guru once told me that each time you stop doing something which you enjoyed as a child, you age another season." He shook his hair and raised his chin. "That's how I still look this good at... well, at significantly older on the calendar than what you see here." He pointed to his face with both forefingers.

I dug my spoon into the Sugar Puffs and munched. Immediately, childhood memories pinged my thoughts. Odd, how taste or smells did that. I took another spoonful and looked up to see Jim watching me. His eyes held a look of expectancy and I realised he'd been awaiting confirmation of his youthful looks. "What? Oh, yes. It's amazing," I said, clearly too late.

Jim huffed. "When did *you* last climb a tree?"

"That's frowned upon in St James' Park. Shouldn't we be having a chat about how to move forwards with the application for independence?"

"I thought you had all that sorted? You said so, about Watt's disks and so on."

"We still have to find a way to get another country to recognise you as an independent country. That's the tricky bit."

Jim seemed to go off into thought for a moment, then, "Vanuatu any good? It's a country in the Pacific."

"I know where Vanuatu is. But for what?"

"Recognition. Would Vanuatu qualify?"

"Of course, but how are you going to get Vanuatu to recognise you?"

"Marek, he owes me one."

"Marek Werner?" I queried. "The tech billionaire you bought the island from?"

"It's complicated. Come on, I'll explain as we go."

"Where are we going?"

"Branok's coming over with some more stuff." He glanced at his watch. "You finished your breakfast? We're gonna be late."

I followed Jim out to the Defender, thankful I had so far not seen him smoke or drink. My relief proved short-lived. The moment he climbed into the Land Rover, a joint magically appeared between his lips. He waited until the cloud of smoke completely encircled his head before pulling away.

We headed straight out across the meadowland, which represented the bulk of the island's interior, bumping and bouncing our way north-west towards Pirate's Cove.

"You were going to tell me about Marek Werner," I said.

"Marek? yeah. Strange dude. Did you know he's got a boat with a garage on board for his Lamborghini? That car travels better than the British Prime Minister." He yanked the steering wheel to the right and my face squashed against the window. "That was close," he said.

"What?"

"There's an old mineshaft there. Forgot about that one for a moment. Apparently, it's got a missile launcher and everything."

"There's missiles in the mineshaft?"

"Huh? No, Marek's boat. Keep up. I sometimes wonder if you're a bit of a stoner on the QT." He looked at me as if trying to detect signs of marijuana usage. "Being unable to concentrate on one thing at a time is… is… what was I saying?"

"Marek?" I reminded.

"Yeah." He returned his attention to the ground in front of us. "He created this platform, MySexRated, the app for rating your past sexual partners."

"I know, I looked into it," then quickly added, "not the platform, dreadful thing. Giving one's previous sexual partners a public star rating. No, I looked into the company."

"Well, he's got more money than God. He bought the island just because he could, but never used it. Then he got into a pickle with the UK tax people and had to move his UK assets before they closed in on him."

"I remember. He got called before the UK parliamentary committee on tax affairs."

"But now he's got this island, and he needs rid. But he can't just sell it, because the revenue bandits will seize the money. That's when he called me."

"Why you?"

"He's a bit of a fan-boy. Loves hobnobbing with the names in rock. Thinks it gives him street-cred or something."

"But he's a nasty little man. Why did you get involved with him?"

"Because he was going to give me the island if we played a gig for his birthday party. And besides, I have a ten-out-of-ten, star rating on the site and I didn't want to jeopardise that. As you say, he's a nasty little shit."

"And you played the gig?"

"Yeah, at his Hollywood place. You'll never believe who was there. Anyway, he keeps his deal, I get the island, and he legs it to Vanuatu, where he's bought himself an estate and a passport. He's got a house bigger than this island just outside Port Vila."

"And how does this help?" I asked.

"Did you know that Vanuatu's main trade is selling citizenships for a hundred grand a time?"

"Yes, I'm aware of that."

"You lot are missing a trick there."

"Not really," I said. "We charge a lot more than that, though it's mostly only Russian Oligarchs who can afford it."

He glanced at me and gave a quick smile. "You're a very unusual government man, aren't you?"

"It's been mentioned."

"Anyway, being as how Marek is now one of Vanuatu's wealthiest citizens, I'm fairly sure he'll be able to persuade somebody in the Vanuatu Government to pick up the phone to the U.N. I'll probably have to give him an invite to my birthday party, but he'll fix it. And anyway, he's a bit of a giggle, you should see him do karaoke to Bohemian Rhapsody."

As we neared the cut, which led down to the beach at Pirate's Cove, Jim pulled the Defender to an unsteady stop far too close to the top of the cliff. A scattering of gravel from the front wheels tumbled over the edge and clattered down the cliff. He shuffled in his seat, rested his hands on his thighs and closed his eyes.

I waited until I couldn't contain my curiosity anymore. "What's up?" I asked.

"Shush." He flapped a hand.

Eventually, he breathed deep, opened his eyes and shook his head as if seeing the view for the first time. "Just centring my chakras. Going down is a bit trickier than going up. Mostly because I can see how soddin' lethal it is. I tried it with my eyes closed once, that's why I'm driving this thing now and not my dirt bike."

"I didn't know you had a dirt bike," I said.

"I haven't anymore." He took a deep pull on the joint, then handed it to me.

"No thanks, I don't—"

"It's not for you." He blinked to clear the smoke from his eyes. "I just need you to hold it while we go down. I need to concentrate. You might want to just look at the sky and imagine you're a cloud. I find that helps me."

I ignored his advice, grabbed the handrail above the door with my free hand while keeping the joint as far away from my face as I could. I thought about closing my eyes, but they refused to cooperate with the instruction, and just widened even more as we commenced our descent. I had to brace my feet into the footwell to avoid a face-mashing on the windscreen. It felt like I was standing upright. I needed both hands, and in desperation, I gripped the joint between my teeth, freeing my other hand to assist in keeping the Defender the right way up.

I tried not to breathe in.

We bucked and twisted down the cut like a bobsleigh running the Cresta Run and landed in a cloud of dust at the bottom. Jim turned off the engine and took the joint from my clenched teeth.

"Thanks," he said and clambered out of the vehicle.

I sat for a moment, trying to decide if the dizzy feeling was down to adrenaline or cannabis. I opted for adrenaline and followed Jim across the beach towards the Pelican. The boat bumped against the makeshift jetty, every little movement threatening to tip the whole lot into the water. The winch arms dangled another Wikihouse panel over the foam gathering on the shoreline. Jake and Branok wriggled the panel onto the waiting trolley as Tiggy operated the yellow remote control to the winch arm. A couple of other men I didn't recognise were busy lining up the next panel.

I noticed Tiggy's own boat moored out a bit, so I guessed they were going to deal with whatever was on the Pelican first, then bring the '300' in. Tiggy flicked her head to acknowledge my presence and continued with her manipulation of the winches.

Another man stood to one side on the beach, watching the goings on with interest.

"Oh, yeah," Jim said. "Come and meet Lin."

We headed over to where the man stood. He turned as we approached and beamed at Jim. "Hey, Jimmy," Lin greeted. He was Asian in appearance, probably Chinese, a touch shorter than me but bigger built.

"John, this is Lin, he's my chef. John, Lin Chao, etcetera. You can work the rest out between you." He relit the joint and turned to watch the offloading.

"You're the government man?" Lin asked, his accent far closer to the East End of London than the eastern end of Asia.

"Not any more. Now I'm the Minister of Scanlon's Rock, apparently."

"Minister for what?"

"I don't know, we haven't decided yet. I guess you're going to be running the Dragon's Palace?"

"Oh, is that what he's calling it? He's got a real thing for dragons. Do you like Chinese food?"

"I love it. In moderation of course."

"You sure you're in the right place?" Lin smiled. "Only, moderation is not exactly the norm around Jim."

"I heard that," Jim said, without turning.

"Do you think we should help?" I asked, watching two men manhandling another Wikihouse side-panel onto the little trolley.

"Nah," said Jim. "That's Shaun, he likes lifting heavy things. He's got prizes for it. Thinks he's builder, but you wouldn't want to trust him with anything substantial. He's a bit of a dickhead, but don't tell him I said that." He waved an arm and yelled towards the men, "Oi, Dickhead," and raised a thumb.

Shaun looked up and returned the thumb, yelling something I couldn't hear.

With the panel safely secured to the trolley, Shaun and another man, just as big, pushed it along the wooden track to where Jim had left the Defender. I tried to help a bit with the transfer to the vehicle's roof, but came to the realisation I was more in the way than of any use.

Once loaded, a couple of trolley loads of shiny cookers and other equipment followed and were packed into the back of the Defender. Jim had to tie the rear door in place as a stainless-steel cabinet protruded from the back. We climbed back inside, and Jim aimed for the cut rising up the cliff.

The wheels kicked at the gravelly track and the vehicle slewed as first one wheel, then another caught a grip. Shaun and the other man walked up the cut alongside the vehicle, and once at the top, they perched themselves on the bonnet like a pair of gargoyles keeping watch.

"Who's the other guy?" I asked.

"That's Shawn," Jim replied.

"No, not him, the other guy."

"Shawn. It's Shaun and his brother, Shawn. One's got a W, the other's got a U. Shaun and Shawn."

"Brothers?" I checked.

"Yeah, their mother, Shauna, was obsessed with Sean Connery."

"And the father?"

"Oh, he was Sean. With an E, A. It was the only reason she married him."

"Was?"

"Yes, funny really, in a sad way," Jim said. "Sean was severely dyslexic. The whole family are. He was working for a demolition company up Truro way, and there was a bit of confusion over the TNT Explosives Locker and the Courier Cupboard. Mind you, they should have known better than to send a dyslexic to fetch a package from the TNT Express Cupboard."

We bounced across the grassland and parked next to the other panels. Shaun and Shawn jumped down and hefted the panels from the roof, then emptied the contents of the Defender into the Dragon's Palace. Once everything had been cleared, we piled back in and returned to Pirate's Cove to collect another panel.

I tracked down Tiggy on the Pelican, she was wrapping a rope into a locker.

"Any chance of a lift over when you go back?" I asked.

"Bored already?" She brushed dust from her hands and slid the locker lid shut with her foot.

"Not yet. I want to fetch the rest of my stuff over."

She straightened up and looked at me. "Where's your tie?"

"Jim took it, he won't give it back." I realised that might have sounded petulant and added, "But it's okay, I've got some more back at the Smuggler's."

"You want to go back to get a tie?"

"No, it's just that... No, I don't need a tie. Not unless somebody... No, no tie. Just the rest of my things. I don't need ties anymore." I opened another button on the top of my shirt.

"Well, glad we've cleared that up. I'm going back over in about half an hour. Just need to help Dad get this back to being a fishing boat. You can give us a hand if you like? Make things quicker?"

She pointed me at another pile of rope which needed storing. I discovered that untangling three miles of heavy rope was a lot harder than untangling a headphone lead. And I always struggled with those.

"It doesn't really matter if the loops aren't all exactly the same length," Tiggy said, after watching me for several minutes.

"But you can get more in the locker if it's even."

"We're not short of locker space, but I have to say, it's very pretty. Dad will be overjoyed." Her eyes flickered with a smile.

Once we'd tidied the ropes, we took the dinghy out to the '300' and headed for Little Didney. The journey was quick and very bumpy, but less scary, or sea-sick making, than before. Or maybe I was just getting used to it.

The dock was empty, so we were able to tie up there and avoid dinghy adventures. I offered to tie the mooring rope, but Tiggy said she didn't have enough time for that and tossed the rope over a capstan where it tied itself beautifully into a double-sheetbend as it landed.

"Thanks for the lift," I said. "I owe you a drink."

"Okay," she replied. "I'll just lock up and I'll be there."

It wasn't quite what I'd meant, but I had no reason to put her off, so just said, "No problem, I'm in no hurry."

I waited as she locked up the cabin and slid a couple of padlocks into place on the hatches, then we headed for the Smuggler's.

Sam Goodenough greeted us with, "I'm not open yet, you know. Haven't even stocked the chill cabinet yet." He turned to point at a carton of soft drink bottles on the floor by the glass-fronted cabinet. "It'll go a lot quicker if you give me a hand."

I resisted for a moment, but he continued to stare in my direction and the pressure proved too much. "You want them in there?" I asked.

"Course there, where d'ya think? Don't you know nothing about bars?"

"I'm learning fast," I said.

Tiggy dragged some chairs off the top of one of the tables and settled herself in one of them. "You shouldn't let him manipulate you like that. He'll have you dragging barrels up from the cellar next if you don't watch out."

"You leave 'im alone, young Tegan," Goodenough grumbled. "He don't mind helping an old man from time to time." He turned to me. "Do ya?"

"No." I squatted on the floor and shifted bottles from box to chiller.

"Not like that," Goodenough said. "You can't put Coke next to Pepsi, I'll have the reps fighting in the car park again."

"Sorry." I shifted the bottles to separate shelves.

"Couple of pints of Doom Bar when you're ready, Sam," Tiggy asked.

"Rush, rush. Used to be a time when a man could take his time to do a proper job of something." Goodenough planted a couple of glasses on the counter and proceeded to fill the first from the Doom Bar pump. "But now, nobody got no time for nuthin'." He poured the second, then pushed them across the bar. "There you go. I'll put 'em on your tab."

I picked up the beers and transferred them to the table to join Tiggy.

"Bit early for me, really," I said, and supped at the beer.

"Fisherman's time," said Tiggy. "When you start work before the rest of the world has got up for their two o'clock pee, then this is lunchtime."

"Okay, we'll call it that."

"How was your first night on the Rock?"

"Quiet. Very odd, not used to anything being that quiet apart from when I ordered a fillet steak, well-done, in the Melchester one time."

"It will probably liven up a bit when Cindy gets back. She likes to party."

"Jim's wife? I thought she was in Rio. Something about a climate change protest?"

"Yes, she's gone out on a trip deep into the Amazon. A helicopter tour party to visit a tribe that has remained hidden for centuries. Jim showed me a selfie she took of herself with the shaman."

"That's nice."

"I have to say, the fresh air seems to be agreeing with you." I felt Tiggy's eyes scanning my face. "You've got a bit more colour to your cheeks. Or it might just be that losing the tie has allowed a bit more blood to your face."

I unconsciously touched my hand to my face, then brought it back to the table when I realised.

Tiggy took hold of my hand and turned it over. "You've got blisters, bless. I can see I'm going to have to toughen you up."

Her hand felt oddly harsh, yet still welcoming. "Maybe, if I stay here—"

A loud scraping of the chair next to mine and Goodenough planted himself in the seat, dumping a plate containing a Cornish Pasty on the table. My hand jerked involuntarily free of Tiggy's, as if in urgent retreat from a fire.

"Is that for me?" I asked.

"No, I need your help," he said.

"With that?"

"Yeah, well, not this one specifically. But pirates."

"Cornish Pasty pirates?" I queried.

"That's what you call 'em innit when somebody copies something to sell it?"

"I suppose. How can I help?"

"Here we go," muttered Tiggy in the background.

Goodenough picked up the pasty again. "This here is a genuine Cornish pasty, the original. You can tell that, 'cause he's got eighteen crimps. Like the ones sent to King Henry in 1536. They had eighteen crimps, down to the fact that Old Man Pengelly's great, great, great." He paused and studied his fingers. "Great, great, great —"

"I recall," I interrupted. "All the way back to Tudor times, yes? Tiggy told me about these the other day."

Goodenough looked disappointed he'd been cut short, paused, then decided he was going to tell his story anyway. "Yeah, well, he lost his finger chopping meat," he continued. "Rumour has it that it ended up in the pasty Jane Seymour had for lunch that day. Anyway, being as how he only had nine fingers, he always crimped eighteen crimps. All other pasties that come after that, they have twenty, you see?"

"Yes, but how does that concern me?" I asked.

"He's wanting you to help him getting all pasties banned from calling themselves Cornish pasties unless they're made in Pengelly's Bakery with eighteen crimps," Tiggy explained. "He's been banging on about this for years to anybody who'll sit still long enough."

"I see. But I still don't know how I can help," I said.

"You're a minister," Goodenough said. "They got rules, like when I had to stop calling my house sparkling wine, Champagne."

"But, Sam, it was just cheap homemade plonk you were trying to pass off as Champagne," Tiggy said.

"That ain't the point. If I can't call that Champagne, then nobody else can sell Cornish pasties."

"But I'm not a minister. Well, I might be, but not in the British Government. You'd need to take that up with DEFRA. It's their domain. I can't help."

"I told you," said Tiggy.

Goodenough grunted and pushed the pasty across to me. "You might as well have that, I can't sell it now." He picked it up, turned it over, and put back down. "It's split."

I shrugged and took the pasty. "Thanks."

"That'll be two-fifty. I'll add it to your room." He pushed himself clear of his seat and headed out the back of the bar.

"Why's he so concerned about Pengelly's Pasties?" I asked, once Goodenough was out of earshot.

"He owns it. Along with quite a few other businesses in the area."

"Ah, that makes sense. Halfsies?" I held up the pasty.

"As long as you don't expect me to pay half," Tiggy said.

I broke it in two and passed one half to her. "My treat."

"Mmm." She raised her glass. "Wined *and* dined. Aren't I the lucky girl?"

"I have to watch the pennies. I don't have an expense account anymore." I bit into my half of the pasty. It may have been cold and a little the worse for wear, but still delicious.

"Yes, I was wondering, what on earth made you chuck away a good career like that? A bit drastic, wasn't it?"

"Hardly a good career. I was never destined to rise above adequate, to quote my last appraisal. It only really dawned on me one day when I found myself fetching coffee for the guy who refilled the paperclip dispensers."

"That must have been a very dark day." She smiled.

"It was." I nodded. "Right up there with the day they changed the Marathon Bar to Snickers."

"So much trauma in one life." She reached forward and squeezed my hand. "Never mind, now you're a government minister."

"So it appears. Just not sure what I'm supposed to be ministering."

"Well, you'd better work it out, you've got your first official function next week."

"What?"

"Jim's birthday bash. You hadn't forgotten, had you?"

"No." I took a long sip of my beer, trying to hide behind the glass. "No. Certainly not. It was... is, indelibly etched into my mental diary. Just one quick question."

"Yes?"

"What day is it, exactly?"

## CHAPTER THIRTEEN

I SPENT THE REST OF the day gathering my possessions together and buying a few basics to ensure I was at least self-sufficient in caffeine and biscuits. The following day, I went back to the village to buy bedding and towels along with some kitchen accessories, including a microwave and grill hybrid contraption. At least I could now survive on the island overnight when needed, and without reliance on Tiggy to get me back to dry land when in need of a proper meal or a bed.

My evening meal consisted of a microwaved lasagne and garlic baguette, followed by a small tub of chocolate ice-cream and a bottle of Chardonnay. Baby steps. I did have a slight panic when I realised I'd forgotten to buy a corkscrew, but then found it was a screw cap.

My sleep that evening was at least under a new duvet and sheet, but the fold-out bed creaked and wobbled with every move, so I spent most of the next day trying to buy a bed. In the end, I had to order one by phone from a store in Penzance to buy one and it was Sunday before I finally slept in something which I could once more call my own bed. A bit small, but functional, and it would do for the moment.

~ * ~ * ~ * ~

DESPITE THE MORE COMFORTABLE BED and cosy duvet, the seagulls once more tore my hard-won sleep from my grasp with their early morning squawking, and persuaded me to start the day at six-thirty, rather than my scheduled seven. I was going to have to learn to tune out the noise of nature, the way I had the dustcarts and street cleaning machines of Pimlico.

When I stepped, blinking into the morning sunlight, I noticed Jim dragging one of a stack of solar panels from the back of his Land Rover. "Ah, just the man," he said.

"I can't lift anything heavy," I said. "I haven't had breakfast yet."

"What?" He looked at the panel. "Oh, this? No, these aren't heavy, and I wasn't asking for help, but as you're here…"

I picked another one from the Land Rover. Jim was right, it was deceptively light.

"Just put it over here." Jim stood the panel against the wall of Government House. "I had a chat with Marek last night. Well, this morning, or *his* morning. *Somebody's* morning, I was a bit vague on the whole time thing last night. Funny how that happens. I lost a whole weekend once when we were touring Ireland. I turned up at the Town Hall Theatre in Galway, but the rest of the band were already in Kilkenny. Still don't know what happened, only that at some point during that time, I managed to acquire a new tattoo." He undid the belt on his trousers, turned round and pushed them down enough to show me the top of his right buttock.

"Who's Tracey?" I asked.

"I often ponder that very question." He pulled his trousers up and redid the belt. "But that aside, it's all good news, isn't it?"

"What is?"

"About the note. Didn't I tell you that bit?" He tapped his pockets and found a joint and studied it briefly to see how much mileage it had left in it. He frowned, then lit it. "They sent a note. Vanuatu, to the United Nations. I don't know what Marek's got on them, but it must be fairly spectacular because they've made him an ambassador for… what did he say? Dealing?"

"Trade?" I suggested.

"Yes, that's it. He's an ambassador for trade now for Vanuatu. Mind you,

Marek does seem to know how to move parcels around the world without everything getting tangled in red tape. He could teach FedEx a thing or two."

"Hang on, you're saying that the Vanuatu Government have already sent notification to the U.N. that they recognise Scanlon's Rock?"

"You know the old saying, if you want something doing quickly, give the job to an unscrupulous billionaire with a dossier on important people's recent sexual activity." Jim slid the last panel against the rest, hopped back into the Land Rover and took off.

The front door opened, and Jeeves stepped into view. "Gone, has he?" he muttered.

"Yes, he seems a bit hyper this morning."

"He's been playing with his new espresso machine. He'll calm down when he gets his hash/caffeine balance back in harmony." Jeeves turned his gaze to the solar panels. "I suppose it's my job to move these now. Move this here, move that there… Oh well, I expect I'll get my rest when I'm dead." He picked up a panel and his whole demeanour sank as if he'd been doing this for a thousand years.

I went back to my house and sat on the little wooden veranda. The low morning sun spread a carpet of jewels across the sea, flashing brightly enough to cause fireflies on my retina. If Vanuatu had sent a notice to the United Nations, this could actually work. The FCO were not going to take it easily though, so the more ducks I could get lined up, the better. I needed a useful idiot. Fortunately, with the current incumbents in government, there was an embarrassment of riches from which to choose. I flicked through my mental file of government minsters. One name jumped out immediately, Stephen Weatherby-Hewitt. For some inexplicable reason, he'd managed to rise to the position of Secretary of State for Arts and Culture. The only thing which could ever be said about the Right Honourable Stephen Weatherby-Hewitt was that he was terminally enthusiastic and highly ambitious. I also happened to know he was a big fan of rock music. Perfect.

I tracked down the phone number to Weatherby-Hewitt's Private Secretary, Linda Herrington. I'd met her a few times. Efficient and terrifying.

"Linda?" I asked as she answered the phone. "John Cabot. We met at Sir Oliver's dinner a couple of years back, when you were in the Foreign Office."

"John, yes, I remember. I heard you'd gone?"

"Gardening Leave, still considering my options. I'm currently acting as an adviser to Jim Sullivan, the leader of the rock band, The Spartans?"

"I know of them. Go on."

"Well, he's celebrating his birthday with an exclusive group of influential people, including an ambassador and several major celebrities. I wanted to check that Stephen had received his invitation, as Sullivan was very keen to meet with him. Something to do with setting up an international exchange programme for music students. Only, we don't seem to have had his reply, and time is pressing."

"I see. I'll check his schedule. When is it for?"

"Week Saturday, the twenty-fourth. Sorry it's a bit short notice, but the invites were sent out months ago."

"I have no record of it. He's supposed to be speaking at a fundraiser for a theatre reformation in Stourbridge, but I don't think he'd be heartbroken to miss it. Can you send another invitation?"

"It's a bit late now, with the post being what it is. I could e-mail one to you, but I'll need it straight back."

"That's fine. Send it to me and I'll see he RSVPs it straight away."

"Excellent. Tell Stephen that Jim's looking forward to meeting him."

I closed the call and slumped back against the little banister on the veranda steps. And breathe.

Once I'd regained control of my pulse rate, I went to my laptop to design the invite and send it on its way.

~ * ~ * ~ * ~

OVER THE NEXT COUPLE OF days, Shaun and Shawn finished off the Dragon Palace and moved on to starting another Wikihouse. Apparently, this one was going to be a bar, or a tearoom. Jim hadn't yet decided which, although, he had decided on the name, the 'Ocean View'.

Lin Chao worked on assembling his kitchen in the Dragon Palace, and gradually, more bits arrived, bringing it into something vaguely resembling a restaurant. Albeit, a sparse one. Branok's boat, the Pelican, seemed to be making two or three trips a day, ferrying in all manner of bits and pieces so I took advantage, and piggy-backed several crossings with some odd bits of furniture I'd found in the Save Our Seals shop. I'd been reluctant to buy anything new until I knew what I was doing with my flat in Pimlico. It also gave me the opportunity to visit the local print shop for various documents I needed.

Most of my time on the Rock was taken putting together the basis for a more formal declaration of independence, including drafting the legal structure of government and outlining the banking and education systems. Mostly, that consisted of lifting standard paragraphs and clauses from documents in the archives of the FCO, to which, fortunately, I still had access. At least until my Gardening Leave period expired, at which point, no doubt, they would delete my authorisations completely.

AS THE DAYS MUDDLED BY, I realised that beyond hearing the sounds of drilling or sawing, I hadn't paid an awful lot of attention to what was going on around me. So it came as a bit of a surprise, when on the Wednesday, as I set out to catch a lift back to the mainland with Tiggy, I noticed for the first time all the tents scattered across the flat centre of the meadowland.

A large marquee stood in the middle of the gathering with several gazebos clustered around. Moving out from those, three slightly smaller marquees, and beyond those, a random collection of bell tents. A couple of small square tents stood on the outskirts, which I presumed were WC facilities.

I diverted my path to go through the middle of the tents and noticed that the central marquee had a stage at one end, so I guessed some sort of entertainment was scheduled. I continued on and resumed my heading to Pirate's Cove. I reached the top of the cliff overlooking the cove in good time and realised I hadn't stopped for a rest. I presumed I must be acclimatising to all this rough walking. A quick glance to the beach confirmed the '300' sat alongside the little pier, now of a slightly more robust construction, although still predominantly built of old scaffolding poles and planks.

"Come on," Tiggy yelled, as soon as I'd reached earshot. "I can't hang about here all morning."

"Sorry," I said, as I scrambled aboard. "Have you seen the set-up back there?" I pointed back the way I'd come.

"You mean the tents and everything?"

"Yes, I was expecting maybe just a single marquee or something."

"You should know by now, Jim doesn't do anything by half measures."

I settled in to the seat next to Tiggy's and she brought the engines to life. "What were you doing over here this morning?"

"Oh, just picking up some cases of drinks and dropping them off."

"From Sam Goodenough?"

She looked at me and smiled. "No, from the little off-licence out there." She pointed towards the open sea.

"France?"

"Not quite. I've been out to meet up with a French boat, stocking up on spirits and Champagne for Jim's party."

"I see. Isn't that illegal?"

"Only if Scanlon's Rock is part of the UK. Hold tight." She pushed the levers forwards, and the bow lifted.

I felt a small sense of exhilaration, then realised I was in a boat, a small boat and travelling very quickly. Exhilaration turned swiftly to unease, but stopped short of outright panic. I forced a smile and wriggled into my life jacket. "Health and safety," I said. "Wouldn't want you to lose your licence."

"I'm meant to have a licence?" She grinned at me. "Don't worry, I'll try not to get you killed. You're fun to have around."

"Fun? You mean with my witty repartee and gregarious personality?"

"I was thinking more of your constant state of total bewilderment, a bit like a new kitten trying to understand how wool works. But we'll go with your version, if that does it for you."

"A bewildered kitten. Well, I suppose it's better than some of the things I'd been called back in the FCO."

Tiggy smiled and swung the boat towards the harbour mouth. I grabbed the seat as the world tipped to the left.

Once docked, Tiggy leapt out and tied up, waiting for me to wobble my way onto the safety of the concrete.

"I've got to go back around six," she said. "There's an urgent package arriving for Jim later and I have to drop it over, so if you're around, I'll give you a lift."

"Thanks, that would be great. Should I buy you a drink or something?"

She paused and looked at me. "Are you asking me out?"

"No, well… I just meant as a thank you. Not that I wouldn't—"

"Oi, Tegan," a voice called from just along the dock.

"Oh, damn," said Tiggy. "I thought he might be here."

"Who's that?" I asked.

"One of those banker twonks I took out to see the dolphins. He's got a grump on because I cut the trip short when they started chucking beer bottles at the dolphins. Thinks he's due a refund."

"Do you need a hand?"

"You offering to be my muscle?"

"What?" I eyed up the irate man. He looked big, And angry. Angry big. "Well, he can't go round bullying people. Especially women, so…" I looked at the man again. He also looked a good twenty years my junior, and fit. "Sometimes one has to make a stand."

"My protector, how sweet. Don't worry, he's all piss and wind. Anyway, you see that big shadow just behind him?"

I looked beyond the man to a warehouse doorway. The shadow was wrong for a doorway. "I think so."

"That's my brother Jake. I think you met him the other day? I texted him earlier as I guessed this twonk would be here."

"Ah, good plan. Well, if you need more back up, I'm just here." I was feeling more confident now.

"I'm sure Jake'll manage, but thanks." She moved more square on to me and I watched her eyes dance across my face. She smiled. "Really, thanks." Her hand briefly touched my upper arm for the tiniest squeeze, then she was gone, marching up the dock to meet the man.

Just as she neared him, the shadow moved and slipped alongside Tiggy. Jake dwarfed her. And the twonk. I couldn't hear what was being said, but the man waved his arms and made noises. Jake moved between him and Tiggy and the man started to walk away. He stopped a couple of times to turn and shout something, and each time he did, Jake closed on him, until finally, he turned and marched away.

I watched a moment longer as Tiggy and Jake chatted briefly, then they set off up the road.

I watched them go, then headed along the dock in the opposite direction.

My first call was to the Smuggler's to settle my latest bill. I really needed to make my mind up where I was staying. Paying for an empty room here wasn't exactly good economics, but it did ease my sense of panic at being trapped on the island.

"Have you used the mini-bar?" Goodenough looked up from his ledger, pen poised.

"There's a mini-bar in the room?" I asked.

"The bottle on the dressing table."

"But that was just tap water."

"It's the mini-bar. Did you use it?"

"Erm, yes, I think. I didn't realise—"

Goodenough made a note in the ledger. "Did you take any snacks from the snack tray?"

"Snack tray? ... Oh, I see, you mean the miniature biscuit next to the water bottle?"

"Did you take anything from the snack tray?"

"Yes. And it was stale."

He made another note in the ledger. When he'd finished with his scribbling, he pulled out an oversized calculator, stabbed at the buttons, then turned it to me.

"Is that the date, or is it an offer to sell the place?" I asked.

"Not my fault, it's the VAT."

"Ah, okay, but I'll need a VAT receipt then, just for the auditors. On the other hand, if you'll take cash..."

Goodenough studied me for a moment, then stabbed at the calculator again. "I've given you the Local's Discount, being as how you're almost local now." He pushed it back at me.

I studied the number again. It still looked more like a holiday for a family of six in Disneyland rather than a few nights in Little Didney. I tapped divide by two and turned it back to him. "How about if I get your pasties into the hands of the Secretary of State for the Environment? He's the man in charge of the Protected Geographical Indication on foods."

He looked at me and smiled. "You're not quite as daft as you look, are you?"

"I think I'll take that as a compliment." I handed him a wad of notes. "Of course, it doesn't mean anything will happen, but at least your pasties are in the right place."

He took the money and counted it. "I'll get your change."

"Don't bother, that'll cover next week as well."

Goodenough looked at the notes. "No it won't."

"Yes it will," I said, and turned for the door.

The next place on my list was the charity shop. I'd remembered they had a big old wooden chair when I'd been in there looking for boots. Luckily, it was still there. Unfortunately, it was more cumbersome than I'd realised, and I had to part drag and part carry it down to the dock where I parked it next to the '300'. I just hoped nobody would steal it. I reasoned that, as it had sat all this time in the charity shop, priced at five pounds, there was a very good chance nobody would be interested in stealing it. I still felt nervous about leaving it though and wished I'd thought things through better and left that one as my last call.

I found a stationer, come printing shop, come bookshop, up near the top of the village. I gave the man my thumb-drive and he printed off the various documents for me. I also managed to find a nice roll of gold coloured wrapping foil. I dropped in on the Post Office on the way back down, posted my letter and found a young King Neptune's plastic play set, which was exactly the thing I didn't know I needed.

As I rounded the corner to the little harbour, my brief moment of nervousness as to whether the chair would still be there dissipated. The chair sat exactly where I'd left it. Only now, it had been joined by a mattress and a pram. I looked around in the vague hope of spotting somebody who looked like a mattress dumper, but the only people there were a couple of men fishing off the dock.

"Did you see who left these here?" I called.

"Nah," said one of the men as he cast out his line. "Probably tourists. Always leaving their rubbish behind."

"Ah, glad you're early," I heard Tiggy's voice from behind me.

I turned to greet her. "Just been buying a few bits and pieces," I said.

She scanned the collection. "I can see. Nice pram, something you want to tell me?"

"No, that's not mine, nor the mattress. Just the chair."

"That?" She pointed at the chair.

"It's for a project."

"I'm not going to ask. I fear the answer would be worse than anything I can imagine, so best you keep that a secret. Get it on board. There's weather on the way."

I looked up to the west. The sky certainly seemed angry. In fact, it looked like it had been in a bar brawl with Tyson Fury, all bruises and puffy lips.

"We'll get back before the weather hits? Right?"

"Only if you get on the boat now and stop fluffing around with your jumble sale."

"Oh, right." I hefted the chair on board and settled in the passenger seat on the top deck.

Tiggy slid into the pilot's seat next to mine and brought the engines to life.

As we skimmed across the waves, clipping the tops of the white horses, I watched the clouds massing, as if building an attack force. My eyes darted from island to clouds and back again, trying to gauge the winner as the race drew closer. So engaged was I that I completely forgot to panic about the speed and the chances of the boat turning over.

We slid into Pirate's Cove, inches ahead of the rain. Tiggy moored the boat out at the buoy, and we took the dinghy for the final hundred metres to shore. Extracting my chair from the dinghy proved harder than I'd anticipated and, in the end, necessitated wet feet.

"Are you going back?" I asked.

"In this?" She glanced up at the sky. "No, I'll stay with Jim for the night. He's got a spare room."

The chair wasn't particularly heavy, but awkward, and by the time we'd reached my Wikihouse, I was exhausted and wet through.

"I'm just going to get into some dry clothes," I said, then immediately felt guilty as I realised Tiggy had nothing to change into. "I've got a jumper and some chinos, if you want to get dry?"

She turned away from me so I could see the rucksack on her back. "Overnight kit. Never leave home without it."

"Good thinking. Do you want a cup of tea or something before you go? To say thank you."

"A cup of tea? Is that what risking my life ferrying you and that damned chair over here is worth? A cup of tea? Should be a slap-up meal at the Dragon Palace at the very least. I believe it's opening tonight."

I studied her for a moment. Her hair, looking jet black under the soaking, clung to her head and dripped water to the floor. Her blue denim shirt, also soaked, now clung to her body, outlining her boyish stature.

"Yes, right. Dragon Palace it is then. It's a date... I mean an engagement."

"A date to engagement so quickly? My, aren't you a fast one?"

"What? No, I meant a dinner engagement. Formal. Let's call it an appointment. Huh?"

"An appointment? You're asking me out on an appointment?" Her eyes glinted with mischief, and a smile tugged at the corners of her mouth.

"You know what I meant. You decide then. You can decide what we call it."

"Okay." She turned towards the door then paused and turned back. "I'll decide what it was afterwards. Eight o'clock?" Another flash of a smile and she slipped out of the door.

## ~ CHAPTER FOURTEEN ~

THE DRAGON PALACE LESS RESEMBLED a plush Chinese restaurant, and more a food hut on a building site. The kitchen sat at the far end and was open plan, in the sense that no wall, or even a counter, yet existed. The equipment was all brand new, but clearly only partly operational. Three fold-out camping tables served as the main dining area, with random seating of stools, deck chairs, or even wooden crates.

Jim occupied one of the tables, along with Stringy, Watt, and Jeeves, while Tiggy and I sat at another. The third table stood available but lacked any seating, so it was just as well there was unlikely to be any passing trade this evening.

Lin Chao came to welcome us as we sat. "Good evening, and welcome to the Dragon Palace. Would you like to see the menu?" He placed a printed sheet of paper in front of each of us.

I scanned the menu. Wonton soup, spring rolls, Sweet and Sour Chicken or Vegetable Chow Mein.

"Can I take your beer orders while you're deciding?"

"Beer orders?" I asked.

"We only have beer."

"I'll have a beer then." I looked at Tiggy. "What would you like?"

"I think I'll have a beer," she said.

"That will be two beers then."

"Good choice," said Lin. "And to eat?"

I picked up the sheet of paper. "Is this it?" I asked.

"Don't blame me," Lin said. "I told him it would take another two weeks, but no, he wanted it open before the weekend. You might want to hurry up and order. We've had a bit of a run on the Chow Mein and the chicken."

We ordered one of each and Lin headed off to the kitchen area.

The wind buffeted around the wooden building, reminding me we were in a wooden box, perched on a rock in the middle of the English Channel. And a storm was brewing.

"These Wikihouses," I started, "they're quite tough really, aren't they? I mean, they have them in some quite remote places I've heard."

She patted my hand. "It's quite solid. Shaun and Shawn put it together and Jim supervised."

"Oh, good. That's all okay then."

"You worry far too much. How did you ever manage in the Foreign Office? Dealing with irate foreign diplomats because a bunch of our football supporters have been and draped their statue of the Virgin Mary in a Union Jack? That must have been fun?"

"It's the Union Flag. It's only a Union Jack when it's attached to a boat. It's a common mistake which..." I caught the message in the way she narrowed her eyes and the manner in which she held her fork. I switched track. "But actually, I didn't have much to do with that end of things. I just do... did research, investigations and data analysis."

"And now you're sat in a wooden hut on a windswept island, eating Chinese food with a fisherman's daughter. Bit of a comedown from dinner at the Ritz with some posh girl from the French embassy?"

"The Ritz is terribly overrated, and besides, a French diplomat is nowhere near as interesting as one might think. All they want to talk about is the expensive places they've been and which designer they're wearing. Give me a fisherman's daughter any day."

Her left eyebrow lifted, and her brow crinkled. "Why, kind sir, 'tis such an honour you bestow on a poor wench."

"Okay, no. That's not what I meant... I only meant to say... that is..." I caught the smile as it spread across her face. "I meant you're much more fun to be with. I really don't like those dinners. Of course, the food is good... although, I prefer the Melchester. If you were my date... I mean, my companion, not date... although not that I'd be against... Can I stop digging now?"

"Probably for the best. Although, can I just check, were you actually asking me out to dinner somewhere in that?"

I scanned her eyes for traces of sarcasm or anger. Finding none, I ventured, "Actually, I was thinking—"

Two shadows descended over us. I looked up to find that Jim and Jeeves had positioned themselves on each side of our table. They lifted the table, complete with our meals, and planted it next to their own. "You're my guests for the evening," Jim said as he repositioned his seat.

We both lifted our seats to follow our meals and sat down again. The smoke from a pair of still burning joints in the ashtray on Jim's table drifted over my Vegetable Chow Mein.

"Can't leave you guys on your own," Jim said. "Order what you like, my treat."

"We already did," Tiggy said.

"Well, have some wine." Jim poured two glasses from a bottle on his table. "My own special cellar. Branok got us a caseload over yesterday. French fishermen have their uses."

"You're importing wine from French fishermen?"

"Not buying as such." Jim grinned at me and hid behind a cloud of smoke from his joint. "That'd be illegal, wouldn't it?" Through a gap in the smoke, his eyes flashed with mischief. "We do a swapsies. The Frenchies are going nuts for Watt's little ammonite disks. Lord knows what they're doing with them."

"I did hear they were selling them to some designer New Age fashion shop in Paris," Tiggy said.

"Bloody daft buggers, if'n you ask me," said Watt.

"Some people'll buy anything." Stringy paused to pull on his joint, drink from his wine and fork a piece of chicken, all in one smooth movement. "Bit like when the Indians sold Manhattan for a bunch of beads?"

"First Nation," corrected Tiggy.

"Huh?"

"First Nation, that's what you have to call them now. Not Indians."

"You sound like my ex," said Stringy. "She was always going on at me about Inuits, Indigenous whatsits, Latinos and China people. She liked to keep up with all the right words. Me..." Stringy bowed his head over his wineglass as if in despair. "I just get to thinking I'd got the hang of it and then, there it was, all changed again."

Tiggy studied Stringy for a moment, as if trying to decide if he needed a hug or a belt over the head with the wine bottle. Clearly, she decided a change of direction was the preferred option. She looked at Jim and asked, "How's Cindy? I thought she was due back by now?"

"She was," Jim said. "But she was flying back from Rio via Cuba. She wanted to see the Che Guevara Mausoleum in Santa Clara. Only they had this massive storm. Ena or Elsie is it? Anyway, she's stuck there for the foreseeable."

"Oh dear, I heard about that. Massive floods. Is she alright?"

"Yeah, she's fine, she's been helping out in one of the public shelters. She likes to get stuck in. She's donated all her clothes from her travelling spring wardrobe to the homeless in Cerro."

"I'm sure they'll appreciate that."

After the meal, Tiggy and I headed back to my Wikihouse.

"I thought you were staying at Jim's?" I asked, when I realised Tiggy had followed me.

"Yes, about that... I didn't realise Stringy was still here and Jim's place has only got three rooms, and it seems he's got a house full. Only..." She shrugged and looked around my lounge.

"I see. Well, of course you can stay here, but I've only got the one bedroom. I can sleep in the lounge. I've still got the camp bed."

"I don't want to—"

"It's not a problem. I'm used to it anyway. Bathroom's over there, if you want a shower. It's solar, but it should still be hot. There's a fresh towel on the stool in there."

"Thanks, I've got one." Tiggy dived into her rucksack and pulled out a large white towel. "Always have a spare everything on the '300'. You never know." She threw it over her shoulder and disappeared into the shower room.

I heard the shower start and then a little squeal. "Sorry," I called through the door. "Forgot to warn you, they set up the pipework backwards so hot is cold, and cold is hot."

"No problem."

I pulled out the spare bedding and set up the camp bed. "Hello, old friend." I patted the made up bed. I'd just finished when Tiggy emerged in a cloud of steam and wrapped in the towel. "Quick nightcap?" She reached into her rucksack and pulled out a bottle.

"You got Mary Poppins in there somewhere?" I asked.

"No, next best thing." She held the bottle out for me to see.

The bottle looked Armagnac in shape, but the label not so. A home printed label with a picture of an oak tree and a corvid, bearing the words, in comic sans font, Raven Oak Cider Brandy. Pengelly's Finest.

"I've not heard of this," I said. "I'm guessing it's local?"

"Pengelly's distillery. Local secret. I brought a bottle over for Jim. But as he's not here…"

I studied the bottle. "I'm sure it's… lovely. I'm guessing it's not licensed?"

"You'll get the hang of this place, eventually. Here…" she took the bottle from me and pulled the stopper. "Where's your glasses?"

"I've only got a couple of ordinary water glasses," I said. "No brandy glasses. Sorry."

She stared at me for a moment, then said, "Just get something to pour this into. Unless you want to drink it from the bottle?"

I retrieved a couple of glasses from the kitchen area and Tiggy poured a generous measure into each. I cautiously sipped. At once, the flavour sprang from the liquor. Fresh and fruity, somehow tasting of outdoors, fields, trees, and with only a hint of apples.

"That's actually very good," I said, and sipped a bit more. Then the fire hit. Like a flow of lava down my throat and settling in my stomach like a hot cup of tea. My eyes started to water, and I blinked them clear.

"Steady on with that," Tiggy said. "It's a bit... what's the word I'm looking for...?"

"Lethal?"

"Yeah, that'll do. It'll toughen you up for the winter though."

I settled into the chair opposite Tiggy. She looked oddly lost inside the big white towel. Smaller somehow.

"What makes you think I'll still be here in the winter?"

"Premonition, I have the gift. Besides, didn't you say it was time for a change?"

"I did? Hmm, maybe it is."

"And why no Mrs Cabot?" Tiggy took a healthy drink of the brandy and squeezed her eyes closed while it bit. "You gay?"

"No, just... Well... I think I just kept putting it off until I felt more settled in my career. But I never quite did."

"How come you stayed so long in the Foreign Office anyway? You're really not cut out for it."

"Didn't want to disappoint my parents, I suppose. Then, I just never got round to thinking about anything different. With Dad being a bit of a hero, it just seemed easier to melt into the lower ranks."

"I bet he wasn't prepared to stand up to some great lump of a drunken banker wanker. That's my kind of hero." Another full sip, more eye squeezing, and this time accompanied by a "pfahh," sound.

I put my glass down. Probably best if one of us stayed reasonably sober, and it clearly wasn't going to be Tiggy.

I heard a tap on the door, then it swung open before I had chance to respond. I had a fleeting mental image of an irate banker, but realised how stupid that was.

Jim, Watt, Jeeves, and Stringy stumbled into the room. He held some helium, penis shaped balloons aloft. "Ah, here you are," Jim said. "Wondered where you'd got to." He glanced at each of us in turn. "Not interrupting anything, am I?"

"What? No," I said quickly. A little too quickly. "Just having a quiet nightcap."

"Good, we have balloons."

"I noticed."

"Sorry, my fault," Tiggy said to me. "I gave him a load of leftovers from one of my hen parties."

"Talking of which," Jim said. "You know that little buzzy toy thingy, the purple one with the ears? You'd think, not much use for a man, but creativity being my forte, so to speak, I found that if you—"

"Uhum," interrupted Jeeves. "Before you share any more of that little tale, do you think it might be an idea to re-examine your privacy settings? Sir?"

Jim looked at Jeeves. "Ah, got ya'. Probably wise. Don't want to lose a minister just yet. Hey, Tiggy, do you want it back?"

"No," Tiggy said, without a moment's hesitation. "Definitely not."

"Good, I was hoping you'd say that."

Jim and his companions settled onto whatever bits of furniture they could find and suddenly, my little cabin felt very small.

Jim noticed the bottle on the table in front of me. "Ah, Pengelly's Brandy. You didn't tell me you had a stash of that. I'll do you a swap for some Jack Daniel's. Don't mind if we light up?" Jim pulled a joint from somewhere in the hair covering his left ear, glanced at it briefly, then slipped it between his lips, lighting it as it went.

The evening drifted into night, becoming cloudier as it went. Jack Daniel's, not one of my favourites, Raven Oak, rapidly becoming one, and the unavoidable fog of cannabis smoke all conspired to rob me of consciousness at about two o'clock. My bladder called me at about four, and

I had a vague recollection of the need to step across several bodies on my way to the bathroom.

I eventually woke about six to the sound of the gulls doing formation fly-bys past the window. I disentangled myself from the camp bed, which seemed to have half collapsed during the night, and stumbled past a couple of sleeping forms on my way to the kitchen area.

"What time is it?" a voice groaned behind me.

"Sixish." I nearly filled the kettle and nearly sat it over the burner. I knew I needed to do something else to make it work and remembered the lighter. A loud woomf reminded me I shouldn't take quite so long between turning on the gas and clicking the lighter. "Coffee?" I asked nobody in particular.

I turned at the sound of unintelligible mumbles. And counted two people who looked in need of coffee. "Tiggy?" I called towards the bedroom. "Coffee?"

Nothing.

I called once more and one of the bodies struggled into a sitting position. It was Jim. "She's gone," he said, pulling something from his hair. He brought the object close to his eyes and squinted. When he realised it was a broken balloon, rather than a joint, he dropped it on the table next to him.

"Gone?" I queried.

"Yeah, said she had to catch the tide. You seen my smokes?"

# ~ CHAPTER FIFTEEN ~

THE NEXT COUPLE OF DAYS were taken up by the final preparations for Jim's Birthday Bash.

I had a couple of things to take care of in the village and caught a lift with Branok on one of his runs. I was, by this time, becoming used to rolling boats, smelly fish, and a face full of sea-spray every so often. A quick drop in to the Smuggler's to catch a draught beer, and a pasty and chips, proved to be an error of judgement though.

"I got one 'o your government men arrive here yesterday," Goodenough greeted.

"I don't have any government men," I said. "I don't work for the UK Government anymore, and besides, none of them were anything to do with me."

He slid a beer across the counter and plated a warm pasty. "He's been down on the beach all day with some fancy telescopes."

"I didn't think you had any more rooms?"

"You weren't using it. Can't have a room sittin' empty. They get damp and then I have to paint it all over again."

I picked up the beer and pasty. "I feel your pain." I turned to go to a table. "And it can't have been thirty years since you last had to do it."

I settled by the window and gazed out. A few boats bobbed in the harbour, but all was quiet. To the west, glimpses of the shoreline peeped through between gaps in the seawall. I visualised a government man with a fancy telescope and tried to work out what Goodenough had actually seen. I needed to go down and see.

Feeling helpful, I took my empty glass and plate back to the bar to save Goodenough's knee, or back, or whatever the current injury.

"Do you want to pay up for another week on the room?" he asked.

"I thought you'd let it?" I said.

"Not let it, as such. It's still yours when you want it."

"That's very kind of you. But you're not expecting me to pay for a room you've let to somebody else?"

"Sub-let, more like."

"Sub-let? You mean this government man is subletting it from me?" I asked.

"In loco parentis, you could say."

"What do you mean, in loco parentis?"

"It's Latin, it means you weren't around," Goodenough said.

"I'm well aware of what in loco parentis means. I'm trying to understand how you want me to pay for a room you're letting to somebody else. Surely, if it's my room, I should get the rent?"

Goodenough sucked his teeth and shook his head. "Tell you what, we'll go halves on it. Half his rent to you, and half to me. Can't say fairer 'n that. After all, I gotta change the bed. You wouldn't 'ave me outta pocket now?" He stuck a hand out. "What ya reckon'? Fifty-fifty?"

I took his hand, trying not to betray my glee at having finally got one over on the man. "Deal."

"How do you want to pay for your half now?" Goodenough asked. "Cash is better, 'cause the machine's broke."

I'd walked halfway towards the Duty-Free shop by the time I realised I'd still, somehow, ended up out of pocket again.

I found the Commodore studying his miniature seascape. I noticed things had changed since the last time I'd seen it.

"This is different," I said.

"The battle of Sluys, 1340. The greatest English naval victory in history, yet all anybody ever remembers is the Armada."

I studied the tiny ships. "There're no cannons," I said.

"They didn't have, back then. Swivel guns, perhaps. But the battle was won by the English longbow men. Greater range and fire rate than the French crossbows." He carefully repositioned a couple of the English fleet, then looked up at me. "What can I do for you? Did you get your charts all sorted in the end?"

"Not entirely. Sam Goodenough tells me somebody's been out on the shore with a telescope. A government man, he said. Although, to be honest, I think as far as he's concerned, everybody who isn't local is a government man. Just wondered if you'd seen anything?"

"Don't know if he's government or not, but there's been some chap out there with a theodolite. Spotted him while I was out patrolling the coastline. Could be taken for a telescope, I suppose."

I thanked the Commodore and headed off towards the beach. I saw no sign of any official looking person with or without a fancy telescope. I did, however, spot a man fishing from the beach about a hundred metres west of the lifeboat house.

"Any luck?" I called as I approached.

"Nothing," he said. "Better when the tide turns."

"Did you happen to see anybody here surveying?"

"Yeah, couple of hours back. He was here yesterday an' all. Said he was looking at coastal erosion. Wants to look at all this plastic if you ask me. I catch more Tesco bags than fish these days." He flicked his rod with practised ease and the line streamed out to sea.

I left the man to his fishing and went to the print shop to pick up the job I'd left earlier in the week.

~ * ~ * ~ * ~

BY THE TIME SATURDAY CAME round, the island hummed with activity. New arrivals drifted in by the hour. Many ferried by Branok or Tiggy, but others seemed to have arrived out of nowhere. I guessed there were a few more boats in the cove, but I didn't investigate.

The Ocean View Tearooms and Bar, as it had finally been decided, had opened for the event, although there was a distinct lack of equipment in the place. A couple of shelves of spirits behind the bar area, and three domestic fridges full of beer, represented the bar side of the business, while an electric kettle and a cake cabinet took care of the tearoom part.

The only occupied table hosted a group of men dressed in camouflage clothing. As they wore binoculars round their necks, I guessed these guys were here for the bird watching, rather than Jim's birthday. Tiggy had told me the island was starting to get a steady flow of 'Twitchers' visiting.

I approached the counter, or bar, or whatever it was. The cake cabinet drew my eye with what looked like a plate of homemade flapjacks.

"You must be Mr Cabot," the woman behind the counter greeted. "I'm Gwen, welcome to my..." She cast an eye around the room. "...whatever it will be when it's finished." She smiled.

"John, please. Are those homemade?" I pointed at the flapjacks.

"They wouldn't be anything else. They're the whole reason I'm here. For my sins."

"For flapjacks?"

"I used to work part-time for Sam Goodenough, you know? The Smuggler's?"

"I know Sam, yes."

"Jim, when he first came to the village, developed a bit of a thing for my flapjacks. Especially after... you know, when he's been on his special herbs."

"So he recruited you to run this place?"

"Jim is a very difficult man to say no to."

"So I've discovered. I'll have one of those and a cup of tea, I think."

"You go sit yourself down, Luv, and I'll bring them right over."

I chose a table by the huge window which overlooked the cliffs. My tea and flapjack arrived a few minutes later.

"You here for the shags?" a voice asked from the twitchers' table.

"Sorry?" I queried.

"Gulosus aristotelis," the man replied. "The common shag. Although, not quite so common now, eh?"

"So I understand." I tried to recall what Tiggy had told me about these birds. "Endangered even," I added.

"We're here to observe the nesting pairs on the cliffs. You too?"

"No, I..." I thought for a moment, stumbling at the words I was about to use. "... actually, I live here."

"Wow, lucky chap," said another of the twitchers. "I'd love to live in a place like this, but I'm stuck in London. Work."

"Yes, I suppose I am lucky."

I finished my tea and flapjack, said goodbye to the twitchers, then headed out to see the goings on out on the main meadowland. I wandered out to the tented area and stalled for a moment at the sheer quantity of people milling about. One visitor I did recognise was the Right Honourable, Stephen Weatherby-Hewitt, member of parliament for Wessex, and Secretary of State for Arts and Culture. He stood in the middle of the main marquee, looking completely bewildered. I headed over to him.

"Stephen, nice to meet you." I offered my hand. "John Cabot, ex-Foreign and Commonwealth Office."

His handshake was firm and practised. "Nice to meet you, John. FCO? Then you must know Ollie Frogmorton?"

"Ollie, yes. I know Ollie." I'd never heard him called that before, "He's my... he was my boss."

"We were at Cambridge together. You've left the service? What are you doing now?"

"This and that. Advising Jim Sullivan on some technicalities, all very boring. I have an idea. While you're here, could you help me with a little birthday surprise for Jim?"

Stephen's eyes brightened at the hint of political opportunity. "Of course, love to."

"There'll be a television crew filming it. Hope you're okay with that? You know what it's like for high profile people."

"Oh, of course. No problem."

"Great." I smiled my best politico smile. "You'll have to excuse me, I have some last-minute arrangements. We'll catch up later, yes?"

"Jolly good."

I scanned the area. The numbers of people seemed to be increasing as I watched. Tiggy and Branok must be making a killing. I found what I was looking for just near the beer tent. Of course, I should have realised. I headed over to the film crew.

"Hi," I greeted. "I'm John, I'm the…" I hesitated. Oh, to hell with it. I was going to have to get used to this. "I'm the minister."

The woman with the microphone in her hand smiled and waved a little signal to the cameraman. I guessed to start filming.

"Minister for what?" she asked, holding the microphone low between us, keeping it out of camera.

"Pretty much everything, at the moment."

"John Cabot. Wasn't it you who contacted the studio? Something about a big announcement?"

"Yes, sorry for the cloak and dagger, but I think you'll find it'll be worth the trip."

I gave them a quick outline of the agenda for the afternoon, without giving too much away. They headed off over to the main marquee to ensure a good position for later.

As the afternoon progressed, and the general party mood took hold, I found time and space to prepare my little contribution, mostly unnoticed.

Mostly.

"What you doing with that chair, then?" Jeeves' voice caught me from behind.

I turned. "Ah, just a bit of a surprise. For Jim."

"But I can see it's a chair," Jeeves said.

"Yes, a chair."

"You ain't done a very good job of disguising it. All well and good wrapping it up in gold paper like that, but I can still see it's a chair. You should have put it in a box, if you'd wanted it to be a surprise."

"No, it's not wrapped to disguise it," I said. "It's... Never mind. You'll see. Where *is* Jim?"

"In the marquee." He pointed. "The Tartan Spartans are setting up."

"Tartan Spartans?"

"Tribute band for the Spartans. Scottish, they are."

"Hence the *Tartan* Spartans?"

"What? Oh yeah, that's clever. Never noticed that. I suppose I'd better go help. They'll all be wanting tea, or something heavy moving, shouldn't wonder." He wandered off to the marquee, and I set back to pressing the gold foil paper around the chair.

Around two, I bumped into Tiggy. She stood with a beer in her hand, watching the tech guys trying to get the amplifiers to work on the little stage.

"Oh, hi," she said when she saw me. "Wondered where you'd got to."

"You heard this lot before?" She nodded towards the band.

"Never heard of them. Jeeves says they're a covers band."

"They played Truro a couple of years back. They're very good. Jim rates them. That's why he invited them to play today."

"Bit odd, isn't it? Getting a tribute act of one's own band to play?"

"Not really. David Gilmour started this when he got the Australian Pink Floyd to play for his fiftieth. You seem very chipper today. You found a new volume of EU law to read?"

"I have a little surprise planned." I pressed my index finger to my lips. "Top secret."

She pushed up against me and, like an over affectionate cat, slid her shoulder across my chest. Her eyes locked with mine and she blinked slowly, saying, "Oh, go on. Do tell."

"No. Foreign Office trained. We know how to keep secrets."

"Even from me?" She smiled and dipped her head slightly. "I can be very persuasive."

"You seen Jim?" Watt Tyler appeared from nowhere. "Can't find nobody in this circus. Not seen so many people since the ninety-six Obby Oss down Padstow."

"I think he's in the area behind the beer tent. He said he was waiting to meet Air Force Two."

"Isn't that the President of America's plane?" asked Tiggy. "What makes him think that's coming here?"

"Actually, Air Force Two is the Vice President's plane," I corrected. "Though why he thinks any plane is coming here, I don't know. But as he's been on the weed since first thing this morning, I thought best not to argue with him."

"You're learning." Tiggy seemed surprised.

"So, where's this 'ere beer tent then?" Watt asked.

I pointed to the southern end of the field. "The beer tent is that one there, so if you go round the side of that and then—"

"That'll do," Watt interrupted my directions. "Beer tent is fine. I'll wait there. Jim'll turn up sooner or later. Or he won't. Not my place to worry."

I watched him wander off towards the tent, then looked back at Tiggy. "You were telling me how persuasive you could be?"

The noise of raised voices gathered around the field, and I scanned the scene for clues. It seemed everybody was talking at once and most were looking skyward. I followed the gazes. A hot-air balloon drifted slowly above my head, and it appeared to be descending. A pair of heads peered out from the hanging gondolier. Somebody in the basket waved to somebody on the ground.

"Air Force Two?" Tiggy asked.

"I'm guessing. Let's go see."

We headed to the area beyond the beer tent to where the balloon appeared to be aiming. We reached Jim just as the basket touched the ground not twenty metres from him.

He turned as we approached. "Oh, hiya, you two. What d'ya think?"

I looked at the balloon, now starting to deflate and settle. The words *'Air Force Two'* had been stencilled on the side. "Impressive," I said.

"My old mate, Tommy Harland, sent it to me for my birthday. Cool, huh?" He sucked on a joint as he studied the monster sinking into the ground.

"Tommy Harland?" I checked. "From The Velvet Beasts?"

"Yeah, I gave him Hendrix's first Strat last year for *his* birthday, so he had to try and outdo me."

"Why Air Force Two?"

"Ah, that's the cunning bit. It's the first craft in my air force, but I wanted it called Two, then everybody'd think I'd got another one hid away somewhere. Make 'em think twice about having a go, like, you know, when we're fully independent."

"Your air force is a hot air balloon?" Tiggy asked.

"Yeah, can't very well land an F15 here, can I?" He waved an arm about, indicating the problem. "Too lumpy. Fancy a ride? We're going to do bungee jumps from it later. When Jeeves turns up with the big rubber band. He's got a load of old inner tubes from—"

"I'll pass on that, thanks," I stopped him.

Tiggy poked an elbow in my rib. "Come on, it'll be a giggle."

"A giggle is when you replace the whole of a minister's inbox with a duplicate from exactly twelve months ago, then wait to see how long before they notice. That's a giggle." I noticed Jim and Tiggy staring at me, and added, "You had to be there. But anyway, leaping out of a hot-air balloon on the end of an elastic band is not a giggle, that's insanity. Especially if Jim's got anything to do with it." I turned to Jim and added, "No offence."

"None taken," he said. "In fact, I have to agree with you."

"But you're still going to do it?"

"I'm still going to do it. What's life without a bit of excitement?"

"Longer?"

"You worry too much." He patted my shoulder and said, "Catch you later. Just going up for a bob." He hopped into the gondolier, and I heard a whooshing noise as somebody opened the burner. The balloon wobbled upwards.

Jim waved over the edge as it drifted higher. I noticed a rope had been attached to a stake in the ground, so clearly this was going to be a very controlled ascent. The balloon came to a halt about fifty metres up and Jim waved over the side, yelling something I couldn't hear. All around, people cheered and whooped.

"I've got some last-minute things to do," I told Tiggy.

"What are you up to?" she asked.

"You can give me a hand if you like."

We made our way to the main tent where the Tartan Spartans were doing a sound check. I showed Tiggy the chair.

"You wrapped it?" She studied the chair. "In gold foil paper. Very...erm, Christmassy. I can still see it's a chair though."

"It's not meant to be... never mind. Give me a hand."

We shifted the chair to the back of the little stage, behind the band, and I found my box of bits and slid it under the chair.

"What *are* you up to?" Tiggy asked.

"You'll see. Little surprise."

Once set up, we moved to the back and found a couple of beers. The Tartan Spartans started their set with 'Moonlight Fire', the same number the Spartans always used to open with. I closed my eyes briefly and listened. Tiggy was right. They were pretty much indistinguishable from the real Spartans. The vocals were not quite as powerful as Jim's, and the guitar not quite as precise as Stringy's, but not far enough apart to know the difference had I not been standing here.

People bobbed in time with the music, or danced a bit and generally seemed appreciative. I noticed several well-known people around. Several members of various rock bands and two or three faces I recognised from films or television. My inner nerd demanded I snatch a few autographs, but my outer grown-up said no.

I noticed Jim had returned and Stringy had now joined him. I also spotted Stringy's battered Les Paul guitar on a stand to the back of the little stage.

The sound of a loud thud outside, followed by raised voices, snatched my attention. We followed the sound to a circle of people stood below where the balloon hovered on its tether line fifty metres above. In the centre of the circle of people, the remains of what seemed to be a fifty kilos sack of rice lay scattered across the ground. Lin Chao stood by the mess and shouted loudly up at the balloon in what I guessed was a stream of Chinese expletives.

"How's your Chinese?" Tiggy asked.

"About as good as yours, but I don't think Lin's very happy," I said.

I looked up. A dangle of something black and twisty hung from the gondolier. Jeeves' inner tubes had clearly failed the test bungee jump. Fortunately, the only casualty appeared to be a sack of Lin's rice.

"Sorry," Jim's voice shouted from up above.

More Chinese from Lin.

The gathering of people dispersed and drifted back to listen to the Tartan Spartans while the balloon drifted earthwards, landing next to the scattered rice. We left Jim and Lin to discuss rice and bungee cords and followed the rest.

The band had come to a slightly uneasy stall and appeared to be waiting for something. Stringy hopped up onto the little stage, looking decidedly more sprightly once in his natural environment. He picked up his guitar and plugged in the lead. The room hushed in anticipation, then Jim appeared and took a microphone. Behind him, the Tartan Spartans played the instantly recognisable opening chords to The Spartans' biggest anthem, *We Are The Survivors*.

As the song picked up, the audience sang along to the chorus, and I felt a thrill spike through my body. When the song came to an end, Jim made to exit the stage, but I scrambled up next to him. Not quite as sprightly as Stringy had done, despite a twenty-year advantage. I promised myself a new fitness regime.

Jim looked confused as I dragged the gold-foil covered chair to centre stage.

"Sit," I said.

He looked even more puzzled, but did as he was told. "What's going on?"

"You'll see." I scanned the people in front and spotted the TV crew. They seemed to be filming. That at once filled me with terror and I froze, wondering what on earth I was doing up here, hijacking Jim Sullivan's birthday gig, and in full public glare. *Breathe. Breathe slowly. Don't panic. Now is not the time to panic.* I scanned the people again and found Stephen Weatherby-Hewitt. He caught my eye and I motioned him to join us.

He looked as confused as Jim, but complied and hopped up onto the little stage.

I pulled him to one side and handed him a certificate. "Can you just present this to Jim?" I said. "He'd be thrilled if you did, and I know he'd love a chat with you later."

Weatherby-Hewitt's face flashed with a mixture of concern and opportunism. For a moment, I worried that concern might win, but the natural instinct of a young, ambitious politician overcame concern. Just as I'd hoped. He glanced at the certificate, but I pushed him towards Jim, seated on his gold throne, before he could study it too closely.

I waved my arms to quieten the people a bit. "Ladies and gentlemen," I started. *Breathe.* "Sorry to interrupt, but we have an important announcement. Today, the island of Scanlon's Rock, having fulfilled the requirements under international law and the criteria of the Montevideo Convention, formally declares independence from the United Kingdom." Lots of mumbles and a few isolated pockets of applause. "Now, I would like to introduce, The Right Honourable Stephen Weatherby-Hewitt, Member of Parliament for Wessex and Secretary of State for Arts and Culture."

The audience gave a subdued, and hesitant, applause. I pushed Weatherby-Hewitt towards Jim.

If the member for Wessex was nervous, he did a great job of covering it. He glanced at the certificate to scan the contents. Another flash of concern, and I worried he might pull out, but his crowd-pleasing programming took over.

"It is my great honour to present this certificate of..." A momentary hesitation as he scanned the contents, extracting the relevant words, as a true professional. "This certificate ratifies the status of Scanlon's Rock as an independent nation state, and Jim Sullivan as King." He handed the certificate to Jim, and they shook hands.

The people shouted and whooped once more, as Jim stood and took a bow. Two consummate professionals on stage, doing what they did best. Performing for their public. I had little doubt that Weatherby-Hewitt's political fortunes were about to take a nosedive, and I should feel guilt. I didn't. He was sharp enough to have spotted the manipulation and, at some point, he'd surely decided it was worth the gamble for the publicity.

The TV crew tried to collar him for a quote, but he slid away. They homed in on Jim instead. I motioned for them to wait, pointing to the throne, where Tiggy was guiding Watt Tyler into position alongside Jim, who'd returned to the seat.

I stood the other side of the throne. "Just one more official announcement." I waited until the tent quietened a bit, then pulled from behind my back the plastic crown I'd bought in the Post Office toy section, and handed it to Watt. "Remember what we practised," I whispered.

Watt puffed himself out, and said into the microphone, "I, as President of this kingdom, hereby crown James Sullivan the King of Scanlon's Rock." He placed the crown on his head and stepped back. I pulled the little string on the furled flag I'd set up behind the throne. It fell out behind Jim. An image of a long-haired skull face wearing sunglasses and flanked by cannabis leaves. A pair of crossed guitars sat in the background. Not my artwork, but worked up by a very talented artist I'd met in the print-shop. I'd just told her who it was for, and she'd said she knew exactly what was needed.

Once I was happy the flag looked okay, I slipped off the stage.

Tiggy arrived at my side. "What on earth have you been up to?"

"Oh, not much. I sent an official letter to the Home Office, pointing out that as the requirements had all been met, they couldn't prevent secession. I also sent a letter to the United Nations, outlining all the steps. And with a UK Secretary of State, albeit a minor one, announcing it on camera, the government is going to have a problem blocking it."

I stayed around long enough to watch everybody making a beeline for Jim, to shake his hand or slap his back, then I slid out of the tent. I stood for a moment in the darkening field. The stars peppered the sky in a way I'd never seen in London. Bright, sharp. Diamonds on black velvet. I'd just destroyed any chance of ever again working for the Home Office, or any other part of the Civil Service, and thrown my lot in with a stoner on a tiny island in the middle of the English Channel. My own version of jumping out of a balloon.

"You alright?" Tiggy asked.

"Yes, I think so. Too much noise and fuss."

"It goes with the territory of being around the force that is Jim Sullivan."

"I think I'm going to head back to my place. I need some quiet." I turned to go.

"Fancy a bit of company?" Tiggy asked from behind me.

I stopped and turned again. "That would be… lovely. I'm feeling a bit odd."

"I've got just the thing for that." She held up a bottle of wine.

The short walk back to my place turned into a bit of a meander along the cliff top. The night sky sparkled on the water, with the low moon tracing a flickering path across the sea. I could imagine walking across it to a magical land. The air felt chilly, but welcoming, after the noise and chaos of the last few hours. By the time we reached my little house, I was beginning to feel more grounded.

I put the heater on and Tiggy pulled the cork on the wine. An unknown Chablis, and probably fresh from the boat. It tasted okay though. I found a KitKat and split it. We settled on the sofa with our supper.

"You really did all that?" Tiggy asked. "Letters to the United Nations, the flag and stuff?"

"Just standard international admin processes," I said. "I may not understand one end of a boat from another, but I understand intergovernmental admin procedure. And with Vanuatu sending the notification of recognition to the UN, that pretty much fulfilled the requirements for statehood."

She slipped a hand over my arm. "A true hero for our times. We should call you Admin Man."

"Please don't."

"You could wear a Lycra suit with a paperclip logo."

"Seriously, please don't. No man ever looks good in Lycra."

She twisted on the sofa to face me. Her eyes scanned me. "Hmm, maybe not Lycra then. Maybe just jeans and a T-shirt? Get you out of these chinos and… what *is* this shirt?" She ran her fingers over my sleeve.

"Burton's. It's a classic," I said.

"But didn't they go pop years ago?"

"I know, but I've got quite a few of these. I stocked up in their final sale. What's wrong with them?"

"Nothing, not if you're going for middle-aged boring. At least wear it with the top button undone." She undid it as she spoke then studied me again. "Hmm, maybe two." And another one opened. "That's better."

Thump, thump on the door and Jim's voice called, "Hello? Anybody in?" without waiting for an answer, he let himself in. "Oh, sorry, am I interrupting anything?"

"No," I said.

"Yes," Tiggy said.

I fumbled to do up my top buttons. "Everything okay?"

"I was looking for Tiggy." He turned his gaze to her. "Stringy's knackered his ankle. I think it's broken. Could you take him over? He'll have to go to hospital."

"Now?" Tiggy asked.

"Yeah, well, it's a bit of a mess."

"What happened?" I asked.

"He fell out of the balloon. We forgot to tie it down before getting out. The thing went up as he was half out, and he landed on his arse. It was very funny. I've got a video of it." He pulled his phone out and aimed it at Tiggy. "Want to see?"

"No thank you." Tiggy stood. "You realise I can't take him? I've been drinking wine all day. I was going to stay here."

I looked at Tiggy. "You were?"

She flapped a hand in my direction. "Shush, not now."

"It's not like you're going to hit anything is it?" Jim said. "I mean, it's a big old sea out there, and not much traffic."

"That's exactly the point," Tiggy said. "I'm not worried about colliding with anything else. I'm more worried about ending up in the middle of the Atlantic."

"I'll get you some coffee," Jim said. "Always works for me." He turned to me. "Where's your coffee?"

"Kitchen. Plastic pot with a label on, saying coffee. Shouldn't we get the Air Ambulance or something?"

"They're not going to turn out for a broken ankle," Tiggy said.

"Cool." Jim looked at me. "You get the coffee going, I'll go tell Stringy that Tiggy's on the case."

Jim disappeared, leaving us standing in the middle of the room, wondering what just happened.

"Coffee?" I asked.

"Better had, looks like it's going to be a late one."

# ~ CHAPTER SIXTEEN ~

SUNDAY MORNING BROKE WITH THE usual squealing of gulls. I dragged myself out of bed, through the shower, and out into a level of bright sunshine which shouldn't be allowed at this ungodly hour. Especially the morning after Jim's birthday bash.

My compensation, though, was my ability to wake Jim at this hour. Especially after his imposed chaos of the evening before.

His door swung open at the first rap. Jeeves blinked at me. "What's the matter with everybody today?" he greeted.

"Hangovers?" I suggested.

"You'd better come in. It's too early for doorstep philosophy." He stepped aside to allow me in.

"Jim up?"

"If you mean, is he conscious, then yes. Beyond that, it ain't mine to speculate." He swept his hand towards the lounge, and I followed it through.

Jim looked up as I entered. "My minister. Greetings, have a drink." He pushed a bottle of Jack Daniel's across the glass topped coffee table. "Glasses." He waved a hand towards a cabinet.

"Bit early for that, isn't it?"

He looked up at me. I wondered if he could actually see through what was left of his pupils. "Well, I haven't actually stopped since last night, so, technically, it's not early. Just very late."

"How's it going with Stringy?"

"Nearly half a million views already. Tommy Harland gave it a thumbs up and a LOL."

"I was thinking more with his broken foot, not YouTube," I said. "Have you heard anything?"

"Oh, yeah, broken meta-something. Having it plastered tomorrow. Or it might be today. He's gonna stay at my house over there for a while."

"Great day yesterday. I thought you might have had the rest of the band at your party?"

"No, difficult getting us all together. Joe's in rehab. Not allowed out until... what month is it now?"

"April."

"April? My birthday's in April."

"I know."

"September it'll be then. Ryan's on bail in New York, he's not allowed to leave the country and Eric... nobody's seen Eric since he met that weird bloke in the orange frock, and went off to Jaipur to learn the thirty-seven-string sarangi. By the way all this stuff with the flag and certificate yesterday? That all for real?"

"Near enough," I said. "The main requirements of the Montevideo Convention have been fulfilled. You've got a currency, Watt's little ammonite disks, cover that. You've been conducting foreign trade—"

"I have?"

"Your booze deals with the French boats, although we probably don't want anybody to look too closely at that. And now Vanuatu recognises the island, it's job done. A few other things to sort out, but just technicalities."

"Cool, we should have a party." He flicked his lighter at the remains of a joint, but it failed to catch. "Don't suppose you've got a light, have you?"

"No, sorry."

I headed out into the morning sunshine. A few people wandered around already, several with black bags, collecting rubbish, but it was a lot quieter than I'd expected. I remembered Jim saying several people had been staying on boats in the cove, and I guessed quite a few had already ferried back with Brannock. I joined in with the clean-up for a while. Shaun and Shawn dismantled the marquee, and were onto the other tents before I'd managed one bin bag of rubbish. They'd used Jim's Land Rover to cart away the collapsed tents and the balloon, which had packed away neatly in its gondolier.

By lunchtime, we once again stood in a wide, open meadow, with just a few areas of flattened grass to show for the previous day's activities. I dropped into the Ocean View Bar and Tearooms for a cup of tea and a snack to fill the gap.

Gwen greeted me like a long-lost friend. "Ah. John, I've kept you a nice flapjack back. A corner piece. I noticed how much you liked the corner piece."

"That's very kind of you."

I settled by the big window and watched the sea roll on the rocks below. I could learn to like this view. I didn't even feel queasy. But that may just have been the tea and flapjack which normalised the terror outside. I decided it was difficult to be frightened of falling off deadly cliffs while eating flapjacks and drinking tea.

After I'd finished, I hitched a ride back to Little Didney with Brannock on one of his trips and headed to the Smuggler's Arms for a late lunch.

The bar bustled with people. I scanned the room but failed to see anybody I recognised. The prevalence of smart casual, as opposed to the usual warm functional, identified this influx as out-of-towners.

"Is my room free for tonight?" I asked Sam Goodenough, as he poured my beer.

"Free's not for free," he said, and pushed my beer across the bar. "Thinking of putting up the rates. I've put a vibrating bed in there now. Got to be up with the jet set, now that we're an international hub."

"Well, don't put it up until next week, though? As I've already paid for this week." I ordered a pasty with chips, then took my beer and looked for a quiet spot.

I'd just settled at an empty table when a woman approached. I started to stand, but she said, "Don't get up. Can I join you?"

I waved my hand at the empty chairs. "Help yourself." I took a sip of my beer.

"I hear the pasties here are something special," she said.

"Originally created for Henry the Eighth. Radio? Television?"

"Press, Keeley Trevellick, Daily Sentinel. You're Mr Cabot? Foreign Office?"

"Everybody calls me John, and *ex*-Foreign Office. But yes."

"You announced yesterday that the island of Scanlon's Rock was declaring independence from England. Was that some sort of publicity stunt? Is Jim Sullivan preparing a comeback of the Spartans?"

"No publicity stunt. The island is outside the Territorial Waters of the United Kingdom, and it fulfils the requirements of the Montevideo Convention. And, as a by-the-by, Scanlon's Rock actually has more claim to independence than does England, which is simply a semi-autonomous region of the United Kingdom. It doesn't actually meet the requirements for being an independent country, which—"

"Yes, interesting," she cut across my explanation. "But does this mean there will be a customs border?"

"That's up to the UK Government, but I assume they will have to create a border."

"Will you be ordering?" Goodenough appeared and gave his best smile to Keeley. He'd clearly aimed for friendly servitude, but came over more as Dracula inviting a maiden into his dungeon.

"Just a coffee, please."

Goodenough grunted and disappeared, and Keeley asked, "Are you going to be in Jim's new government?"

"I *am* Jim's government. Certainly for the moment."

"Do you have any comments on the Foreign Secretary's statement this morning that it's all just a stunt and will never be allowed?"

"The Foreign Secretary's already made a statement? On a Sunday morning?"

"Yes, on the BBC this morning."

I'd thought I'd have a couple of days before this all blew up. Change of plans. "I'm sorry, you'll have to excuse me." I stood, drinking the last of my beer. "I need to attend to something quite urgent."

"Here's your pasty." Goodenough dropped my plated pasty on the table. "What about the chips?"

"They'll be along dreckly. Got a rush on."

"Okay, forget the chips. Can I take this to go?"

"Do what you want with it. But the plate stays here."

I picked up the pasty and a paper napkin from the dispenser. "Pleasure meeting you, Ms Trevellick. Sorry I have to rush off like this."

THE SUNDAY ROADS BACK TO London proved unusually smooth and trouble free. I dumped my bag in the hallway of my apartment and stared around. Everything seemed strangely unfamiliar. Everything was the same: the hatstand, the full length mahogany framed mirror, the painting of ice skaters on the Thames. All just as they should be, yet somehow, oddly alien. I made a pot of tea and wondered why. I only wanted one cup. I opened the curtains and windows, letting the dying sun tint the room in shades of amber. With it came the noise of traffic and the smells of burnt diesel and city dust.

I changed and headed out to a local Hawksmoor for steak and chips. The place was desirably anonymous and efficient. I ate the meal on autopilot, without really tasting anything, my mind constantly rehearsing the conversation to come with Froggy. I played through various scenarios before realising I was simply torturing myself. Froggy was like some deranged magician, always able to pull something revolting out of a hat when one least expects it. I took a taxi back to my apartment and spent an hour deleting all the rubbish my cable box had recorded in my absence. I found an old episode of Sherlock and was asleep before he'd lit his first pipe.

~ * ~ * ~ * ~

THE PHONE CALL CAME AT nine o'clock exactly, by which time, I was already in the ante room of Froggy's office, nursing my cardboard Starbuck's cup.

"Sir Oliver would like you to attend a meeting at your earliest convenience," said the voice on the phone.

"How about now?" I suggested.

"Oh, you mean…"

"I'm outside his office at this moment." I terminated the call and knocked on the door.

"Come," Froggy's voice demanded.

I did as ordered. Leaving the door purposefully open, as I knew how much that annoyed him, I walked through the ankle-deep carpet and settled in the seat opposite him. I planted the cardboard mug on his shiny desk

"I didn't realise you were in today?" Froggy's eyes drifted to the door as he spoke.

"I was just passing, so I thought I'd drop by to keep you up to date."

"Hmm. Tell me, this sideshow the other day, with the funny hat and the certificate." He lifted up the Starbuck's mug and slid a coaster underneath it. "That was all some publicity stunt for this idiot's pop group, right?"

"Not at all. The island meets the requirements of the Monte—"

"Yes, yes. I'm sure you're going to give me chapter and verse complete with all the relevant sub-clauses, which, if you didn't have them all covered, you wouldn't be here today? Is that a fair assessment?"

I felt somewhat deflated. I wanted to tell him about Watt's currency and the trade deals with the French fishermen. "Yes, however—"

"However, blah, blah." He slapped both hands on the desk and leaned forwards. "You're still technically in the employ of His Majesty's Government, yet you're gallivanting around like some Robin Hood plotting the overthrow of the rule of law."

"Robin Hood never plotted to overthrow the rule of law, he simply—"

He held up a hand to cut me off. "Here's the problem. You seem to be working for, in your own words, what is now known to be a foreign power, and probably a hostile one at that."

"I don't think—"

"Not only is that sedition, but it's a damned poor show to boot."

"Sedition might be a bit—"

"Here's what we're going to do." Froggy pulled a blue folder from a drawer under his desk and opened it. "I have your termination agreement prepared." He slid a pile of paper towards me.

I scanned the contents. My trained eye quickly picked out the relevant bits. "You're expecting me to sign this? I'm not relinquishing my severance pay and pension rights."

"Your choice. If you don't, you will be charged with incitement to treason."

I opened my bag and placed a red folder on the desk. "I didn't know we were doing presents, but here we go." I pushed the folder towards him.

"What's this?" He opened it and idled through the top few sheets.

"It's a report on the directors and interested parties in an oil company. You might know of it, Valdez Oil?"

The raised eyebrows indicated he did indeed know of it. I continued, "I noticed your name here, just here." I reached over and pointed to a section of text. "It's a log of meetings involving you, Member of Parliament Sir Guy Serrick, and a certain Saudi prince, over the course of several months. Also, you'll see there's a copy of a payment made by the aforementioned prince, to an account of yours in the Cayman Islands for... hang on, here it is... 'Assistance with the procurement of an oil, and or, shale gas exploration licence for the English Channel.' Just to clarify, this Saudi prince, from whom you have accepted payments, he's in the employ of a foreign power?"

"Where did you get this?" His eyes looked ready to explode.

I retreated slightly in case there was a mess. "I'm a researcher. It's what the department paid me to do. I'm very good at it."

His eyes darkened and appeared to be trying to read my mind. *Good luck with that,* I thought. *I'm surprising myself here.*

"It appears we have reached a stalemate," he said, finally.

"A zugzwang, more like. A stalemate indicates a drawn position, whereas—"

"Have you any idea how irritating your pedantry can be?"

"Yes. But have you any idea how much fun it is?" I pulled a second file from my bag and dropped it on the desk. "This is a full statement outlining how each of the requirements of the Montevideo Convention has been met and the official declaration by the new government of the Kingdom of Scanlon's Rock of its independence from the United Kingdom. A copy has been sent to the U.N." I stood. "Now, unless there's anything else, I have a legislative architecture to design."

I left the building and found the first bar I could. Beer number one did nothing to calm my trembling hands and the hammering in my chest. I called on beer two for support. That did it. Once my nerves had steadied, I took a cab back to my apartment.

My phone rang just as I was paying the cab. I handed the driver the cash and checked the caller I.D. at the same time. My sister Jane. I clicked answer while waving the cab driver off.

"Where are you?" Jane asked, before I even had chance to speak.

"Just outside my apartment. What's happened?"

"What's happened? What's happened? You're all over the news declaring secession from your own country and you ask what's happened?"

"Oh, that—"

The call waiting tone bleeped. I glanced at the screen, Tiggy.

"Hang on a sec," I said to Jane and clicked answer on Tiggy.

"Where are you?" asked Tiggy.

"Just outside my apartment in London."

"Why? What's happened?"

"Nothing's happened. Well, not really. Hang on a sec." I clicked Jane.

"Sorry, that's a friend from Little Didney."

"Who?"

"The other call," I said. "A friend from the village where I've been staying."

"Who's that then?"

"Can we meet up for lunch tomorrow? I'll explain then."

"In London?" asked Tiggy.

"What? Sorry, I thought I was talking to my sister?"

"You are," said Jane. "Who did you think you were talking to?"

I pressed Tiggy's avatar on the screen. Now I didn't know whether I'd just put her on hold or connected. "Tiggy?"

"Who's Tiggy?"

"Did I ask you about lunch?"

"Yes," said Tiggy. "I'll come up on the late train this afternoon. It'll be fun."

"Jane?"

"Oh, there you are, John. Shall we meet for lunch tomorrow?"

I finally managed to disentangle myself from both calls with a growing dread that I'd just booked a lunch date with Jane and Tiggy. That was going to be complicated.

I collected the accumulated mail from my box and took the stairs to my apartment. Mostly offers of credit cards or insurance renewals. I made a strong coffee and vowed to never drink two beers on an empty stomach again. The process of reading junk mail, then dumping it, brought a welcome calm to my thoughts. I scanned the apartment; I would need to make some decisions soon about all this. I probably needed to take the important stuff down to Scanlon's Rock, then put the place to bed for a while. I had no idea how long my tenure would be down there. Maybe I could persuade somebody to pop in from time to time, just to check for leaks or something.

I changed out of my suit, which was beginning to feel very odd, and into some chinos and a polo shirt. I hung the suit back on the rail with the others and paused, seeing the row of suits as if for the first time. Each was different, but in a subtle way. The majority, traditional pinstripe, a couple of rope stripe and even a chalk stripe for when I was feeling rebellious. Even the colours changed from dark blue through to charcoal. My shirt rail was mostly given to plain white Egyptian cotton. One could never be mis-dressed in a white Egyptian cotton.

The casual side of my wardrobe consisted primarily of chinos and polo shirts, albeit in a slightly more diverse colour set than the suits. I even had a red polo shirt.

None of which seemed a high priority for my little house on the rock. Maybe I'd take a couple of suits, always best to be prepared. I piled up on the bed a collection of suits for packing, then put half of them back on the rail again. I looked at the reduced pile and put another couple back on the rail. That left four suits. That should be enough. I repeated the process with the casual clothes, and in the end, my whole going-away wardrobe condensed into one suit carrier and a suitcase. I definitely needed more walking boots, thick shirts, and pullovers.

I gathered another pile of miscellanea, books, CDs, a few bits of artwork and such. If only I knew how long I would be likely to spend there, it would help. I assumed at the most, it would be six months, the period of my paid notice. If I hadn't found a new position by then, I was going to be in trouble. Six months, plan for a maximum of six months. I added another suit and three extra white shirts.

I spent the rest of the day buying a few more casual clothes, and even a pair of jeans. I hadn't worn jeans since university. In the evening I packed everything into some plastic crates and stacked them in the hallway, ready for transportation down to my car.

~ * ~ * ~ * ~

MY PHONE RANG JUST AS the host on Radio Four's Today programme announced they were going over to their reporter in Westminster. Apparently, the resignation of a front bench politician had just been announced following the disclosure of some unexplained property investments, a construction company collapse, and a call girl. I didn't get to find out who it was.

"Where are you?" asked Tiggy as soon as I connected the call.

"I'm in the kitchen, having breakfast."

"Not helping. I meant more in terms of your current location relative to Paddington Plaza Hotel."

"The Paddington Plaza? I've not heard of that. Is it a new place?"

"I think it probably was, back in the 1800s. I stayed here last night."

"Oh, I see. Well, Paddington's about four miles, twenty minutes by taxi."

"And by bus?" Tiggy asked.

"Bus? I haven't the faintest idea. What's wrong with a taxi?"

"To be honest, I was trying to decide between getting a taxi or paying my rent next month. Odd as it may seem, I went for the rent."

"It's not that expensive. Maybe twenty-five pounds. I'll pay it, if you're short."

"No you won't." Tiggy sounded snappy and I wondered what was wrong. "Text me your address, I'll figure it out."

I sent the text and turned the radio up again. An interview with some celebrity who's just written a book about peacock farming in Suriname. I turned to Classic Rock, and *Hotel California* drifted through the kitchen.

My door intercom buzzed after about half an hour and Tiggy's voice announced her arrival.

"Second floor, the lift's to your left." I pressed the button to unlock the door.

I opened my apartment door and watched the lift. A strange feeling of anticipation rose with the flashing floor numbers. The lift didn't stop, then Tiggy appeared a moment later from the stairwell.

"I hate lifts," she announced. "Got stuck in one in the Penzance council offices once. I was only going there to argue about my rates bill, and we had a power cut. Have you any idea how depressing it is to be stuck in a dark lift in a council office with only a rates bill for company?"

"I can imagine. How was the journey?" I stood back to let her enter.

"The train was late, the bus was squashed, and I missed my stop as I couldn't get to the door." Her eyes settled on my stack of plastic crates. "I guess there's not much storage room in a flat here. Ikea do some hanging wardrobe things."

"No, that's not storage. It's just some clothes I'm taking down to the island."

She studied the label of the topmost crate. "Suits? You're taking a crate full of suits?"

"I'm a minister. You never know when ministerial duties call, and I have to represent the government."

"The government consisting of Jim and Watt? That government?"

"Okay, but it pays to be prepared. Come on through, coffee?"

"Thanks." Tiggy stopped as she entered the lounge. "It's big. Bigger than it looks, like the Tardis." She craned her neck upwards. "Wow, high ceiling. There's space for another floor up here. You could have a secret upstairs room, nobody would know."

"I could. But I think there's probably a clause in the lease about that. There's certainly a prohibition on changing the ceiling architraves, so it probably comes under that."

She went to the window and pulled the curtain back a bit further. "Is that the Thames over there?"

"Yes, you can just see it from here. Smog permitting. How do you like your coffee?"

"Just one spoonful and a dash of milk. Where are we going for lunch?"

I switched on the coffee machine and let it do its thing. "The Melchester. It's Jane's favourite. They do very nice sardines in a tomato and garlic sauce with thyme."

"Sardines in tomato sauce, goodee. I wonder if they'd pop them on a slice of toast for me?"

# ~ CHAPTER SEVENTEEN ~

WE TOOK A TAXI TO the Melchester Hotel, and the waiter showed us to the table.

He pulled the seat out for Tiggy and said, "The chef's recommendation today is honey glazed, fresh Atlantic salmon."

"Fresh?" questioned Tiggy. "How is it fresh? Atlantic salmon can't be fished anywhere close to Britain."

The waiter looked confused. "I'm sorry. The chef sources the menu. I wouldn't know where it comes from."

"But it's on the endangered list, we shouldn't—"

"We're expecting a third," I interrupted.

"Very good, sir. Would you like me to ask the sommelier to come over?"

"No, thank you. I'll order from the list."

The waiter slid away and Tiggy said, "But how can it be fresh?"

"They do very nice steak. I'm sure that's fresh. And local," I said.

She looked ready to start again, but fortunately, Jane chose that moment to appear. "Sorry I'm a bit late. We got stuck in a protest march against homeless people. Or it may have been *for* the for homeless people, I wasn't paying attention. You must be Tegan? Lovely to meet you, dear. John's told me *all* about you."

"He has?" Tiggy asked, looking at me.

"Not really," I said. "I just mentioned that you've been helping me get to the island, and other things."

"It's the *other* things that I'm worried about." Tiggy's eyes flashed with mischief.

"How's Gerald?" I asked, attempting to derail Tiggy's desire to provoke.

"Oh, he's in a meeting with the Secretary of State for Defence. I forget his name, Gerald did say. They want to sell Rapiers to Iran, or Iraq. No, I think it's Italy."

"Rapiers?" asked Tiggy.

"Rapier Surface to Air Missiles," I said. "Jane's husband is an import/export broker in military ordnance."

"What's that?"

"He's an arms dealer, dear," said Jane.

"Oh. How exciting. Guns and things?"

"Mostly military hardware. Tanks, boats, helicopters, that sort of stuff."

"Isn't that illegal?" Tiggy asked.

"Not at all," I said. "He's on contract to the British Government, who are actually the second biggest arms exporters in the world."

"Oh, can he get hold of a gunboat? Jim would love a gunboat."

"Of course he can't," I said.

"I'm sure he can," said Jane.

The waiter appeared again and took our orders.

"How much would a gunboat cost?"

"Millions," I said.

"No," said Jane. "He did say he'd done a deal with the government of... Esperanto? No, that's in Argentina... Eswatini and he's taken a gunboat off them as part of some deal."

"Eswatini?" I trawled my geography. "But that's a tiny country, and landlocked. What on earth do they want with a gunboat?"

"Don't ask me. That's probably why they want to swap it for some new tanks."

"They've got tanks as well?" asked Tiggy.

"No," I said.

Tiggy gave me a sharp smile which said, '*Be quiet*,' and continued, "Have they got any old ones going? Tanks?"

"I'll ask for you, dear. If they haven't, I'm sure Gerald knows where there's one lying around. He always seems to end up with some leftovers."

"Leftover tanks?" I queried.

"All the time. Tanks, Jeeps, he usually sells them off to film companies. Anyway, enough about tanks, I want to know all about this independence business. It all sounds terribly revolutionary."

"I suppose it is a bit," I said. "Although, in actual fact, it's fairly straightforward. You see, in the Montevideo Convention of—"

"I don't really want to interrupt you," Jane interrupted, "but if you're going to launch into one of your complicated explanations, would you mind terribly if we ordered the wine first? Only, I find they go much better on a nice glass of Prosecco."

"It's really not that complicated."

"Just hang on a tick." She waved her arm towards the waiter, "Could we have a bottle of Santa Margherita?" She turned back to me, "Okay, carry on."

"I was just saying... Well, it's just that the island's fulfilled all the criteria, currency, population, trade—"

She reached out and grabbed my arm. "Yes, yes. I'm sure you've taken care of all the little details. I was only saying to Gerald, the other day, whatever disasters John gets himself into, he can always be relied on to take care of all the little details." She squeezed my arm as a signal to not talk while she smiled her thanks for the incoming bottle of Prosecco. "So now, I suppose this means you're now living in a foreign country?"

I thought for a moment. "I suppose, I hadn't really thought of it like that."

Our meals appeared in front of us, almost without our noticing.

"Now, tell me about you two." Jane sat back and allowed the waiter to place a white napkin on her lap. "How long have you been dating?"

"We're not," said Tiggy and I, in perfect unison.

Jane smiled. "Just what I thought. Well, I think this calls for a little celebration." She gave an almost imperceptible gesture with her hand and the waiter materialised by her side. "I think we'll have another bottle of the Santa Margherita."

After the meal, I managed, with Tiggy's help, to pour Jane into a taxi, then asked Tiggy, "Do you want to go straight back to Paddington?"

"My train doesn't leave until ten tomorrow. And there's not much to do in my hotel. It's very... functional."

"I see. I could show you some of London. Have you ever been to the National Archives? You can look up your family history, or even see the original of Shakespeare's will."

"Or you could take me on the London Eye?"

"It's very high," I said. "How about a boat trip up the Thames?"

"A boat trip? Seriously?" Tiggy said. "You could take me to the Tower of London?"

"Where the secessionists were executed? We could do the Cutty Sark?"

"What *is* it with you and boats? Let's go shopping. How about Oxford Street? You can buy you a decent pair of wellington boots."

"I don't think they sell wellington boots in Oxford Street."

"Then we'll have afternoon tea in Selfridges, or somewhere equally posh."

"Okay, tea in Selfridges it is. I'll find us a taxi."

Tiggy muttered something about busses, but I tuned that out and intercepted a passing Black Cab before she could get started on how Black Cabs were elitist eco-monsters which ran on radio-active rainforest juice.

"WOULDN'T THE UNDERGROUND HAVE BEEN quicker?" Tiggy commented, after five minutes sitting in a tailback to Marble Arch.

"Underground's always quicker this time 'o day, luv," said the driver over his shoulder. "But then you'd've missed 'aht on my scintillatin' repartee, wouldn't ya?"

"Plus, I don't like being stuck in an underground coffin with screaming babies and drunks," I added.

"I should have guessed," Tiggy said, and continued staring out of the window.

My phone bleeped at me, and I checked the number on the screen. A London number, but not one my phone recognised.

"Excuse me," I said to Tiggy, and pressed the green dot on the screen. "John Cabot."

"Ah, good afternoon, Mr Cabot. My name is Marcel Dallemagne. I think we've met before?"

"Marcel, yes, how are you?" I muted the phone briefly and said to Tiggy, "Marcel is the Deputy Head of the EU Delegation to the UK."

"How exciting," Tiggy said. "Is he important?"

I studied her to see if she was being serious, but her face was implacable.

"I have some news and I wanted to inform you personally," Marcel said.

"You know I'm no longer with the Foreign Office?" I replied.

"Indeed, that is why I'm calling. The EU is quite keen to recognise Scanlon's Rock as an independent state. As I understand it, you are now their diplomatic representative. I thought it prudent that you should be advised without delay."

"What's the quid pro quo?"

"Quid pro quo? Not at all. Why would there be?"

"Because with the EU, there's always a catch."

"Ay, and there is the rub."

"Huh?"

"You are no longer the British, true? You are now... how shall we say? ... Scanlons? Scanlonians? Hmm, either way, I would estimate that you are, or very soon will be, experiencing similar problems with the British Government as have beset ourselves for the last seventy years? That would make us allies, would it not?"

I pondered that for long enough that Marcel thought the line had dropped.

"Mr Cabot?" he checked.

"Sorry, I was just trying to work through your motives. You're going to have to help me. What is it exactly that you want in return?"

"Mr Cabot! It is good we can talk openly, but your suspicions are unfounded. We are just… reaching out, extending the hand of international friendship to an emerging country."

The taxi started to move again, and the driver spoke to his mirror, "'Ere we go, guv. 'Ave you there in a jiff."

"Thanks," I acknowledged, then returned to my call. "So, just good friends, then?"

"Of course, and perhaps we could have a Diplomatic Delegation office there? You would be welcome, of course, to submit your own mission to Brussels."

"You want to put an embassy on Scanlon's Rock?"

"Delegation, and as we are to become near neighbours, what could be more natural? Nothing grand, a simple office would suffice."

"I would have to put your request to the Government," I said. "I will raise it at the next parliamentary meeting."

"I see." He sounded disappointed. "I'm sure you would find such a liaison mutually beneficial."

"I'm sure, but it is not my decision. I'll keep you updated on developments." I closed the call and stared at the blank screen for a moment.

"What does he want?" Tiggy asked.

"I'm not entirely sure. He wants a foothold on the island, that much is obvious. At a guess, he probably sees us as a stepping stone into the UK. A backdoor trade route, a way of slipping round EU trade regulations."

"But I thought the EU were great believers in regulations?"

"They are," I said. "They created lots of them, but they also don't always believe the rules should apply to them."

The taxi finally broke free of the traffic and dropped us outside Selfridges. We did a patrol of the floors and managed to find some Xtratuf wellington boots for me and a Banksy T-shirt for Tiggy. As that brought me to the emotional limit of my shopping ability, we adjourned for tea and scones.

As we emerged back onto Oxford Street, I scanned for a taxi.

"Do you want to go back to your hotel?" I asked. "The taxi could drop you first. Save you fighting with busses or the Underground."

"You trying to get rid of me?"

"No, not at all, I was just—"

"Good. As I said, my hotel is very basic, there's not even a TV in the room. Not that I'd be able to hear it, even if there was. How do you put up with all this noise all the time?"

"One gets used to it. Triple glazing helps."

"The Hotel Paddington Splendide has only just got round to windows. How about we pick up a Chinese and a video and just chill?"

"I don't have a video player," I said.

"DVD?"

"No, I do have Netflix. We could watch a movie on that?"

"Netflix, huh?" Tiggy squinted in thought. "That hasn't got to Little Didney yet. We still have wind-up internet. Okay, Netflix and a Chinese."

"Or Thai?" I suggested. "I prefer Thai. I find it a bit lighter for an evening meal."

"Have you ever thought that your taste buds might be better travelled than you?"

"Who needs to travel when I have food from more countries than make up the U.N. within a five-minute taxi ride, and also, I've just got myself a pair of winter boots from Alaska?"

"Hmm, you sure you're not slightly over-prepared for a Cornish spring? I mean, I know we get rainy days, but…"

"The assistant assured me they were the best boots one can get, for all weathers."

A passing taxi finally acknowledged our existence and slid alongside us. "Where to, guv?" the driver asked.

"Pimlico, Cumberland Street."

As we joined the traffic chaos that is Oxford Street, I pulled up the takeaway menu for the Phuket Garden. "What do you fancy? I usually have the Chu Chi Goong prawns."

"I don't think I've ever had Thai food. Do they do a Sweet and Sour Chicken?"

"The Gai Yang is similar. Bit spicy."

Tiggy's phone started ringing from deep in her bag. As she dived in, in search of it, she said, "You choose, surprise me." She dragged her phone free and studied the screen. "It's Jim." She stabbed the green button. "Hiya, Jim, what's wrong?"

I couldn't hear Jim's response, but Tiggy said, "When? ... You're on your way?" She put her hand over the phone and whispered to me, "Jim and Watt are coming up here."

"Why?" I asked.

"Why?" Tiggy asked. She listened, then turned back to me. "He says he wants to do a State Visit."

"A State Visit? He can't just do a State Visit. They take preparation. Itineraries, security."

"John says you can't do a State Visit." She listened again, then to me, "He says, why?"

"Because it's... Let me talk to him." I took the phone from Tiggy. "You can't just suddenly do a State Visit," I said.

"Why not? I'm the King, and the President's coming with me. Can't get much more State than that."

"These things need a lot of arranging. Who are you expecting to meet?"

"The King, of course. Or the Prime Minister, if he's not in. Just want to let him know we're not miffed with him, personally like. I thought, keep him onside, you know?"

"I'm sure he'll be very pleased to hear that," I said.

"Yeah, that's what I thought. Anyway, seemed like a good time, seeing as how you're already in town, just in case I need a bit of diplomatic support. We could meet up later. I've booked a suite at the Melchester. Got a few pals coming over, the King as well, if he's up for it. Seven o'clock alright for you?"

"I was going to—" I started, but the line went dead. I looked at Tiggy. "I think Netflix and Thai is on hold."

I diverted the taxi to the Paddington Splendide, so Tiggy could pick up some different clothes, then we headed to my place.

Tiggy stood in my lounge and dropped her rucksack on the floor. "I'll take the sofa then." She nodded towards my corner lounger set.

"No you won't," I said. "Here…" I led her through the short passage to the guest bedroom. "It's not been used for a while… In fact, I'm not sure it's ever been used. I'll find some bedding."

By the time we'd made the bed and moved some packing crates, so Tiggy had space around the bed, it was nearly time to think about getting ready. I opened my wardrobe and studied the racks. Mostly formal suits. Daytime, Evening, Dinner, Tuxedo, Lounge, Linen for summer evenings, Black Tie for ultra-formal, Semi-casual for afternoon garden parties. But nothing which really said Jim Sullivan party in the Melchester. I heard a movement behind me and turned.

Tiggy stood in the doorway to my bedroom. "I thought you'd broken."

"What?" I asked.

"You haven't moved for five minutes. I thought maybe you'd broken, or your batteries had died or something."

"Just deciding what to wear. It's a difficult one. On the one hand, this is the Melchester we're going to. On the other, it's Jim Sullivan."

"But they're all the same? Well, apart from the white one at the end. Although, you're pretty much good to go as you are, if you want."

I glanced down at my current attire and was about to explain this was just afternoon-about-town when my phone rang from the lounge. I hurried to it and scanned the screen. Not a number I recognised.

"Hello?" I answered.

"This is Desk Sergeant Dobson at Belgravia Police Station. Are you mister John Cabot?"

"Yes, what's happened?"

"We have a mister... er, hang on... James Sullivan in custody here. He claims you're his Diplomatic Minister and that... To be honest, I don't really know what he's on about. He's higher than a pigeon's arse."

"Ah, I see. What's he done?"

"Well, currently, he's been charged with parking in a security-controlled area, being in possession of a class B drug, obstruction, and I'll probably add being a mouthy git if he doesn't shut up in a minute."

"Oh dear. Shouldn't he have a lawyer? I'm not sure I'm much use."

"He's claiming diplomatic immunity."

~ * ~ * ~ * ~

BELGRAVIA POLICE STATION LOOKED LIKE any other modern office block on Buckingham Palace Road, with the only thing really differentiating it, a large Metropolitan Police coat of arms on the corner face. We had to wait a few minutes before the desk sergeant extracted himself from the berations of a very drunk man dressed as a squirrel and holding a sign reading, 'Everybody's going nuts over our prices'.

"I'm John Cabot," I introduced. "We spoke earlier."

"Ah yes. The diplomat. Come through." He led the way to a small side office and sat us at a wooden desk. He opened a file of paper. "Your man, James Sullivan, was found parked in a security area outside Buckingham Palace. An SO14 officer arrested him after he refused to move on. He claimed..." The sergeant ran his finger down the paper. "...Diplomatic immunity on the basis he was on a State Visit to see King of England, and that he's the King of... The Kingdom of Scanlon's Rock?" He looked up at me with tired eyes. "To say nothing about the fact that His Majesty's currently enjoying a well-earned in Balmoral, SO14 wanted him brought up on terrorism charges."

"Terrorism?"

"Well, I convinced them he was probably harmless barmy, so they

~ 200 ~

dropped that. To be honest, I didn't have time for the paperwork, you any idea how much paperwork's involved in a terrorist charge? Besides, he's clearly off his meds. He keeps banging on about trying to find his President. A president in a kingdom? I mean… come on."

"I know," I said. "I've had this exact conversation with him, but he won't have it."

"I blame the education system. They don't teach proper history anymore."

"When you two have quite finished," Tiggy said. "It's his island. He can do what he wants. He can be King, or President, or even King President if he wants."

We both stared at her for a moment, then Sergeant Dobson said, "Island? Is he that pop singer what bought that island and declared independence? I read about that."

"Rock God," corrected Tiggy. "But yes, that's him. What about the other guy that was with him? Watt Tyler, is he locked up as well?"

The sergeant studied his file once more. "No mention of anybody else. You mean there's another one on the loose?"

"Yes, he's the President."

"The President?" He scanned his papers again. "No, no presidents. We've got a couple of queens down in the drunk tank, you're welcome to take them."

"So, what happens now?" I asked.

"Well, he's been charged with possession and parking in a security-controlled area. We're considering obstruction. After that, and considering his form, he will probably be held overnight and put up before the magistrates tomorrow."

"Held? But he's no risk," I said. "Surely he should be bailed after charging?"

"Normally, yes. That would be standard procedure, but as you've just told me he lives on a foreign island, of which he thinks he's the King, that's changed things. That makes him a flight risk."

We left the police station and made our way to the Melchester. My best guess was that would be where Watt would head.

This proved to be right, and wrong.

"Oh, Mr Tyler? You just missed him," said the receptionist in the hotel foyer. "He's just gone away with the police."

"What happened?" I asked.

"The maître d' called them when he refused to pay his bar bill."

"I don't understand," said Tiggy. "That doesn't sound like Watt."

"I wasn't there," said the receptionist. "But he'd been drinking all afternoon with some ladies who were... let's say, of interesting vocational persuasions, and then when he was asked to pay he just handed over a bag of old stones and told the barman to keep the change."

"I see," I said. "Anything else?"

"Yes, he knighted the hall porter on the way out."

~ * ~ * ~ * ~

SERGEANT DOBSON GREETED US AS we entered Belgravia Police Station for the second time. "Usually, people can't wait to get away from here. And yet, here you are again."

"I think you've arrested another friend of ours," I said. "Watt Tyler?"

The sergeant scanned his screen, then looked up at me. "Ah, yes. Theft of goods and property valued at £1,232.19 from the Melchester Hotel. I'll say this for your chums, they have style. Usually it's half a dozen cans of Carlsberg Special Brew from the Tesco Metro."

"Can I just pay the bill and get him out?" I asked.

"You'd have to take that up with the Melchester. We've charged him now, so they'd have to formally withdraw their complaint. Although, there may be other charges. He tried to bribe our custody officer with a handful of pebbles."

We intercepted a taxi outside the police station and headed back to the Melchester.

"Sorry," I said to Tiggy. "Looks like no Netflix or wild party."

"It's not really your fault." She squeezed my arm in reassurance. "You weren't to know they'd keep him in."

"I should have realised. It's supposed to be my job. I'm the diplomat, after all." A thought niggled to be heard. Diplomat. I pulled out my phone and scrolled the list of contacts. One name caught my attention. Philip Whitethorn, a Home Office Deputy Director, Policing. I pressed call and Philip answered on the first ring.

"Hi, Phil, it's John Cabot. We met at that interdepartmental team building exercise down on Exmoor."

"Yes, I remember. We had to get a ladder to get you down off the zip-wire."

"As I said at the time, it didn't look quite so high from the ground."

"I hear you've left the Foreign Office. Aren't you involved in some sort of independence coup on a Cornish island? Renegade John, they're calling you here."

"Renegade John, huh?" I pointed at my chest and smiled at Tiggy. "Renegade John."

She gave a pursed-lip smile, shook her head slightly and returned to studying her phone.

"What can I do for you, John?" Philip asked. "Looking for a new position in the Home Office? Not quite so many foreign junkets as your previous lot, I'm afraid."

"I wondered if you could help expedite a small problem?"

"If I can."

"The person I'm doing some consulting for has managed to get himself arrested. Silly thing really, just possession of a small quantity of Class B drugs."

"Oh, you mean your president, the pop singer? Yes, we had a bit of a giggle about that."

"Rock God," I corrected. "And actually, he's the King. The President is also under arrest, but that's not a problem."

"You have a king and a president? How does that work?"

I drew a deep breath and held it. Try not to annoy the man who can help. I glanced at Tiggy, she seemed to be deep in conversation with somebody on her own phone.

"I did try to point it out to them," I said, "but they were never going to listen to me. Anyway, I wondered if you could drop a word in the right in-tray and get bail granted for him? I mean, technically, he's a head of state, so it's more of a diplomatic issue than one in which UK law needs to become involved."

"Hmm, I would say that makes it more of a Foreign Office problem, not Home Office. Besides, I don't have that level of influence over decisions taken by an individual police station. Have a word with Sir Oliver Frogmorton. He should be able to pull a few strings."

"Okay, never mind." I closed the call and turned to Tiggy to tell her the news.

She was still engaged on her own call. "Really? He never told me any of that." She listened as the other person spoke, then, "Yes, that would be lovely... Thanks, I owe you one... No, not that! ... I'm quite sure Mrs Werner would do that for you, if you asked... Well, buy her some flowers and try. Anyway, I must go now, thanks for your help... Yes, you too." Tiggy dropped her phone back in her bag.

"Marek?" I asked.

"Yes, he's going to have a word with the Home Secretary and get Jim bailed. Apparently, he owes Marek one. Something to do with Marek removing some less than flattering reviews from his website."

The taxi drew up outside the Melchester and I said, "Okay, so we just need to pay Watt's bar bill. You hang on here, then we'll go back to my place."

"Oh, Marek sorted that as well. He knows the General Manager and I think he has some financial interest in the place."

"Hmm, it's not what you know, or even who you know. In the end, it all comes down to what you know about whom." I leaned forward to the driver. "Sorry, change of plans. Pimlico, Cumberland Street."

The taxi pulled away again and Tiggy said, "But at least we have it sorted, now we can enjoy the party."

"Perhaps we shouldn't have interfered," I mused. "We could have gone back to Plan A, Thai food and a movie."

"Maybe we just turn up, mingle a bit, then slope off?" She smiled and caught my gaze.

"How long do you think we have to stay?"

"Well, Jim said seven, so one of us could develop a headache by... what, say eight?"

"That long?"

"I'm sure you can manage an hour. We can still pick up a takeaway on the way back."

"That's a plan then."

Tiggy's phone rang, and she retrieved it from her bag. "Sam Goodenough? I wonder what he wants?" She pressed to answer. "Sam? What's up?" As she listened, she appeared to grow more agitated. "Okay, thanks, I'll come straight back."

"What's happened?" I asked, as she closed the call.

"Gawan's demolished a big chunk of the harbour wall with a bulldozer."

"Gawan?"

"Yes, he a sort of builder. Allegedly."

"Why would he do that?"

"You're new to Little Didney." She patted my hand in a patronising way. "Where Gawan's involved, we never ask why. The question should be, which idiot let Gawan anywhere near a bulldozer." She looked at her watch. "I need to get back, the '300 is moored to that wall, and Sam said the whole section of wall could collapse at high tide tonight. It would take my boat down if it did."

"Can't your dad move her?"

"No, he's out fishing, he's at least half a day out. What time do the trains go back?" She looked more stressed than I'd ever seen her. "How do I find out? Is there a phone number?"

"I'll drive you down. I was going back in the morning anyway."

"You sure?"

"Absolutely. We'll go back to mine and pick up the car, and then stop by your hotel to collect the rest of your things and checkout."

She wrapped an arm around mine, leaned her against my shoulder, and said, "You're a hero."

"Just as long as you don't expect me to change my clothes in a phone box."

## ~ CHAPTER EIGHTEEN ~

WE FINALLY CLEARED THE OUTSKIRTS of London minutes before the full force of the rush hour hit and joined the M5 at Bristol, just as the sun slid below the horizon in front of us.

"How long do you think?" Tiggy asked.

"It'll be late," I said. "Probably eleven'ish, or midnight, depends on traffic and how often we stop."

"I can share the driving if you like? Save having to stop."

"You sure?"

"Of course, it's a Volvo, can't get much easier to drive." She paused for a moment, then, almost under her breath, added, "Or more boring."

"I like boring. If I'd wanted exciting, I'd have bought a Peugeot."

Radio Four kept my attention with an investigative report into the refugee crisis, during the leg to the A30 at Exeter, but then lost it with a play about a single mother of five, cocaine addict, who tried to sell her children on eBay. I turned to a Virgin Music, just bland enough to burble away in the background.

"Does Gawan do this sort of thing regularly?" I asked.

"What. Demolishing the harbour wall with a bulldozer? No, that's a first. We usually keep him away from heavy machinery. Although, he did once drive a forklift truck through the front of Pengelly's bakery."

"How did he manage that?"

"To be fair, he was only trying to be helpful with a delivery of flour. He misjudged the width of the door. It doesn't help that he's very dyslexic, and the concepts of left and right are a bit of a mystery for him."

"That must make life difficult."

A slow-moving clutch of caravans forced a heavy lorry to move out to overtake, blocking my lane. I forced myself to relax and just let them sort themselves out.

"It does, but mostly for other people," Tiggy said. "He's always been the same. Good for labouring, but you wouldn't want him anywhere near something you want to keep. He built an annex on the church hall last year. Whole lot fell down in the first wind. He used a job-lot of old cement that he'd bought on the cheap."

As evening drew in, the traffic lightened, and our progress quickened. We finally reached Little Didney by half ten. We parked up and headed straight down to the harbour. Fortunately, a clear sky, and a nearly full moon, threw enough light to see the situation. The first thing to catch the eye was the tail end of what I guessed to be a yellow bulldozer. It sat skewed at an alarming angle, in a crumbled section of the harbour wall, its nose, completely submerged by the rising tide. A large section of the harbour wall, on either side of the machine, lay like a crumbled piece of cake out of which somebody had taken a bite. Beyond the sorry-looking bulldozer, the wall still stood with some semblance of its previous self, and it was here that the '300' lay at her berth.

Tiggy gave a short gasp as she saw it, followed by a comment on Gawan's parentage, IQ, and general usefulness.

"At least she's in one piece," I said, immediately regretting it when she turned her attention to me.

"Not for long, she won't be. And how do we get to her? The sea's going to pull chunks out of what's left of that wall, and I don't have my dinghy free to get to her."

I looked around on the off-chance there was somebody nearby with a portable bridge, or at the very least, a salvage vessel. "I see," I said, helpfully.

"I'll have to get across the gap," Tiggy said, staring at the mess. "It looks as though it should hold up."

As the words left her lips, a huge chunk of rock slid gracefully out of the wall and disappeared silently into the dark water.

"Don't you think we should call the fire brigade or something?" I asked.

"Why? Does it look like it's about to burst into flames?"

"No, but I just thought... But, probably not. We might be able to—"

Another chunk of rock slid into the water. This time, not so quietly. The bulldozer's rear end gave a little shuffle, the way a dog's backside does when it's investigating a rabbit hole.

"Ah, I think we need another boat," I continued.

"You think?" Tiggy said. "Slight problem," she turned to face the harbour and threw her arms wide. "Do you *see* any other boats?"

I scanned the harbour. "There's one over there." I pointed to a large shape moored to a buoy just inside the harbour. "Isn't that the Commodore's?"

"Yes, but not only is it far too big, and ancient, to manoeuvre, but the Commodore will also be fast asleep under the best part of a bottle of brandy by now."

I looked again at the destroyed section of the wall and the bulldozer, gradually enacting its own suicide. "We could try to get across that thing before it sinks completely. Or somebody could. Probably somebody very quick and agile."

"And probably suicidal?" Tiggy added.

"Yes," I said. I drew a quick breath and said, "Give me the keys." I held my hand out.

"Are you mad?"

"Yes. Probably. Give me the keys before I realise how stupid this is." I thrust my open hand.

"But even if you get there, you don't know how to drive the boat. Look, I can—"

"Keys," I demanded, with a firmness that surprised me.

Tiggy raised an inquisitive eyebrow and dropped the keys in my hand. I tucked them safely in my pocket and stepped with great purpose onto the secure section of the harbour wall. The second step lacked some of the confidence of the first, and by the third step, my bravado had evaporated completely. I tested the wall with my foot, then pressed my weight on it. No movement. I took another step. This one brought me up to the beginning of the damaged section. I kicked at a block of stone, and it felt solid. I transferred my weight onto it. So far, so good. I repeated the kick on the next section and a large block slid out of the wall and splashed into the sea a metre below. Tiggy gave a sharp squeak, and I froze.

"Okay, you've proved you're very brave," Tiggy said. "Now get back here."

I studied the challenge in front of me. A crumbled mess of blocks and concrete, gouging a four-metre-long gap in the wall. The unhappy bulldozer filled some of the gap, for the moment at least. I estimated two steps to get me onto the rear end of the bulldozer, and it looked like a couple more to clamber over that, then another two steps of rubble would bring me to the remaining intact section. I pushed forwards and twisted my foot slightly. A few loose stones skittered over the edge into the water, but underneath, it felt firm.

All my instincts told me to step backwards, to weigh up the risks properly, maybe create a spreadsheet on the possible outcomes. What's the worst that could happen? I could fall in under a pile of crumbling rock and get squashed underwater by a falling bulldozer. Okay, looking at worst-case scenarios was probably not a good idea. I felt my body lurch forwards, as though I'd just been launched from a catapult. I didn't remember taking a conscious decision to move. It just sort of happened. With no way now of changing my mind, all I could do was make tiny decisions as to which bit of stone to entrust with my next step. A couple bounces and my foot hit the yellow metal of the bulldozer. My feet skidded on the smooth, painted surface, and I found my hand contacting with the beast to steady a slip. I heard Tiggy yell something, but couldn't catch what it as I regained my balance and jumped again. I landed on what looked like a solid block, but which turned out to be anything but. The block gave way, and I collapsed forwards, landing on my front. The breath I'd been holding exploded from me and my hands scrabbled for purchase on anything they could find. They found a piece of rock which didn't move, and fingers dug into a gap. I waited for a moment, expecting everything to give way under me. It didn't. I shuffled forwards on my stomach until I lay on a relatively undamaged section of wall. I stayed still for a moment to let the worst of the panic subside, then pushed myself to my feet.

"Are you alright?" I heard Tiggy call.

"I think so." I brushed dust from my clothes. "I think I've torn my trousers." A flash of panic, the keys! I thrust my hand in my pocket and found them. "All good." I held them aloft.

"You're quite mad."

"I know. What now?"

Tiggy shouted simple instructions. Unlock the wheelhouse door. Keys in the control panel red button to start the engine. Lever forwards very gently. Steer like a car to the dockside.

"What then?"

"Don't worry about that. I'll be waiting. Don't forget to slip the mooring rope first though."

"Aye, aye, Skipper," I shouted.

The boat responded well to my trembling hands, although I found aiming it tricky. I'd start going in one direction, but it wouldn't stay pointing where I'd set it. In the end, that didn't really matter, as Tiggy seemed to know indistinctly where I'd end up, and she was there waiting. As I neared the quayside, she leapt onboard with the fluidity of a cat's shadow.

"That was completely insane," she said, as she took over the controls. "You could have got yourself killed."

"I'm not thinking about it. I'll probably have a panic attack. In fact, I think I still might."

"Just breathe slowly." Tiggy tucked the '300' neatly against the dock, then hopped up onto it to drop the mooring line over a post.

"It had to be done," I said. "What other choice was there? I mean, how else were you going to get it back?"

She shook her head. "You didn't give me chance to tell you, did you?"

"Go on then, what was your plan?" I challenged.

"You want to know?" She reached down to take my hand to steady my climb out of the boat. "I was planning to swim out to it. Easy swim. I was just about to get my clothes off and jump in, when, all of a sudden, off you go like a twelve-year-old playing Batman."

I paused, then said, "You were going to take your clothes off and swim? Naked?"

"Well, you didn't think I'd go swimming in my clothes, did you?"

"I… erm… I didn't think about swimming."

"I'm a fisherman's daughter, born to the water. How else did you think I was going to get to the boat?" She straightened up and studied me. "Although, I have to say, you were very gallant."

"Gallant?" I toyed with that for a moment. "Okay, I'll take gallant. But don't let me stop you if you still want to take your clothes off and go for a swim. If you feel like it, you know."

She smiled and held my eyes. "You can dream on." She leaned forwards and touched her lips to mine in the briefest touch. "Come on. Let's get you up to the Smuggler's before Sam locks up, or you're going to be sleeping on the '300'."

Sam had already locked up and was not overjoyed at having to let me in. "Don't know what you're doin' in an' out this time o' night," he grumbled as he opened the door.

"Sorry, bit of an emergency," I said. "I wasn't planning on coming back until tomorrow."

"We had to rush back to rescue my boat," Tiggy explained.

"Oh, yeah," Goodenough said. "Damned fool. If'n I'd known he was going to go charging around on that machine, I'd never have served him all them whiskies. Boy can't tell 'is arse from 'is elbow at the best of times." His eyes scanned the area just outside the door. "'Ere, give us a hand to get those tables in, will you? Looks like a wind is gettin' up and they'll be in the harbour by morning if it does."

"I'm going to leave you to it," Tiggy said. She turned to Goodenough, "And *you*, stop taking advantage of him." She flashed me a smile and headed off.

"Don't you pay no mind to her," Goodenough said. "Always got something to say for herself. Just put them over there." He nodded towards a spot just behind the door. "Save you havin' to carry 'em so far in the morning."

~ * ~ * ~ * ~


I WOKE WITH THE DAWN and briefly wondered where I was. The frilly canopy over the bed reminded me I was in the Honeymoon Suite of the Smuggler's Arms. And I ached. Not the normal ache of fifty-year-old bones protesting the new day, not even the usual knots caused by the overly soft bed. No, these were the aches of a body which felt like it had been trampled on by the Oxford Street hordes on the first day of the January sales. I gradually remembered the boat, and the harbour wall, and the bulldozer. I also remembered the idiot who had jumped along a crumbling wall, and over the bulldozer, in the dead of night and within inches of the watery death which lurked just below.

I groaned.

Then I remembered Tiggy's plan, the swimming one, and I groaned again. Once I'd finished beating myself up, I showered, dressed, and slipped out before Goodenough could catch me to rearrange his furniture, or whatever project he had going.

I headed along the harbour front to survey the damage from last night. There was now a gap in the harbour wall where the bulldozer had been. I guessed the machine itself was now languishing at the bottom somewhere. After observing the wrecked wall, it became clear we had taken the right decision to come back and move the '300', as the section of wall where she had been moored no longer existed. Quite a few people milled about the scene, chatting and taking pictures. I turned and continued along the waterfront. I'd intended to pop into the Fisherman's Plaice for a quiet coffee, but my plans were thrown when I spotted a new Portakabin had appeared in the last couple of days. Its red, white, and blue racing-stripe logo immediately marked it out as a Border Force unit. A notice on the door advised 'New arrivals to proceed this way'.

I climbed the three wooden steps and pushed open the door. A counter faced me as I entered, and a bored looking Border Force officer sat at a desk behind the counter. He eased himself upright as I closed the door behind me. A tall, well-padded man, with a beard and horn-rimmed glasses.

"Good morning, sir," he greeted. "Welcome to the United Kingdom. Where have you arrived from?"

"London," I said.

"Well, you don't need to be here. This is for international arrivals only."

"This is new…" I studied his I.D. card hanging round his neck. "Leonard, I'm John Cabot, Minister for Scanlon's Rock, ex-Foreign and Commonwealth Office."

"Len, actually." He waggled his I.D. card. "Len Bickerstaff. Yes, I only opened yesterday."

"So, how does this work? You have no secure shore-side area for arrivals."

"It's a bit of a problem, to be true. For the moment, we're working on an honour system."

"You expect visitors to come and find you?"

"It's the law."

"I see. Well, I suppose it will take time to build proper facilities."

"Don't know. Nobody tells me nothing. But I did hear a whisper that they don't think this'll be here for long, anyway." He poked his glasses up his nose with his finger.

"And it's only you on duty?" I asked.

"Yup, only me here. I open at nine and lock up at five."

"A nine-to-five Border Unit." I turned to head back through the door.

"You can't go out that way," Len said. "You have to go through either the red or the green channel. It's the law." He pointed at another door just to the right of his desk. A red circular disc hung on it.

"Okay, where's the green channel?"

"We ain't got no room for two channels. You just turn the disc round before you go through."

"Then what happens?"

"If you turn it to red, I'll be waiting outside for you, then I search your bag."

"And if I turn it to green?"

"Then I *might* be waiting for you. Randomised checks and all that."

"Well, it seems like an efficient system. Thank you, Len. No doubt we'll meet again on my visits from Scanlon's Rock."

"Right you are, sir. You have a safe onward journey now." He gave a little salute.

I turned the disc to green and stepped through the door, along a very short passage, then out through another door, back onto the seafront.

Len wasn't waiting for me.

I'd just turned once more to head for the Fisherman's Plaice for a morning coffee when I spotted Tiggy coming towards me.

"Good morning, Spiderman." She grinned.

"Hmm, not so much Spiderman this morning, more Peter Parker," I replied. "You look in a hurry."

"Just been told Gawan's in the Smuggler's. I want a word with him before he disappears back into his hole."

I took up alongside her and matched her pace. I felt quite out of breath by the time we reached the Smuggler's Arms.

Gawan stood with his back to the end of the bar. He already had a glass of something amber in his hand, and looked like he was having trouble keeping a gap between himself and several other, quite angry looking, people.

"I tell you," he was saying, "it was a faulty accelerator. Cable stuck, probbly, or summat'. Not my fault."

"What on earth did you think you were doing?" A tall man in a fawn sports jacket asked.

"I got a contract, didn't I?" Gawan said. "Rebuild the shoreline defences where it got washed away. It's all official, like. I got papers and everything."

"Who, in their right mind, would give you a contract like that?" the man demanded. "I tendered for that job, and never even got a reply."

"Who's that?" I whispered to Tiggy.

"Tim Calderman. Runs a building company up Penzance way, but he lives here. Well, half the time anyway. Rest of the time, he's got a place down near Marbella."

"P'raps they thought you was overpriced," Gawan taunted. "I ain't got no Porches to keep up."

Calderman pushed forwards a bit and Gawan tried to press himself back against the bar.

"Have you even drawn up a plan?" Calderman demanded. "Or did you just take off with that bulldozer to make it up as you went along?"

"That's why I got the job, see?" Gawan said. "Don't need no fancy plans or Risk Assessment bollox. Easy job, just shift a pile of rocks back where them's meant to be, and fill 'em with concrete. You lot, and your management strategy, health 'n safety, natural beauty impact rubbish this, that and the other. Ain't no wonder that they just want somebody who just gets on with it. None of yer chit-chat." He made a talky motion with his fingers and thumb to illustrate his point.

Calderman looked like he was about to launch himself at Gawan, but the Commodore slid between them.

"And who's going to pay to get that bulldozer out of the harbour?" the Commodore asked. "That's what I'd like to know. It's a maritime hazard."

"Leave it down there," said Gawan. "It was broke anyway. Brakes didn't work. It'll soon rust away. Look at the Titanic."

I spoke quietly to Tiggy, "Any chance you can calm this down a bit? I'd like a quiet word with Gawan before somebody dumps him in the harbour."

"No problem." Tiggy stepped into the middle of the group. "Right, you lot," she said loudly. "It was *my* boat nearly lost through this fiasco, so I want first dibs at him." She made eye contact with each of the group, almost challenging them to contradict her.

Mumbled noises of acquiescence greeted her, and they dispersed to continue grumbling with each other in corners.

Gawan looked relieved. "Thanks, Tiggy. I'd've handled 'em sure enough though. Sorry about your boat. I'll make it up to you."

"Leave it, Gawan. Come on, John wants a chat with you."

He looked around nervously, clearly wondering who this John was. When he saw me, he relaxed. "Oh, yeah. Jim's ministry man."

"I do wish people would stop calling me that," I grumbled. "Makes me sound like an evangelist."

Tiggy paused and looked at me. "Nah, that would be *way* too exciting for you." She smiled.

We led Gawan to a quiet corner, and I finally managed to get a cup of coffee.

"Gawan, this contract," I started. "How did you come to get it?"

"My reputation, must be. Get a job done, see? Good price. Word must've got around. Was only a matter of time."

"Okay, but what actually happened?"

"Got a phone call, didn't I? Posh bloke. Said his company had got this job from the Very Mental Agents, or somebody, to rebuild the sea defences at Little Didney."

"Environment Agency?" I suggested.

"Could'a been." Gawan shrugged. "Said he hadn't got the men with the skills that could do the job and he wanted to sub it out to me. Good money too. He said it was government money, so I thought, here we go, fill yer boots, Gawan. No brainer, really. He sent me the drawings of what he wanted. Looked easy enough, just pushing rocks and lots of concrete. Though I'm gonna need a new bulldozer now."

"Can I see the plans?" I asked.

"Yeah, no problem. I'll drop 'em down to Tiggy later." He downed the last of what I guessed was whisky, and slipped out of the pub before anybody else noticed.

"What's got you so curious?" asked Tiggy.

"Not sure. It's probably nothing. After all, the sea defences needed rebuilding, and it's not unusual for such contracts to be passed down to smaller contractors like this."

"Even to idiots like Gawan?"

"Mostly to idiots. Big construction companies off-load the low profit jobs to smaller contractors, who think they can do it cheaper. Which often they can, but usually by cutting specifications, or safety or quality of materials."

"So what's got you addled?"

"The timing. Just way too coincidental. I don't believe in coincidences."

The doors swung open, and I turned to see Jim and Watt enter. Jim spotted me immediately and came over.

"John, you missed a humdinger of a party, and hey, you'll never guess who I bumped into in the Melchester?"

"Probably not," I admitted.

"Your brother-in-law, Gerry. Cool dude, you didn't tell me he was an arms dealer."

"Yes, there's a very good reason for that."

"He's going to get me a tank."

"And that's it, right there."

## ~ CHAPTER NINETEEN ~

THE '300' SKIPPED ACROSS THE shallow waves, bursting spume from each one as the boat breached their crests. I sat in the seat next to Tiggy, eyes squinted against the spray. Jim and Watt had settled in the small cabin, wind and sea spray made it too difficult to keep their joints burning, apparently.

"You alright?" Tiggy asked, across the sound of the engine and buffeting hull.

"What? Oh, yes. Just thinking."

"That's a new look on you. Usually you spend this trip brain-numbed, and staring into the bottom of the boat."

"I guess it must be calmer today. Gawan landing that contract, something's not right."

"You think? I wouldn't trust him to build a rockery."

The cabin door opened, and Jim's head popped into view. "Hey, Tiggs. Can you calm it down a second? Trying to load a spliff and I've just lost a load on the floor."

She eased back the throttle and Jim held a thumb up and disappeared back inside.

"Since I've been ferrying him to and fro, I've swept up enough grass that would have kept Bob Marley going for a year. I just hope I never get pulled for a random search for drug smuggling."

"I need to see the plans. Did Gawan drop them off to you?"

She nodded to her rucksack. "He gave me a big brown envelope, so I guess that's what's in it. Have a look."

Although the sea crossing didn't seem to be affecting me so much today, I didn't want to risk it. "I'll have a look when we get there," I said.

The cabin door opened again, and a cloud of smoke billowed out, followed by Jim's slightly surprised face. "All good," he shouted. "You can open her up again now."

Tiggy pushed the levers forwards, and the prow lifted as the engines dug deep into the water. Now I grabbed the sides of my seat.

~ * ~ * ~ * ~

WE LANDED AT PIRATE'S COVE, where things had clearly stepped up a gear. The wobbly, thrown-together jetty, now looked more substantial, to the extent that Branok's boat sat tied to it and it hadn't collapsed yet. A more serious track had been carved up the shallowest part of the cliff, and a couple of quad bikes were busy ferrying building materials up to the waiting Land Rover Defender.

We squashed ourselves inside the vehicle, amongst cable drums, another generator, and all manner of electrical oddments. The roof lay laden under a stack of solar panels and a trailer behind was barely visible under what looked like a bundle of wind turbines.

As we bounced along over the now well muddied track, a case of Jack Daniel's tumbled onto my shoulder, and I had to spend the rest of the trip holding it clear of my windpipe. When we neared Jim's gradually expanding settlement, the place was a hubbub of activity. A pair of large satellite dishes had appeared and already scraped the sky.

"Two dishes?" I eased the case of whisky off my neck and leaned forward to ask Jim.

"Yeah, one's internet and phone, the other's TV. I'm told we can watch the Latvian football league now. Or Russian porn, if you prefer. No censorship here, we're a free state." He paused to gather a thought.

"Although I'm not having any punk music here. That's a royal decree, no punk music. Oh, and TV programmes about celebrities going fishing or riding tandems and cooking crap for each other. They're all banned as well. But, apart from that, we're a free state. And no Kardashians. And people with topknots, they're banned."

We pulled up alongside a large metal framework which extended for about fifty metres at a width of about five or six. Pipework and racks lay scattered in its footprint, and several huge rolls of polythene stood waiting.

"Is that what I think it is?" I asked.

"Quite possibly. It's going to be my major export, and there ain't enough room in Watt's lighthouse to keep me in smoke, let alone export."

"Cannabis? That's your export plan?"

"Why not? Massive market sat on my doorstep. Shame not to exploit it."

Tiggy shook her head. "And you think the British Government is just going to let you do that?" she asked.

"They can't complain. They're the biggest exporter of cannabis in the world."

"Medicinal cannabis," I said. "Not recreational."

"You say potato, I say dope dealers. And anyway, how can they stop me? Sovereign territory," he said. "Besides, I'll have a tank in a minute. I'd like to see them try." He flicked his lighter at the joint. It failed, and he shook it, that time it caught. "Clapton, phah, he can keep his custom built Ferrari. I've got a tank!"

I climbed out of the Defender and stepped through the timber piles of another half constructed Wikihouse, "You do realise a tank's only of any use once somebody actually lands on the island with their own vehicles?"

Jim hopped across the timber with the agility of a fourteen-year-old girl playing hopscotch. He paused. "Good point," he said. He looked around the landscape. "See, that's why you're the minister. You think of stuff like that."

"Maybe you should cancel the tank?" I suggested, helpfully.

He turned to face me, a look of a new idea on his face. A look I had come to fear. "No, but you're on the right track."

"I am?"

"Yeah, I've got an air force, and a land force now. What I need is a boat." He looked at Tiggy. "No disrespect, Tiggs, but the '300' is not much use in a sea battle. I need a warship." He patted my shoulder. "Good call, John. I'll give Gerry a ring, he said he had one." He headed off to Government House with a terrifying level of enthusiasm in his step.

"That went well," Tiggy said. "Let's hope your brother-in-law is out of stock on warships."

"I shouldn't worry. A warship would cost... what... millions? He couldn't afford one of those. Could he?"

"I don't know. Two subjects there I know very little about. Jim's finances, and the current price of warships. I'm just a poor fisherman's daughter. Besides, didn't your sister say Gerald gets leftovers?" She gave a quick smile.

"I'll try to get hold of Gerry, see if I can find out a bit more. You got time for a cup of tea?"

Tiggy checked her watch. "I'm supposed to be taking Shawn back to the village. Apparently, he knows a man who's got a bulldozer for hire and he's trying to get a finder's fee out of Gawan."

"You see, there's another thing. If this contract is legitimate, Gawan would be able to hire more than one bulldozer." I glanced at the huge satellite dish. "Do you think that thing's working yet?"

"I'll put the kettle on," she said. "You can check out the internet."

The internet proved to be a simpler task than making the tea. Tiggy ended up having to change gas cylinders halfway through the kettle boiling procedure, while the internet set-up took mere seconds. I didn't even have to track down the passwords, as the default settings hadn't been changed. User Admin, Password Admin. And Jim was right, the speed was blisteringly fast. Faster than my Pimlico flat. Even faster than the FCDO network.

Tiggy placed a mug of tea next to me. "How's it going?"

"The good news is, I still have access to the systems. The bad news, the Environment Agency only has a record of a sea defence contract being awarded to a company called Valdez Construction, registered in the Cayman

Islands. No mention of Gawan. I'm guessing that Valdez Construction is related to Valdez Oil. The same company who were leasing the IRV Xerxes, the boat that was sounding in the Channel."

"What does that mean?"

"It could be perfectly innocent, though I doubt it. Companies subcontract out work all the time. On the other hand, it's not unknown for certain politicians, let's say those with more morally ambidextrous stances, to lobby for contracts to go to companies who pay them consultancy fees. It's quite feasible that Valdez secured this contract via such a route, then subbed it out to a local contractor, at a reduced rate, probably a fraction of what they're getting paid, and they keep the extra."

Tiggy leaned across me to stare at my screen. I felt her breath on my cheek. "And you think that's what's going on?" she asked.

"I'm certain of it. I just can't figure out how to track them down."

"Is it important?" She straightened up and supped at her tea.

"Not really, I suppose." I closed the lid of the laptop. "The question is, why now? Why, all of a sudden, has the Environment Agency decided to spend, what was probably, the best part of a million on sea defences in one small, and very insignificant, fishing village?"

Tiggy pursed her lips in thought, then she shrugged. "Beats me. I've long ago stopped trying to make sense of what government does." She drank the last of her tea and dropped her mug in the sink. "Plans are on the side there, when you want them, by the way. I'm going to track down Shawn then head back." She kissed the tips of her fingers and wiggled them in my direction. "Catch up later, yeah?"

"Oh, yes, okay then." I watched her leave, wondering if I should have asked her to stay awhile.

I opened the laptop again and accessed the Parliamentary Publications records. Fortunately, this particular part of the government machine is actually open to the public, although trawling through the records of members' interests is no easy task, as it runs to several thousands of pages. After a few minutes playing with various search terms and dates, I had a solid looking hit. Sir Guy Serrick, the Honourable Member for Berrow upon Thames, and Minister for Financial Oversight. Recent financial interest declared. A payment of twenty-thousand pounds from Valdez Construction, consultancy fees. A scan back showed regular payments of similar amounts stretching over several years.

I turned to call for Tiggy to show her what I'd found, but there was no sign of her. I picked up the plans and unfolded them across my table. Building plans had always been a mystery to me. Even when my corner of the FCDO Main Building was being refurbished, it wasn't until the paint was dry that I realised my office was going to be in the basement.

After ten minutes studying random lines and numbers, I finally determined that the brown lines represented what already existed, and the blue, what was planned. In addition, and after much puzzling, I figured out that the drawings of the section of the proposed defences had been drawn in the sea to save paper, and not because that's where it was going.

I fished out the Hydrographic Office plans I'd brought along, and lay them alongside. Of course, they were on a different scale and used different symbols for the same features. I tried to recall what the Commodore had explained about the sandbank, but none of it made sense. I rolled them all up together and investigated the fridge and cupboards in the hope I'd left something which could be turned into a meal of some sort. A packet of ginger hobnobs, two tins of tuna and a Family Pack of Pot Noodles, which I'd certainly never bought.

A double knock on the door, and it swung open before I had chance to invite whoever it was, inside.

"Shawn's not going back to the village tonight," Tiggy said, and dropped her rucksack in the middle of the floor. "Jim's cracked open a new case of Jack Daniel's, and I think he plans to see it off before the football starts. Or finishes. I can't remember, I zoned out when they started on about how somebody had lost the dressing room and somebody else wanted to park the bus. Then, when the popcorn machine came out, I decided it was time to make my excuses."

"Which were?"

"That I'd planned on cleaning the oil filters on the '300'."

"And did you?"

"Really?" She opened her arms to draw attention to her figure. "Do I look like somebody who has to clean her own oil filters?"

"Not really," I admitted. "In fact, if I knew what one looked like, I'd probably offer to change it for you."

She smiled. "Well, there you go then. Now, why don't you pour me something nicely alcoholic and we'll have a look at these plans?"

I opened the cupboard. "I have a bottle of Roulot."

"That sounds like a wine."

"Yes, it's a chardonnay from one of the…" I caught the look in her eye. "I'll open that, then, shall I?"

"Good idea." She shrugged her denim jacket onto the back of the chair and flopped into the sofa. "Are these your hydrographic plans?" She picked up the roll of sea charts I'd left there.

"Yes, I was trying to compare them with the survey plans we got from Gawan."

Tiggy rolled them out onto the coffee table. "Wow, these are up to date. You can even see where they extended the slipway for the inshore lifeboat. That was only built a few months ago."

I sat next to her and planted the two glasses on the chart to hold it down. "They're kept up to date by satellite."

She stabbed a forefinger on a part of my chart where the Commodore's pencil line intersected the harbour front. "That's where Gawan is starting work, look." She pointed to the plans of the sea defence.

Now I had a point of reference, I was able to see how the two sets of plans married up. "I suppose that would be the natural place for a new defence. It's not so deep there. Less cost."

"Hmm," Tiggy muttered, and rolled up the charts. "You got anything to eat here? I'm starving."

"I seem to have acquired a thing of pot noodles from somewhere. We could go two's-up?"

"And people wonder why you're still single." She nodded towards my television. "Can you get Netflix on that?"

I looked at the television. "I suppose so, now that we've got this super-duper internet satellite. I haven't tried."

"Okay, while you figure that out, I'll go get us a takeaway from the Dragon's Palace. Sweet and Sour Chicken okay?"

"Is that still all he's got?"

"No, I think Lin's got a full menu now. Why, what did you fancy?"

I caught her eyes and couldn't help smiling. "Well…"

Her left eyebrow flicked. "I'm talking about Chinese food here. I haven't eaten all day, and if I don't get something soon, I might have to kill somebody."

"Okay, I'll let you choose then," I said.

"Good choice." She turned and slipped out of the door.

I turned my attention to the television and within ten minutes, I had Netflix up and running. I found a pair of plates and some cutlery and gave them a quick rinse for good measure. Tiggy returned after a few minutes with a pile of tinfoil containers and lay them out on the table.

"I haven't the faintest idea what we've got," she said, lifting lids from containers. "I just asked Lin to give us a selection. You haven't poured the wine yet."

"I was waiting for you. It's a Chardonnay, it should be served chilled, and I didn't want—"

"Just pour the damned wine," she cut in. "And is your phone still on?"

I picked it up and checked. "Yes, are we expecting somebody to call?"

"Yes, any minute now. Turn it off, quickly."

"What? Oh, yes, I see. He wouldn't, would he? I mean, it's eight o'clock and the football's probably started. He'll also be high as a kite by now."

Tiggy took the phone from my hand and switched it off. "There, see, that's how it's done. Now pour the wine before I start to get snippy."

The meal proved to be far better than expected, although I wasn't sure what most of it was. We finished eating and, at Tiggy's not-so-subtle request,

I opened a second bottle of wine. Netflix offered a good selection of movies, and we chose a spy adventure chase, with somebody I vaguely recognised from a programme about gangsters. By the time the credits rolled, we had somehow gradually become more entwined. I turned the television to background music, and let the entwining continue to its natural, and long delayed, conclusion.

## ~ CHAPTER TWENTY ~

MY BED WASN'T MADE FOR two. When I'd ordered it, I'd figured a standard sized double would be plenty big enough. The trouble was, I'd become spoiled in my London apartment, a king-sized bed, and that was just for me. It had been a very long time since I'd shared a bed and I'd forgotten that double beds were not really designed for two people. Two people need a king-size, at least. Maybe I should get it shipped down?

The morning forced its way through my curtains and Tiggy groaned. I dragged my way clear of the bedclothes and headed for the kitchen in pursuit of coffee.

"How many bottles of wine did we have?" Tiggy called from the bedroom.

"I had about half, not sure about you."

"That explains it. Why didn't you stop me?"

"I rather value my testicles."

"Probably wise." Tiggy stumbled into the kitchen, wearing one of my white Egyptian cotton shirts and not much else. "Are you making coffee?"

"It's number one on my list." I lit the gas under the kettle and measured coffee into a couple of mugs. "I guess you're heading back to the village?"

"I've got a booking this morning, a school group to go find some dolphins. That'll probably mean spending the afternoon cleaning cola, ice cream, and vomit out of the seat covers."

"I've got some digging around to do in the Whitehall records. I also need to create a dummy account while I have administrator privileges. That way, when they cut me out, I'll still have access." I handed her a mug. "I'm surprised they haven't blocked me already."

Tiggy finished her coffee, took a quick shower and headed off while I cleaned up. It felt slightly odd, washing up two plates, two glasses, and two mugs. My mind drifted back to the night before, remembering how strangely comfortable and familiar it had all felt. A very natural path that seemed both completely out of my normal reality, yet oddly, totally inevitable since the day we'd met.

I tracked down my phone and called Gerry.

"Hello, John," Gerry greeted. "I bumped into a chum of yours the other day. At the Melchester, no less. That pop singer chap."

"I heard. That's why I'm ringing."

"He's certainly a bit of a card, that one. Wanted me to sell him a tank."

"Yes, about that..."

"Normally, I'd say no, of course. We don't usually deal with private individuals."

"Normally?" I asked, dreading the answer.

"Well, as he's a friend of yours, I thought, why not?"

"I can give you a few reasons."

"I can see why you two get on so well," Gerry said. "Your sense of humour and his enthusiasm. Must make for some lively banter on the 19th hole."

"Indeed. But how could he buy something like that?" I asked. "I thought they'd cost millions?"

"New, yes. But this is an old Scimitar. You can get them on eBay these days. I can sell you one of these for less than you'd pay for a new Mondeo, or whatever it is you're driving these days."

"Volvo."

"Really? I suppose that fits. Anyway, we end up with a load of these things every time some new junta somewhere wants to upgrade their military hardware. We usually move them on to collectors or film companies. eBay, if push comes to shove. Generally lucky if we get back the cost of shipping them."

"Can you tell him no? Say you've sold it to somebody else?"

"Can't do that, Old Bean. That would be my reputation in the cat box. In my business, reputation is everything."

"Maybe just delay it a bit then? He gets bored very easily. If you can hold things up a bit, he'll go onto some other idea."

"Sorry, already in motion, along with the frigate."

"Frigate? As in the navy type frigate?"

"Of course." Gerry sounded surprised. "He said you'd told him he had to have one."

"I did?" I thought for a moment. "No, that's not what I meant, what I meant was... never mind. A frigate? A navy warship frigate?"

"Of course. Sailing boats are not in my bag."

"He can't buy a frigate. How can he buy a frigate? I know Jim's not short of a penny or two, but he can't afford a frigate. Can he?"

"HMS Raven, type 22 frigate. She's been around a bit. Pick these things up for less than you'd pay for a year's membership to a decent golf club. After the Royal Navy decommissioned it, it went to the Kenyan navy, then to the Gambia, where we had to take it as part of another deal, and now it's back here. To be honest, I'm glad he's taking it. It was destined for a Turkish scrap dealer. Twenty dollars a ton doesn't even pay the insurance for the journey. No fate for an old girl like her, but it's where most of them end up."

"But it must be bigger than the island? That's insane."

"It's a frigate, not a carrier. Only about half the length of the eighteenth at St Andrew's."

"That doesn't really help," I said.

"Ah, umm..." Silence for a moment as Gerry searched for an alternative comparison. "About the length of the Harrods' frontage on the Brompton Road."

"Okay, probably still not something I'd like to try to park though," I said.

"Funnily enough, I was going to give Jim a call today. I've just taken a job lot from Albania, including a LARC, thought he might fancy one of those. Perfect vehicle for him."

"Lark? What's a lark?"

"L-A-R-C. Amphibious landing craft. Just the job for him. Drive it straight from sea up to his front door. Twenty-five grand, dollars, if he's interested. To be honest, if he takes that, it will make it easier for me to deliver his tank."

"Does it have any guns?"

"Good Lord no. Well, none that function, anyway. I think."

"Okay, I'll let him know."

"Good show, we must do a round and lunch sometime, next time I'm in the country."

I closed the call and went to find Jim.

Jeeves answered my knock on the door of Government House with his usual enthusiasm.

"Don't know why you always come knockin' when I'm sat on the toilet," he greeted.

"Sorry, I didn't mean to."

"Have to keep regular, doctor says." He swung the door open, then turned and walked up the short passage. His cue for me to follow. "Though how he 'spects me to keep regular with all this up and down, I don't know." He pushed open the door to Jim's lounge area and extended his arm forward. "In you go, then."

Jim and Watt sat facing each other in front of the huge picture window. They both turned to face me as I entered.

"Hey, John," Jim said. "Just in time, you'll never guess what."

I noticed Watt trying to re-sheath a large samurai sword. His first couple of attempts defeated by the length of the thing and a combination of unsteady hands and poor eyesight. I wondered if I should help, but then it slipped smoothly away.

"You've declared a Shogunate?"

"What? No, although, that's not a bad idea."

I was going to have to learn to stop my flippant comments from turning into horrible realities.

"Go on then, I give up," I said.

"I've just knighted Watt. He's now Sir President. Cool, huh? Or is it President Sir?"

"A republican monarchy is constitutionally new territory, so I think you're free to choose."

"Sir President it is, then." He flapped a hand towards a collection of bottles and glasses on the sideboard. "Help yourself."

"Bit early for me."

"Well, at least have a smoke with me." He pulled a ready-rolled joint from his shirt pocket and tossed it in my direction. I caught it without thinking. "You have to celebrate the occasion. It's the rules."

I placed the joint on the sideboard and poured myself a very small Jack Daniel's. "Cheers." I raised my glass. "To Sir President Tyler."

"Watt," he said. "Sir President Watt. Don't want to get too formal, might go to his head."

"Of course not. I spoke with Gerry this morning. He told me about your frigate."

"Yeah, how cool is that?"

"Very. But have you thought about what you're actually going to do with it? I mean, these things need a crew of hundreds. Even just to turn on the lights, you'll need an engineering team."

Jim studied me and grinned. "You don't know anything about these things, do you?"

"Not a clue," I admitted. "But, I'm fairly sure you can't just turn a key and aim it, the way you can with say, something like Tiggy's boat."

He patted my shoulder on his way to retrieve the joint I'd turned down. "Neither do I. But I know a man who does, Old Salty."

"The Commodore?"

"Yeah, apparently, he was Second Lieutenant on this thing when it was down in the Falklands, back in… whenever the Falklands was."

"Eighty-two."

"If you say. To be honest, I don't actually remember a lot about eighty-two. Or three. Well, the eighties in general."

"Gerry asked me to tell you that he has some sort of amphibious landing craft you might be interested in. Something called a Lark. He'll do you a deal, as it makes it easier for him to get your tank here."

Jim lit the joint and breathed deeply. "That sounds fun. Makes sense really. A bit like reusing the wooden crates they send my JD in. Recycling, Cindy would be chuffed."

"How's she doing?" I asked. "I thought she was coming back soon?"

"Was." He drew a lungful of smoke and held it until his eyes started to water. "But she decided to fly up to Kugaaruk," he finally said, through a blue cloud. "Top of Canada somewhere. They're doing helicopter flights over the glacier so people can see the damage being done by global warming. She's into all that conservation stuff."

"Yes, you've said. Let's hope she likes the idea of recycling 5,000 tonnes of frigate."

"Haven't told her yet. I'll wait till she gets back, catch her in a good mood.

"Here, do you want to be a knight?" Jim asked. "I need to get some practise in."

"Practise? Why do you need practise?" I asked.

"'e nearly 'ad my ear off with that sword." Watt nodded towards the katana. "Waving it around like a demented ninja."

"It's heavier than it looks," Jim said. "We need something smaller."

"What d'ya suggest?" Watt asked. "You can't do no knighting with a kitchen knife. It's not proper, gotta be a sword, ain't it? You don't see King Charles with a bread knife, do you? He got a proper sword."

"Um, can I just clarify something?" I asked. "What's all this talk of knighthoods?"

"Ah, yes," said Jim. "Of course, you weren't here last night. We had a summit. A strategic planning initiative to plan... er... strategies."

"And plans," offered Watt.

I looked around the room. The debris from the previous night's strategic planning meeting lay everywhere. Several empty Jack Daniel's bottles, ashtrays overflowing with the remains of joints, and a stack of foil takeaway containers.

Jim noticed me eyeing the evidence. "It wasn't really like that. And Stringy was here, and Shawn."

"The knighthoods?" I persisted.

"Oh, yeah, you know this cash for honours business is all the thing now?"

"Hmm, I think I can see where this is going."

"Well, I got to thinking, if there's people about who are happy to cough up a few grand just to get a 'Sir' in front of their name, then we should be having a bit of that."

"You're planning on selling knighthoods?"

"Part of our overall GDP strategy. Just think how much somebody like Trump or Kim Jong would pay to be able to call themselves 'Sir'. Or the Kardashians. They'd go for it big time. Can women be knights?"

"They can be dames," I said. "So your economy is going to be based on selling cannabis and titles?"

"And tea with the President," said Watt. "Don't know why King Charles ain't done that 'imself. Missed a trick there."

"All the thing in your Parliament, buying knighthoods and stuff," said Jim. "And then there's... er, what do they call it when the Prime Minister sells tickets for breakfast with him?"

"Corruption," I said. "But I'm not sure it's a good basis for an emerging economy's balance of payments. Have you thought about something more... let's say sustainable? How about eco-tourism? Set up a glamping area, yurts or some of these Wikihouses, where people can come and watch the dolphins and birds?"

Jim paused and stared out across the sea. "Hmm, you know, you might have something there," he said, finally.

His reply took me by surprise, being used to normally having my ideas dismissed. "Really?"

"Yeah, we do the glamping stuff, dolphins and whatnot, then they get a tour of the special farm, with a free sample, tea with the President and a Knighthood. Full Monty package like."

"They can 'ave a ride in yer battleship, too," Watt added.

"Of course." Jim's eyes sparkled with an enthusiasm which triggered all my self-preservation synapses. *Run, now!* They screamed.

"That wasn't quite—" I started.

But Jim was in full idea mode and was way beyond stopping. "And Air Force Two. They can have a flight over the island. Maybe even fly over the French coast. With croissants and champagne for breakfast."

"Waste o' time, bleedin' French rubbish," muttered Watt, pouring himself another drink and spilling most of it. "Croissants are just empty pasties. Give 'em proper Pengelly Pasties. They got history, they have. Only the French could go, *ooh, let's make a Cornish pasty wiv' nuffin' in it,*" he caricatured, in an appalling, comedy French accent. "*Oh mon dew, wee-wee, how French of us.*"

I looked at Jim. He shrugged, and said, "Don't worry, I'll work on him."

A Cornish pasty with nothing in it. Interesting take. I suppose to a Cornishman, brought up on substantial meat pasties, the light fluff of a croissant might well seem a bit of nothing.

Of course. A bit of nothing. A fake. Several niggling threads suddenly crystallised into a network of coherent paths. Why hadn't I seen this before? Idiot.

"I've got to go," I said.

Jim looked surprised. "You need to chill a bit. All this rushing about, you'll have a heart attack. Happened to Des, our original drummer. Always rushing about he was, never stopped. Until one day, out of the blue, his heart just went pop, and he keeled over, dead. The girls he was in bed with at the time were hysterical. Hell of a state it was. There he was, sprawled on the bed, covered in lacy underwear, chocolate sauce, and Colombian marching powder."

"Warning taken," I said. "I'll try to slow down."

I left the two of them to their planning and headed back to my house. A thought had been niggling in my mind, and I wanted to check something.

I made myself a coffee and pulled out the two sets of plans again. The line on the blueprints for the new sea defence followed the old sandbank exactly. This wasn't a sea defence project at all, it was land reclamation.

I scrolled through my contacts list on my phone. Simon Culthorpe, Oversight Manager at the Infrastructure and Projects Authority.

He answered at the first ring.

"Simon, it's John Cabot, FCDO, or was."

"John, how are you doing? I heard you'd left. What can I do for you?"

"I'm doing some consultancy work, and there's a bit of construction work involved. I just wondered if you could help me avoid a costly mistake."

"If I can."

"I just want to make sure my clients avoid getting stung by dodgy contractors, you know how it is."

"Tell me about it. You'd be amazed at the number of shady building companies who pop up out of nowhere each time we issue a project for tenders. Most of them, shell companies coming in on the recommend of a cabinet minister who just happens to have a seat on their board."

"I know you can't recommend companies," I said, "but do you have a blacklist of the worst, the ones to avoid?"

"Hmm, well, we wouldn't confess to such a thing as a blacklist. But... in what field are you thinking?"

"Primarily, concrete suppliers. I'd just hate to see something like that Essex school roof collapse happen again."

"Yes, well, I suppose," Simon said. "Given the circumstances, it wouldn't really be a problem to give you a couple of names to avoid. I can text them to this number you're calling on, if it helps?"

"Excellent, thank you."

# ~ CHAPTER TWENTY-ONE ~

JIM'S FRIGATE ARRIVED A WEEK later. It looked nowhere near as big as I'd thought it would, I guessed only about four or five times the length of Branok's trawler. I think I'd probably had something about the size of the Ark Royal in mind. Whoever was driving it clearly knew their business, as it slid smoothly under the rocky face of the western promontory part of Pirate's Cove, where it dropped anchor. I guessed the water at that part of the cove was much deeper than I'd realised. Four figures clambered down the ladder into two semi-inflatable rubber boats, then headed up to the jetty.

Jim, Watt, and me, headed to the shore to greet them.

A large man, in combat clothes and green woolly hat, tossed some keys to Jim as they drew closer. "All yours, mate," his Australian accent at odds with the Royal Marine's DPM of the jacket. I assumed it was probably courtesy of an Army Surplus store somewhere. Maybe even something to do with Gerry.

"Do I get a lesson?" asked Jim. "Only, the nearest I've been to driving anything that big, was a double-decker bus we hired when the band was starting out. And that didn't turn out too well. I lost the top deck under a low bridge."

The man looked at Jim quizzically, then grinned. "Piece of piss, just remember, she's an old lady, so treat her gentle. Where's the bar? I'm as dry as a dead dingo's donga."

"Hop in," Jim waved towards the Defender. "I'll take you to the best bar on the island."

Seven in an old Land Rover Defender proved cosy. Even with the rear, fold-down seats deployed, it wasn't something I'd want to endure for more than a few minutes. The cramped interior, combined with the bouncing of a tortured suspension system and the clouds emanating from Jim's ubiquitous joint, brought me to the verge of losing my breakfast. Fortunately, the journey was short.

Jeeves greeted us all at the door, but when he saw Jim was with us, he just muttered, "You might have told me you were bringing company. I'd've got out the best china." He turned and started walking through to the lounge. "This way, gents."

Jim signalled the crew to sit, then pulled a stack of beer cans from the fridge and dumped them on the central coffee table. "Help yourselves. Or there's JD, if you'd rather, or some nice homegrown. First crop of the island. But be careful, it'll have you floating out of your socks."

The men stuck to beer, and as it looked like turning into a session, I looked for a reason to escape. Rescue came as a barbed lifebelt when my phone bleeped. I glanced at the screen. Foggy's office.

"Sorry." I held up my phone. "Got to take this."

Nobody objected, in fact, nobody even seemed to notice. I slid outside as I pressed answer.

"Mr Cabot?" a female voice asked.

"Yes."

"Please hold for Sir Oliver Frogmorton."

"It's no longer *Mr* Cabot, it's—" But she'd gone, and I found myself talking to the FCDO's automated telephone system.

"*Thank you for holding,*" said the patronising computer voice. "*Your call isn't important to us, and we really don't give a toss about whatever petty grievance you have with the authorities of some foreign country, but you can continue to hold for some jumped-up, overpaid twat to tell you the same thing. Here's some music to annoy you with while you wait.*"

The sound of The Sex Pistols', *Anarchy in The UK* drifted through the phone's speaker.

I held.

Eventually, Froggy's voiced barked, "Cabot?"

Always a bad omen when he just uses my surname.

"Did you know your phone system's been hacked again?" I said.

"Damned hooligans. What is it this time?" Froggy demanded.

"The Sex Pistols, *Anarchy in the UK.*"

"Hmm, it was *Won't Get Fooled Again* last week. Anyway, listen, Cabot, we have a problem—"

"It's actually *Sir* John Cabot now," I said.

"Sir? What are you blathering about, man?"

"I've recently been knighted. I think you should use my official title from now on. Sir John Cabot. Or Sir John is okay too."

"Don't be ridiculous, man. Now, I want to discuss this warship that your pop singer chum has acquired. What the devil does he think he's doing?"

"First, he's not my 'Pop singer chum', he's the King of a sovereign state, second, it's actually none of your business, and third, it may have escaped your notice, but I no longer work for the FCDO."

"Well, first," said Froggy, "it *is* the business of this department when somebody aims a warship at us, second, it's a constitutional impossibility for a country with a president to create a knight, and… er, fourth—"

"Third," I corrected.

"What?"

"Third. You went from second to fourth."

"Have you any idea how much I miss these little conversations with you?" Then, without waiting for an answer, he continued, "None. That's how much. Fourth, you'll never work for this office again if you persist in displaying such a belligerent attitude to your superiors. Tell your king that he provokes the mightiest navy in the world at his own peril."

"What's the USA got to do with all this?" I asked.

"The USA? I never mentioned the USA?"

"Well, numerically speaking, *they* currently have the mightiest navy in the world. The UK only has seventy ships, the USA, four-hundred and ninety. And besides, I don't think you need worry too much about a forty-year-old boat, which until a few weeks ago, was heading for a Turkish scrapyard to be turned into baked bean tins."

"I'll be raising this matter with the Defence Secretary. Good day." The line went dead.

As I stared at my phone, I noticed a text message. I opened it up. A strange list of company names confused me for a moment, then I noticed it was from Simon Culthorpe. The list of concrete suppliers best to be avoided. One name, Crumblee's Discount Concrete and Tarmac, had three asterisks against it, with the legend, '*definitely one to avoid*'. That would do nicely.

I headed back into Jim's lounge to find Jim, Watt and the crew from the Raven glued to the PlayStation, as Jim and the Australian skipper commanded a destroyer in Battle of Midway. The acrid smoke of cannabis gathered around Jim's head as he juggled a game controller, a joint, and a glass of JD in his hands. A whoop of laughter and chinking of beer cans signalled the death of another Japanese aircraft carrier.

"Um, guys," I ventured.

"What's up?" Jim asked without turning his eyes from the screen.

"You know that knighthood you offered me?"

"Yeah, we're going to call them Knights of the Suspender. Cool, huh?"

I thought about not asking, but curiosity won out over my desire to retain some sanity to the conversation. "Knights of the Suspender?"

"I looked up this knighting stuff on Wikipedia. Did you know they call them Knights of the Garter?"

"Yes, I did know that. It's to do with—"

Jim interrupted me with a wave of a momentarily free hand. "Yeah, yeah, let's pretend I know all that, whatever Latin stuff you're about to fill my head with. Mick, get that anti-aircraft turret, will ya? So, what's higher than a garter? Huh? A suspender belt, that's what. So *our* knights are gonna be Knights of the Suspender."

"Ought to be Knights of the Bra," suggested Watt. "Them's is higher than both suspenders and garters."

"How would you know, you silly old sod?" Jim teased. "You ain't seen neither for twenty years. Not that turret, Mick. *That* one. I thought you knew about boats. You just got me shot down again."

"They're ships, not boats," Mick said. "And at least I know how to skipper one."

"You don't know what I seen on the island, them years past," Watt grumbled. "Some 'o those Frenchie boats what brought me stuff. Well, they 'ad lasses as crew, some of 'em. Course, I ain't gonna say nothin', 'cus that ain't gentleman like. But, just say…" He tapped the side of his nose. "I know what a bra looks like."

Jim handed his joint to Watt. "Here, have a pull on that, give your lips something to do other than talking bollox all the time."

"These knighthoods," I tried again. "Any chance I could have one? Quickly? Only I might have accidentally told Sir Oliver Frogmorton that I was a knight now."

Jim actually turned away from the screen to study me. "How do you accidentally tell someone you're a knight?"

I drew a breath, ready to answer, but Jim cut across me. "Go, John. Cool," he said, with a big grin on his face. "I once told a Russian woman in a Moscow nightclub I was a secret spy. Just for the shits and giggles, you know how it is. We were there doing a series of gigs in Russia, and I got bored. Anyway, long story short, I got arrested by the KGB, or whoever they were. My manager went nuts. Good tip, don't ever tell anybody you're a spy in Russia. They've got no sense of humour about these things."

"I'll try to remember that," I said.

"We'd better make you a knight, then. Or a lord? Would you rather be a lord?"

"Just a knight," I said.

"Or a lord knight. That would shut him up, if you were a lord knight."

"A knight is fine."

"Okay, knight it is. Watt!" Jim called. "Get me sword, we're on."

Watt stood and paused, seemingly to gather his legs for walking. He gazed across the room to the corner where the katana stood propped against the wall. He handed the joint back to Jim in passing and retrieved the sword. It wobbled dangerously in his hands as he passed it to Jim.

Jim made a couple of sweeping movements with the sword, and a cushion on a nearby chair exploded into a cloud of feathers. He looked surprised, then adopted a faux martial arts stance as a cover.

"What you doin' with that thing, mate?" asked Mick. "You sure you should be waving that thing about in your state? You might want to leave that a while."

"Nah, I'm alright," said Jim. "Just need another quick smoke. Calms the JD-shakes a bit."

"We could always leave it till the morning," I said, watching him as he tripped over a rug. "There's no hurry."

"Best catch 'im while he's still upright," Watt said. "Kneel yourself down on the rug, and you might want to hold your ears in a bit. Just speaking from experience."

I studied the katana in Jim's hand. It looked older than the man holding it, streaks of rust dulling the metal. I wasn't sure I wanted that anywhere near me. If I didn't die from massive blood loss, it would probably be tetanus.

"Do you have a different sword, perhaps?" I asked. "Maybe something… erm… less sharp?"

"I've got a light sabre," Jim offered.

"Is it real?"

"If it's not, I'm going to leave a shit review on Amazon." Jim wobbled the sword back in its sheath and disappeared into the next room for a moment. After some rummaging noises, and a couple of faint grumbles about Jeeves' Lego collection cluttering up all the available cupboard space, he returned with the light sabre in hand. He switched it on, and it gave a loud buzz, instantly recognisable to Star Wars fans everywhere. "Cool, batteries still work. Here we go, let's have a try with this."

"Yer gonna have to get him to kneel down, son," Watt told Jim. "You don't wanna be reaching up that high. I do that, and it makes my trousers rise up, and the gusset gets into places that—"

"Yeah, yeah," interrupted Jim. "I don't think John wants to know all that. Let's just get on with it."

With the unwanted image in my mind of Watt's travelling gusset, I knelt on the rug. The light sabre wobbled in front of my eyes in a hypnotic dance of pulsing lights and buzzes. It then clipped against the edge of my right ear and landed with a gentle thump and buzz on my shoulder before repeating the operation on the other side. I was very glad we'd gone for the light sabre, and not the rusty katana.

"I now pronounce you Sir Knight of the Suspender," Jim said and fiddled with the switch. "I've forgotten how to switch this thing off. Here, sort this." He handed the light sabre to Watt. "I'll get your certificate." He turned to the writing table in the corner and busied himself for a moment.

"Is that a real thing?" asked Mick. "Being a sir, and all? For defo?"

"Of course," said Jim. "I'm a proper king. Why? Do you want one?"

"Too right. That'd go down a storm with the boys back home."

Jim paused for a moment, then. "Hundred quid. Or you can be a lord sir for one fifty."

"How about I forget to take the reading for the invoice of the amount of diesel left in the tanks in the Raven?"

"How much is in them?"

"Dunno, I ain't read the gauges." He shook his head. "Maybe a hundred gallons. About enough for a turn round your island."

Jim thought for a moment. "Okay, deal."

"Hundred gallons to circuit a two-kilometre-long island?" I queried.

"Pretty much," said Mick. "If you'd wanted something cheap to run, you should'a bought a Prius."

"And I thought my Volvo was fuel hungry."

"Here's your knight's certificate." Jim shoved a large parchment sheet at me.

I took it and studied the content. Overly flowery language declared, 'This day forthwith and witnesseth that John Cabot now be declared a Knight of the Great Order of the Suspender and from this day forwards hereafter be known as Sir John. By order of King Jim, King of Scanlon's Rock and Lord of all his domains. Given under the Great Seal of the Kingdom Republic of Scanlon's Rock'.

A scrawled signature nestled alongside a black ink shape resembling something from a Rorschach test.

"What's that?" I asked.

"The Great Seal of Scanlon's Rock," Jim said.

I studied the shape. "How?"

"It's a paw print from Clarence."

"Clarence? Oh, Watt's tame seal?" Then it dawned. "Clarence is the Great Seal of the island?"

"Yeah, clever, huh?" Jim said. "Every country has a great seal of state, but we're the only ones with a *real* seal."

"Yes, that's sure to be the subject of the dinner table at the next UN Assembly."

"Oh, about that, can you get us into that? I've got a few ideas they might like."

"No."

~ * ~ * ~ * ~

JIM'S LARC, THE AMPHIBIOUS LANDING craft, arrived the following week. We were told it was on its way, so there was quite a reception committee waiting on the beach at Pirate's Cove. We watched as it approached, looking for all the world like a simple grey barge, about the length of Branok's boat, but significantly lower, and wider. The machine chugged steadily to the shore, then climbed up on the beach without breaking its stride. It stopped just clear of the water, and the forward ramp dropped down, bringing its cargo into full view.

The Scimitar tank, or armoured reconnaissance vehicle, as Gerry preferred to call it, started up with a cloud of black smoke belching from its rear. The engine grumbled like a reluctant tractor, then settled into a steady thrub, not much louder than one of those noisy American motorbikes.

Mick, the Aussie skipper who'd delivered the Raven, sat inside the top of the open turret. It rolled forward, out of the LARC, and with effortless grace, headed up the steep cut to the top of the cliff. I guessed it to be about the size of Gawan's bulldozer, which I'd last seen disappearing into Little Didney's harbour.

"That's one beautiful machine," said Jim. "Did you see how easy it made that?"

"Certainly beats your Land Rover," I said.

Piled behind the position the Scimitar had occupied inside the LARC, stood a stack of timber panels, probably another Wikihouse, or two, and dozens of crates. Not much point in sending over a half empty transport vehicle, I supposed.

The front of the LARC lifted again, and it rumbled forwards to follow its companion up the cut. I noticed Shaun and Shawn peering over the side as it passed by us.

"That's going to make bringing supplies over a whole lot easier," I heard Tiggy say from my right.

I turned. "Hello, I didn't see you arrive."

She nodded towards the far end of the cove where I now saw her boat. "You were busy having boy wet-dreams over the big machines." She grinned at me. "I had to lead them in. The cove is tricky if you don't know where the rocks are."

"You staying for tea?"

"Only if you've got some chocolate hobnobs."

"Got them in especially. McVitie's."

"You know how to tempt a girl."

"You two gonna get a room?" asked Jim.

"It's on the back of that thing," Tiggy said, pointing at the LARC, just cresting the cliff.

"What is?" I asked.

"My own house. Well, sort of office come house. My accountant suggested that basing my business here was better for tax. Or indeed, no tax."

"That makes sense. If I had an income, I might do the same." I stared pointedly at Jim.

"No worries," he said, and patted my shoulder. "I now appoint you officially as Minister of..." He paused in thought. "No, you're now the First Minister. Sir First Minister."

"If you're going to be appointing government ministers, you should really have a constitution."

"A constitution?" Jim queried. "That sounds very boring. That's your first job then, as First Minister. Make a constitution."

"What sort of systems do you want it to cover? Law, democratic processes, governmental structure?"

"Yes."

"Yes what?"

"What you said. Yes. You've got to wear the official uniform, though. Can't have you representing the Kingdom of Scanlon's Rock in a suit. They're now officially banned, by the way. No suits on the island."

"What's the uniform?" I asked, imagining all sorts of horrors.

"They're in that." He nodded towards the LARC, disappearing over the top of the rise. "Come on, I'll give you both yours when we get back."

Tiggy and I shared worried glances, shrugged, and followed Jim back to his Land Rover Defender.

After a furious, bouncing chase across the grasslands, where Jim seemed intent on beating the LARC home, we slid to a halt alongside the already parked amphibian outside Government House.

The front of the LARC lowered once more, and Shaun and Shawn set about unloading the crates. Jim surveyed each one as they emerged, indicating where they should go. One crate in particular caught his eye, and he told them to leave it with him.

"What size are you?" he asked.

"In what?"

"Suits, what size suit do you take?"

"I don't know," I admitted. "I usually have them made to measure."

He studied me for a moment. "Hmm, medium, I reckon." He dived into the crate and rummaged among the packages. "Here you go, medium and medium." He tossed two plastic bags at me.

I pulled open the first one. "Jeans?"

"Levi's, stonewashed. Only the best. Open the other one."

I tore open the second and pulled out a dark blue sweatshirt. I unfolded it and held it up. The front displayed the image I'd commissioned for the flag. The skull face with long hair, flanked by cannabis leaves, and a pair of crossed guitars in the rear.

"Cool huh?" Jim asked. "Better than your pinstripe Gulag uniform."

"Jeans and sweatshirt?" I checked. "That's the official code of dress for your government."

"It's your design," Jim said. "They came out good." He went back into the crate and pulled out another pair of bags, which he tossed to Tiggy. "Small?"

She opened the bags and held them up against herself. "They look about right. But why me? I'm nothing to do with your set-up here."

"You are now, I'm officially appointing you as Minister of Getting us some Visitors."

"Getting Visitors?" Tiggy questioned.

"I think he's probably thinking of Minister for Tourism," I suggested.

"Yeah, that one, what he said. That sounds better," Jim said. "You're good with all that stuff, Tiggy. I don't know how you keep a straight face with some of the drongos you take out. I'd tip 'em over the side."

"You'd be surprised how close I've come at times. Are you really sure you want me as Minister for Tourism? I'm not actually that good with people."

"It's either you or Jeeves," Jim said.

"I see. Maybe that offer's not quite as flattering as you hoped it might sound."

Jim looked puzzled. "Oh, but you'll do it though? Right?"

"Yes, Jim, I'll do it."

~ * ~ * ~ * ~

THE PHONE CALL FROM FROGGY came the next day. Just as I'd started work collating headings for the constitution.

"What's this about tanks and marine landing craft?" he demanded, dispensing with the usual opening niceties.

"Nice to hear from you too, Mr Frogmorton."

"Sir, it's Sir Frogmorton. Have you forgotten all sense of social decorum? Tanks, I want to know about these tanks."

"I'm sorry, I thought we'd dispensed with official titles when you thought it appropriate to not use mine."

"What title? His Majesty's Government doesn't recognise this island as independent. Therefore, any titles issued by persons claiming otherwise, are invalid. Now, tell me what's going on. Is your chappie building a private army? From what I hear, it's just the sort of thing he'd do."

"I don't think you can expect me to comment on matters of state security." I would have given anything to see his expression. "You need to make a request to the Scanlon's Rock Ambassador to the UK."

"And who is that?"

"Sir John Cabot."

"Sir John... you're not making any sense. That's you. I'm talking to you already."

"No, you're talking to me as a Research Analyst for the FCDO, which I no longer am, even though you don't seem to understand that. If you want to talk to Sir John Cabot, the Scanlon's Rock Ambassador to the UK, then you have to ask nicely."

"Well, talk to me as the Ambassador then."

"You have to ask nicely. Ask if you can have a telephone summit with *Sir* John Cabot, Ambassador to the UK."

The line went dead.

~ CHAPTER TWENTY-TWO ~

THE LARC HAD MORE THAN proved its worth as a versatile transport, chugging to and from the mainland on an almost daily basis. I'd decided to take advantage of improved logistics, and arranged for my bed to be shipped down from London for the LARC to bring over.

Tourists had started to visit the island, thanks in no small part to Tiggy's energy as Minister of Tourism. Not that there was much infrastructure on the island yet to support visitors. Just a Wikihouse Ocean View Tea Room and Bar, a Wikihouse Spartan's Museum, and a Wikihouse souvenir shop selling shells, postcards of the views, and of course, packets of Jim's Organic Weed. This proved very popular with a particular type of tourist. Nobody mentioned how it bypassed the Custom's Post in Little Didney when they returned. But as Len Bickerstaff was still the only Border Force guard, and he only worked Monday to Friday, nine to five, and was inclined to long tea breaks at the Smuggler's, trade flowed seamlessly. All paid for, of course, in the local currency, the moni, Watt's little ammonite disks.

Sam Goodenough had messaged me to tell me my bed had arrived a couple of days back, so I'd decided to take a break from working on the Scanlon's Rock constitution and get some fresh air. I'd been struggling with it non-stop for over a week, and I felt I'd earned a little R&R, even if it was only to travel to the mainland to collect an item of furniture.

I peered over the edge of the LARC, now re-christened the Leonidas, as we neared the Little Didney harbour. My tendency to seasickness and terror had largely calmed over the months, but was now severely tested by the rolling of the LARC. This thing could roll in an indoor swimming pool. As its primary function had been to transport a company of Royal Marines with their vehicles and kit, passenger comfort had never figured highly in the design specs.

As we approached, I was able to see the progress of the sea defence. It now extended out from the section of the harbour the bulldozer had trashed a few weeks ago, and reached out to what I guessed to be about halfway to where the sandbank had previously been. A good hundred metres out, although only about half the length seemed finished so far. I squinted against the sea-spray to see the work being done. I knew nothing about building methods, and even less about sea wall defences, but even I could see that this probably fell short of what it should be. Being able to compare the finished section, with the further reaches still under construction, the methods became clear. It seemed like Gawan had essentially been pushing lorry loads of quarry rocks into the sea, then tipping vast amounts of concrete over the top of them. Some smoothing of the top layer had been necessary to give access to the lorries carrying the next loads out. But apart from that, it all looked fairly hotch-potch, and resembled a Picnic chocolate bar which had been through a washing machine. A lonely cement truck trundled along the undulating surface, heading to its drop point at the far reach.

The Leonidas slid smoothly from sea to slipway with barely a rumble to indicate we were now running on wheels. We came to a halt at the special bay which had been built for passenger transfers. The front dropped open, and we all disembarked, filing straight past the Border Force Post with its signs demanding we report to the Port Authorities upon arrival. A group of outward-bound passengers waited by the barrier. A disparate group. A gathering of twitchers, with binoculars and flasks of tea at the ready, a couple of families with children and a mingling of hippy types.

I waved at Officer Len Bickerstaff as we passed. He seemed slightly disappointed that nobody had gone his way. He gave a small shrug and headed back into his Portakabin.

I made my way along to the Smuggler's Arms to collect my bed from Goodenough's storeroom. For this early hour, the place was already busy. Mostly local, but quite a few visitors. I spotted Tiggy sitting with a coffee and a newspaper.

She looked up as I approached. "Hiya, thought you'd got lost."

"The Leonidas was late leaving. I can't believe how busy it is."

"I know." She scanned the room. "As Minister For Tourism, I'd like to be able to take credit for this. But sadly, I think it's more to do with Jim's Happy Farm, as he calls it."

Sam Goodenough spotted me and came over. I half hoped he'd come to take my order for coffee and toast, but no. "You come to get yer bed out of my shed?" he greeted.

"That was the plan," I said.

"Good job too. Losin' me money."

"I'll collect it later this morning, before the Leonidas goes back. Any chance of a coffee and two slices of toast?" I glanced at Tiggy. "Do you want anything?"

"Depends what you're offering." She gave a coy grin, then, "But in the meantime, I'll have another coffee, thanks."

"Might be awhile," Goodenough muttered, scribbling on his pad. "Bit stacked up in the kitchen. Chocolate cake, of all things. Who wants to eat chocolate cake this time of a mornin'?" His mumbles faded as he headed off back to the kitchen.

"Chocolate cake?" I looked at Tiggy.

"And fudge, apparently," Tiggy said. "Mrs Pomfrey has sold right out of her homemade fudge. She's got her mixing machine going round the clock."

"It really is busy." I spotted a crowd at the bar, laughing loudly. "What's going on there?"

Tiggy twisted in her seat. "Oh, that's Gawan in there somewhere. He of the bulldozer. Busy buying rounds for everybody. He's obviously come into some serious money from this contract. He's always popular when he's got money. Never lasts long with him, though. What he doesn't spend on booze and gambling, he tends to squander on his mates until it's all gone."

"I'm just going to be nosy." I wandered over to the bar with as much nonchalance as I could pack into a two-metre stroll.

I sidled up to the bar, as near as I could, without raising suspicion. I fixed my gaze on the row of coloured liqueur bottles on a shelf behind the bar and tuned my ear to the conversation going on. My trigger word, 'concrete', came within two minutes.

"With the deal I got on the concrete," Gawan said, "I'm gonna make enough on this job to buy my own machines. Won't have to rent 'em no more."

"If you have any concrete left over, my drive needs a surfacing," a man in a Burberry flat cap said.

"Be plenty left," said Gawan. "Odd though, the way they just rang me up out'a the blue like that."

"Who was that then? Readycrete?" somebody asked.

"Nah, Crumblee's Discount Concrete and Tarmac, it was. Never 'eard of 'em before, but quarter the price of Readycrete, so I ain't gonna argue, am I?"

"Yes, sir. What can I get you?" A girl suddenly appeared behind the bar in front of me.

"Um." I panicked, and my eyes raked the shelf in front of me. A bright orange bottle with what looked like a red dragon on the label caught my eye. "Two of those…" I squinted. "Fireballs," I said.

She picked the bottle off the shelf and poured two generous glasses. "Anything else?"

"No, thanks. Oh, yes toast." I paid and took them back to our table.

Tiggy studied the drink as I placed one in front of her. "That's not coffee and toast," she said.

"I noticed that too," I said.

She took a sip and flinched. "Tastes like Christmas."

"It's a Fireball, apparently."

She took another sip. "I can see why. So, not that I'm in any way ungrateful, but why?"

"I was going to do some subtle conversation with Gawan about—"

"Practising for your new career as a P.I.?" Tiggy interrupted. She smiled and lifted an eyebrow.

"Not really. Well, maybe. But anyway, he was so full of himself that all I needed to do was listen in. And then the girl behind the bar surprised me by asking what I wanted, and—"

"Always comes as a shock when they do that."

"Are you going to keep interrupting me?" I scolded.

"Sorry." She touched her lips with a finger. "I'll stay silent."

"Well, I didn't want to engage in conversation with her..." I paused and watched Tiggy. She touched her lips again and shook her head, all the while trying to hide a smile which threatened to spread. I continued, "... In case it drew attention. So I just pointed to the first thing I saw. Fireball."

"And what did you find out on your Secret Squirrel undercover mission?"

"That Gawan has just ordered a huge load of very cheap concrete from a very dodgy company with a reputation for supplying dangerously poor quality product."

She eyed me carefully. "That's unfortunate. For him, anyway. I wonder how they knew he was in the market?" She studied me like a cat watching a mouse.

"Hmm, I wonder."

"Toast," Goodenough announced as he closed on our table. "It's a bit wonky. Had to do me own slicing, we've run right out of sliced. Everybody wants toast, all of a sudden."

I noticed Tiggy still staring at me. "What?" I asked.

"Nothing." She smiled. "On a separate subject entirely, why do you think they decided to rebuild this sea defence now?"

I broke a piece of toast and munched as I gathered my thoughts. "Clearly, they want to bring the coastline back to where it was before the storms of

1987. That would effectively put Scanlon's Rock back within the twelve-mile limit. The question is, why are they so keen on the island not being independent? And that, well that depends on what that survey vessel, the Xerxes, found in the channel. My guess is shale gas, possibly oil, but whatever, if Scanlon's Rock remains independent, the UK loses the rights for further exploration, or the granting of expensive drilling licences." I took a paper napkin and dabbed toast crumbs and butter from my fingers. "And, I wouldn't mind betting there are one or two high ranking civil servants, or even ministers, who have second jobs as consultants with Valdez Oil."

"Can you prove it?" Tiggy asked.

"No, not easily. I did have a go, but Valdez Oil is a maze of shell companies and offshore entities. It would take an army of lawyers an age to sort out. Did you know there are more than half-a-million companies registered in the British Virgin Islands alone, yet it has a total population of about the same as Penzance?"

"That's insane."

"Maybe it'll all come out one day in another Panama Papers leak who knows. Meantime, we have to keep ourselves out of the clutches of Whitehall until the UN recognises us."

"So, what next?"

"Next, we go rescue my bed, which is being held hostage in a shed out the back."

We finished our toast and coffee, then Goodenough led us through behind the bar. We came into a small yard where his shed backed on to a narrow alley running behind the businesses fronting the harbour.

He dragged open a wooden door. "There you go. Light switch is on the right, but mind the wires. Rats have been at the insulation again."

My tentative fingers found the switch, and despite myself, I closed my eyes as I flicked it on. A forty-watt light bulb fought bravely against the gloom. I'd expected my bed to be in sections, as it had been shipped, so seeing it fully assembled, and made up with sheets, pillows and a floral quilt, came as a bit of a shock.

"Why is my bed all made up?" I asked.

"Had to make use of the space it's been taking up," Goodenough answered. "Can't have a bed sat there doin' nothing, not when I got paying customers wantin' somewhere to kip."

"You've been taking bed-and-breakfast in this shed? In my bed that I was paying you to store for me?" I scanned the shed. Stacked boxes filled one wall and cobwebs decorated the corners. A wooden workbench, now covered in a lace cloth, doubled as a dressing table. The remains of an old Chinese rug attempted to disguise an oil stain on the concrete floor. "And somebody actually paid you to sleep here?"

"Nothin' else in town. Can't turn away people in need. I'm like that publican in the bible, always room in my inn."

"For a price," Tiggy muttered.

"The least you can do is give me a hand to dismantle it again," I said to Goodenough.

"Love to, only I've got this back. Doctor said it's too much bendin' and liftin'. Easy enough though, there's a toolbox under the dressing table. I'll go make up yer bill."

"It is a nice bed though," Tiggy said, as we watched Goodenough go.

I thought about the strange people I'd seen in the bar this morning. "Not sure I want to sleep on it now."

"Don't be silly." She crouched down and dragged an old, rusty toolbox out from under the so-called dressing table. "I'm sure we can think of a way to reclaim its virtue." She handed me an adjustable spanner.

After separating the bed into its component pieces, we carted them through the bar to the LARC boarding gate. On my last journey, Goodenough called me from behind the bar. "Here's yer bill," he said, sliding a handwritten sheet of paper to me.

'To the storage of bedroom furniture for three days, £25.'

I took the pen from his hand, and added, 'Less £25 for the rental of bedroom furniture = £0'. I slid it back to him and locked his eyes. He grunted, screwed up the paper, and tossed it into a bin behind him.

The late spring sunshine had brought an influx of visitors wanting to get to the island, forcing the Leonidas to increase its runs to two a day. We had to prop the bed pieces against the side of the craft, rather than laying it flat. Fortunately, the vessel was well equipped with lashing points. The speed with which the visitor flow had taken off had meant no time to make any concessions for passenger comfort, and we were still essentially in a functional, military vehicle. The fold-down bench seats racked along the sides were limited, and most had to stand. And given that the beast had been designed for hauling heavy equipment, not humans, it wasn't exactly Royal Caribbean.

As we approached Pirate's Cove, the Leonidas swooped out in a wide arc, and a voice drew everybody's attention to the Raven, still moored just outside the bay.

"Please see our newest attraction, the SRN Raven," a voice spoke across the tinny loudspeakers. "A veteran of the Falklands war. You can book your guided tour of this historic vessel on board here at a special discount."

"That's you?" I asked Tiggy.

Tiggy nodded. "Jim got me to record it a few days ago. Said I sounded suitably seafaring and touristy. My guess is, I was the only person he could get to do it."

A small queue formed at the front of the boat for tickets. "I wonder why Jim never told me he was going to do this?" I asked.

"Oh, I don't know. Maybe it's because he knew what you'd say?"

"Which is?"

"About twenty-five pages, verbatim, of Health and Safety statistics, listing every possible thing which could go wrong with the idea?"

"Hmm, okay. Fair point. But it's really asking for trouble to have tourists—"

"Aaaannd, here we go," Tiggy interrupted.

I stopped talking and just watched the beach approach in silence.

The Leonidas slid out of the water and clambered up onto the beach without a break in its momentum. It shuddered to a halt, and the front dropped down. A voice yelled. "Pirate's Cove. All out here for trips to the SNR Raven or stay onboard for Paradise City."

Once those leaving had disembarked, the front lifted, and we climbed the side of the cliff and onto the top fields. Ten minutes later, we arrived outside the Ocean View Tearooms and Bar. Once more, the front dropped down and people filed out.

We waited until everybody had gone, then lifted out the bits of my bed and carried them into my Wikihouse.

"We'll just dump it all in the bedroom," I said. "I'll put it together later. I want to have a quick chat with Jim about the Raven."

"I'm sure he's looking forward to that."

I found Jim signing autographs and posing for selfies outside the Ocean View Tearooms and Bar. I waited until the crowds cleared a bit, then persuaded him to join me along the clifftop for a chat. He didn't need much persuasion, as it gave him a chance to have a smoke out of the public eye. Not that he was worried about being seen smoking cannabis, it was more that he didn't want to be hassled for free samples.

"How's the constitution going?" Jim asked as we walked.

"I've got the basics down. Although, I'm having a little trouble really nailing down the concept of a republican monarchy. I was wondering if—"

"How about we just move on to the bit where you've told me lots of complicated stuff and I've said, I understand it all, and then you make a suggestion, and I say, 'yes', then you go work out the detail?"

"But… I suppose. I was also going to talk to you about the Raven—"

"Isn't it great? People love it. You should see the way the kids slide down those stairwells between decks."

"Yes, do you think it's altogether wise letting them do that? I mean, they could fall and break something, and then where would you be?"

"The thing's forty years old and built like… I was going to say a tank, but that's a bit silly, isn't it? Looks nothing like my tank. Built like a battleship. They're not likely to break anything. Nothing that matters, anyway."

"I was thinking more in terms of bones or skulls."

"Ah, I see, yes. I'll tell you what, how about you work up a disclaimer, or waiver, or whatever it is? We'll get them to sign that first. Good catch."

"I thought you were going to use it as a flagship or something," I said. "I had no idea you were going to turn it into a theme park."

He pulled thoughtfully on his joint and gazed out over the sea. "I was," he said, through a cloud of smoke. "But I had no idea how much fuel those things use. Had Salty come out to have a look. I was going to get him to give it a whizz around Plymouth harbour, give the navy boys a fright, but he said there was nowhere near enough fuel. He reckons it'll use fifty gallons just to turn it round. And, I have no idea how to fill it up again. I can't just pull in to the local BP station and ask for five gallons of four-star."

"I did wonder about that when you said you'd bought it."

"But what was I supposed to do? Somebody offers me a warship for less than the price of a '59 Gibson Les Paul?"

"Buy the guitar instead?"

"I've already got one of those. Mind you, I'd like to get my hands on a '62 Strat. Anyway, I've got another idea."

"Oh, good."

"You'll like this one. I'm going to do paintball games on it. Two teams, invaders and defenders. Or pirates. Maybe laser guns, rather than paintball. Less mess. Hey, you haven't seen the President's Grotto yet, have you?"

"I didn't know there was one."

"It's new. Come on, we'll take the tank."

We found the tank behind Jim's house, and Jim clambered up, then dropped down inside. "You have to sit up top," he said.

"But I can't drive this thing," I said.

"No, I'm driving it from down here. You just keep a lookout."

"What am I looking out for?" I asked.

"Mostly to make sure we don't drop off the side of the cliff. Can't see sod all from down here."

The engine spluttered into life, chucking a cloud of black smoke out of the rear end. I glanced down at Jim. He squinted through the small window, a lever in each hand. The machine jolted, like a train had just rear-ended us, then we snaked forwards, following a zig-zag movement for a short distance while Jim brought his levers into harmony.

"You watching out?" he yelled above the noise.

"Yes. Little bit to the left... No, the other left... that's the one. Now straight... Straight. That's not straight."

"Have you ever tried driving one of these? It's like steering a double-decker bus from inside a letter box."

"Not something I've had much experience in," I said. "More straight. Okay, you're getting a bit close to the cliff edge on the left, so go right a bit."

The tank veered violently to the left, kicking topsoil over the edge of the cliff. "Stop! Stop!" I yelled.

We jerked to a halt, and Jim popped up out of the hatch and peered over the edge. "You said right," he said.

"Yes, but you went left."

"I pushed the right lever. Why would it go left if I pushed the right lever?"

"I don't know," I said. "Have you ever driven a tank before?"

"I've got to bronze level on Tank Commander."

"I'm guessing that's a video game?"

"They're very accurate. They use similar to train tank crews now, you know."

"Really?" I shook my head, then squinted down into the machine. Two levers sat either side of the driver's seat, no steering wheel. "I'm guessing each lever controls one side," I said. "Bit like the levers on Tiggy's boat. Increase the power on the right side lever, and the boat turns left. It's probably the same with the tracks on this thing."

Jim waved a cloud of smoke to one side and stuck his head back into the interior. Then he came back out and peered over the edge at the tracks. "I think you might be onto something here. I'll give it a go. Right to the left, and left to the right."

"You don't need me up here for this," I said and jumped down onto solid ground. "I'll come back onboard when you're clear of the cliff edge."

"Coward," Jim said.

"Maybe reverse it, rather than trying to steer it?" I suggested.

"I don't think it's got reverse. I couldn't find anything which said 'R'. Maybe tanks don't have reverse?"

"It must have. What about pulling both levers back, like on Tiggy's boat?"

Jim appeared to go away while he thought about that. "Cool," he said after a moment. "You stand here and yell loudly if I start going the wrong way. It's difficult to see from down there."

"Are you sure this is a good idea? How about we leave it here until we find somebody who knows how these things work?"

"You worry too much." He slid back inside, and the engine revved. It gave a little jolt backwards, then stopped. "How was that?" his voice called.

"That was right," I yelled.

"Your right or my right?"

"No, I meant you did it right, it went backwards."

His head popped out of the hatch again and he looked around. "Backwards?"

I nodded. "Yes."

"Cool, so that's how it works. Who'd've thought? Hop in."

"I'll just wait here a minute to see you back safely."

He disappeared again. The engine revved, and the tank hurtled backwards about twenty metres before coming to a skewed halt. Jim's head popped out and stared around, like a meerkat checking for predators. When he saw the ground he'd put between the tank and the clifftop, he smiled and said, "Come on then."

I clambered back up the tank and settled in one of the top seats. The engine noise increased, and we wriggled our way towards Watt's lighthouse.

The noise of our approach caught the attention of a handful of tourists ambling around outside the lighthouse. Hands pointed, children stood wide-eyed, and cameras followed our coming. Jim stopped outside the low wall which surrounded the area. Just as well, as the gap was not much wider than the tank itself, and I didn't trust Jim's bronze level Tank Commander credentials.

As we dismounted, a couple of kids started climbing up on it. I tried to dissuade them, but Jim shushed me, telling me to let them have fun.

The ground floor of the lighthouse thronged with people, albeit in an orderly queue which wound round the room and headed up the staircase. We pushed our way through to a mixture of complaints or requests for autographs in about equal proportions. At the top, in the light room itself, where Watt's original cannabis farm had been, several tables and chairs had been set in a circle around the old light in the centre. Groups of people sat at the tables drinking tea, which was supplied by a girl in a white apron and white hat.

Watt sat on the gold throne I'd given Jim, behind an old oak table. A pile of papers littered the table and Watt was balancing a child on his knee as he wrote on one of the sheets. A pair of proud parents flanked the child, and many photographs were being snapped.

Watt finished whatever he was writing, stuffed the piece of paper in the child's hands, then lifted him to the floor where the parents promptly scooped him up. The next child shuffled forwards for Watt's attention.

"What's going on?" I asked Jim, as I watched Watt hoisting the next child onto his lap.

"Tea and presidential honours with the President." He unconsciously picked a ready-rolled joint from his shirt pocket and slotted it between his lips.

I frowned and shook my head, nodding to the family groups hovering around. He took the hint and returned it to the pocket.

"Honours?" I asked.

"Yeah, the kids get to be made Junior Knights, and get a presidential medal of honour, and the parents can be full Knights of the Suspender. Then they get a cup of tea and a toy seal so they can tell all their mates they had tea with a real-life president. Hundred quid a go, and we can't keep up with it. You need to put this in our constitution."

"That's not really what a constitution is for. That's to deal with the basic laws and principles of a state, rather than—"

"Yeah, yeah, yeah," Jim interrupted. "That's the trouble with the world, too much stuck in history. We're *making* history, not doing it all over again like… like…" He struggled for a comparison.

"Like countries that do it all over again?" I offered.

"Yeah." His eyes widened, and he nodded. "Exactly. There you go. I knew you understood. We're going to do it different. Our constitution can be whatever we want it to be. So, add the bit about Junior Knights and tea with the President. Oh, and a bit about the weed farm as our state export."

"I'll include it." I had a feeling that the constitution was going to be a lot bigger job than I'd expected.

"I'll probably have a bit more for you later. I've had this idea about a national anthem, but Stringy's back in rehab again, so we haven't been able to work out the riff yet."

"I'll allocate a section for that."

He patted his shirt pocket where the joint hid. "Now, I've got to slip outside a minute. All these ideas make my brain fizz."

# ~ CHAPTER TWENTY-THREE ~

"PLEASE HOLD FOR SIR OLIVER Frogmorton."

I stared at my phone and wished I could reach down into it and strangle the pompous twit who thought it a good idea to instigate a phone call, then put the recipient on hold as a display of self-superiority.

Instead, I just hit the red button to terminate the call, and returned to my cooking. I'd promised to cook supper for Tiggy tonight and I needed to learn how to make macaroni cheese from scratch. It wasn't going well, as YouTube kept playing adverts in the middle of the critical bit of the cheese sauce making bit and I'd already burnt one batch. I measured out the butter and flour once more and I'd just put it on the heat when my phone rang again.

I lifted the phone to my ear and continued to tickle flour into the bowl. "John Cabot."

"Please hold for Sir Oliver Frogmorton."

I clicked 'End' once more and left a floury fingerprint on my screen. I'd hardly returned my attention to the job in hand when the phone bleeped once more.

"John Cabot."

"Cabot?" Froggy's voice greeted.

"Frogmorton," I returned.

"Hmmph. What's this I hear about you selling titles?"

"Did you want one?" I added what I thought looked about 325 millilitres of milk to the bowl. "We're doing a discount on lords at the moment. It would go well with your knighthood." I whisked at the mixture.

"You can't go round selling titles, it makes a mockery of the whole thing. It devalues the sterling service given by loyal, and humble, servants of the Crown."

"*Your* Crown, not my Crown anymore. Besides, your chums started it by selling titles to Russian oligarchs and party donors. We're just more democratic about it." I turned up the heat under my mixture and squinted at the screen to see what setting YouTube was suggesting. What on earth is electric mark five in gas?

"Listen, Cabot, it's been decided that your little island can become a British Overseas Territory. Subject, of course, to certain criteria being met."

"And the advantage to us is what?" I stirred at the gloop in the saucepan and wondered if it was meant to look like that.

"Industry, trade. You can host certain companies who... let's say... have a need for anonymity, and favourable tax treatment, yet still retain close links with the UK."

"A bit like British Virgin Islands, only with easier access?"

"It seems like we are on the same page."

"We're not even in the same book, but I'll have to put it to the First Minister. Hang on, I'll ask him."

I silenced the microphone, then rewound the video. More adverts. Back to the phone. "Sorry to keep you." Video resumed but went back to the beginning, not helpful. Phone on again. "You still there?" I asked.

"Yes."

"Sorry, the First Minister says no. You have a nice day now." I closed the call and tried to extract my spoon from the strange mess in the bottom of the pan. The pan came up with the spoon. That didn't look right at all.

~ * ~ * ~ * ~

"I THOUGHT YOU WERE MAKING macaroni cheese?" Tiggy said, watching me dishing the Chinese food from the containers.

"I just thought you'd like Chu Chi Goong prawns. Lin Chao made it especially. He doesn't usually do Thai food, but for a special occasion..." I caught the look in her eye.

"So, what went wrong with the macaroni cheese?" she asked.

"I may have underestimated the nuances required for that particular dish."

"The sauce went lumpy, then?"

"Lumpier than I thought you deserved to witness. I may have given you a slightly optimistic expectation of my cooking abilities. You see, when I cook for myself, which is rare, it's usually these menus-in-a-box. You know, the things with all the ingredients arrive in little plastic envelopes along with an idiot's guide in pictures. Even then... well... let's say you dodged a bullet there."

Tiggy smiled and emptied the bag of prawn crackers into a bowl. "How goes the constitution?"

"I fear it's going to be an ongoing project. Jim keeps adding things. His latest, is he wants to ban the shuffle option on all music playing devices that are brought to the island."

"That's very specific."

"He thinks it's the work of the devil. Also, no pictures of the Kardashians, jeans which hang down round the knees, and country and western music. He was particularly firm about the country and western music. Is that enough rice? I think I may have over-ordered."

"Plenty, thanks." Tiggy started into her meal. "Mmm, it's good. Have you seen the sea wall lately? I can't believe how quickly it's going up."

"No, I've been busy setting up standard forms and paperwork. I've got the passport all designed now, ready for printing. The bank is a little bit more complicated, but, after long video calls with an old pal in the Treasury, I think we have the basis for a formal currency. It's just whether we stick with the physical moni disks for the moment, or dive straight into fungible tokens, that's banknotes, or whatever. How far has it got?"

"I'd say it's not far off the full length of where the sandbank reached. Not that I remember it that well. I was just a kid when the storms took it."

"That means we'll be hearing from London soon, then. Probably demanding we give up our secession, as they'll claim we're now within the twelve-mile limits again."

"You really think that's what this sea defence thing was all about?" Tiggy asked.

"Absolutely. I was hoping it would take longer to build. He's using substandard concrete, but I don't know how long before it fails. Or even if it's likely to. It's not an area I know much about."

"Really?" Tiggy looked at me in mock horror. "I'm sure there's a spreadsheet on it somewhere." She paused as another thought occurred to her. "And, how exactly do you know he's using substandard concrete?"

"Well... it's possible there was a leak about the awarding of a construction contract by the Environment Agency... and erm... subsequently, it's just possible that a known rogue supplier of substandard concrete came to hear of this and... well... knowing Gawan's proclivity for doing things on the cheap... and... How're the prawns?"

"Lovely. Tell me more about concrete rogues."

As we ate, I brought her up to date on my digging around into the tangle of offshore companies and ministers with special interests in what was happening around the island.

"Do you think I should tell Jim?" I asked.

"That's a difficult one, you know what he's like. I'm in two minds on that. He could demand to speak to the King, or he could just sit back and smoke another joint. He might even decide to drive his tank up to the Houses of Parliament."

"That's three minds."

"Don't you start with me." She wagged a scolding finger. "You've done well so far this evening. Don't spoil your chances."

"I'll do the washing up," I said. "Would you like another glass of wine?"

~ \* ~ \* ~ \* ~

I KNEW IT WAS A mistake the moment the words left my mouth.

"You mean, they're extending England?" Jim waved a cloud of smoke away from around his head, as if that might make my words clearer.

"It wasn't quite what I meant, but close enough," I said.

"They can't do that. Can they?" He paused and raised his eyes upwards, a good sign he's usually about to come up with some crazy plan. "I've got a plan," he said.

"I thought that might happen."

"We dig away the same amount from the island. That way, they'll be the same distance apart. Genius, huh?"

"How do we dig away that much?" I asked.

"We just get Gawan and his bulldozer. He's far better at knocking things down than building stuff anyway. Tell him that what he digs off the north of the island, he can dump on the south. That way, the island stays the same size. Get hold of him. He can start now."

"Only one small flaw in that plan," I ventured.

"Always one. No wonder you never got to be head of the Civil Service, always looking for the Nazis, never the Holy Grail—"

"Actually, it was the Ark of the Covenant the Nazis wanted, not the Holy Grail. When Indiana—"

"And there you go again. Shush…" He held a finger to my lips. "That's better. Now tell me what's wrong with *this* idea?"

"If we keep taking a bit of the north, then adding it to the south, the whole island is going to end up in France."

He studied me for a minute, then a huge grin spread across his face. "Good point, don't want to end up in Calais."

"Umm…" I hesitated.

"What? What is it?" Jim demanded.

"It'd be Roscoff, not Calais. Calais is about five hundred—"

"Still France though?"

"Still France," I confirmed.

"Okay, no more geography lessons. I've got tour managers to do the geography. Besides, I've got a better plan."

"Oh good."

"We get the Raven, and we blow Gawan's giant rockery penis out of the sea."

"Oddly, that's where I thought you'd go first. And I've just lost ten quid to Tiggy."

~ * ~ * ~ * ~

THE CREW OF THE RAVEN assembled by the shore, waiting for Tiggy to ferry us out. Although, crew was probably an optimistic description. The Commodore stood proud in his peaked hat and white blazer, every bit the old sea dog he aspired to be. Branok and Jake stood chatting, staring out at the Raven in the far reach of the bay. At least those three had some idea what they were doing. The rest of us, not so much. Shaun and Shawn swapped a joint between themselves and skimmed stones into the surf, while Jim and I hovered, ankle deep in the surf, waiting to snag Tiggy's dinghy as it approached. I hadn't the faintest idea what either of us were doing there, save the fact that the Commodore had said the boat needed at least six people on board just to get it to move.

"I'm still pissed with your mate Gerry," Jim said.

"He's not my mate," I said. "He's my brother-in-law. And, to be honest, I think he's being unusually circumspect, given his occupation, by not selling you ammunition for the Raven."

"Humph, but it would be far easier if we just blasted it to hell."

"And just how long do you think it would be until you find yourself staring at a fleet of Royal Navy warships? This way, everybody will just think it's failed concrete."

"You've got to admit though, even you, that blowing it up would be much

~ 268 ~

more fun." Jim waded a bit further into the surf as Tiggy's boat rode a small wave and grounded.

The others joined us, and we all squashed ourselves into a dinghy which had been designed for five, at best. It certainly never took into account the size of people like Branok or Jake. The little outboard motor pushed us bravely back through the surf, and we puttered over to the waiting frigate.

So far, I'd managed to avoid setting foot on board this thing, or indeed, any warship. At close-up, the condition of the boat did nothing to allay my growing panic. Rust patches covered the greater area of the hull, interspersed by multiple sheets of steel welded over signs of the worst of the damage. Somebody, at some point, had painted some red, blue, and green stripes near the bow, in a vague representation of the Gambian flag. Unsettlingly, a scattering of what looked like bullet holes traced a line across the upper part of the bow.

A rusty set of steps hung from the deck above us, culminating in a small platform just above the lapping water. Tiggy tied her mooring line to the steps, then held on to a handrail to stop the dinghy swinging out. Branok and Jake stepped onto the platform and headed up the steps like it was a staircase at home. Shawn and Shaun followed with equal ease.

"Go on then," Tiggy commanded. "It'll be dark soon, and we want to be there while we can still see what we're doing."

I hesitated to see if Jim wanted to go first, but he seemed more interested in poking at a particularly large patch of rust on the hull. "Just needs a lick of paint," he said, as a large flake dropped off with a little splash. "And some filler."

I navigated the steps with the same care I'd give a staircase to the top deck of a London red bus whilst the driver was negotiating Marble Arch during rush hour. Only this was much bigger, and slippery. And with certain death below.

Once up top, I took a moment to catch my breath and enjoyed the view. The island looked quite different from up here, compared to onboard the '300'. I turned my attention to the superstructure of the ship, then wished I hadn't. Some signs of battleship grey still survived, but rust was the predominant colour. More steel plates were welded at random places, and piles of miscellaneous lumps of metal scattered the deck. I felt a rumble beneath my feet. Somebody had managed to get the engines going, and the noise travelled up through my legs.

I heard a shout from above and looked up. The Commodore already stood on the small high deck just outside the bridge. He yelled something at me.

"I can't hear you," I yelled back.

He leaned over the guardrail and yelled again. "I want you up at the prow." He pointed towards the front of the boat.

"Okay," I yelled, and headed forwards, threading my way through old oil drums, cables and bits of abandoned pipework. As my knowledge of battleships was limited to the children's game with little plastic pegs, the Commodore had appointed me as chief pointer. With none of the ship's communication, radar, and navigation systems working, the only way of telling those doing the steering what lay in front, was either mobile phones or pointing. I was doing pointing.

I settled myself in the prow and gave the guardrail a firm yank. It seemed secure, but I wasn't going to take any chances.

Jim appeared just behind me. "Fancy giving it a Leonardo DiCaprio from Titanic? King of the World?" he asked. "Come on, you've got to, ain't you?"

"No." I shook my head. "I really haven't. And if you remember, it didn't turn out well for him?"

Jim clambered up onto the guardrail and braced himself forwards, arms wide. "Woo-hoo!" he yelled, his hair blowing behind him in the wind.

"More Kate Winslet, I think."

Just then, the ship gave another shudder, and Jim's foot slipped from the rail. He grabbed the top bar, stopping his headlong descent over the side.

"That was close," he said. "That could've been... whoops." The rail came away from the deck, and he held a large section of it in his hand.

I reached forward and grabbed the first part of him I could reach. My fingers closed hard around the collar of his denim shirt, and he wobbled briefly, then collapsed backwards onto the deck.

"Might need to get that fixed." He tossed the piece of railing to one side. "I'll ask Shaun, he does welding."

The engine noise increased, and I felt the deck tilting to one side. "Looks like we're off," I said. "I'm supposed to be pointing." I inched forwards and tentatively took hold of a remaining section of rail. I tugged at it, and it held.

"I'm gonna go find a shady spot for a smoke." Jim pulled himself upright on a pillar. "Do you want to join me?"

"No. Pointing." I pointed forwards to explain.

Jim shrugged and headed back towards the hatch.

I turned my attention to scanning the sea in front of us, and strained my eyes against the gathering gloom of evening. Apart from the deep rumbling coming up through the floor, and the sound of the sea, far below, splashing against the bow, I would have been hard-pressed to know we were moving.

I studied the view, or lack of, in front of me. Just grey. Everything grey, the same colour as the remaining sections of the original ship. I couldn't even make out where sea turned to sky.

"What are you doing up here?" I heard Tiggy's voice from behind me.

I turned, moving away from the gap in the guardrail as I did so. "Pointing," I said.

"Okay, but why?"

"The Commodore said as there was no navigation or radar, we had to rely on visuals to spot hazards."

"I see. But there's no need at the moment. Jake unhooked the satnav from the '300' so they've got that up on the bridge. Although you're right, when we get closer, it'll be down to human lookout."

"Oh, I wondered why nobody was watching me." I glanced up at the bridge.

"What happened here?" Tiggy nodded towards the gap in the guardrail.

"Jim, Titanic."

"Ah."

I peered down at the fluorescent surf ploughing against the bow. "It's very stable. I thought this would roll a lot more."

"That's only because the sea's so calm, and we're heading into the wind," Tiggy said. "The stabilisers aren't working, so if it were any rougher, we'd be bobbing like a plastic duck in a Jacuzzi."

"Eyes out," a shout came from above.

"Oh, looks like you're on," Tiggy said. "You'd better get pointing. And I need to get up there. I'm supposed to be the communications between bridge, aft steering room, and engine room. Have fun." She took my hand and gave a quick squeeze, looked around, then sneaked a brief kiss.

I returned my attention, trying to find anything in front of us that would be best avoided.

My eyes soon tired of the strain and started presenting me with shadowy shapes which disappeared by blinking. I closed my eyes and massaged them with my fingers. Peering forwards once more, I noticed one particular shadow persisted. Exactly in front of us a slightly greyer line than the grey of the sea, spread out across my field of vision.

"Ooh, ooh," I yelled, pointing furiously as I did so. "Lookout, big thing. There." I pointed again, looking up to see if anybody had noticed me.

"What's going on?" Jim's voice asked from behind me.

"Something there, can you see it?" I asked. "I think it's the sea defence wall."

"That's a relief," Jim said. "I thought it was a giant sea snake."

"A giant sea snake?" I twisted to look at him. "That's your go-to?"

"It's this new weed." He held up his joint to show me. "I got the seeds from this guy who—"

"Can we focus on this?" I looked up again. Still nobody paying attention. "You stay here, watch the giant sea snake. I'm going up there."

"Hang on," said Jim, peering into the dusk. "What's that? There's a Decepticon out there, on the snake."

"Decepticon? What on earth is a Decepticon?"

"They're the sworn enemies of the Transformers. Have you never played Dark of the Moon?"

I squinted out towards where he pointed. "It's a bulldozer," I said. "Gawan must have left it on the sea defence."

"You sure?"

"Maybe that particular crop is best left to mature a while longer?" I had no idea how these things worked.

Jim looked at the joint in his hand. "No, it's good."

I paused, wondering if I should continue to try to dissuade him from smoking that stuff while on a battleship. I decided no. "Just stay there and watch the... whatever it is you're watching." I turned and ran for the steps leading up to the upper decks.

Dark, wet, slippery steps. Just as well we're not bouncing around, I consoled myself, just as the ship twisted under my feet. I slipped, but luckily, had hands on both handrails. I held tight while my feet flailed, looking for purchase. The ship bucked again, and the engine noise increased to a roar. At a slightly slower pace, I resumed my climb, landing on the platform at the side of the bridge, just as the Commodore opened the door.

"What are you doing up here?" he asked. "We nearly ran into that thing. In my day, you'd be up on a charge."

"I couldn't make anybody hear." I followed him into the bridge. "What's going on?"

"Blasted thing's further out than I thought."

A sudden shock through the ship and a loud creaking noise. The Commodore froze, as if waiting for something even more dramatic to happen.

Nothing did.

"We hit the sea defence?" I asked after a while.

"I thought that was the general idea? That's what I was given to understand?"

"Yes, but I was expecting something a bit more controlled." I thought about the rough panels of steel welded over sections of the hull. "Are we okay?"

"Take more than a little bump like that to disturb this old girl. When she was down in the Falklands, we had an Exocet come through here..." He cast his gaze around the bridge. "... right about where you're standing. Didn't go off, fortunately. Went straight through that wall over there." He pointed to the far wall of the bridge.

I studied the wall, wondering if the different colour paint meant anything.

The door opened and Tiggy came in. "Everything all right?"

"We hit Gawan's sea defence," I said.

"Any damage?"

"No, we're all okay."

"I meant to the sea defence," Tiggy said. "Any damage to that?"

"Oh, I don't know. We'll need to get a spotlight on it."

We felt another jolt, and the floor shifted under me.

"She's just swinging round," said the Commodore. He picked up his walkie-talkie and clicked a button. "Can you hear me down there?"

A buzzy, crackling noise came from the little device, then the Commodore said, "Stop. Stop. All stop."

The engine noise subsided. A few minutes later, Shawn had rigged up a spotlight on the front of the boat and we had a clear view of the sea defence wall. The construction was a mess. Nothing to do with being hit by 5,000 tons of warship, it was just a mess. Random lumps of rock and what looked like general building rubble, mixed in a hotch-potch manner and all held together by over generous helpings of concrete. But there were no signs of any damage by the ship.

"It's not as big as I thought it would be," I said. I scanned the monstrosity. It climbed maybe only a metre above the water, though difficult to judge from up here. It looked about three metres wide, although it varied wildly, and gave the general impression of something somebody had just knocked down, rather than recently built.

As the spotlight scanned more of the construction, it became apparent that we'd come into contact with the newest section. Which probably explained why we hadn't realised it came out quite this far. Sat atop of the last completed part, Gawan's bulldozer graced the top like a mechanical hobgoblin staring out to sea.

"No damage," said Tiggy. "I thought it'd crumble away with just a nudge. Most of everything else he builds does."

"Can we hit it again?" Shawn asked. "Bit harder this time. Maybe take a run-up?"

"If we hit it too hard, we'll ride up over it," said the Commodore. "It's too low, and we'll tear the bottom out of the ship."

"What do we do then?" I asked.

The Commodore scanned the construction as the light moved across it. "There's a section there, a bit higher than the rest. If we can push up against that bit, we might get enough power to shift it." He clicked on his walkie-talkie. "Branok, are you there?" A garbled reply and the Commodore continued, "Dead slow, twenty degrees starboard rudder." More garbles, and the engines rumbled.

The ship moved smoothly at first, then a jolt. "Full ahead."

The engines rattled through the floor and the deck juddered. I took hold of a pillar and felt my heart going almost as fast as the beat of the engines. "Is it working?" I asked.

"Nothing yet."

The vibration continued for a moment, then I felt a huge thud reverberate through the whole ship. Everything swung violently to the left, and the floor tilted beneath me.

"What's happened?" I forced an unfelt calmness into my words.

"I don't know," the Commodore said. "Branok? Report."

I heard the words come through the little device this time. "Port engine's blown. Any idea if there are any working fire controls on this thing?"

"Fire?" I said. "That doesn't sound good. Should we call the fire brigade? Or the lifeboat? Is there a fire lifeboat?"

I felt Tiggy stroking my arm. "Shh, we're not sinking."

"But I heard him say fire. Fire's not good. Not on a ship. Have you never seen the Poseidon Adventure?"

"It's not going to sink. We still have a working engine. And even if it did sink, you see that lump of concrete out there?" She pointed to where the light shone on Gawan's sea defence.

I nodded.

"You could just step out onto that and walk back to Little Didney for a nice cup of tea and a rest."

"Ah. Yes. Although…"

"Although?"

I squinted out at the sea defence. "What happened to Gawan's bulldozer?"

"What?" Tiggy turned to look out. "Oh, it's gone. Commodore? What happened to the bulldozer? It was just there a minute ago."

The Commodore peered through the window. "We must have bumped it into the sea when we hit the wall."

"Gawan's not going to be best pleased," Tiggy said. "That's the second one he's dunked."

Jim appeared in the doorway. "Hey, guys, did you see that giant sea snake eat the yellow Decepticon?"

# ~ CHAPTER TWENTY-FOUR ~

THE RETURN JOURNEY IN THE Raven proved decidedly unpleasant. With only one functioning engine, progress was slow, and the sea had turned angry. We'd lost some manoeuvrability, which meant we were more of a victim to the vagaries of the waves. By the time we landed on the beach at Pirate's Cove, I'd lost my newfound, but very short-lived, bravado with all things watery.

I sat on the sand for a while, trying to persuade my stomach it didn't need to keep swirling, now we were on solid ground. It didn't believe me. Jim had offered to drive us back to Paradise City in the tank. I'd declined, and despite the walk in front of me, the thought of seven of us jammed in, and on that thing, was almost enough to pull my stomach inside out.

Tiggy had stayed with me, saying she needed the walk, but more likely, wanting to keep an eye on me.

"What now?" Tiggy asked.

I ventured into an upright position and checked my feet. "Now, we walk back," I said.

"No, I meant what now with the sea defence. It's obviously stronger than we thought, despite Gawan's dodgy concrete. Maybe we should consider Jim's plan?"

"What? Blowing it up?"

"Well, perhaps some strategically placed dynamite or something. Nothing huge."

"Have you been at Jim's new crop?"

"No. Maybe just a little. But that's nothing to do with it. If we don't get rid of that, the British Government will never let the island go. You said."

"I know, but we need something more subtle than explosives."

"Okay, how?" Tiggy challenged.

"I don't know. I've got this meeting with Marcel Dallemagne tomorrow. Let's see what comes up there." I glanced up at the moon, which had just risen above the cliff. "You fit? I'd like to get back home and into a nice warm bed while it's still worth it."

~ \* ~ \* ~ \* ~

THE MEETING WITH MARCEL DALLEMAGNE took place in the new Houses of the Holy, in reality, just another Wikihouse, but with a big meeting room at its centre. Jim had named the community house after a Led Zeppelin album, and it served as a parliament house as well as a potential general purpose space for group events.

Marcel arrived exactly eleven minutes late, and with a young woman who he introduced as Irina Werth, his PA. A very attractive looking young woman, with more legs than were necessary for a political PA.

"Apologies," Marcel said, as he settled at the round conference table. "I had to change clothes. I didn't realise the ferry over would be... what do we say? ... quite so rustic?"

"No worries," said Jim. "We're quite chilled here."

Marcel scanned us, taking in Jim, Watt, Tiggy, and me, all in our uniforms of stonewashed Levis and Scanlon's Rock sweatshirts. "Yes, I see. I feel slightly overdressed." He smiled and loosened his tie. "There, that feels better."

I remembered that feeling.

The door swung open and Jeeves shuffled in. He dropped a pair of six-packs of beer on the table with a, "There ya' go," and turned to leave.

"Hang on," Jim said. "This is a proper, official meeting here. A bit more class needed, come on."

"Yes, of course," Jeeves said. "Mea culpa. Do forgive my transgressions." He bent down by a wooden cabinet, fished out a roll of plastic glasses, and dropped them on the table. "Don't know what I was thinkin' of. I'll go and flagellate myself at once."

Jim smiled and looked at Marcel. "He's the life and soul of parties, though."

Marcel watched as Jeeves left the room, then "Hmm, so, to business. As we previously discussed, the EU are of the opinion that your nascent territory is at a critical juncture in its developmental trajectory, and given that, and subject to ratification by the council, we feel that a closer relationship between the Union and your administration would be advantageous to all parties. With that objective to the forefront, we propose an exchange of delegations to facilitate efficient channels of communication and cooperation between us." He sat back and smiled around the table, as if expecting applause.

Silence hung in the air for a moment, then Watt asked, "What's he on wobblin' about? I didn't catch a bleedin' word 'o that."

"He's French," Jim offered, as if that explained everything.

"Belgian," I corrected.

"Pardon," said Marcel. "What did he say?" Looking at Watt. "I did not understand. What language is that?"

"It is English," I said, glancing at Watt. "But it's a strong south west dialect."

"Oh, ladi-da," Watt mumbled under his breath.

Jim leaned towards me. "I think you're going to have to act as translator here. Seeing as how I don't understand what he's talking about neither."

"Really?" I looked from Watt to Marcel to Jim. All three shrugged in unison and shook their heads. "For goodness' sake. Right, Marcel was explaining that he's proposing an EU, Scanlon's Rock, joint strategy for international cultural and trade relations which would create a strategic partnership between us and the EU."

Jim studied me for a moment, then said, "Nope, still not getting it." He looked at Watt. "How about you?"

Watt shook his head. "Don't mean nothin' to me. It's all attle, that's what it is."

I looked around the faces, held my arms out, palm upwards. "I give up."

Tiggy pressed her hand on my arm. "Let me try. Marcel is suggesting the EU has an office on the island, so we can have meetings about stuff when we need."

"Why didn't he say that?" Jim asked.

"He did," I said.

"Do we get an office in Paris, then?"

"Brussels," Marcel said. "But yes, I'm sure if you want, that can be arranged."

"With a guard outside and a posh car? A black one, bulletproof?"

"If you like."

"What about taxes and stuff? We don't want none of that. Or rules on what we can grow. If we want to grow stuff."

"Ah yes, I noticed your... um, farm, on the way here. We can be flexible. For example, you can apply for full membership of the European Economic Area, the EEA, like say, France or Germany. Or the European Free Trade Agreement, the EFTA, which is similar, but more favoured by Norway and Iceland as well as Switzerland, but of course, although they're not actually part of the EEA, they are part of the Schengen free movement area, unlike Ireland, who are in the Eurozone, and the EEA, but not Schengen. They also opted out of NATO but remain in the EFTA. Then there's Austria, who is in the Eurozone and the EEA but not NATO. Or, you could favour the Polish option where they are in the EEA, EFTA, and NATO but not the Eurozone, although they are in Schengen." He folded his hands on the table and smiled.

All eyes turned to me.

I looked at Tiggy. She shook her head. "I've got nothing," she said.

I turned to Marcel. "Let's say, just for the moment, that you have a simple delegation here. Nothing else at this stage. Would that still allow the EU to recognise our independent status?"

"Certainly," Marcel said. "On the proviso, that your claim that the island is indeed outside of the UK's territorial waters is confirmed when our hydrographic surveyors complete their own study."

~ * ~ * ~ * ~

AFTER MARCEL HAD LEFT THE island, we reconvened in the Dragon Palace for a sort of celebratory meal.

"Of course," I said, "this will only work if that sea defence is not there. But the problem is, it is there."

"Perhaps we could bribe them?" suggested Jim.

"Give it another whack wiv yer battleship," Watt offered.

"The port engine's blown," said Tiggy. "Besides, I don't think there's enough fuel to get her out there and back again."

"Bribe, it is then." Jim leaned back in his seat and picked up his bottle of Tsingtao beer.

"You can't bribe an EU hydrographic surveyor," I said. "For a start, it's unethical, and it would be sure to come to light. And anyway, there'd be satellite imagery available for all to see."

"What if we painted the sea defence blue?" asked Jim. "It wouldn't show up on the photographs. It'd just look like sea."

All eyes turned to Jim for a moment. He looked around the faces. "What?" he said. "It could work. They paint the ships so they don't show up. What's the difference?"

"Moving on," I continued. "I think we should lodge a formal notice to the British Government informing them that we intend to refer this to the United Nations."

Now all the eyes turned to me.

"Well, it's the proper course of action." I looked around the room for support. None came, so I continued, "Or, we could swap the signs of Little Didney with those of Porth Cullen, so that when the EU hydrographic surveyor arrives, he goes to the wrong place, and measures the distance from there." I pushed back in my seat and folded my arms.

Tiggy smothered a giggle, and Jim said, "There, see, now you're thinking outside the box."

The evening drifted through several courses of Lin Chao's wonderful food and into unfettered alcohol and cannabis abuse. I slipped away and headed back to my house.

A few minutes later, Tiggy knocked lightly on the door and let herself in.

"You don't need to carry on knocking," I said.

"My mum taught me to be polite. It's not my house." She smiled and settled next to me on the sofa.

"Maybe it should be your house as well?" I suggested.

"Why! What are you implying, Mr Cabot?" She feigned shock.

"Just that... well, you spend more time here, and you only use your place as an office... so, maybe we both use your place as our office and this place... you know..."

She snuggled up against me and put her head on my shoulder. "That all sounds very permanent. But are you sure we're going to be here long enough to go making plans like that? I mean, we're only here because Jim thinks this is going to remain an independent island. What happens if the UK pulls it back somehow? Will Jim stay here under British laws? Or will he get bored and move on?"

"I know. I've been thinking the same. Jim's boredom threshold is about one step below that of a butterfly with ADHD."

"Then we have to make sure we stay independent," Tiggy said. "That's if you want me to move in, otherwise, it's not really worth me making the effort to move my stuff."

"No pressure then," I said. "Anyway, what stuff? Most of it's here already."

~ * ~ * ~ * ~

"PLEASE HOLD FOR SIR OLIVER Frogmorton," the computerised voice dribbled through the little speaker on my phone. *Why does he insist on instigating calls to* me *when he's not there when I answer?* I'd been listening to this for nearly ten minutes now, the repetition only broken by three bars of Four Seasons every thirty-seven seconds. I'd timed it. Thank goodness for hands-free speaker phone. As I waited, I trawled through pages of recent ministers' declarations of interests, to see if anything new had turned up. Nothing had. It also gave me the opportunity to check to see if the fake identity I'd created within the FCDO intranet system still worked. It did. Surprisingly, not only did I still have access to the systems, despite the real me being removed some weeks ago, but it appeared that the mythical me was in the pay system now. I looked up the HR file and found it was 'Pending Payment' due to missing bank details. I pondered supplying some bank details just to see if I actually got paid, but decided against that. Unauthorised access to the FCDO computers was one thing, but fraud, Froggy would love to be able to pull me into court on that one.

"Cabot?" the phone shouted at me.

I stabbed answer. "*Sir* John Cabot," I corrected.

"Don't get bumptious with me. What's this damned notice of yours that I've just been sent by the King's principal Private Secretary?"

"You're going to have to help me here, to which notice are you referring?"

"This one," he snapped.

"I'm sorry, but this is a telephone, not a magic eye machine. I have no idea what you're talking about."

"This nonsense about challenging the sovereignty of the United Kingdom with your claims about territorial waters. For goodness' sake, man. Don't you know what notices you're sending out?"

"No, still no idea. You're going to have to give me a clue. Are you sure it's from me?"

I heard rustling of paper, then, "It's signed by your idiot pop singer, King Jim."

"Ah, he never told me about this. You'll have to read it to me. That is, if you want me to know what it says. Otherwise, lovely as it always is to speak with you, this is a fairly pointless phone call."

"Hrmph, I will quote, *Dear your majesty.* Dear your Majesty? For heaven's sake, the man has no breeding at all—"

"Just read the letter."

Froggy continued reading, "*It has come to my kingly notice that you have had built an extension to your lands, and that therefore means the land of your kingdominion...*Kingdominion? *Your kingdominion now extends into waters owned by my country, so now under the law of international laws, this means I can therefore claim England as belonging to Scanlon's Rock. You can keep your palaces and carriages, but could you please ask all your minions to move out of the Houses of Parliament, as I will be putting my own crew in there forthwith.*"

I had to pause before answering, for fear of breaking into a fit of laughter. Once I'd gained control, I said, "I see..." another pause to stifle a giggle. "Well, to be honest, I had no idea about this, but..." I clicked the phone to mute as the laugh broke free. "... Sorry, somebody came in. I'm not sure I would have phrased it quite like that, but... you have to admit, he has a point."

"A point?" I felt the phone actually vibrate under my fingers. "The man has taken leave of his senses. This is lunacy of the highest order. And why does he think he has a right to involve the King in all this? This is a matter of territorial integrity, it's nothing to do with the King."

"Hmm, in a historical context, it has most often been the reigning monarch who did resolve matters of territorial integrity. Generally from the back of a horse and with sword in hand."

"Don't quote history to me, I have a first from Oxford in history. His Majesty's Government has been remarkably tolerant, and this is the final straw. We have made allowances for your man's obvious lack of education, but this... this is an affront to any sense of common decency. You are forcing us to take steps."

"I hardly think—" I started, but the phone went dead.

I closed my computer and failed to control the laughter, which had been threatening. Once I'd finally settled myself, I went out in search of Jim.

He wasn't difficult to find, as the moment I stepped out of my door, I noticed the shape of Air Force Two in a state of semi-inflation, looming just beyond the House of the Holy. I didn't need to be a detective to guess Jim wouldn't be far away. I was right. He seemed to be in a full-blown argument with Tiggy as he and Shawn loaded cardboard boxes into the gondola under the tethered balloon.

"John," Tiggy greeted as I neared. "Thank goodness, perhaps you can talk some sense into him."

"What's going on?" I asked.

"Jim's planning on dropping explosives onto the sea defence."

I studied the cardboard boxes. "They're full of explosives?" I asked, stepping back slightly. "Where did you get that?"

"A mate of mine does the pyrotechnics for festivals and so on. He was having a clear-out, and he had loads of old fireworks that'd gone past their best by date. Who'd have thought? Fireworks don't go out of date, not like chocolate. That's gotta be just a con to make people buy new ones?"

"Or that perhaps they become unstable over time? And therefore dangerous?" I suggested.

"Yeah, well, whatever. Anyway, he wants shot of them, and doesn't want to end up with a bill for *'Controlled disposal'*, another con, so I said I'd take 'em."

"And now you're going to drop fireworks onto a concrete and rock sea defence from a hot-air balloon?"

"Nah, not fireworks, just the powder. Me 'n Jeeves spent most of last night breaking them open and getting the powder out." He nodded towards the boxes. "That's just the powder."

I paused and studied him.

"What's up?" Jim asked.

"Just checking. You've still got your eyebrows, I'm impressed."

"It wouldn't work otherwise. Drop all the powder onto the thing, it'll fall into the cracks, set it on fire, boom, Bob's your uncle, no more sea defence. That's how they do it with granite mines. I saw it on YouTube."

"I told him it would be an environmental disaster," Tiggy said. "But he's not listening to me. You try."

"It's only gunpowder, or something." Jim tossed another box into the gondola. "It'll burn off and disappear. No problem. I even made sure the boxes are eco-friendly. Thinking of the fishes, see?"

"And at no point did you stop to consider that filling a hot-air balloon with explosives was probably not one of your better ideas? A balloon, which by its very nature, relies on an open flame?"

Jim paused and squinted up at the burner, currently on idle, positioned under the opening of the envelope, then down at the cardboard boxes. "Okay, there may be a small flaw in my plan. Maybe if I..." He scratched his head. "Hmm, might need to rethink the delivery system."

"In the meantime," I said, "I've just had a phone call from Oliver Frogmorton, Foreign Office."

"Ah, that explains the negative vibes I'm picking up off you."

"Can we have a new rule? That you don't send letters to the King of England when you're stoned?"

"Oh, that? Yeah, but, in my defence—"

"You don't have a defence," I interrupted. "You're a stoner. And when you're stoned, you have a tendency to do very stupid things."

He paused in thought for a moment, then, "To be fair, that was actually going to be my main defence."

"What we doing with these boxes?" Shawn asked.

"Put 'em back in the shed," Jim said. "We're going to need a helicopter." He looked at me. "I don't suppose your brother-in-law—"

"No," I said. "He hasn't. He said so, just the other day. He said, '*John, do you know what? I haven't got any helicopters at the moment.*' Last Tuesday I think it was."

Jim looked at me, then broke into a grin. "I'll give him a ring, see if he's had any come in."

I shook my head, turned, and headed back to my house. As I passed Tiggy, I said, "I tried."

~ * ~ * ~ * ~

BACK AT MY HOUSE, I logged in to the FCDO portal under my dummy account. I couldn't access any critical areas, but often, the mundane can reveal more of what is truly happening. I set up a meta-search to trawl for any internet searches recently made which mentioned Little Didney or the surrounding areas. Among the results was one which caught my eye, a search some junior admin officer in the MOD had made for tide times and weather in the area.

I widened the search, looking for any memos being sent to the local police, notifying them of any forthcoming activity in the area. Nothing. I included anything vaguely related to shipping in the area and noticed a request to clear a maintenance wharf and provide a security detail. Probably just routine nonsense, although I did try to access further, but it was beyond my clearance. As most things were. What was of slight interest was the same person, at the same time, put in a request for a private minibus hire to go from Plymouth docks to Poole in Dorset. Not seeing any obvious connection, or anything significant, I closed the access and logged out.

~ * ~ * ~ * ~

THE MORNING BROUGHT A GREY sky that looked reluctant to lift. I'd spent the night on my own for the first time in quite a while. Tiggy had gone back to Little Didney, as she'd had an early morning booking for a documentary film crew to video the seals at sunrise. The house felt oddly empty, and I didn't fancy making toast and coffee on my own, so I went off to the Ocean View Tearooms and Bar for breakfast.

Gwen greeted me with a cheery, "Hello, my dear. Nice bacon sandwich and a mug of tea?"

"Coffee and hot buttered toast, please."

"Right you are then. Just be a jiffy."

As the only visitor at this time of the morning, I had the pick of the seats, and chose my favourite table by the huge window overlooking the cliffs. The place had matured quite quickly, outgrowing its Wikihouse origins, and now just one of a number of these forming Paradise City. Its open-plan layout made it seem much airier and spacious, and the use of almost seamless windows showed off the beauty of the island to all who visited. Gwen had more than proved her value, and her permanent smile and homely manner made her popular with the residents and visitors alike.

The toast and coffee arrived with a, "There you go, love. That'll set you up for the morning. You on your own today?"

"Tiggy's got an early trip out." I tapped a little envelope of sugar into my coffee. "Honeymoon couple, I believe."

"Now, ain't that just the most romantic? You could take a lesson there."

"I don't think Tiggy would thank me for a seal trip."

"You daft buggins." She headed back to the counter.

The sound of the old bell over the door drew my attention, and Branok and Jake came in and planted themselves at a nearby table.

"Mornin'," greeted Branok. "Bit early for you, init?"

"I was planning on getting a full day in to finish the constitution before Jim adds anything else."

"He'll be 'ere in a minute, so you might want to hide."

Jake giggled.

Gwen dropped two huge fried breakfasts in front of each of them. "There you are, my ducks. Perfect timing."

Branok looked at his watch. "You're eleven minutes late," he scolded with a smile.

"So are you," Gwen said, and patted his head. "Never change."

"Should I be worried that you're both here instead of fishing, and Jim's involved?" I asked.

"Depends." Branok swirled a lump of bread in his fried egg. "If you're given to worrying, then you should probably've stayed away from 'imself in the first place." He popped the egg-laden bread into his mouth and chewed slowly.

The door opening jingled the bell once more, and a cloud of smoke entered, with Jim somewhere in the middle of it. I remembered seeing something similar on Penn and Teller once.

He spotted me. "Hey, John, I was going to come find you. You're just the man."

"I'm sure I'm not," I said.

"How are you with a camera?"

"Useless. I have a smartphone full of pictures of my right ear to verify that."

"No, I've got you a top of the range camera." He rummaged in his shoulder bag. "Here you are." He planted a small black camera on my table. "It's German, five-hundred megapixels. Apparently that's good."

"It looks complicated." I turned the beast round in my hands. "Why do I need a complicated camera?"

"We're doing some pictures for the website."

"We have a website?" I asked.

"We will have as soon as we've got some pictures. Going to get on Trip Advisor and probably the telly. It's the treasure hunting, see? It'll go viral when the pictures get out there. You'll see."

"Treasure hunting? Why do I feel I've come in halfway through this conversation?"

"Oh, I didn't tell you, did I? It's this idea I had the other day. I was sat out over the top at Pirate's Cove. You know, just chilling with a spliff and a JD, and I got to thinking, there's this wreck out there somewhere. Spanish galleon or something. Probably a treasure ship, most of them were."

"Can I just check something?" I asked.

"Go ahead, brainstorming, that's the thing."

"Um, yes. Do you actually know there's a wreck out there?"

"Branok does." He nodded towards Branok.

"You're in on this as well?" I asked.

Branok grinned and loaded bacon onto his fork. "Warned ya to make yerself scarce."

"You're talking about the Vagabunda?" I asked. "Do you know where it is?"

"Course we do. Wouldn't be much of a fisherman if I didn't know where the wrecks lay now, would I? Fastest way to lose my nets."

"And there's treasure there?"

"Could be. Could be not. Not for I to know."

"Back to the camera…" I looked at Jim.

"Yeah, you're gonna take pictures of me diving and coming up with a bit of treasure, then—"

"Hang on, you said diving?"

"Yeah, Branok's got all the gear. So, I go diving and—"

"Whoa, too fast," I said and looked back to Branok. "Diving?"

"Course. We sometimes go scallop diving. Best way to get 'em. That fancy TV chef down Porth Cullen, he pays good for them, so he does."

I turned back to Jim. "And you know how to dive?"

"Not yet, but how hard can it be? Just swimming and breathing. Besides, I'm only doing a little bit, just for the camera. Dive down, come up with a handful of doubloons, snap snap, suddenly we have loads of people out here wanting to go treasure hunting."

"And you're up for this?" I asked Branok.

"Man's gotta turn a penny," he said. "Fishin's gettin' harder, and I ain't gettin' no younger. Taking a boatload of yahoos out to go diving's gotta be easier than hauling nets twelve hours a night."

"And where's this treasure that you're planning on finding for the camera?" I asked Jim.

He dug deep into the bag again and came out with an oversized plastic gold coin. "Got a load of these off my mate. He's got an amusement arcade up in Newquay and he uses them to dress up the crane machines. Nobody'll know."

Despite all my protestations, an hour later, we were bobbing on Branok's boat, half a mile outside Pirate's Cove. The troubled sky turned and twisted above our heads, although Branok assured me it wouldn't rain until tomorrow.

Jake strapped the scuba tanks to Jim's back and showed him how to use the regulator mouthpiece. Jim held a joint in one hand and the mouthpiece in the other, and seemed conflicted as to which he should suck on first.

"You might need to give up the smoke for a moment, Jim," I suggested. "I don't think even you can manage to keep a joint going while scuba diving."

"I'll take that as a challenge," Jim said, eyes wide with the excitement of a new venture.

"Please don't."

"It's only pretend. Well, sort of." He removed the regulator and took a pull of the joint. "I'm not really going down to the bottom or anything. It's just for the pictures." He swapped joint and regulator again.

"You ready?" asked Branok.

"As I'll ever be." Jim wobbled down the wooden steps hung over the side of the Pelican. "It's not easy with all this stuff strapped on your back. I'm gonna have more sympathy for snails in the future."

"It'll be easier once yer in the water," Branok said.

"You ready with the camera?" Jim asked. At least, I guessed that's what he said, as he'd confused regulator and joint and was trying to speak through the mouthpiece. He paused to sort things out, took a lungful of smoke, and slipped into the water.

"Is he going to be alright?" I asked Branok.

"Him? He can't come to too much harm." Branok held up a line which snaked from a cleat on the gunwales to a clip on Jim's belt. "Providin' he remembers to breathe, that is."

I aimed the camera and started clicking as Jim disappeared under the water in a flurry of bubbles. A few seconds later, he reappeared, arms flailing and coughing smoke out from the sides of the mouthpiece. He grabbed hold of the steps with one arm and dragged the mouthpiece clear with the other. More coughing and smoke. Finally, he spluttered, "Did you get pictures?"

"Yes."

"Best, delete those. I wasn't ready. Have you seen my stash tin? It's up there somewhere."

"You can't roll a joint in the water," I said.

"I know that, but get Jake to skin one up for me, will you? Gonna need a smoke after this. Right, here we go, lights, camera, action." He replaced the mouthpiece and let himself slip back under the water.

I clicked. Several times, as he bobbed and resurfaced. Each time, his flailing became more frantic. I clicked. A flotilla of gold plastic coins suddenly appeared, and floated around him in a strange pastiche of the death of Ophelia. I clicked.

"Cor, bugger," Jake said loudly. "Better get him out o' there, 'afore he goes down for the third time."

I realised Jim was no longer flailing and seemed to be slowing in his movements.

Jake slid down the steps as Branok pulled the line and between them, they hauled Jim up onto the deck. Jim spluttered and coughed as Jake slapped his back. "There ya go. Cough it all up."

"What happened?" I asked.

"Prob'ly forgot to breathe. Easy done," Branok said. "Instinct see, people go under water first time and hold their breath. Just the thing to not do, but lesson learned 'n no 'arm done."

Jim sat hunched forwards still coughing while waving a free hand towards Jake. "Where's my smoke?" he finally managed to ask.

Jake found a joint and guided it into Jim's hand.

After a few minutes, Jim's breathing had recovered, and he looked at me. "Did you manage to get any good pictures?"

"I don't know. All the coins were floating around you though, so probably not much good for the website," I said. "It'd probably give the game away."

"Sod it. Give me a minute, and we'll go again."

"No we won't," Branok said. "We're done 'ere for the day. We gotta go out tonight, if we want to be on position to shoot the nets at first light."

I looked up at the gathering night clouds. "You're going out in this?"

"If we stayed in harbour each time a bit of wind or rain promised, we'd soon have nothin' to put on the table."

"Never mind," said Jim. "You got some picture, right?"

"Yes, but the plastic coins?" I asked.

"Nothing that can't be fixed with a bit of Photoshopping."

"Maybe, if I knew the first thing about Photoshopping. Which, I don't."

"Opportunity to learn then. Expand your skill base." He looked at the joint in his hands. It had become sodden by his wet hands. He tried to suck on it, but it disintegrated on his lips. "Somebody needs to invent waterproof skins. There's an opportunity waiting for an entrepreneur. Maybe I should give Elon Musk a call. What d'ya think?" His eyes looked wide and wouldn't settle.

"I think you probably need to get back and have a hot shower and a lie down."

## ~ CHAPTER TWENTY-FIVE ~

THE USUAL SHAFTS OF SUNLIGHT and squawking gulls were noticeable by their absence as I woke. I peeled the curtains back and stared into a sky of ominous grey. I felt little balls of wind pummelling the side of my house, and the wood creaked in protest.

"What's up?" Tiggy mumbled from under the bedclothes.

"Looks like rain," I said, reluctantly extracting myself from the warm bed.

"Told you so. Mackerel sky and mares' tails last night. Always brings the wet and wind."

"I still prefer the BBC for my weather," I said. "At least I can understand what they mean. Mackerel tails and little boys' noses... Do you want coffee?"

"Yes, please. And it's mackerel sky, not tails. Like fish scales in the clouds. How do you think sailors managed before the BBC?"

"The daily Met office reports in the Times?"

"I'll have you know, the old ways are still the best."

I ducked the pillow heading in my direction and slipped into the kitchen. The rain had just started to patter at the window. I switched on the radio and tuned to a local station. Lots of jabber about the upcoming Royal Cornwall show, and hopes for fine weather. The voices faded into the background as I made coffee and loaded the toaster.

I felt Tiggy's presence and turned to see her just behind me, straining to see through the rain covered window. "Dad's not going to be happy," she said, wiping at the condensation with her hand.

"Not a day to go fishing, that's for sure."

"Oh, they're used to the weather, it's just that the catch won't be so good. And stocks are shrinking anyway. He's going to be in a right fug when he gets back."

"I'll keep out of the way."

"I'm supposed to be taking a school group out to see the grey seals. Hmm, I think I'll have to cancel."

The front door swung open, and Jim greeted with, "The boat's crashed."

"Crashed?" Tiggy looked alarmed. "The Pelican? How?"

"What?" said Jim. "Oh, no, not *that* boat, *my* boat, the Raven. It's crashed."

Tiggy visibly relaxed, then asked, "How can it crash? It was anchored out in the bay."

"How do I know?" said Jim. "Do I *look* like Captain Birdseye?"

I studied him for a moment. His normally well-controlled, shoulder-length hair tangled round his head like it had just come out of a tumble dryer, and his eyes told of a dangerous caffeine/weed imbalance. "I'd have to say no to that," I said. "More like the captain of the Hesperus, perhaps."

Jim's eyes searched mine. "Huh?"

"From the poem, The Wreck of the Hesperus, Longfellow. It was a… never mind. Explain crashed."

"What do you want? A spreadsheet with probability factors and projected outcomes? It was out there last night," he threw a hand in the direction of Pirate's Cove, "and now it's tangled up in the rocks with its nose in the sand. Crashed."

Tiggy wiped at the window again. "There's not enough of a sea out there to tear it loose from its anchor. It's choppy, but not enough to do that. We'd best go have a look." She headed back to the bedroom to get dressed.

I managed to persuade Jim to go by Land Rover, and leave the tank, and we bounced across the growing mud of the meadowland to the descent to

Pirate's Cove. With the rain gathering in intensity, and the sand of the cliff always unstable, even at the best of times, the drive down to the beach tested my ability to crush a metal door handle with my bare hands. My controlled exit from the Defender failed when my legs wobbled on the wet sand and dumped me in a heap.

"You alright?" Tiggy asked.

Jim laughed.

"Yeah, tripped on the step," I lied, struggling to my feet.

The wind threw the rain into my face and made seeing difficult. The low clouds churned towards the sea, darkening as they touched the horizon. The morning sun had long given up the battle for the day and gone back to bed.

"Ah, yes," Tiggy said. "I see what you mean." She squinted against the rain. "Although, round here, we call that a shipwreck, not a crash. They were quite popular with the Cornish wreckers in days past."

I followed her gaze and saw the frigate, listing steeply to one side, and wedged firmly between two huge black rocks which climbed from the angry waves. She looked much bigger here, her nose out of the water and up against a mound of sand she had pushed up on her arrival.

"How?" was all I could manage.

"Dunno," said Tiggy. "It's not unknown for a ship that size to drag an anchor, but very unlikely. Especially given it was Dad and Jake who anchored her. They know what they're doing. Besides, the sea's not that rough."

We moved closer to have a better look. About a quarter of the length lay out of the water, with the rear end still buried in the waves. The lower section of the hull looked covered in what I guessed were barnacles, although I'd never actually seen any in real life. I could also make out various patches of different metals which had been added at various points. Testimony to the poor girl's history of numerous hostile encounters.

"How do I get it back in the water?" Jim asked, craning his neck up to the beast in front of him.

"You don't," Tiggy said. "Even if you could hire something big enough to pull her off the beach, she's not going to float. Not after hitting those rocks."

"Was it insured?" I asked.

Jim turned to stare at me. "Insured? It's not a sodding Ford Escort. Who's going to give me fully comp on this?" He waved an arm at the boat. "And before you ask, no, I'm not in the RAC either."

A beam of light suddenly pierced the gloom and danced across the sand. It stopped when it found us, containing us within its bright circle.

I heard Jim say, "What the..." as we all craned our necks upwards, following the source of the beam. It seemed to originate on the main deck of the Raven.

"Ahoy!" a voice called from far above us.

"Who the hell is that?" Jim asked.

"Did you leave Shawn on the ship?" Tiggy asked.

"Shawn?" Jim yelled upwards. "Is that you?"

"No," came the voice. "No Shawn here. I am Lieutenant Commander Hunter, Special Boat Service, and I am seizing this ship under the orders of His Majesty's Government."

"And how's that working out for you?" Jim yelled.

"We appear to be grounded."

Jim paused for a moment, then yelled, "Looks like it. That was a bit careless."

"I'm coming down. Stand by."

Three pilot's ladders dropped down the side of the hull, and six shadowy shapes slid down at impossible speed and landed in front of us. The men were dressed all in black, with balaclavas, goggles, and each carrying a short-stocked gun.

One man stepped forwards, his gun slung over his back, and he pulled the googles clear of his face as he approached. "Lieutenant Commander Hunter," he announced. "Who's in charge here?"

"I'm the King," said Jim. "The President's sleeping off a hangover."

"You have a president *and* a king?" He pulled a black balaclava from his head and ran his hand through his hair.

"I was going to be an emperor, you know, like Ming the Merciless? But then… What the hell are you doing with my warship?" Jim took a joint from his shirt pocket and lit it.

"I have orders to take control of this vessel and move it into Plymouth naval docks."

"Off you go then."

"We would, only the port engine's out of commission and we've run out of fuel."

"Yeah, you'll probably also find that the toilet on the top deck is blocked, so you might want to give that a miss." He took another deep pull on the joint, then handed it towards Lieutenant Commander Hunter.

Hunter shook his head. "No, thank you. Not really my bag."

Jim shrugged. "Suit yourself. So, what now?"

"You're not going to resist?"

"Resist? Nah, to be honest, I'm a bit over the whole warship thing now. Have you any idea how much fuel they take? Probably best get rid of it before Cindy gets back. She'd have a fit."

Hunter looked bewildered. "Cindy?"

"Jim's wife," I explained. "She's very green. Makes Greta Thunberg look like Donald Trump. Speaking of whom…" I looked at Jim. "I thought she was coming back about now?"

"Yeah, she's attending a gala dinner in Venice. They're trying to bring attention to the fact that massive tourism is destroying the city. Everybody who's anybody is going, so she has to go."

"I see," Hunter said. "But doesn't that involve—"

"Best not think about that," I interrupted. "You do know you have no jurisdiction here? This is a sovereign state, and under article two, section four, of the United Nations—"

Jim nudged me with his elbow. "Hey, can't you see he's got a gun?" he said. "Don't piss off the man with the gun. If you'd toured as many South American countries as I have, you'd have learnt not to piss off the man with the gun." Jim turned to Hunter. "Talking of which, how do you get a gun like that?"

"Five years in the Royal Marine Commandos," Hunter said. "Then complete selection for special forces, followed by twelve months of the hardest training in any army in the world."

"Yeah, I was thinking more like, where do I buy one of those?" Jim turned to me. "Do you think Gerry's got any of those?"

"Shouldn't we leave these people to do whatever it is they want to do with that thing?" I nodded towards the Raven. "It's cold and wet here, and I haven't had my breakfast yet."

"I don't think we're going anywhere anytime soon," said Hunter. "Unless you fancy giving us a push back into the sea?"

"I would," Jim said, "only, I've got the wrong shoes on for that. Sorry. But I tell you what, before you set out, can I just get something off the boat?"

"I don't see why not, what is it?"

"My yellow Freddie Mercury jacket, I left it in the Wardroom?"

"You have Freddie Mercury's jacket?" Hunter asked.

"Yes, we both played Music for Refugees, Wembley. We swapped jackets at the end."

Hunter studied Jim as if seeing him for the first time. "You're Jim Sullivan? *The* Jim Sullivan? The Spartans?"

"Last time I looked. The jacket? I'd like it back. I was wearing it when I captained the ship. I thought I looked very sort of captainy, don't you think?"

"I don't know. It's not—"

"It's such a great colour. So Freddie. I was going to get uniforms in that colour for my navy when I set it up. Cindy was going to design them. She's got her own range of sunglasses, so she knows about designing."

Hunter turned to one of his men. "Scotty, go get the man his jacket."

"Sir." The man turned and headed up the pilot's ladder almost as fast as he'd come down it a few minutes ago.

"How are you going to move that now?" Tiggy asked, looking at the ship. "I mean, even if you could get a boat big enough to tow it, I'd be fairly certain the hull is damaged now."

Hunter turned to study the Raven. "No doubt. But it's not my problem from this point. We can't move it, that's for sure. Salvage job now."

"I'm going to demand compensation," said Jim.

Hunter shrugged. "Don't blame you, mate. But, like I said—"

"Not your job?"

Hunter smiled.

The SBS man returned with Jim's jacket and handed it to him.

"Thanks," said Jim. He held out the joint to Hunter again. "Sure you don't want a toke?"

"I'm sure. More of a whisky man, myself."

"Got some Jack Daniel's Single Barrel back up top." Jim nodded his head towards the cliff.

"Now you're talking."

"Isn't it a bit early for a session?" Tiggy asked. Her eyes flitted between Jim and Hunter, almost challenging them.

"Yes, you're probably right. And I shouldn't leave this unattended." He nodded at the Raven.

"You're worried we're going to nick it back off you? I've got a steering lock in the Landy you can borrow if you like."

"How about a nice cup of tea and a bacon butty instead?" Tiggy suggested.

Hunter eyed his men. "Well, it has been a long night, and there's nothing we can do with this, so... under the circumstances, perhaps a short break wouldn't be amiss."

Nods and mumbles from the men.

"We're not all going to get in the Land Rover," Tiggy said.

"A Defender?" Hunter asked, eyeing the vehicle on the sand.

"Yeah," Jim said. "1980, long wheelbase. Classic."

"Good show," said Hunter. "We got eighteen men, women and children in, and on, one of those once, when we were e'vaccing the Stan. Plus three dogs and a goat. Lay on, Macduff." Hunter waved his arm towards the cliff.

We opted to walk up the cut to the top of the cliff and let Jim drive the Defender up on his own. We set off up the track, the eight SBS men, graciously bringing up the rear, and not humiliating us by running up the cliff at ninety miles per hour, as they were, no doubt, inclined to do.

Once at the top, Tiggy and me squashed in the front of the waiting Landy, while the SBS men filled the back, with the remainder sitting on various outside parts of the vehicle. The Defender took it all in good grace, and we trundled across the top meadowland towards Paradise City.

We arrived outside the Ocean View Tearooms and Bar just as the wind and rain took on a new urgency. Gwen looked slightly shocked at the sudden invasion, eyeing the black-clad men with suspicion, until they removed their balaclavas.

Tiggy explained the situation to Gwen, who smiled then set about making teas, coffees, and bacon sandwiches. We all settled around a group of three tables, and the men relaxed, although they kept their weapons close.

"So, you're really the King, then?" Hunter said. "They never told me it was you."

"Yeah, and Tiggy is the Minister for Tourism, and John here is the Minister." He nodded towards me.

"Minister? Minister of what?"

"Mostly everything else," I said. "What do you plan on doing now? Taking the island?"

"Good grief, no." Hunter sounded genuinely shocked. "We were purely sent to capture the frigate, and if we couldn't, to disable it. Job done."

"Disable it?" I queried.

"Well, scuttle it. If we couldn't get it safely into Plymouth, we had orders to take it out deep, and lay explosive charges in the bilges."

"More trash in the sea," Tiggy muttered.

Gwen dropped a pile of bacon and egg sandwiches on the table in front of the men. "There we are, ducks. Get yourselves outside of that lot."

"I hope I'm going to get compensation for my boat," Jim said.

Gwen set a bottle of Jack Daniel's, a glass, and an ashtray in front of Jim.

She looked at Hunter and said, "You make sure he does, mind. He was very fond of that."

"Was it actually worth anything?" Hunter asked. "From what we could see, it was a miracle it was still afloat."

"It's the sentimental value." Jim poured a whisky and lit a joint. "You can't put a value on that. Although…" He took a big pull on the joint. "… I am open to offers." His head disappeared in a blue cloud.

Hunter mopped egg from his lips. "I'll see what I can do. If I put in my report that the engine failed, and we had to run it aground for safety, they'll probably give you a decent amount, if only to shut you up."

"You'd do that for us?" asked Tiggy.

"No skin off my nose. Besides, it's not very often we get greeted with bacon butties when we turn up unannounced. Usually, people are trying to kill us." He turned to Gwen. "Have you any ketchup, my dear?"

"Cool." Jim flapped a hole in the smoke cloud so he could see the others. "You get me a good price, and I'll get you some tickets for our next gig. How's that? We're planning another farewell tour for next year."

"That seems like a deal."

"What gives with this place, anyway?" asked one of the SBS men. "Seems like quite a set-up here."

"It's a proper community," I said. "We're independent from the UK, although they are trying to force us back by building a so-called sea defence to prove we're within the territorial limits."

"That's a bit off, ain't it?" said the man.

"You mean that lump of concrete and rocks out there?" Hunter asked.

I nodded. "That's it."

"Hideous mess," said Hunter. "We wondered what that was about, when we reccied the area. It doesn't show on our charts."

"It won't wash. The EU is set to recognise us as independent, but the UK is worried about losing oil rights in the area. Plus, they don't like the tax-free status, of course."

"Or my agriculture." Jim waved his joint.

"Is that legal here?" asked the SBS man.

"Of course," Jim said. "It's me who says what's legal here and what ain't. And this…" he held up the joint, "is definitely legal. I'm even thinking about making it compulsory."

"And if they start exploring for oil round here," Tiggy said. "Well, they're going to destroy what's left of the marine life here. We've got one of the last remaining pods of bottlenose dolphins left in UK waters out here. And grey seals."

"Amazing creatures, dolphins," said another man. "They're extraordinary to swim with."

Tiggy's phone started ringing. She picked it up and looked at the screen. "It's Dad," she said. "That's odd." She stabbed the screen and put the phone to her ear. "Dad? What's up? Can you hear me?"

A noise hissed and crackled through the little speaker.

"Dad? Are you there? Yes, I've got you, but you're breaking up… Say again… How bad is it? Dad? Can you go to VHF?"

We all froze. I remembered he was supposed to be out fishing, but I didn't know where.

"Are you there? I can just hear you. Can you send your GPS? … GPS… Hello?" She stared at her phone and turned to us. "He's gone."

"What's happened?" I asked.

"They're tangled in something. I think the propeller's snagged on a cable or old nets, but I couldn't catch it. They're a bit far out for a good signal."

"What type of vessel is it?" Hunter asked.

"It's a fifty-five-foot beam trawler. Single Cummings engine. I'm going to have to go out and help." Tiggy glanced out of the window. "If they're adrift without engine, and this gets—" Her phone rang again. "Dad? Yes, that's better. What's happening? … Why? … Okay, I'm on my way."

She stared at the screen for a moment, then it bleeped. "Got it," she said.

"Okay, tell me exactly what's happening," Hunter demanded.

"They think it's a steel cable of some sort. Tangled in the prop, they think the prop is probably damaged, so they have no power. Sea's picking up, and without control... I need to get out there." She held the phone up. "I've got the GPS, they're about fifteen miles out from here."

"Shouldn't we get the Coastguard or lifeboat out?" I asked.

"The inshore lifeboat's on its way," Tiggy said. "But it's a long way to go, and they can't save Dad's boat anyway, they're too small. They'd have to abandon it. That's his livelihood gone."

"You have a boat?" Hunter asked.

"Yes, thirty-five-footer, sports fishing boat, 300 horse power, so she should be able to tow it. That's if they can free themselves."

"Okay," Hunter said. "We've got two RHIBs with full dive equipment and cutting gear. So we can cut it free, but the RHIBs can't tow something that size, not in bad weather."

"RHIBs?" I asked Tiggy.

"Rigid Hull Inflatable Boats," she said. Turning back to Hunter, "You'll be able to get under the boat to cut them free?"

Hunter simply said, "It's what we do." He turned to his men. "Okay, lads, let's go."

# ~ Chapter Twenty-Six ~

WE BOUNCED THROUGH THE GATHERING storm towards the cove, the wipers barely functioning against the heavy rain.

"You don't have to come," Tiggy said to me.

"I know. But another pair of hands. I can hold a torch, or a rope, or something."

She squeezed my arm and forced a smile.

"They'll be alright," I said. "These guys seem to know what they're doing."

Tiggy fell to silence, and I stared out of the windscreen, wondering how on earth Jim had any idea where we were going. As soon as we started our descent, I hung on tight. Jim was already several joints and a JD or two in. We were in a hurry, the slope was wet, and we were eleven-up on an ancient Land Rover Defender. I held on and concentrated. The vehicle tipped and slid, the four-wheel-drive bit firmly into something, and we kicked back into a rough nosedive down the side of the slope. More of an uncontrolled descent, rather than a drive, but still we made it onto the beach, with the three external SBS guys still clinging on.

We pulled up close to the two RHIBs, which had been lashed to a rock.

"We'll take both RHIBs," said Hunter. "The kit's already loaded on them, and we can get in closer than your leisure boat can manage safely in this weather. Let's hope your boat can tow it."

Tiggy nodded, and we randomly dispersed ourselves across the two boats, pushed them into the water and jumped onboard. I sat near the front of one, and before I'd had time to summon up a panic attack, the engines fired into life, and we skimmed across the angry waves out towards where Tiggy's boat lay at her mooring. The short, violent journey threatened to rattle all of my bones loose inside my skin. I managed to make it all the way to the '300' on one held breath. Once there, the SBS men divided three to each RHIB, with Hunter and one other man joining us on the '300. Within seconds, all three craft were crashing through the tops of the waves, heading into the thickening rain, and out to some geo-point in the middle of nowhere.

I hadn't notice it happen, but both Hunter and the other man were now wearing wet suits, with headgear which looked like something out of a sci-fi movie. I saw Hunter talking, but whatever he was saying was drowned under the roar of engines, driving rain, and the exploding waves as we burst through them. I guessed he was in communication with the other boats, which flanked us like a pair of black chariots, barely in contact with the water.

I did more holding tight and concentrating. I promised myself a proper panic attack later, but for now, I tried to do my bit by squinting into the driving rain in the vain effort of looking out for anything that wasn't water.

The whole journey felt more like being in a go-kart, hurtling across an endless cattle grid than any boat trip I'd ever experienced. Thankfully, we'd only been going about twenty minutes when I noticed Hunter suddenly becoming more alert, and started pointing. He talked constantly into his headset. I strained my eyes against the wind, trying to see through the gloom and rain, but nothing caught my eye.

The sound of the engines changed, and I felt the boat swinging round underneath me. For a moment, I was convinced something had gone horribly wrong, and we were going down. But then, on my right, a grey wall reached up, blanking out the rain. And the sky. The mournful sound of a ship's horn broke through the sounds of engines and rain. I guessed this was the Pelican, and she was calling us. We bumped against the hull of the trawler a few times, and then some ropes appeared, snaking down onto our deck. I grabbed one, without understanding why I'd done so, or what I was going to do with it once I'd got it.

For a moment, I stood, holding my rope and looking for something to tie it onto, then it was taken from my hands by the SBS man, who gave it a quick twist, and it dropped over a cleat in some complicated knot. I made a mental note to ask him how he did that, when all this had stopped.

The door to the cabin swung open, and a cloud of smoke drifted out, with Jim in the middle of it somewhere. "Are we there yet?" he asked.

Tiggy threw him a look. "You see that bucket?" she said to Jim.

Jim followed her pointing finger and spotted a large blue bucket hanging on a stowage hook behind the door. He nodded.

"Grab hold of it, fill it with fresh water from the tap in the sink, and hold onto it. Make sure it doesn't spill. Right?"

"Right, I'm on it. You can rely on me," Jim responded and grabbed the bucket to disappear back inside.

"Why?" I asked.

"No reason. It'll just keep him busy. We don't need a stoner cluttering up the place in this."

"What about me? Do you have another bucket?"

Tiggy smiled and indicated a spotlight attached to the roof overhang above my head. "Aim that at the water-point at the rear of the Pelican."

"But try to keep it out of the faces of my men," said Hunter.

"I get it. They have to keep their identities secret."

"No." He looked at me in the way my schoolmaster used to do. "I just don't want you to blind them."

I turned to Tiggy, "Maybe I should just hold a bucket. I'd feel safer with a bucket."

Tiggy ignored me and turned the wheel of the '300' while increasing the revs.

Keeping a spotlight still on a moving boat, while aiming at a small part of a different moving boat, proved harder than I'd thought. Probably akin to trying to thread a needle while drunk and riding a roller-coaster. Not that I'd had a lot of experience with roller-coasters before. Or threading needles.

The two RHIBs bounced around near the rear of the Pelican, although one seemed to be holding out a bit. One of the RHIBs moved in very close to the flat rear end of the trawler and I aimed my spotlight puddle on that one, trying to hold it still for them. There were two men in that RHIB, both wore wetsuits and masks, and with tanks on their backs. One rolled backwards into the water and the other lowered what looked like a heavy piece of machinery down to him.

"That's what I've always wanted to know," I ventured to Hunter, hoping to de-idiot myself after the last comment. "Why do they roll backwards into the water?"

He brought that look to bear on me again, and said, "Because, if they rolled forwards, they'd still be in the boat." He smiled.

I turned my attention back to the man in the water. He clipped a strap to the machine he'd been given, which I assumed was some sort of cutting gear, but I wasn't about to ask. Once secured, he disappeared into the water. I tried to keep the light trained on where I expected him to be. My puddle of brightness flashed and undulated on the turbulent water.

Another light appeared. This one brilliant blue, and it came from just underneath where my own light struck the water. It flickered and flared, giving off sudden spikes of white. I kept my light still. I'd figured out that my legs could bend at the knee to compensate for the rolling of the boat. That way, it was easier to keep the light more focused. For a moment, I felt quite pleased with my new skill, then realised that probably everybody else who'd ever set foot on a boat had no doubt worked this out long before me.

More movement on the RHIB. The two men were now moving more equipment around, although I couldn't see what. The first man slipped below the water once more, along with whatever new contraption he'd been given. More blue light glowed from beneath the surface, fighting for dominance with my own white circle.

An arm broke the surface of the water, and right in the middle of my spot. The hand held in a thumbs-up position for a moment, then disappeared again. For a few moments, nothing seemed to happen, then the surface broke once more, and the diver scrambled back into the RHIB, and they pulled away from the Pelican.

Hunter turned to Tiggy. "All clear. Take up the strain on the towline." Then, to the other SBS man, "Jamie, keep your eye on the line. Let's see if we can get this thing moving."

Tiggy increased the throttles and the lines between the '300', and the Pelican, ran taut. I heard the engines strain at the same time as the deck heaved and vibrated beneath my feet. We violently skewed side to side for a moment, then the screws seemed to find their purchase in the water, and we groaned forwards.

I moved to the front of the wheelhouse and peered through the rain-lashed windows. I could see nothing, just shades of grey, and higher up, gathering bundles of black.

"I need to call off the lifeboat," Tiggy said.

"Of course," said Hunter. "Just don't say anything about us."

Tiggy turned to glare at the SBS Lieutenant Commander. "Really? After you invaded sovereign territory, stole our ship, then trashed it? You think I'm going to keep this quiet? Oh, no, this is going all over the news."

"To be fair, we did rescue your father's boat."

"And what good is that going to do him?" She turned and fixed his gaze. "What good's a fishing boat when there are no fish left because the oil companies have destroyed their grounds?"

Hunter seemed to struggle for words, and I almost felt sorry for him. "I really don't know the politics. We're simply the tools the politicians choose to use."

Tiggy gave a low grumble and turned her attention to the storm in front of her.

The boat rocked and twisted far more than we had on the way out. Breakers even crashed over the front at one point, and I pulled my lifejacket tighter, and glanced around for something floatable to hang onto when this all went wrong. I'd seen Titanic. I knew how this was going to work out.

I noticed nobody else seemed concerned, and that worried me. After all, it had been overconfidence which had done for the Titanic in the first place. I noticed the seat under which the cushions were stored. They'd float at a push. I edged closer to it.

Hunter noticed me move. "Wouldn't get too close to the edge, if I were you," he said. "We get hit by a big one, it'll take you away, or dump you under the other boat. Either way, the end's the same."

I slipped back to where I was and held tight.

Just as the sea seemed to be picking up in its attempts to drag us all down, I caught sight of the headland of Pirate's Cove. I'd never been so grateful to see a lump of rock. I now understood the relief people like Columbus must have felt, when the lookout yelled '*Land ahoy!*'

Tiggy moored the '300' up against a buoy, and Branok secured the Pelican to anchor. We spread ourselves between the two RHIBs. The journey from mooring point to shore took a matter of seconds and felt like being shot out of a catapult. We didn't even seem to slow down when we hit the shore, skidding to a halt on the sand.

"Wow, cool," Jim said, as we landed. "Can we have another go? I wasn't ready."

After the boats had been secured, some of us piled in the Land Rover, but several of the SBS guys decided to walk. They didn't arrive much behind us.

Gwen welcomed us into the Ocean View Tearooms and Bar.

"What can I get you, dearies?" she asked. "You all look like you could do with a nice cup of tea. Not a day to be out in this. I've got some nice scones, just come out of the oven." She spotted the disappointment on the various faces around the table and tried again. "Or a beer? Sun's probably over the yardarm." She glanced at the rain-soaked window. "If we could see it."

Hunter gave a big grin. "Beers all round, my dear. His Majesty can pay. And a plate of your best scones."

Gwen smiled and scuttered back to the kitchen.

"You get a beer allowance?" I asked.

"Strictly speaking, it's a grey budget we can use in trying to win support from locals in a potentially hostile situation."

"Are we viewed as hostile locals, then?" challenged Tiggy, her eyes narrowed.

"Only if you try to come between me and my beer."

"So, what are you folks doing here anyway?" asked Branok.

"They came to steal Jim's ship," said Tiggy. "That's what."

"Crashed it on the beach, they did," said Jim.

Gwen returned with a huge plate of scones and a plate with knife, butter, cream, and jam for each.

Branok took a scone and cut it open. He turned his gaze to Hunter. "Stealing a man's ship, is it? Indebted as I am for the rescue, stealing a ship is bad business. Especially hereabouts. We have a name round 'ere for folks who steal another man's vessel."

"Pirates?" suggested Hunter.

"Aye, that's a word too. Mostly, we call them 'Missing'."

"Missing?"

"Missing. As in, gone missing. No bugger knows where they be anymore."

"I see," Hunter said. "I'm sure that, given the circumstances, His Majesty's Government will offer some fiscal recompense."

"I thought you said I'd get compensation?" queried Jim.

"That's what he meant," Tiggy said.

"You mind he does, now." Branok wagged the knife at Hunter. "You don't want unfinished business 'tween us. You hear me?"

"Loud and clear," said Hunter. "Trust me, they'll pay up. Or they might simply give up one of their decommissioned Type Twenty-twos. There's several in dry-dock in Devonport they don't know what to do with."

"About that," said Jim. "Any chance of getting one with a few less miles on the clock next time?"

As the beer warmed the conversation, the barriers started to drop. By the third round, Branok and Hunter were swapping sea stories.

"So there he was, bold as brass," Branok said. "Russian trawler, my arse. Those buggers wouldn't know a sardine if it leapt out'a the water and bit their peckers off. So, me and another couple 'o boats, boy's out of Porth Cullen they were, don't wanna mess with them boys, we just ran along each side of him until he buggered off. Nosin' about here, doin' no good. Think some o' your lot picked them up as they went past Plymouth."

"Bit before my time," Hunter said, cracking the cap on his next beer. "All spy planes and drones now. Fly Boys' problem, not ours. They don't bother with spy ships so much these days."

Branok held up his bottle and chinked it against Hunter's. "Ya know? You ain't no different to us. Born of the sea. Probably die on her too."

"Let's hope not," said Hunter. "I've got my eye on a villa in Spain, just down from Granada. Tell me, what *is* going on here, anyway? We just had orders to take the ship. I didn't even know this place existed."

Jim looked at me. "John, that's your cue, you're on." He patted his pockets, presumably in search of a missing joint.

Hunter turned to me, so I started to explain. "It all really comes down to the Montevideo Convention of 1933, which states—"

"Here we go," interrupted Jim. "Hope you've brought your duvet, this could be a long night." His fingers found a joint in his shirt pocket and he looked genuinely surprised.

"As I was saying," I persisted, and ran through a brief summary of the legitimacy of the claim to independence and the tangle of corruption behind Valdez Oil's bid to gain exploration rights in the area.

When I'd finished, Hunter asked, "And their sole claim rests on that lump of concrete out there? It's just to reduce the twelve nautical mile distance?"

"Exactly. And strictly speaking, under the Territorial Sea Act of 1987, there is no retrospective—"

"Way too much now, John," Jim said. "You're losing your audience. You need to learn when to change key."

"But, it's—"

"I think he's got it." Tiggy pressed on my arm. She turned to Hunter. "Sorry, he gets passionate about the detail."

"Detail saves lives," Hunter said.

"It's just that..." Tiggy, took a deep breath. "Well, the eco system in the English Channel is fragile enough. The fishermen barely survive as it is. The UK has nearly half the planet's remaining population of grey seals, and most of those are around here. And as for the Leatherback turtles... best I don't start on those. Just saying that if Valdez Oil starts exploration out this far... well... Sorry, I know, not your job."

"I think we should open a bottle of JD Single Barrel," Jim said. "It's all getting a bit too heavy." He motioned for Gwen to bring a bottle over.

"Well, technically, we're still on duty until we return to base," said Hunter.

"Tell them you had to appease the locals," Jim said, grabbing the bottle from Gwen before she had chance to place it on the table. "Mission on." He slopped the whisky into one of the glasses provided and slid the bottle towards Hunter. "I hope you're not going to let me drink this all on my own?"

"Wouldn't think of it." Hunter matched Jim's pour, then sent the bottle on its way to the next of his men.

Jim chinked his glass with Hunter's. "I know what I'm going to do."

"Oh dear," Tiggy mumbled under her breath.

Jim looked at her, not quite catching what she'd said. Tiggy gave a quick flash of a smile, so Jim continued, "I'm going to knight you guys." He waved his glass in an arc around the group of men at the far end of the tables. "Services rendered to the nation of Scanlon's Rock and the saving of precious human lives... and Jake," he added with a grin.

Branok stood unsteadily and held his newly refreshed glass high. "To the courage and... um... courage of His Majesty's Special Boat Service... and all who sail in her." He collapsed back into his seat with a crash.

Hunter stood, with a little more control, and replied, "To the brave men of the sea, who everyday risk their lives to make sure the nation's fish and chips are secure."

Everybody held up their glasses and drank a toast. We then drank a toast to the Kingdom of Scanlon's Rock, the sea, and Cornish Pasties. Jim wobbled to his feet and, for a moment confused by his joint in one hand and JD in the other, announced he was going to get his Knighting Sword. He made his way out of the door.

"This is going to get messy," Tiggy whispered in my ear.

"I know. I think we'll just make sure he doesn't cut somebody's ear off with his sword and then leave them to it," I said.

She nodded and nudged her shoulder against mine momentarily.

Jim returned a short while later with Watt in tow.

"Meet the President of Scanlon's Rock," he said. "You don't need to bow or anything."

Watt looked around the room. "Who's this lot then?"

"They're my mates," Jim said. "They rescued Jake and Branok under extreme conditions of hazard and exceptional danger to life and limb, without regards to their own safety and generally jolly good blokes, and I'm going to knight them with my Knighting Sword." He waved his samurai sword high.

Hunter leaned towards Tiggy, a slightly worried look in his eyes. "What's he doing with that thing?"

"You're going to be a knight."

"For real?"

"Actually, yes. This, at the moment anyway, is a sovereign nation, and a monarchy. So yes, King Jim is constitutionally able to give real knighthoods. If you want to know the details," she glanced in my direction, "John will explain the constitutional ins and outs."

Hunter flicked a glance in my direction, gave a small smile, and returned to Tiggy. "I'm good."

"Word of warning, though," I said. "You might want to tie your ears back."

The Knighting Ceremony proved unusual, even by Scanlon's Rock standards. The men decided that in the interests of keeping various parts of their anatomy intact, that wearing their balaclavas was probably the order of the day. Add to that, the fact that none of them would give their names, the whole thing became even more surreal.

As Tiggy stood shoulder to shoulder with Jim, helping him keep the sword steady, and looking like a bridal couple cutting the cake, Jim said, "I now pronounce you Sir Knight of the Suspender," to each in turn.

When he'd finished, he settled to sign the certificates. That bit at least went smoothly. Probably years of practice with autograph signing.

More drinking and toasting followed, at which point Tiggy and I made our escape. I picked up Jim's sword on the way out and Tiggy gave me a puzzled glance.

"Best that's out of his reach for the rest of the evening," I said.

She smiled and nodded.

As we stepped outside, the full rising of the storm became apparent. The rain drove into our faces as if somebody had turned a hosepipe on us. We had to pause for a moment to gather our balance as the wind fought against our desire to remain upright. The sky should be just turning to sunset by this time, but no light broke through the black clouds that boiled above our heads.

We fought our way to our house, and despite the distance being no more than a hundred metres, we arrived no less sodden than if we'd swam there. Our legs were spattered in mud, where the driving rain had torn into the earth, throwing it up almost to our knees.

I pushed the door closed behind us and leaned against it. "Well, *that* was a day."

"Certainly glad it's over, that's for sure," she said.

We pottered around the kitchen together in a way we'd subliminally developed, and emerged with a sort of a meal of new potatoes, veggie burgers, and a variety of salad vegetables. Most of which had come from the hydroponic poly-tunnels in the farm section of the island. We settled in front of a movie, ate, and nodded off, slumped against each other.

I awoke with a start and glanced at the clock. Four AM. I looked down at the sofa. Tiggy stirred, but didn't wake. I wondered what had woken me. The storm still swirled outside, but maybe at a slightly more subdued level of violence. I listened to the wind and rain. A sudden boom of thunder rattled the windows, followed by two more in quick succession. Short, violent claps. Somehow, they didn't sound quite right, but then, this was the first storm I'd experienced stuck out on a rock in the middle of the English Channel. I listened again. Just the wind and rain vibrating against the house.

I nudged Tiggy, and we both stumbled into bed to see out the rest of the night snuggled against each other.

# ~ CHAPTER TWENTY-SEVEN ~

THE RINGING OF MY PHONE dragged me into the day. I followed the ringing to the kitchen work area and squinted at the screen. Nine-thirty, and caller ID, Marcel Dallemagne.

"Marcel?" I answered.

"I have good news for you, John. The Council have decided to recognise Scanlon's Rock as an independent nation, just subject to final verification of the lack of foundation for the territorial waters claim being made by the UK."

My brain still swam with sleep fog. "Sorry, Marcel, can you clarify that? You mean that if they confirm the island is outside of the twelve nautical mile limit, then the EU will recognise us?"

"Indeed, good news, yes?"

"Um... yes. When will they do their measurements?"

"This morning. This is why I call you now. The International Hydrographic Organisation surveyor is taking readings this morning."

"Oh... that's... wonderful. I think. How do they do it?"

"Helicopter, I understand. If you are on the island, you may see them. En tout cas, I must go now, I am in a meeting. Your former compatriots are demanding to call their pathetic little sausage a bratwurst so they can win contracts in German supermarkets. Crazy, yes? So, good luck." The phone went dead.

"Was that Marcel?" Tiggy called from the bedroom.

"Yes."

"What did he want?"

"Apparently, there's an IHO surveyor on their way to check the distance between us and the mainland."

"Is that good?" She came into the kitchen and filled the kettle.

"Depends. If their measurements confirm the distance, we have recognition."

"And?" Tiggy paused, kettle in hand, and studied me.

"As soon as they spot that concrete monstrosity out there… well, basically, we've about as much chance as getting a plumber out on a Sunday."

"Ah." She planted the kettle on the cooker and lit the gas. "Perhaps we can try again in a few years, you know, when that thing finally crumbles away?"

"In theory, yes. In practise? If Jim doesn't get his way, he'll probably kick his ball over the fence, and move on. Or he'll swap the island for some rare guitar once owned by Clapton, or Gilmour, or an unsung Mississippi bluesman who tragically died in a car crash at the age of twenty-seven."

Tiggy stared at me.

"What?" I said. "Don't tell me I'm wrong. You know what he's like as well as I do."

"I know. I'm just a bit surprised, that's all. You seem to be almost disappointed that you might have to leave here and return to normal life in… where is it? … Pimlico?"

"Well, I've sort of settled now. And you know I don't do change very well." I wiped steam off the window with a tea towel and peered through. "Weather's cleared up. Going to be a nice day."

"Okay," she said. "Let's talk about the weather. Fancy taking a walk down to The Eye later? We could take a picnic."

"We'd better warn those SBS guys we might have company coming," I said. "EU officials bumping into a squad of British Special Forces on a disputed island. Could provoke a diplomatic incident."

Tiggy studied me, but said nothing. Just a gentle shake of her head, then returned to making tea. I wondered what I'd said wrong.

After a rushed breakfast, I headed over to Jim's house. Jeeves answered the door. He looked like he'd just been dragged from his coffin.

"Bit early for all this door knockin' on a Sunday, ain't it?"

"It's Tuesday," I said. "And it's urgent. Is he in?"

"Better see for yerself." He stepped to one side to let me in. "I'm not his keeper. I just answer doors. Sometimes telephones too. But not so much of that these days. Not with all this Skippy internet nonsense. Got no time for it me-self."

I slid past Jeeves and tapped on Jim's door. No answer, so I tapped louder.

"You're fired," yelled Jim.

"It's me, John."

"Then you're fired as well."

"It's urgent. We might have some EU officials arriving."

"So? That's your job, EU officials. Deal with it. I don't want to know."

"But you just fired me."

"You're rehired. Now let me sleep."

I turned back to Jeeves. "Have you any idea what happened to those SBS men?"

"The puppet men?"

"Puppet men?"

"Yeah, all dressed up in black like those guys who do puppet shows, and you have to pretend you don't know it's them hiding in the dark, and moving the puppets about the stage."

"Really? Did you tell them that? No, I don't want to know. Where are they?"

"We opened up one 'o the new houses for 'em to kip in. Number thirty-two, over yonder." He nodded towards the door.

"Thank you. I think." I headed out and crossed the grass to house number thirty-two. I knocked on the door but no answer. I waited, knocked again, and when there was still no answer, I tentatively opened the door. Silence. They were probably hiding behind the door, ready to pounce.

I knocked again. "Hello, it's only me." Still nothing. I pushed at the door, it swung open. No men with guns rushed me. "Hello?" I repeated. Silence. I stepped inside and reached for the light switch. The room broke into full brightness. The empty room. Not a trace that anybody had been here. Maybe it was the wrong house? I repeated the procedure with the three other empty houses. All empty. It was as if they'd never existed. I turned and headed back to my own house.

"Well?" greeted Tiggy.

"Nothing. Nobody anywhere. Apparently Jim let them sleep in one of the empty houses, but they're not there now."

"Where did they go?"

"Back to their base, I guess. Probably on their RHIB things. Bit of a trip though, I'd've thought."

"Maybe they got picked up by a secret helicopter?"

"Possibly. Anyway, no international incident. Maybe we'll take that walk after all."

"I'll put some beers in the freezer."

We fixed a light breakfast, more coffee, then tidied up. By the time I'd checked my emails, the sun had positioned at a comfortable point for a walk. We wandered through Paradise City, and out past the hydroponic section. This seemed to spread more each time I saw it. I wondered what would become of all this if Jim abandoned the project. Maybe he'd have to stay on, if only just for the weed farm. How else could he expect to feed his passion for the smoke?

An approaching noise caught my attention. I glanced around, then up. A yellow helicopter circled above our heads.

"Is that the survey helicopter?" asked Tiggy.

I shielded my eyes against the sun, peeping under my fingers. "Looks like it." I watched as the machine circled, and then descended to a clear space just to the west of the poly-tunnels. "It's coming in to land."

"Best get your Minister's hat," Tiggy said.

We looped back to our house, dropped the beers in the fridge, then headed out to where the helicopter had landed.

By the time we arrived, a small gathering clustered around the machine. Jim was already there and engaged in conversation with the pilot.

A man and a woman slipped through the people and appeared to be looking for someone or something.

I moved towards them. "Hi, I'm John Cabot, Minister for the Scanlon's Rock."

"Good morning." The woman spoke in a clipped and precise English, with a noticeable German accent. "Minister? Minister for what?"

"Everything."

She smiled. "I am Lena Stassner, Hydrographic Officer for the IHO. This is my colleague, Technical Assistant Thomas Diehl."

"I was told you were on your way. Have you taken your measurements?" The question I didn't really want answered.

"Yes. The measurements are confirmed, and I will submit my findings to the EU once I have prepared my report."

I hesitated, the question stalled on my lips. I took a deep breath and prepared for the worst. "What did your measurements confirm?"

She studied me as if I'd just asked what colour the sky was. "At the closest point, this island is exactly 12.11 nautical miles due south of the United Kingdom baseline mark for this area."

"I see. Oh well, to be expected." My shoulders slumped as the tension I'd been holding fell away. That was it. All over. I felt a weight of failure settle on me.

Tiggy nudged me. "What's the matter?"

"We tried," I said. "We tried, but they won in the end."

"What are you talking about?"

"You heard, 12.11 nautical miles, that's…" my head buzzed. I turned to Lena. "12.11? You said 12.11 nautical miles?"

She checked the screen on her tablet computer. "I did."

"But that's… that's *outside* the UK's territorial waters?"

"Of course."

"Are you sure? Absolutely sure?"

"Mr Cabot, I am not in the habit of making mistakes over such data."

I turned to Tiggy. "We did it!" And then, "But how?"

"I don't know. Just go with the result," Tiggy said, a wide grin spreading across her face.

"There is, however, one thing with which I would like your help," Lena said.

"Of course. Anything."

"We found some anomalies. My technical assistant made some film. He will show you."

Thomas opened the cover on his own tablet and moved to where I could see. "We noticed a series of unusual constructions," he said.

I peered at the screen as he swiped a video clip into view. The sea glinted in the image, but I could see nothing else.

"Here is the first one," he said.

I looked harder. A concrete lump drifted in from the top of the screen as the helicopter had made its pass.

"And again," Thomas said, as I watched another one, this time larger, move across the screen.

I felt Tiggy at my shoulder. "That looks—" I dug an elbow gently in her ribs to cut her off. "… strange," she said.

"Very strange," I said. I knew exactly what it was. The final remains of Gawan's construction. I kept quiet.

"Do you have any idea what this is?" asked Lena.

"No," I lied.

"Hmm, we think this is a deliberate series of constructions to disrupt shipping in the area. This is strictly against international maritime law."

"It's nothing to do with us," I said.

She stared at me. "Clearly. You have no resources for such a construction. Evidently, this is something created by the United Kingdom. My report will say this."

"What will happen?" Tiggy asked.

"They will be invited to remove these constructions. They are a hazard to vessels in the area. This is not allowed."

They both turned and started back to the helicopter, separating their pilot from Jim's clutches en-route. We all stood back and watched the machine climb into the sky, circle once, then head south.

Jim sidled up to me. "I'm going to get one of those," he said.

"Oh, good."

"Apparently, they're easy to fly. Bit like a car, only they go up and down as well. I'll give you a ride."

"Did you hear anything odd last night?" I asked.

"Like what? Somebody was playing reggaeton at midnight."

"No. Not that sort of odd. Doesn't matter. What happened to the SBS guys? Any idea?"

"Nah, we drank until about two, those guys can drink. Tip, don't try to keep up with SBS men when they're on one."

"I'll remember that. Did you see, or hear, them go?"

"Have they gone?"

"Never mind."

Tiggy and I left Jim and wandered back to our house. Once inside, I slumped onto the sofa.

"What's going on?" Tiggy asked.

"Those images, the ones they took on their fly past. That was the remains of Gawan's so-called sea defence."

"I guessed. I also got your hint about not saying anything."

"Yes, sorry about that. It's collapsed."

"So I saw. How?" Tiggy pulled a beer from the fridge and placed it in my hand.

"That's the puzzle." I twisted the cap off the beer and drank thirstily. "That thing was solid."

"Could the storm have done it? It was a bit fierce."

"It didn't leave a mark when we rammed it with the Raven, so I doubt it."

"Maybe the Raven weakened it, just enough? And then, with the storm..."

"Did *you* hear anything odd last night?" I asked.

"Like what?"

"Loud noise?"

"I heard thunder."

"Yes, so did I. At least, that's what I thought it was."

We sat together in silence on the sofa and ate the picnic Tiggy had prepared.

After a while, Tiggy said, "I think we probably need to send a case or two of Jack Daniel's to those SBS guys. You know, a sort of a thank you."

"Odd, I was thinking exactly the same thing."

AS I WANDER THROUGH THE endless array of tents and marquees, my mind drifts back to Jim's last birthday bash, exactly one year ago. In some ways, it felt just like yesterday. That one had been a hasty, haphazard affair, built on the excitement of the new adventure, and Jim's relentless enthusiasm for the next experience. A lot has changed.

This one was different. This was professional and engineered like a Swiss watch. This would also be the first time that the Spartans had played together as a full band for ten years, and the music world was alive with anticipation.

Despite the expansion of Paradise City in the last year, and the commencement of a second village, just up from Pirate's Cove, accommodation for visitors was non-existent. A tented city lay on the meadowlands in the north of the island, and many of the wealthier visitors had boats moored out in the bay. The little airstrip ran a continuous flow of light aircraft in and out, day and night, while the LARC bobbled to and fro, bringing a steady procession of visitors. Already, we had overtaken Glastonbury in sheer numbers, and still they came. Yet despite being an island, all ran smoothly.

The support bands, most of whom were normally headliners in their own right, flew in by helicopter, Jim's latest toy. Although thankfully, he wasn't piloting.

The press tent teemed with not only local reporters, but international, as well as the music press. The buzz was that this would herald the first of many music festivals yet to come. I hoped so.

Even Cindy had finally made it to be at Jim's side for the event, declining an invitation to fly to Australia to speak at a conference about how global warming was contributing to the wildfires there.

I squeezed Tiggy's hand as we walked. When this was over, we were heading to Lanzarote for a relaxing week. I was actually feeling quite excited about the trip.

I felt somebody approach to my left. I turned to see Jim, somehow managing to escape the usual entourage, who had been glued to his tail for the last twenty-four hours.

"There you are. Been looking for you everywhere. I've just had the most brilliant idea."

The End

*Author Note*

*I do hope you enjoyed this tale, if so, I would be grateful for a few words as a review on your favourite book buying website or Goodreads. Reviews are very important to us authors and I always appreciate them.*

*Many thanks.*
*David*

# ~ *Find my books and sign up for the newsletter* ~

IF YOU WOULD LIKE TO subscribe to my Newsletter, just enter your details below. I promise not to sell your email address to a Nigerian Prince or send you adverts for various biological enhancements.

I will however, at entirely random moments, send you a newsletter containing my writing updates, competitions, giveaways, general meanderings and thoughts on the latest Big Thing.

luddington.com/newsletter

Or to find out more about the author

To Follow On Facebook: facebook.com/DavidLuddingtonAuthor

The Website: www.luddington.com

Twitter: @d_luddington

*~ Other Books From This*
*Best Selling Author ~*

TONY RYAN IS BEMUSED. HE thought he understood the way the world worked, but now, as a sacrificial lamb of the credit crunch he finds himself drifting... drifting into the clutches of the ever resourceful Pete who could find the angle in a Fairy Liquid bubble... and into the arms of the enigmatic hippy girl, Astrid, who's about to introduce Tony to rabbits, magic caves and the joys of mushrooms.

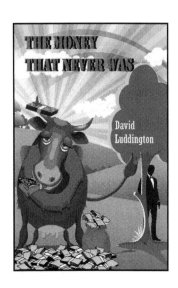

CHARLES TREMAYNE IS A SPY out of his time. After a long career spent rescuing prisoners from the KGB or helping defectors across the Berlin Wall the world has changed. The Wall has gone and no longer is there a need for a Russian speaking, ice-cold killer. The bad guys now all speak Arabic and state secrets are transmitted via satellite using blowfish algorithms impenetrable to anybody over the age of twelve. Counting down the days to his retirement by babysitting drunken visiting politicos he is seconded by MI6 for one last case. £250,000,000 of government money destined as a payoff for the dictator of a strategic African nation goes missing on its way to a remote Cornish airfield.

Tremayne is dispatched to retrieve the money and nothing is going to stand in his way. Armed with an IQ of 165 and a bewildering array of weaponry and gadgets he is not about to be outmanoeuvred by the inhabitants of a small Cornish fishing village. Or is he?

TINKER'S COTTAGE NESTLES IN A forgotten corner of deepest Somerset. It also happens to sit on a weak point in the space time continuum. Which is somewhat unfortunate for Ian Faulkener, a graphic novelist from London, who was hoping for some peace and quiet in which to recuperate following a very messy breakdown.

It was the cats that first alerted Ian to the fact that something was not quite right with Tinker's Cottage. Not only was he never sure just how many of them there actually were, but the mysterious way they seemed to disappear and reappear defied logic. The cats, and of course the Pope, disappearing literary agents, mislaid handymen and the insanity of Cherie Blair World.

As Ian tries to untangle the mystery of the doors of Tinker's cottage he risks becoming lost forever in the myriad alternate universes predicted by Schrodinger. Not to mention his cats.

Schrodinger's Cottage is a playful romp through a variety of alternate worlds peopled by an array of wonderful comic characters that are the trademark of David Luddington's novels.

For fans of the sadly missed Douglas Adams, Schrodinger's Cottage will be a welcome addition to their library. A heart-warming comedy with touches of inspired lunacy that pays homage to The Hitchhiker's Guide whilst firmly treading its own path.

*"...And there will be a corner of some foreign field that will be forever England."*

ONLY THESE DAYS IT'S MORE likely to be a half finished villa overlooking a championship golf course somewhere on one of The Costas.

Following an unfortunate encounter with Spanish gin measures and an enthusiastic estate agent, retired special effects engineer Terry England is the proud owner of a nearly completed villa in a new urbanisation in Southern Spain.

Not quite how he'd intended to spend his enforced early retirement Terry nevertheless tries to make the best of his new life. If only the local council can work out which house he's actually bought and the leaf blowers would please stop.

Terry finds himself being sucked in to the English Expat community with their endless garden parties and quests for real bacon and Tetley's Tea Bags. Of course, if it all gets too much he can always relax in the local English Bar with a nice pint of Guinness, a roast beef lunch and the Mail on Sunday.

With a growing feeling that he might have moved to the 'Wrong Spain', Terry sets out to explore and finds himself tangled in the affairs of a small rustic village in the Alpujarras. It is here where he finds a different Spain. A

Spain of loves and passions, a Spain of new hopes and a simpler way of life. A place where a moped is an acceptable means of family transport and a place where if you let your guard down for just a moment this land will never let you go again.

*Forever England is the tale of one man trying to redefine who he is and how he wants to live. It is a story of hope and humour with an array of eccentric characters and comic situations for which David Luddington is so well known and loved.*

*"Overall, this is a very warm and funny book. It is filled with wonderful characters and many laugh out loud moments." book-reviewer.com*

*"Genuinely funny, with many laugh out loud moment..." Matt Rothwell - author of Drunk In Charge Of A Foreign Language*

*Reading David Luddington is like "Like reading your favourite sitcom." –*
*Nigel Planer*

RETIRED STAGE MAGICIAN TURNED PROFESSIONAL mystic debunker, John Barker, finds his sceptical beliefs under fire when he encounters a strange man who claims to be Merlin. After several unsuccessful attempts to rid himself of his increasingly unpredictable companion, John finally relents and agrees to assist in the man's crazy mission, to find the true grave of the mythical King Arthur.

Following a hidden code contained within the text of a soft porn novel, they gather a growing entourage of hippies, mystic seekers and alien hunters as they leave a trail of chaos across the south west of England. When the group comes to the attention of a TV Reality Show producer looking to make a fast profit out of harmless eccentrics and fading celebrities, John decides it's time to take charge and prove one way or the other, the identity of this mysterious person who claims to be a fictional wizard.

*"Whose reality is this anyway?"* is a warm-hearted tale of what it means to be an individual and to follow one's dreams. With his trademark cast of oddball characters and absurd situations, David Luddington once more

transports us into a world where who you are is more important than what you are.

*"David Luddington epitomizes the elusive quality of writing that he perpetuates - the British Comedy." – Grady Harp*

"Like reading your favourite sitcom"
Nigel Planer

CAMP
SCOUNDREL
Doing what it takes to survive paradise

DAVID LUDDINGTON
Author of the Best Seller - 'Forever England'

WHEN EX-SAS SOLDIER, MICHAEL PURDY, comes in front of the judge for hacking the bank account belonging to the Minister for Invalidity Benefits and wiping out his personal wealth, he braces himself for a prison sentence.

What Michael doesn't expect, is to be put in charge of a group of offenders and sent to a remote location in the Sierra Nevada Mountains in Spain to teach them survival skills as part of their rehabilitation programme.

But Michael knows nothing at all about survival skills. He was sort of in the SAS, yes, but his shining record on the "Escape and Evasion" courses was more a testament to his computer skills than his ability to catch wildlife and barbecue it over an impromptu fire. Basically, he was the SAS's techy nerd and only achieved that position as a result of a bet with a fellow hacker.

Facing a stark choice between starvation or returning home to serve out their sentences, the group of offenders under Michael's supervision soon realise that the only way to survive is to use their own unique set of skills – the kind of skills that got them arrested in the first place.

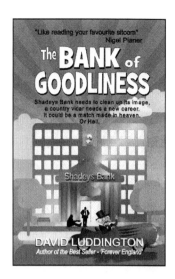

WHEN SHADEYS BANK LOSES YET another C.E.O. to a major scandal, they are desperate to show they've reformed. Who better to present their redemption to the world than a country vicar with a reputation for being annoyingly good?

Reverend Tom Goodman is ousted from his job as a country vicar for allowing a homeless family to stay in the church hall. Meanwhile, a major bank is trying to rescue its image after the latest in a long string of financial scandals.

It seems like the perfect match and Goodman is hastily appointed as the bank's new C.E.O. All they have to do now, is promote him as the new face of Shadeys Bank whilst at the same time, keeping him away from the day-to-day business of dubious banking.

However, Tom Goodman has other ideas. He's not going to be satisfied with being used as an empty puppet for a PR stunt. Unfortunately for Shadeys, Tom is planning on actually making a difference.

And so begins an epic battle of wills. The might of a multi-billion pound bank versus a seemingly naïve country vicar.

No contest.

*"Yes Minister meets The Vicar of Dibley."*

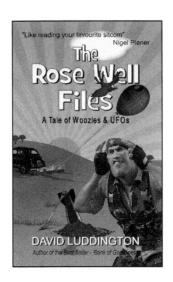

"Like reading your favourite sitcom"
Nigel Planer

The
Rose Well
Files
A Tale of Woozles & UFOs

DAVID LUDDINGTON
Author of the Best Seller - Bank of God...

ROSE WELL HOLIDAY PARK NEEDS a hero.

This once shining icon of the Great British Holiday Camp is dying, and the last residents are more interested in preparing for a zombie apocalypse or fighting off imaginary UFOs than playing Crazy Golf or Bingo.

In addition, a foreign bottled water company is attempting to force a sale so they can seize the last asset of Rose Well Park, the Rose Well Spring. The famous spring water claimed to bestow great health and longevity.

And then there's the bomb...

What Rose Well Park could probably do without, is a hero whose belief in a better tomorrow far outweighs any of his past achievements. But William Fox is all they have.

Armed with nothing more than an undying sense of optimism and a box of books about alien conspiracies, he slowly draws up his plans to make Rose Well Park famous.

"Dad's Army meets X-Files"

• *Woozle: Noun*

*A presentation of evidence by citation only. A woozle occurs when frequent citation of publications, lacking evidence, mislead individuals, groups, and the public, and nonfacts become urban myths and factoids.*

Printed in Great Britain
by Amazon

20594546R00194